LIN CARTER

CALLISTO

Linwood Vrooman Carter was born in St. Petersburg, Florida in 1930. A veteran of the Korean War—having served in the U.S. Army infantry from 1951-1953—he used the GI Bill to attend Columbia University, then worked as a copy writer for advertising agencies, book publishers, and law firms before becoming a full-time freelance writer and editor of fantasy and science fiction stories in 1969. Influenced by the works of such genre masters as J.R.R. Tolkien, Robert E. Howard, L. Frank Baum, and Edgar Rice Burroughs, Carter's vast body of work includes his first published novel, *The Wizard of Lemuria* (1965), as well as three popular fantasy series: *Green Star*, *Callisto*, and "Thongor of Lemuria." Carter is also known for his numerous collaborations with Robert E. Howard and L. Sprague de Camp on a series of novels and short stories featuring Howard's classic character Conan the Barbarian. As an editor, Carter assembled more than two dozen anthologies, including *The Year's Best Fantasy Stories* (1975-1980), *Flashing Swords!*, *Weird Tales*, *The Spawn of Cthulu*, and *Realms of Wizardry*. He died in Montclair, New Jersey in 1988.

AVAILABLE NOW

The Deceivers
by Alfred Bester

The Computer Connection
by Alfred Bester

Arthur C. Clarke's Venus Prime: Volumes 1, 2, and 3
by Paul Preuss

Isaac Asimov's Robot City: Volume 1
by Michael P. Kube-McDowell and Mike McQuay

Isaac Asimov's Robot City: Volume 2
by William F. Wu and Arthur Byron Cover

Mirage
An Isaac Asimov Robot Mystery
by Mark W. Tiedemann

Heavy Metal: F.A.K.K.²: The Novelization
by Kevin B. Eastman and Stan Timmons

X-Men: Shadows of the Past
by Michael Jan Friedman

COMING SOON

Isaac Asimov's Robot City: Volume 3
by Rob Chilson and William F. Wu

West of Eden
by Harry Harrison

The Science of the X-Men
by Link Yaco and Karen Haber

Moebius' Arzach
by Jean-Marc Lofficier

X-Men: The Chaos Engine Trilogy
by Steven A. Roman and Stan Timmons

The Sentinel
by Arthur C. Clarke

Sailing to Byzantium
by Robert Silverberg

CALLISTO

VOLUME I

LIN CARTER

ibooks
new york
www.ibooksinc.com

DISTRIBUTED BY SIMON & SCHUSTER, INC

An Original Publication of ibooks, inc.

Pocket Books, a division of Simon & Schuster, Inc.
1230 Avenue of the Americas, New York, NY 10020

ibooks, inc.
24 West 25th Street
New York, NY 10010

The ibooks World Wide Web Site Address is:
http://www.ibooksinc.com

ISBN 0-7434-0005-4
First Pocket Books printing June 2000
10 9 8 7 6 5 4 3 2 1
POCKET and colophon are registered trademarks of
Simon & Schuster, Inc.

Cover art by Steranko
Cover design by Jason Vita
Interior design by Michael Mendelsohn at MM Design 2000, Inc.

Printed in the U.S.A.

Dedicated, with respect and admiration, to
EDGAR RICE BURROUGHS
the greatest master of the
fantastic adventure story who ever lived.

Share your thoughts about Lin Carter's *Callisto*
and other ibooks titles
in the new ibooks virtual reading group at
www.ibooksinc.com

INTRODUCTION

by JOHN BETANCOURT

In the 1960s and 1970s, Lin Carter proved himself one of the most energetic and popular fantasy authors and editors in the world. Few fans missed his sword & sorcery books, from his Conan novels (some written in collaboration with L. Sprague de Camp, some on his own) to the saga of barbarian warrior Thongor of Lemuria to the epic *Callisto* series.

Carter's *Callisto* books, in particular, brought him legions of new fans. They quickly became Dell Books' best-selling science fiction & fantasy series, going into multiple printings and racking up an impressive 1.5 million copies in print.

I'm not surprised: the eight volumes in the *Callisto* series—the first two are collected herein—comprise perhaps the most startling work in Carter's long career. Neither sword & sorcery nor science fiction—though they contain elements of both—these books capture the feel of an exotic alien world on par with the best imaginings of Edgar Rice Burroughs, Jack Vance, or any of the other great world-builders in the field. One might almost think Carter had actually *been* to that fantastic fifth moon of Jupiter.

More on this later.

Linwood Vrooman Carter (1930-1988) was born in St. Petersburg, Florida. He served in the U.S. Army infantry in Korea from 1951-1953, then attended Columbia University in 1953-54 under the G.I. Bill. An ardent science fiction fan, he wrote copiously from his high school days onward, and his poetry and short fiction began to appear in fan magazines soon thereafter.

Upon college graduation, he pursued a writing career, becoming a prolific copywriter for law firms, ad agencies, and book publishers. Finally, in 1969, he became an editor for Ballantine Books and launched the still-classic Ballantine Adult Fantasy line, which reprinted scores of classic fantasy novels, from William Morris to Lord Dunsany, from Evangeline Walton to Katherine Kurtz. Fantasy in particular was Carter's driving passion, and the largest volume of his work lies in this field: some sixty novels, hundreds of short stories, and twenty-five anthologies bear his name.

My first meeting with Lin Carter occurred at the 1984 Empiricon Science Fiction Convention, which was held in New York City. I found Lin to be a cheerful, energetic, loquacious man, with a Van Dyke beard, silvering hair, and a love for storytelling. We ended up spending six hours chatting about the field, his work, and his thoughts about publishing.

At one point I commented that his *Callisto* series had always been my favorite work of his, and he just laughed and shook his head. "I'm just the editor," he said. "Jon Dark is the author."

I thought it a little odd that he'd let the fictitious narrator of the series take credit for writing the books, but then—why not? Carter's own introductions to each volume of the series tell how Jonathan Andrew Dark, a twenty-four-year-old helicopter pilot, crash-landed in a river in Cambodia during the Vietnam War. After making his way to shore, a weird beam of light drew Jon Dark into the jungle and to a lost and ruined city: Arangkôr.

(Arangkôr, you may remember from the various features in *National Geographic* and *Life* magazines, was excavated in the 1970s by the distinguished British archaeologist Sir Malcolm Jerrods. This ancient city, in the Mekong Delta, is one of the three great "lost" Khmer cities in Cambodia. Overrun by dense jungles, its walls tumbled to ruin, you can still see evidence of its former magnificence in the brooding statues which still surround the Jade Well and several other famous monuments. Doubtless it would be a popular tourist destination today if not for the political troubles in Cambodia and the fact that it's located in the middle of one of the hottest, swampiest, least civilized, and least accessible spots on Earth.)

When I asked Carter if more *Callisto* books might be forthcoming, he said, "I have a bunch of them in my files. I just haven't had the time to prepare them for publication yet."

More and more curious!

In early 1999 I was asked to prepare the *Callisto* series for new editions to be released by ibooks, the present publisher. To that end I contacted Bob Price, Carter's literary executor, and asked to look through Carter's files.

Since Price lived about half an hour away, it was no big deal for me to drive over, and we spent a pleasant morning chatting about Lin Carter and the fantasy field. Finally, he led me into the basement vault, where Carter's files are preserved, and he showed me where the working files for all of Carter's books are stored: several filing cabinets, neatly arranged, containing voluminous correspondence, working notes, drafts of manuscripts, proposals for books and series, and the other literary "footprints" of a working writer. My own filing cabinets look much the same, so I felt right at home digging in.

There were plenty of surprises: an unpublished Thongor novel—completed just before Carter's death—and a lengthy synopsis for another; several unfinished short stories; folders of poetry and artwork by Clark Ashton Smith; unpublished fragments by Robert E. Howard . . . a veritable treasure trove for any fantasy fan!

Finally I found the *Callisto* files: one for each book in the series. They were slim, almost empty. I couldn't help but feel a bite of disappointment. What had happened to everything—the drafts of manuscripts, the outlines, the working notes?

When I took out the *Jandar of Callisto* file, I found it contained nothing but the old contract with Dell Books, a few check stubs, and royalty statements. Nothing else. It seemed odd to me that someone who had so methodically saved every scrap of paper he'd ever written on—and some of the Thongor notes were on *cocktail napkins!*—should have saved *nothing* on this book.

The Black Legion of Callisto file also held little of interest; ditto all the others. It was only when I reached the *Renegade of Callisto* file—*Renegade* being the eighth and final published volume in the series—did I find a clue: a faded computer print-out dated February 11, 1988—four days *after* Carter's death.

It was an airline itinerary, I realized as I scanned the contents. One L. V. Carter had booked passage from La Guardia to Tokyo via American Airlines, and thence to Bangkok. At the time I supposed it to be a planned vacation which he had never managed to take.

When Mr. Price noticed what I'd found, he became quite agitated and all but ripped it from my hands. "That shouldn't have been there," he snapped. He started for another filing cabinet—on the other side of the vault—produced a key from around his neck, unlocked it, and hurriedly stuffed the itinerary inside. I had followed him, and I saw only a glimpse over his shoulder, but that second filing cabinet seemed to contain another complete set of file folders, these holding rough-edged, brown pages which looked almost like papyrus—and they had been cut to unusual, almost square dimensions. The one title I could read said, *The Ice Kingdom of Callisto.*

I stood there, staring, hardly able to believe my eyes, hardly able to breathe. It had to be one of the unpublished *Callisto* novels which Carter had mentioned to me fifteen years ago!

Even when Price slammed the drawer shut and locked it again, the image lingered in my mind. *The Ice Kingdom of Callisto!* What images it conjured!

And most intriguing of all, *those rough, brown pages exactly matched Carter's description of Jonathan Andrew Dark's original manuscripts.*

But why wouldn't Price have told me of its existence?

When I asked about the filing cabinet, he quickly changed the subject, rushed me out of the house with claims of a pressing appointment, and locked the door behind me.

The later years of Lin Carter's life had been filled with various tragedies. His literary career wound down; his personal life was turbulent; he gambled and drank heavily, running up debts with various unsavory people. In the last months of his life, he became a virtual recluse, with no surviving family and few close friends besides Bob Price. Reports of his cancer trickled out, and the fantasy field collectively held its breath, fearing the worse. Word finally came that Carter had passed away, via a press release from Price's office.

I tried to visit Carter's gravesite in West Orange, New Jersey last week. Unfortunately, I couldn't find it—nor had the caretakers ever heard of Carter when they tried to locate his plot on their computer.

"Could he be buried under a different name—maybe an old family name?" they asked.

I couldn't answer and left, ultimately unsatisfied.

Fifty-eight is not a particularly great age these days, when so many people now live into their eighties, nineties, or even beyond. I cannot help but wonder if Carter—somehow—faked his own death with the help of Bob Price, left his literary affairs in order under Price's careful administration, and set off for Cambodia on his own. The airline reservation would have supported this theory, but unfortunately I no longer have it.

Still, quite a few facts remain: The lost city of Arangkôr has been found, studied, photographed. Its famous "Jade Well"—its lip composed of one of the largest single pieces of green jade ever discovered—has been thoroughly documented. Perhaps, to Carter's mind, it really *did* form a gateway to the fifth moon of Jupiter when the planets align properly. Perhaps he *did* run off on a last great adventure.

I cannot say. But one thing is certain: there are more than enough unsolved puzzles here for a dozen books. Unfortunately, they are likely to remain unsolved, at least for now. Bob Price no longer returns my phone calls or letters. American Airlines doesn't keep records going back twelve years (yes, I checked). And Lin Carter's gravesite is . . . *missing*.

I wish I could have gotten a better look inside that locked filing cabinet. I have the strangest feeling it holds quite a few secrets.

John Betancourt
Berkeley Heights, New Jersey

PART ONE

JANDAR OF
CALLISTO

CONTENTS

A WORD FROM THE AUTHOR
ABOUT THIS BOOK

A uthors, as any of you who may have met one are likely to agree, are surely among the least modest or humble of God's creatures. To some degree this is natural and even desirable, for a certain amount of egotism is required to give one the boldness necessary to placing his work before the public in open competition with all the other good books there are in the world to read.

To this common failing I of course plead guilty—although I console myself with a maxim uttered by a much better writer than I, the late Damon Runyon, who once and wisely wrote: *"He who tooteth not his own horn, the same shall not be tooted."*

This mildly philosophic preamble appears at the opening of this novel in order to reassure you that the statement I am about to make is not prompted by any unprofessional and amateurish affectation of humility. This understood, then let me make the following statement in all solemn and sober honesty:

Although my name appears, I trust prominently, on the

cover, spine, and title page of this novel, *I am not in any way the author of this book*. At best, I am its editor, and my labors in that direction have been limited to a small degree of correction in terms of spelling, punctuation, and grammar, and to the addition of an occasional footnote here and there amid the text, each such clearly marked with my initials.

Why, then, should Lin Carter's name appear at all on this book? Mainly because Gail Wendroff Morrison, the charming editor at Dell who buys my books, has insisted on it with a most unladylike firmness. When I had prepared a typescript of this book (the original, which we shall shortly discuss, was written—and in a most strange way—in longhand), I brought it into her offices myself, rather than having my agent handle the submission as usual. I did this because I wanted to explain that I had only edited *Jandar of Callisto*, but that its author was someone else. I don't know just how much of my account she believed, but a week or so later she phoned my home to say she would buy the script, but only if she could use my name as its author.

"But, Gail, I didn't write it. Jonathan Andrew Dark wrote it!" I protested. Her rejoinder was crushing.

"Okay, maybe he did," she said firmly. "But the name 'Lin Carter' on the cover is going to sell more copies than the name 'Jonathan Andrew Dark.' "

Of course, I could see her point. But I still felt a mite uncomfortable about claiming the work of another man as my own. So I agreed, but not until I had extracted grudging permission to tell the truth about the novel's authorship in a preface. *This* preface. . . .

On November 27, 1969, the postman handed me a rather bulky parcel whose brown-paper wrapping was torn, battered, and soiled, but bright with a profusion of stamps and, surprisingly, a Saigon postmark. My wonderful wife Noël is, by now, accustomed to my receiving unsolicited manuscripts from would-be authors who want either my opinion on the salability of their effusions, or my help in finding a publisher for such. So she watched without comment as I snipped the cord and removed the wrappings, putting them on the living room floor so the dogs could sniff and play with them while I examined this curious gift from the other side of the world.

There was, as I had assumed, a large, shabby-looking manuscript, which I put aside for later perusal, and a covering letter on U.S. Air Force stationery, which I read at once. It went as follows:

Hq & Hq Co
U.S.A.F. Group
Saigon
August 19, 1969

Mr. Lin Carter
Hollis, Long Island,
New York, N.Y.
U.S.A.

Dear Mr. Carter:

I hope you don't mind a stranger writing to you. At least I am a stranger who comes bearing gifts.

I write to you, rather than to someone else, because you seem the person most likely to be interested in the story I have enclosed. Perhaps you don't know it, but here in Vietnam we read an awful lot of American science fiction paperbacks, and you and Edgar Rice Burroughs and Andre Norton are about neck to neck when it comes to reading for relaxation and fun. Because my buddy Jon Dark was fond of your Thongor books,

I think he would have liked you to read his own attempt at a novel. At least, I guess you could call it a novel.

Jon was not in the Air Force, although he tried to join up over here; there was some problem about his citizenship (he wasn't born in the U.S., but in Rio). The best he could do was get in with the International Red Cross as a chopper pilot. But because quarters are crowded here in Saigon I saw a lot of him and we got to be good friends.

Jon was shot down, or anyway disappeared on a flight, early in March this year. His copter was the only one of the flight lost and nobody knows what happened, but he seems to have strayed across the border into Cambodia, which as you probably know lies right next door to Vietnam. About the first of August this year (a good five months after he was first reported missing) some natives came out of the Cambodian jungles with his dogtags and the enclosed manuscript. As Jon had no family at all, and as I am about his closest friend, I ended up with the manuscript. I got to admit that I had no idea Jon was trying his hand at writing books; and for the life of me I can't understand why he would have bothered to bring the manuscript along on a flight, but that's the way it was.

I'm sending it to you because it sounds a lot like one of your own books, and because about the last time I ever saw Jon alive he was talking about a novel of yours, The Star Magicians *I think it was. You can do anything with it you want, keep it as a sort of souvenir, or even try to get it published if you like. But I don't know what else to do with it except to send it to you.*

It's a strange story, you will have to admit. And the strangest thing about it is that the early stuff, all about Jon's family and even the stuff about his flight, is all straight fact as far as I know. Jon must have survived in the jungle long enough to write down a fanciful opening to his story, based on his copter crash . . . at least, that's the only way I can explain it.

I don't dare believe in what the book says. Neither will you!

Excuse me for taking up your valuable time, and here's hoping you write some more Thongor books.

Best wishes,
Gary Hoyt
Major, USAF

The rest of that morning of November 27, and most of the day and the night as well, I spent in deciphering the manuscript, which I have given the title *Jandar of Callisto*. Let me tell you something about its odd appearance.

The paper, for one thing, was unlike any I have ever seen. It was coarse and fibrous, brown and crudely made. It reminded me of old papyrus. It happens I own a scrap of old Egyptian papyrus among the collection my wife and I have built of Egyptian antiquities. I compared the two, and they share a marked similarity. The paper on which the novel was written seems to be composed of coarse reedy fiber, interwoven, pounded flat, just like the brown Egyptian papyrus that hangs in a gilt frame in my dining room.

I have said the manuscript was handwritten, and this is true, but it was not written with any kind of pen I have ever seen. Neither a ball-point nor a felt-tip, nor even an old-fashioned fountain pen would leave marks quite the same. It looks for all the world as if somebody had used a quill pen—a bird-feather quill, trimmed off with a sharp knife at an angle, then dipped in ink.

I suggest a quill pen because the quality of the writing periodically deteriorates, as if the quill were wearing down, losing its sharpness; at which point Captain Dark seems to have either cut a new one or trimmed afresh the one he was using. The writing on the first few pages starts off crisp and clear, gradually becomes rough and blurred, then abruptly becomes sharp and clear again.

The ink, even, is odd stuff. It seems homemade: at least I know of no commercial brand of ink that would give the muddy, uneven darkness of the ink on this manuscript.

The manuscript consists of exactly fifty-six sheets of the queer parchment, or papyrus, or whatever it is; written in close, fine handwriting on both sides of each sheet, with very narrow margins; and each sheet of the manuscript measures about ten by twelve inches, almost square, in other words. I can think of no reason for such an odd size. Commercial brands of writing paper come generally in the $8\frac{1}{2}$ by 11-inch size—the size of paper I use in my typewriter, for example. I have seen Japanese rice paper in my time, and it comes in a smaller size—6 inches by 8 inches, if I recall correctly. But all of this is neither here nor there. I seem to be avoiding the big questions that stand out:

Is this a true story, or just a novel?

Is the lost city of Arangkôr a real place?

Is there a strange well, lined with milky jade, amid the jungle-grown ruins of antique Cambodia—a well that somehow serves as a mysterious link between two worlds?

And *is* there at this moment a Yank on Callisto, moon of Jupiter, heroically fighting against incredible odds to rescue the beautiful woman he loves from the clutches of her enemies?

Truth—or romance? Fact—or fiction? An honest narrative account of the most astonishing adventure ever lived—or merely an entertaining and exciting novel written somewhat in the style of my own yarns?

I have told you everything I know about the genesis of this most remarkable book. As for the answers to those questions above, I am afraid we shall never really know for certain.

> Lin Carter
> Hollis, Long Island, New York
> December 9, 1969

Note: Mr. Henry J. Robinson of the headquarters of the International Red Cross in Washington, D.C., has kindly searched the personnel records of his organization, and he assures me that a volunteer pilot named Jonathan Andrew Dark, attached to an Air Rescue Group in Saigon, has indeed been listed as missing in action in South Vietnam since March 8, 1969. He is presumed dead or a prisoner. His personal record gives no next of kin, no single name and address of any relative. I am uncertain as to my legal standing in this, but I have decided after some thought to use Captain Dark's real name, since he himself employed no pseudonym for his central character.

Here follows his own account of his adventures, just as he described them in his own words. I have added chapter titles for the pleasure of the reader, and have taken the liberty of dedicating Captain Dark's book to one of his—and my—favorite authors, Edgar Rice Burroughs.

> —L. C.

CHAPTER I
THE LOST CITY OF ARANGKÔR

That the most far-reaching and momentous historical events often spring from minute and seemingly inconsequential accidents is a fact which I can attest from my own experience.

For the past four months now—insofar as I have been able to measure the passage of time—I have dwelt on an alien world, surrounded by a thousand foes, struggling and battling my way through innumerable perils to win a place beside the most beautiful woman in two worlds.

And all of these adventures, these wonders and terrors, sprang from a single cause, and that cause was a crumb of dirt half the size of my thumbnail.

As I sit, painfully and slowly setting down these words with a quill pen and homemade ink on a sheet of rough parchment, I cannot help but wonder at the obscure vanity which prompts me to record the tale of my incredible adventures—a tale which began in a lost city deep in the impenetrable jungles of southeast Asia and which ventures from there across the incredible distance of three hundred and ninety million miles of infinite space to the surface of a weird and alien planet. A tale, furthermore, which I deem it most unlikely any other human eye will ever read.

Yet I write on, driven by some inexplicable urge to set down an account of the marvels and mysteries which I alone of all men ever born on earth have experienced. And when at last this narrative is completed, I will set it within the Gate in the hopes that, being composed entirely of organic matter, paper and ink as well, it may somehow be transported across the immeasurable gulf of interplanetary space to the distant world of my birth, to which I shall never return.

In the night sky, at certain seasons when the Inner Moons are on the other side of our primary and the starry skies are clear, I can (I fancy) see the earth. A remote and insignificant spark of blue fire it seems from this distance; a tiny point of light lost amid the blackness of the infinite void. Can it truly be that I was born and lived my first twenty-four years on that blue spark—or was *that* life but a dream, and have I spent all of my days upon this weird world of Thanator? It is a question for the philosophers to settle, and I am but a simple warrior.

Yet I can well remember my father. He was a tall man, stern-faced and powerfully built, with scowling brows and thick black locks. His name was Matthew Dark; a Scotsman from Aberdeenshire, an engineer by profession, and a wanderer by inclination, he tramped the world to its far corners searching for the joy of life, its richness, its color, which always eluded him and always seemed to beckon from over the next horizon.

From him I seem to have inherited my inches, for like him I am something over six feet; from him, as well, must come my strength, for among men I am reckoned a strong man of great endurance and stamina. But it was from my mother came the gift of my yellow hair and blue eyes, which have none of the dour, darkling Scot in them. She was a Danish girl from a town whose name I cannot pronounce and she died when I was a small child. All that I can remember of her is a soft warm voice, a sweet smiling face bending over me, the touch of a gentle hand. And I seem to see laughing blue eyes, as calm and deep and sparkling as the lakes of her homeland, and the gleam of pale gold hair woven in thick braids—alas, it is only a shard of memory, a brief glimpse into a past which I can never recapture, never completely recall.

The color of my hair and my eyes, these were the only gifts she ever gave me, besides my life itself. But in an odd way I owe her a double debt: for it was for reason of my yellow hair and blue eyes that my life was spared when I fell into the cruel hands of the savage and inhuman warriors of the Yathoon—but I am getting ahead of my own story.

If I owe my mother the double debt of life given and life saved, I at least owe my father for my name, Jonathan Andrew Dark. He was building a great hydroelectric project in Denmark when he met and loved and wed my laughing, blue-eyed mother. She went with him to South America for his next job, for an engineer must go where his work leads him, and wanderers have no home. And thus it chanced that while my mother was a Dane and my father a Scot, and I am now a naturalized American, I was born in Rio.

Of my early life there is little enough to tell. Or, rather, I run the risk of telling too much—for it has little bearing on the saga of my adventures on the fantastic world that has now become my home. A tropical fever carried off my lovely mother when I was only three; my father I seldom saw, for he was off building a highway in Peru, a dam in Bolivia, a bridge in Yucatan. But when death took her from us I became his constant companion. Prim and proper folk might be scandalized to think of a tender child amid the savage surroundings of a jungle camp, but I thrived on the rough, exciting life, and to this I am sure I owe my love of peril and adventure. For I saw the green, stinking interior of the Matto Grosso before I ever saw the interior of a schoolroom, and was familiar with the dangerous rope bridges that span the airy heights of the high Andes before I ever saw a paved city street.

I became a sort of pet or protégé to the engineers of my father's camp. It was that laughing bandit Pedro who taught me to throw a knife before I ever learned my letters, and the big Swede, Swenson, who taught me every trick of rough-and-tumble fighting his brawny, battered body had ever learned. I could bring down a hunting jaguar with one cool steady shot straight between its burning eyes even as it sprang for my throat—long before I had mastered the occult mysteries of long division.

Yes, long division—for my formal schooling had been somewhat neglected while I had learned to brew coffee with water taken from a snake-infested jungle stream and heated over kerosene flames in a battered tin pot, to hunt and fight like a man, to climb like a monkey, and to survive where a city-bred boy would have succumbed to fever ticks, snakebite, or cholera. It happened when I was about thirteen. My father had had enough of the banana republics by now; he yearned for the dry, parched air and gorgeous nights of the desert after years spent in the sweltering sinkhole of marshy jungles; he was thinking of an oil-drilling project in Iraq.

But in the back alleys of a vile little jungle town named Puerto Maldonado he ran into an American geologist named Farley, an old friend of many years standing. Puerto Maldonado is in the back country of Peru, on the shores of a river called Madre de Dios, "Mother of God." God, however, had nothing to do with Farley being in Puerto Maldonado: he was hunting for the place where the Incas had gotten their gold.

He had found nothing but ticks, mosquitoes, and a particularly nasty breed of snake the natives called *jararaca*. It was a nip in the ankle from the venomous fangs of this particular denizen of the jungles that had laid up Farley in the backroom of the only gin mill in Puerto Maldonado for three weeks. My father and his friend celebrated their chance meeting with copious toasts of bad gin in fly-specked glasses, and somewhere between the second and the third bottle my father conceived the notion that I required schooling. Here was Farley, a distinguished geologist with a string of college degrees after his name, like paper tags in the tail of a kite. And here was I, a tall, raw-boned, broad-shouldered and sunburnt boy, able enough to hack through the tangled and snake-infested swamps of the Matto Grosso like a veteran, but a green-eared novice when it came to the mystic doctrines of long division.

In less time than it takes me to describe the event, a decision had been reached. Farley was on his way to the coast when the next mail packet came chugging down the coiling silver length of the Madre de Dios; thence overland to the burgeoning young city of Santo Domingo and a bush pilot named O'Mara who would fly him to civilization. He was on his way back to what he described as "God's Country," but what the geography books call the United States of America, and with all possible haste, for there was a professorship open at Harvard for a seasoned field geologist, and he was hungry for the world of cinema, cocktail lounge, and campus. And, besides, he had been lucky this time to have spent only three weeks sweating *jararaca* venom out of his guts. He preferred not to give the wriggling little monsters the chance for a second bite.

So I was off to America with the would-be *Herr* Professor, and, to tell the truth, I didn't at all mind the idea. I had become aware in recent months that we men shared the world with a delectable species called girls, and I would find few specimens here in the muddy jungles of Peru, while I was given to understand they were as common in America as was *carrapato do Chão*, the humble ground tick, in this part of the world.

I never saw my father again. An exploding oil pocket in the uplands of Iraq nine months after this sent him to that El Dorado or Valhalla where all old adventurers spend their eternities. God bless him, for the world's a poorer place without him in it.

Not to occupy these pages with an account of the wonders of small-town America, which must be already familiar to my reader—if ever this most unusual journal is fortunate enough to find its way across three hundred and ninety million miles of space to the nearest reader capable of understanding English—I shall pass over the next several years without much more than a summary.

My lack of anything in the way of schooling proved a bit of an impediment. But Mr. Farley—now Assistant Professor Farley—serving *in loco parentis*, lined up enough tutors for a crash program. I proved, rather surprisingly to all, and especially to myself, an alert, bright student, and before long I was almost up to my age group. I had seen the interior of a schoolroom at last, and found it no less of a jungle in its way than the Matto Grosso had been. And the abstruse mysteries of long division were at last conquered.

Farley was teaching at Harvard, but somehow or other I ended up at Yale. I shall pass over these years briefly: they were happy years. I broke no fewer bones on the football field than do most undergraduates, and no fewer hearts in Lover's Lane, under the stimulus of a ripely golden Connecticut moon. Nor did my own heart escape without a fracture or two; but it's all part of the mystery of what philosophers call "growing up"—as if there was any other direction in which to grow!

Oddly enough—for all the heady pleasures of the football field—I found more intoxication in the feel of a rapier in my hands. Quite by chance I discovered a natural affinity for the sword, and for two years running I was captain of Yale's famed fencing team. This, too, like the color of my hair and eyes, was to prove an unexpected blessing when I came to wandering and warring through the black and crimson jungles of barbaric Thanator—but again I am ahead of my story.

Although I was an American citizen by now, the wanderlust had bitten too deep, had struck me too young, for the quiet academic life to hold many attractions for me. I yearned, always, to see what lay beyond the dim horizon . . . over the next range of hills . . . beyond the bright waters of the shining sea.

Before the ink was dry on my sheepskin, I was off. A hasty farewell to the Professor, and I began to wander. The next couple of years took me far and wide. The restlessness, the wanderlust I had inherited from my father took me about the globe. A brief stint of journalism in New York, then I shipped as an ordinary seaman on a merchant tub to Stockholm. I learned to fly in India, of all places, and this led to a bit of refugee-running out of Cuba, arms smuggling in the Near East, and a few flights of medicine and food supplies into blockaded Biafra.

I ended up in Vietnam, and when some technicality over my naturalization papers looked to keep me out of the fight, I joined the Red Cross as a pilot, running supplies and medics into the trouble spots. My thirst for adventure had frequently carried me into trouble from which my fighting instincts had, till now, rescued me without permanent damage. But in Vietnam, something happened. . . .

The Viet Cong terrorists had made a strike at a small village and medical help was needed urgently. So urgently that they hauled me out of my billet on thirty minutes notice. I was to ride herd on a squad of choppers flying in medics and food and flying out the seriously injured.

I had just spent a couple of weeks in Saigon on leave so I was fresh and rested, so to speak. My group was stationed at a temporary field hacked out of the brush on the outskirts of Hon Quan, which is about sixty-five miles north of Saigon and only some ten miles or so from the borders of Cambodia.

We were a half hour out of Hon Quan when my chopper began to develop a bad case of the chokes. Something was wrong with one of the fuel lines, probably a morsel of dirt that had clogged the line. The sort of thing a full mechanic's checkout would have spotted and corrected, but we had been scrambled on notice too short for a full-scale check.

And that meant I was in trouble. We didn't have the big two- and three-man combat choppers the American army used; on rescue missions like these all I had was a little one-man copter. The cargo craft were up ahead, needed to fly out the injured. So I was all by myself.

I radioed the rest of the squadron and told them my second-in-command would take over as I was having engine trouble and would probably fall behind. They went on ahead while I dropped back, trying to figure out what to do. We were flying over some of the densest jungles on earth and there was nowhere to sit her down safely. If I could find a flat space to sit her down I could probably fix the trouble in no time, even if I had to unscrew one of the lines and blow the obstruction out.

I circled for a while, hunting. There was a chance, a slim one, that the line would clear itself, but I couldn't count on it. If the motor conked out I would crash in the treetops. A chopper comes down slowly, even without power, because the air catches and turns the blades, braking the rate of fall. That's the nice thing about these flying eggbeaters.

The bad thing is you are flying too low to bail out with a parachute.

I began to sweat.

For a half-hour I played with that chopper like a virtuoso with a Bach concerto, getting every ounce of go-power I could squeeze from my laboring engine. I couldn't return to base because I knew there was no landing area between there and here, having just flown over the same piece of countryside. But— who could say? Off to the west a bit there might be a clearing. I nursed her carefully in that direction.

A while later I spotted a flash of light, the yellow-brown glisten of a jungle river. My chopper was fitted out with pontoon gear, of course. Half the land in this desolate corner of the globe is swamp and marsh. If I could make it to that river I could at least make a landing.

I began wondering just where I was. No river of that size should be in my neighborhood. I must have flown farther afield in my search for landing space than I had suspected.

Could it be the Mekong? If so, I was in trouble. The Mekong isn't in Vietnam at all, but over the border in Cambodia. It traverses eastern Cambodia from north to south and empties into the South China Sea. And Cambodia is a place we were not supposed to be. A so-called "neutral" country, its ruler, Prince Sihanouk, might be a jolly host to visiting American

VIP's like Jackie Kennedy, but he was mighty inhospitable when it came to lost or strayed or crashed American pilots who violated what he laughingly called the neutrality of his borders—which the Cong are suspected to cross regularly.

But beggars cannot be choosers. Just as my chopper came over the broad, gliding floods of the jungle river, my exhausted engine gave one last strangled croak and died. The chopper fell like a stone. Then the uprush of air caught the dead blades. They creaked and began to turn. The rate of descent lessened—not much, but just enough.

The muddy yellow river swung up to smash me like a flyswatter in the hand of a giant. Just before I hit I caught one fleeting glimpse of thick green jungle lining either bank like a solid wall. Then I smacked the water and everything went black.

Well, as Carmody, the guy who taught me how to fly in India, used to say, any landing you can walk away from is a good one. I have a hunch even Carmody would not have thought much of the way I hit that river. Yellow-brown water smashed over the bubble canopy as we hit the surface with a jolt that knocked me against the panel. When I came to I had a cut on my brow streaming blood. I ached all over like one big bruise. But I was alive, at least.

But that belly flop had sprung leaks in both pontoons and they were filling up fast. I tore off my safety harness and inflated a rubber raft. Then I grabbed the emergency gear, prepacked in a knapsack for just such a spot, and got out.

The knapsack was packed with everything from snakebite serum to signal flares, and it made a bulky package. I wrestled it into the bobbing raft and climbed out dizzily. One pontoon was underwater already and the chopper was riding at a forty-degree angle, just about to slide under. I pushed away from the pontoon with one paddle, backed water a bit, and sat glumly, watching my one link with civilization go under. Then I roused myself and took a long sour look around at the depressing scenery. The jungle was packed, green and thick, on either side of the river. It looked unpleasant. But with the raft I could get down-river and maybe be lucky enough to find a settlement of some kind. I began to paddle a bit, but the river whipped right along and I didn't need to work very hard to keep moving.

Pretty soon I was soaked with sweat and busy keeping off the bugs. The air was thick and soupy and hot. It stank of stagnant water and rotting vegetation and slimy mud, but I wouldn't have traded that river for the jungle. I could stand flies and stink and sweat, but the jungles hereabouts are somewhat less wholesome. They are crawling with unfriendly creatures, of which cobras are only one variety. Not to mention tigers and wild boar and elephants. I would take my chances with the river.

After a while, I sat and rested aching arms and sourly watched endless jungle whip by on either side of me. The Cambodian jungles are among the world's least hospitable places, thick with teak and dense bamboo and rubbery rhododendron bushes, the ground a sloppy quagmire of knee-deep leaf mold and greasy mud. I had carried off a machete from the helicopter, but I had no desire to have to use it. Let the river current do the work, was my motto. If worst came to worst, I was perfectly willing to simply glide downstream all the way to the sea.

I began to do some serious thinking about where I was. Our base at Hon Quan was some ten miles or so on the other side of the Cambodian border, but the Mekong itself lay farther away. I cudgeled my memory, trying to picture the maps I had seen. There was a map case in the bubble canopy, and a compass as well, but I had gotten out of the chopper so fast they had been left behind.

Could this be the Mekong? As far as I could remember, the Mekong at its closest point to the border lay some fifty miles northwest of Hon Quan. Was it possible I had flown that far afield while searching for a spot to bring her down safety? Well . . . it was possible, but just barely. A chopper eats up the miles unobtrusively. I *could* have come that far, but I wondered: could this be another river? I recalled to mind the maps of Cambodia that I had studied. In the center lay something called the Tonle Sap, the Great Lake. This, I vaguely remembered, was supposed to have been the last shrinking remnant of a mighty prehistoric sea. Lots of rivers fed into it: I might have crashlanded on one of these tributaries and not on the Mekong. In which case, God alone knew where I was being carried by the swift gliding current of the muddy waters.

It was late afternoon by now and getting dark. The startlingly sudden night of the jungle was coming down across the sky. And here was another problem. Up to now I had been kept busy not so much by paddling, for the current was very swift, but by the necessity of shoving my rubber raft clear of half-sunken teakwood logs and other river debris. All I needed was to brush up against one of those half-submerged snags. My raft would tear and sink in seconds. Then I would *really* have problems!

But how could I continue keeping the raft clear of snags when the impenetrable darkness of the jungle night closed down over the river? As it would be doing before very much longer. . . .

I decided on the only course that seemed advisable, and began to put in towards the nearer shore. I would just have to take my chances on spending the night in the jungle, and push on down river with dawn.

It was tough work breaking free of the rushing current, and it was pitch dark by the time I came to shore. I got out, my boots sinking to the knee in the foul-smelling mud, and dragged the lightweight raft up out of the water. It was marshy and soft on this part of the bank, and I fought my way through tall stiff grasses up to solid land, tying the raft securely to the limb of a fallen tree.

Then I sat down on the log and made a meal of sorts out of the emergency rations, washing it down with a swig of fresh water from one of the canteens. I was thirsty enough from the sweltering heat of my river journey to drink the whole canteen, but I knew that would be most unwise. It might be days before I came to a riverfront town or settlement, and I would need every drop of my water supplies. I had half a pack of cigarettes, so I rationed them as well. I sat and smoked and batted flies and watched the stars come out by the score. They burned bright and fierce against the night, like fistfuls of blue-white diamonds strewn across black velvet.

It was a beautiful sight, but I was in no mood to appreciate beauty just then. I began to wonder how I was supposed to sleep. I could lie down on the ground and take my chances with the cobras, or I could curl up in the rubber raft. But the raft would hardly be a barrier to any really determined cobra, and anyway there were other creatures infesting these jungles who might be inclined to come down to the banks of the river for a little drink.

The only alternative was to climb a tree and find a comfortable crotch. Then all I would have to worry about was falling asleep—and falling out. But it was too dark to see clearly and most of the trees nearby were unclimbable.

And then I saw the light.

It shone in the heavens above like a pale beacon. I froze, snuffing out my cigarette in the leaf mold, wondering about Viet Cong. Who else would have a searchlight operating in these jungles? If this was Cambodia, there certainly could be no friendly American camp nearby.

And I began to sweat again.

I was in enough trouble already without falling into enemy hands. I had seen some examples of what happened to Americans during "interrogation" at the hands of the Viet Cong. I began to wish I had kept going on the river awhile longer.

The light shone on. It was pallid and ghostly, a stationary pillar of faint light standing up against the stars. It seemed to waver rhythmically. It throbbed. It pulsed like a beating heart. My curiosity became overwhelming. And I knew that I could never dare sleep this close to whatever was making that jungle beacon without satisfying my curiosity. I had to discover the cause of this mystery.

Whatever was causing the light was not very far inland from the river. A few hundred yards at most. Surely, if I watched my step, I could make my way close enough to the source of the weird pulsing column of light. I resolved to try, anyway.

Taking up my machete and slinging the pack across my shoulder, I started straight for it. I went slowly and tried to be as careful as possible, to avoid making any more noise than was necessary. But I really didn't have to worry about the noise my passage made as I squeezed through the thick underbrush. For the whole jungle had come alive around me with the onset of darkness. For night is the jungle's day. The big predators are aprowl, and the little scuttling things scurry through the brush seeking food and water. Only the monkeys sleep in the trees above, huddled together along the branches.

With every step my boots sank to the ankle and sometimes halfway to the knee in the slimy mulch of decaying leaves and reeking mud. I wormed through thick groves of bamboo and crept through gigantic rhododendron bushes. Their rubbery leaves swished against my face and slapped my shoulders. I hoped I would not disturb a sleeping boar. Or, for that matter, one of the slithering reptiles that infested this rotting hellhole.

Soon the light became dimly visible through the densely packed trees. It waxed and waned like a living thing of light. I paused from time to time to listen. No sound of diesel engines, no guttural Viet Cong voices, no chatter of radio static. Just the slap and wash of the river against the reedy shore, the rustle of small things sliding through the leaves, the thousand little ordinary sounds of the jungle.

I pushed forward, and came to the edge of a clearing. And stopped dead in my tracks, staring.

Before me, rising tier on tier out of the swampy bush, were the crumbling ramparts of an old stone city. Conical towers, covered with carved faces and wreathed with jungle vines, loomed up into the darkness.

I had stumbled upon a lost city, buried for ages in the jungles of Cambodia.

CHAPTER II

THE GATE BETWEEN THE WORLDS

T o this very hour I can remember the thrill of shock that went through me as I first gazed upon the gates of the dead city. I can remember catching my breath with amazement, and the prickle of awe that roughened my skin and tingled at my nape as I stared at the uncanny spectacle that lay before me, drenched in the silver glamor of a brilliant moon.

The very unexpectedness of the discovery added to the air of the supernatural that hung about that timeless moment. One moment ago I had been worming my way though the dense black jungle, and in the next I stood before the frowning gates of a fantastic stone city left over from another age!

The transition was so miraculous, so swift, so unexpected, that it was as if some unseen magician had conjured the city into being before my eyes. Still, frozen, timeless, bathed in the mystery of moonlight, the city seemed an apparition. I thought of the glimmering mirages of the desert, and of that persistent image of an unknown city the Italian mariners have seen for centuries, hovering above the waters of the Straits of Messina—*Fata Morgana*, the superstitious fisherfolk call the floating mirage, and to this day the scientists have yet to solve the baffling mystery of the illusion that has haunted those Straits from the age of the Crusaders to this day.

Strange and very beautiful was this unknown and ruined metropolis of the Cambodian jungles that lay before me. I stood, frozen with awe, my nerves prickling with the cold premonition of the supernatural, almost as if in another breath I expected the moonlit ruins to evaporate into darkness—to vanish as swiftly and as mysteriously as they had flickered into being.

There were conical and many-sided stone towers that loomed up into the star-gemmed sky, their sides heavy with sculpted faces that glared down at me with blind eyes. Walls were thickly graven with weird hieroglyphic symbols in a tongue unknown to me, perhaps unknown and unreadable by any living man. What lost wisdom, what forgotten science, what mysterious lore, lay hidden in those huge and cryptic symbols?

Well did I know that the trackless jungles of old Cambodia were whispered as the haunt of legend and marvel and mystery. I had heard of the baffling stone ruins which lay far to the north—the jungle-grown cities and temples known as Angkor Vat and Angkor Thom. For untold centuries the jungle had concealed those colossal ruins, those vine-grown temples left over from the mysterious reign of the little-known Khmer race who had so curiously vanished from the face of the earth ages before. Was this mystery metropolis yet another monument abandoned in unknown antiquity by the strange and forgotten people we knew only as the Khmer? Lost in the unexplored jungles, had I stumbled across the threshold of an age-old secret city left behind in time's remotest dawn?

The stone gates towered before me, covered with weird glyphs. From the lintel above the arch, a heavy face of cold sandstone stared down at me with an enigmatic expression. Controlling a little shiver of uncanny awe, I stared back at that stone mask. Broad cheeks, flat nose, thick lips, wide glaring eyes—it was not a face of smiling welcome, that much was certain.

Was it a trick of moonlight and shadow, or did the faint trace of a mocking smile lurk in the dim, shadowed corners of those stone lips? Was it an illusion of my overstrained imagination, or did I glimpse the flicker of an impersonal, aloof intelligence in those wide and staring eyes, and—a chill, remote amusement?

What secret lore of unknown antiquity lay hidden behind the frozen smile of that guardian deity or demon whose face was set high above the gates of the lost city? In the cold glory of the moonlight, the stone metropolis was like a labyrinth, all black inky shadow and faint rose sandstone.

A rose-red city, half as old as time. . . .

Unbidden, my memory conjured up that famous line from the old poem. Dimly I recalled that John William Burgon, the author of that poem, had been writing about the stone city of Petra in the deserts of Arabia. No matter: the line fit here just as well.

Almost without volition, my feet had carried me through those frowning portals, beneath the enigma of that stone guardian with its mocking smile, and into the rubbish-choked courtyard that lay beyond.

All about me rose a forest of megalithic stone towers, built of colossal blocks hewn from solid sandstone the color of pale coral or of the faint skies of early dawn glimpsed over the gliding floods of the Orinoco. Whatever elder wisdom this vanished race had possessed, they certainly knew the secrets of stone construction. Blocks of stone weighing tons apiece were so closely fitted together to build these soaring walls and tapering spires that they needed no concrete to hold them firm. And measureless centuries of wind and rain had dislodged but few of the great building stones.

I remembered that when the French explorer and naturalist Mouhot, the first to stumble upon the vast ruins of Angkor to the north, had questioned the natives about the mystery cities, they told him they were the work of many-armed giants. It had been Pra-Eun, sorceror-king of the Dawn Age, who had commanded captive titans to raise the walls of the ancient city. Gazing now upon these mighty towers and megalithic bastions, I could well believe them to be the work of primal colossi enslaved by some mighty magician from an unknown age.

I could not resist the urge of my curiosity, and began to explore the ruined metropolis. I prowled through stone-paved streets, down long galleries where weird and monstrous caryatids bore up stone architraves carved with snarling devil-masks and beaked demons. Time hung heavy here; its invisible weight pressed on my soul. There was an almost palpable aura of an immense and unbelievable antiquity that hung about these moldering ruins from time's dawn. I felt the shudder of superstitious awe go through me. It was as if I walked through a shadowy necropolis where gods themselves lay buried; as if with every step I risked awakening mummified wizards or unseen guardians who had slumbered the ages away, and into whose time-haunted precincts mine was the first intruder's step.

Who were the mysterious Khmer kings who had built these sprawling metropoli of ancient stone? Where had they gone, leaving behind this wilderness of carved stone, the haunt of shadows and silence, a kingdom given over to the whispering dominion of the patient spider? And I thought of the lost and ocean-whelmed cities of elder Atlantis and pre-historic Mu ... of the stone enigma of the Ponape ruins, which A. Merritt had described in the opening pages of his great romance, *The Moon Pool.*

With every step I ventured deeper and deeper into the labyrinth of aeon-lost and time-forgotten mysteries. A fragment of a verse by Clark Ashton Smith came to my memory:

> . . . *search, in cryptic galleries,*
> *The void sarcophagi, the broken urns*
> *Of many a vanished avatar;*
> *Or haunt the gloom of crumbling pylons vast*
> *In temples that enshrine the shadowy past.*

Were these dim colonnades and glyphic walls and mega-lithic temples the work of the long-lost Khmer kings? I knew the remains of Angkor Vat were among the most curious and baffling ruins on earth, and that science has for many years sought to solve the enigma of their antiquity. But I knew, as well, that the vast stone wreckage of Angkor lay far to the north of this place, in the jungles north of the Tonle Sap, on the right banks of the river Siem Reap, a tributary of which fed into the great lake at Cambodia's heart. Never had I heard of any mysterious ruined cities this far south—*unless* . . .

Could this stone city be long-lost, legendary Arangkôr itself, the primal city from which the mighty line of the Khmer kings had sprung in mythic aeons before the beginning of time? I knew something of the weird epic literature of this mystery-haunted corner of oldest Asia; science had never found the lost and secret city wherein the first of the Khmer kings had arisen to rule the dawn age. Could this shadowy city of moonlight and silence be the fabulous and antique Arangkôr? Why, even the Khmer themselves had forgotten the whereabouts of the cradle of their own race.

> *. . . long-lost and legended Arangkôr,*
> *Thou age-forgotten City of the Dawn,*
> *Wherein doth stand the Gate Between The Worlds,*
> *Handwork of ancient Gods whose very names*
> *Are long since silence on the lips of men . . .*

Dim and tall, a column of throbbing radiance thrust above the lost city into the star-gemmed sky.

Enthralled in the crumbling mystery of lost Arangkôr (as in my heart I somehow knew this forgotten city to be), I had forgotten the beacon of pulsing light that had caught my attention in the jungle, and which had called me to the stone gates of the ruined metropolis like a beckoning finger of lambent light.

Now, as I glimpsed it above the conical towers, I remembered how I had come here to investigate that light. And instantly caution awoke within me. I had, for some unknown length of time, been prowling the rubbish-choked avenues and squares of the dead city, careless of the noise my boots made, not thinking it possible that ruins of such evident neglect and antiquity could be inhabited.

But now I froze, cursing my carelessness. That throbbing beam of mysterious light was no natural phenomenon, surely. Some stranger shared the lonely streets of the dead city with me, and it was yet to be determined if he were friend or foe!

I went forward more cautiously now, watching every step, my machete in my hand like a sword.

The pillar of pulsing luminance rose from the very center of lost Arangkôr. As I made my way towards that glowing beacon, I puzzled over its cause and purpose. Straight up into the midnight sky it blazed, that ray of pale light that throbbed and flickered and throbbed. Looking up, I saw the yellow spark of distant Jupiter directly overhead. I thought nothing of this at the time.

I came at last into a great stone-paved plaza at the very heart of the deserted city.

Stone colossi squatted in a vast ring about that which lay at the center of this plaza. Tailor-fashion they sat, raising many arms, hands clutching meaningless attributes, skulls, keys, flowers, wheels, swords, and stylized thunderbolts. Heavy stone faces glared inward to the unknown thing at the center of the circle of gods: some howled, some smiled, some wept, some leered, and some looked down at the source of the column of radiance with the placid and immobile features of a Buddha.

Nowhere could I see a sign of life, although my eyes searched the shadows that clung about the bases of the circle of stone gods.

I went forward between two of the stone titans and looked at last upon the source of the mysterious light. A gasp broke from my lips.

In the very center of the great plaza, encircled by the towering carven gods, lay—*a well!*

Wide was the mouth of this well; a man could fall therein with ease; and that it descended to a very great depth I did not question. Sunk deep in the stone pave was this curious well, and its margin was a thick lip of some pallid translucent stone that reminded me of milky jade, although were that lucent substance truly jade, the mineral must have been the most gigantic piece of worked jade known to archaeology. Fifteen feet across from side to side the mouth of the great well stretched, and the lip of the well was ten feet broad, set flush with the stone floor of the plaza. The imagination reels, imagining the boulder that had yielded up so huge a single slab of the semiprecious mineral. A very mountain of jade would have been required! For I could see no jointure in all that flawless circle of milky stone: incredible, almost impossible, but it was *all of one piece.*

Up from the mouth of the jade well the mighty beam of radiance shone. Fifteen feet across, the throbbing pillar of luminance sprang into the night sky, pointing, as it seemed, at the distant spark of Jupiter.

The column of light had only the faintest suggestion of color. Dull white, a cold hue as of moonbeams, the colossal ray rose up from the bottom of the world to fling a shining spear against the citadels of the stars.

Rhythmically, a wave of sparkling gold ascended the luminous shaft of that beam of pallid radiance. A mist of gold-dust, a calyx of powdered gold, a tissue of flickering, gemmy golden sparks—I blinked in fascination and awe at the mysterious phenomenon. The ripples of gold light were what gave the illusion that the shaft of light dimmed and grew brighter, dimmed and again grew brighter. The secret of the throbbing rhythm I had glimpsed from afar was solved—one mystery, at least!

For when the wave of sparkling gold particles went gliding up the dim shaft of the beam, the beam seemed brighter through the added brilliance of the fiery mist.

But what were those rising flakes of golden fire? What unseen and unimaginable lamp deep in the bowels of the planet thrust forth this shining beacon against the stars? And why?

Incautiously, I stepped forward to investigate this luminous enigma.

As I stepped out on the shimmering ring of milky jade, I

lost my footing. For the lucent substance was as slick as oiled glass!

I fell headlong, my machete flying, the knapsack slipping from my shoulders to thud against the sleek stone.

And now I saw something I had not noticed earlier. The broad ring of milky, luminous stone was ever so slightly *concave*.

The jade lip of this mysterious well sloped inward towards the mouth, and I was helplessly sliding into the throbbing beam of light that speared up against the midnight sky!

My palms struck out but slid futilely, unable to stay my progress. Frantically I groped for a handhold, but there was none that I could find or feel.

Feet first, I slid into the golden, pulsing glory of the ray.

Strange—strange beyond words—is the uncanny experience I must next relate.

My vague, distorted memories of that flashing and timeless moment are blurred and meaningless.

For months I have pondered over the sensory record stamped in my mind. At length I believe I have pieced together some explanation of what followed as I slid down the sloping mouth of that mysterious well, straight into the throbbing beam of luminance. Perhaps my imagination has contributed something to the account I must give you now; perhaps remembered fragments from a hundred science fiction stories I have read have gone into the crucible of memory, and result in the following description of that which cannot adequately be described. If so, so be it! But here, as accurately as I can picture the experience in the inadequate medium of written words, is what seemed to occur.

A blinding light enveloped my body.

I squeezed my eyes shut against the awful brightness, but

to no avail! The blaze of radiance pierced through me. I could feel it beating against my flesh. I could feel it warm against my very bones, like desert sunlight.

Then all bodily sensation left me. Numb, I seemed to float like a cloud of insubstantial vapor amid a glory of dazzling light. But—no—a ghost of sensation filtered to me through the shining splendor.

I felt a storm of fiery particles beating against naked flesh. The particles I had seen before—the flakes of golden fire that swept up the column of the ray? I cannot say; I will never know.

Like a drumming hail they beat upon me from beneath, and I felt myself rising, rising up that column of shining glory . . . faster and ever faster, until my velocity became a soundless rush of hurricane force.

I could not see, I could not speak. I felt bodiless, devoid of substance, without weight. A ghost of streaming mist, impelled upwards by some unthinkable force, I hurtled into the sky.

Had the unknown radiance, in some manner inexplicable to me, sundered the bonds of interatomic energy, the binding force that holds matter together? Was I now but a dematerialized cloud of racing neutrons and electrons, driven up that beam of radiant force by some ionic thrust?

Science would scoff at the thought. But I know of no other explanation whereby to explain the inexplicable.

Now I was vaguely conscious of intensest cold—a supra-arctic cold such as might lie in the dark abyss between the stars.

There was a moment of utter blackness.

A sensation of incredible speed, as though I now traveled faster than light itself.

The cold bit deep—the blackness closed about me—I flew

like a meteor through unguessable immensities at the speed of thought itself.

Ahead of me I caught one flashing glimpse—incredible sight! A colossal, banded globe of brown and orange flame, with a cyclopean eye of fire!

A cold, dead orb of jagged rock swung towards me, like the frozen, airless satellite of some planetary giant.

For a single flashing instant I stared down—or up?—at splintered mountains of frozen black rock—valleys of frozen blue methane snow—a jumbled, jagged, wintry wilderness in which a man could not survive for a second.

Then the features of the frozen stone orb hurtling towards me with unthinkable velocity *blurred*.

Changed—in a miraculous transformation!

I caught one single swift flying glimpse of thick jungles, shining rivers, cloud-crested mountains, glittering barbaric cities—and the next instant I felt as if the walls of the universe had closed with a deafening crash upon the flying mote of light that was myself.

And I knew no more.

CHAPTER III
WORLD OF MANY MOONS

Nature is, in many ways, a merciful mother. When the flesh of her puny children has endured shock upon shock to the very limits of the intolerable, she extends to them the benison of unconsciousness.

From a heavy coma, I awoke slowly.

Awoke to a torpor of body and soul—a languor that lapped me soothingly in its folds. For a long while I simply lay without thought or feeling, in a dim stupor like the aftereffect of some powerful narcotic. I lay flat on my back against some slick, cool stone surface, staring up at the moons in the dim golden sky. Sleepily I blinked at the three shining moons in the darkly golden sky above me.

Something clamored in my mind for attention. But it felt too good to lie here motionless and numb. So I firmly closed my mind against the intrusion of unwanted thoughts and idly gazed at the triple-mooned sky of golden vapor—for now I could see that it was indeed vapor, a crawling, curdled film of dim gold light that wrinkled and glided and whorled and eddied above my head like foam on the surface of a disturbed pool, or the coiling and panchromatic arabesque of an oil slick on the pavements of New York.

There was something about that sky that obscurely troubled my placid semiconsciousness. A sky, I reasoned, ought not to be gold vapor, but some other color—blue?

I could not remember.

But there should not, I felt most definitely, be *three* moons aloft in that strange sky. And especially not such moons as these. For moons should be pallid white, not like these three monstrous orbs, one of which was cold lime green, the second dim rose, and the third a luminous blend of azure and silver.

And then I woke fully, tingling with shock as if a drenching gush of ice-cold water had sluiced my naked body from head to heel—

My *naked* body?

Wildly, I cast an involuntary glance down at myself and saw that I was bare as a new-born babe. I stared around me at the broad disk of milky jade whereon I had lain upon awakening, the broad disk of jade that lay athwart a field of thick-leaved grass that was the crimson of fresh blood—

A gold sky—three moons—and crimson grass!

I sprang to my feet with an inarticulate cry, and reeled, staggering for a moment. My body felt numb, as if the circulation had been suspended in every extremity. Pins and needles lanced through me with excruciating pain as the circulation began. I lurched to the edge of the milky disk of stone and fell sprawling in that springy field of thick-leaved grass that was so impossibly crimson.

Panting, my heart racing with shock, I stared around me wildly.

From dreamless sleep I had awakened into—*nightmare!*

The jade disk was ringed about with nine towering monoliths—featureless pillars of dark, smooth stone. All about, a field of heavy-bladed crimson grass stretched away. To one side it sloped down to a gurgling stream some fifty yards below.

Behind me, and to my right, a wall of dense foliage blocked my view of whatever lay beyond—a heavy jungle, but like no jungle I had ever seen. For the trunks of the trees, and the branches, even to the most minute twigs, were *black*—black as any velvet—and gnarled and twisted into knotted, malformed shapes unlike any terrene trees with which I was familiar.

And the leafage of those trees was, again, that impossible, incredible, fantastic *crimson!*

It was a scene of nightmarish strangeness and phantasmagoric beauty, like something from the dreams of a painter like Hieronymus Bosch, or Hannes Bok.

And yet it was real! There was no question of that. Every detail of the scene lay clear and sharply defined before me, limned in the triple brilliance of those impossibly huge, fantastically colored moons. No dream or vision, no illusion or hallucination, could possibly have sustained such a detailed and lucid reality.

Another thought struck me as I lay there, my stunned mind striving to grapple with the impossible scenes that lay to every hand.

Could it be that I was—dead? And that this weird world of uncanny beauty and strangeness was the Afterlife? I uttered a mocking burst of laughter. Perhaps . . . perhaps . . . but, if that were so, the religions of my world were thoroughly wrong in their conceptions of the Afterlife, for this weird place of black, monstrous trees, golden sky and triple moons, and blood-colored vegetation, this was neither Hell nor Heaven, Purgatory nor Limbo.

It didn't look much like Valhalla should, or any other

world that myth described beyond the portals of life and death.

These first few moments of my life on the surface of Thanator (as I later discovered to be the name by which its strange natives called their curious world) are a blur to me. But I know this: I never for one moment entertained any serious doubt as to the state of my sanity. Never once did I really question that what I saw about me was not actual but some sort of dream or hallucination.

I knew that I was alive, sane, and that the scenery about me was a real place, no figment of a mind driven into the refuge of madness. I could feel the crimson blades of grass tickling the soles of my bare feet; I could feel the warm sunlight (or what I took to be sunlight) beating upon my bare body; a slight breeze stirred the unruly locks of yellow hair that fell over my brow, and passed invisible hands over my nakedness. My nostrils drank in the unfamiliar spicy aroma of jungle growths such as I had never seen or heard of before. My ears heard the faint clashing of thorny-edged leaves struck together in the light wind, the gurgling of the brook below, the coughing grunt of some unknown creature of the jungles.

This world was real. And I—however I had come here—was *here*.

I examined myself curiously.

Every article of clothing had somehow been stripped from my body. Even my underwear, my socks, the wristwatch on my arm, the ring on my right index finger, given to me when I was a boy by my father on some forgotten birthday—everything I had worn was gone.

Putting my hand to my chest, I discovered that the identification tags which had hung about my neck on a chain were also missing.

Most baffling of all: I'd cut my thigh on a tool a day or two ago, and had affixed an adhesive bandage to the cut.

The cut, half-healed, was still there. But the bandage was—gone!

Memories came tumbling back to me now, as if the shock of these discoveries had driven everything else from my mind, making room for the recent past. I remembered the helicopter crash on the Mekong, the trek through the Cambodian jungles, the way I had stumbled by accident upon the lost city, *the pillar of throbbing light into which I had fallen*—

Could it be—

That ancient verse from one of the old epics of Indochina, that reference to Arangkôr—

Wherein doth stand the Gate Between The Worlds

It was fantastic, incredible—like something out of the wildest, most imaginative piece of science fiction ever written, but—could it be? Was that beam of throbbing radiance that flung up against the cold glitter of the stars some weird means of transportation between worlds—some surviving mechanism of an elder science otherwise lost to the knowledge of man?

Almost instantly my mind came up with a term—*transporter beam*. I recalled the sensory illusions of speed and flight across dark and frigid immensities at frightful speed—the sensation of being not solid heavy matter, but a dematerialized cloud of electrons.

It was a staggering conception. All I had ever read about the mysterious scientific wizardry of lost and legendary peoples of the Dawn Age came tumbling back to me. Ancient Atlantis, whose glittering cities the green throat of the sea drank down before history began—primal Mu, whispered of in dark surviving myths—Lost Lemuria, whose colossal stone cities are long since submerged beneath the mighty waves of the Pacific, save for the cryptic ruins on Ponape and the huge, enigmatic stone faces that stare forever out to sea from the legend-haunted, lonely hilltops of Easter Island—

Did the Ancients possess the secret of transmitting matter across space?

Had I stumbled onto the secret of a lost science forgotten for uncounted aeons?

Was there a network of intangible pathways linking the planets together? Pathways of unknown force down which one could travel at unthinkable velocities to materialize upon the face of another world?

If so, what world was I on? What planet of the solar system had three moons?

I cudgeled my wits, remembering that Mercury and Venus were not known to have any satellites. Mars, I remembered, had two moons called Deimos and Phobus—it was no use: no planet known to me had three great moons to light its golden skies!

After a while I went down that sloping crimson lawn to bathe my face in the rushing stream below.

In a world of weird and terrifying strangeness, it was curiously heartening and gratifying to discover that water was still—water. Cold and pure, the water of this stream, as I drank from cupped hands, tasted no different from the water I had drunk from a score of jungle rivers back on Earth.

I went back up the hill to investigate the black and crimson jungle. It was thick and dark and I did not care to venture within its depths. There was no telling what savage predators might roam those gloomy aisles—and I had no weapons.

Neither did I care to squeeze through that thick foliage unclothed. The thick, broad leaves were edged with sharp, thorny serrations like a saw blade. My naked body would show the red trace of those razory thorns before I had penetrated a yard—and who could say what unknown venom such leaves might secrete?

Yet I could not stand in this place forever.

And the sky was darkening now. The gold vapor dimmed. The luster of the three immense moons brightened slowly, like goblin lanterns. I resolved to explore the edge of the jungle, and began walking.

I had become aware of two curious facts.

One was that the gravitation of this planet was the same as the gravitation of the world on which I had been born, or very similar. This suggested that the red and black planet must be nearly the same size as Earth—which seemed impossible. For, unless I had incorrectly read my astronomy text in college, the only planet in the solar system that is anywhere close to the size of our own world is cloud-wrapped, moonless Venus.

And the three moons that lit the darkening skies reduced to zero any chance of this planet being Venus.

The other fact was the air. I had been breathing it now for half an hour. I felt no ill affects therefrom; in fact, the air seemed to be the same as Earth's atmosphere—perhaps a bit fresher, perhaps even a bit richer in oxygen.

And my astronomy classes had given me to understand that no other planet in our solar system had an atmosphere breathable by human lungs. Mars, they said, had a cold rarefied atmosphere like that of the crest of Everest; the outer planets were supposedly wrapped in smothering blankets of poisonous methane and ammonia.

But my chest rose and fell calmly, and I breathed this air without discomfort.

It was a mystery, and but one of the myriad that surrounded my experiences thus far. I gave over as fruitless the attempt to puzzle it out, and resolved to wait for further data.

Night had fallen now, and with the advent of darkness came new mysteries—and a marvel beyond comprehension.

Glancing up, I glimpsed a *fourth* moon ascending above the horizon! It was very small and faint, compared to the three great orbs whose multicolored light illuminated the darkness—but it was visibly a disk, and adrift on the tides of night.

I could think of no planet with four moons. Did this mean the mysterious transporter beam, as I called it, had hurled me beyond the limits of the solar system into the orbit of some unknown planet which revolved about a distant star?

The answer to this new riddle was very swift and definite!

As I prowled along the margin of the dark jungle, the world about me was suddenly illuminated by a rich red glow that lit the sky like some unthinkably colossal explosion.

I turned to witness this new marvel and cried out in my astonishment.

Above the horizon a titanic arch of brilliance rose into view.

The fifth moon, if moon this was, must be either unthinkably huge or incredibly close to the planet whereon I stood—for the arch of its sphere bisected a considerable span of the dark horizon. If any body so huge were so close, it was difficult to understand why the gravitational forces did not bring the two globes together in a terrible collision.

As I watched, I became aware of an incredible fact. *The arch of light was broadening visibly.* As it rose steadily in the skies of this jungle world, instead, of rounding into a globe, it became ever more obvious that this new fifth moon was even larger than I had at first imagined.

More and more of this luminous globe arose above the horizon. Now it seemed almost to occupy *one-quarter of the visible horizon!*

I stared at this astounding vista with an awe so vast and thrilling as to be beyond description.

No stargazer of ancient Babylon, no great astronomer in his mighty observatory, has ever looked upon such a marvel of the skies as rose before me now.

Brilliant beyond belief, vast beyond comprehension, beautiful beyond dreams, the titanic globe rose at last fully above the horizon. Its surface was banded with horizontal zones, and an infinity of colors made it radiant with hues. Vast portions of its surface were colored an indescribably beautiful peach. Stripes of brown and glowing amber, rich orange and luminous ocher, brick-red and velvety purplish gray marked off the surface of the colossal glowing shield into ten belts or zones, of which the central or equatorial belt was easily twice the width of the others.

And burning like an unholy blemish, like a colossal pit of flame, the southern hemisphere bore into view a terrible glaring crimson eye.

And I knew now where I was.

This was not the unknown planet of some distant star.

There was no mistaking that brown and yellow-banded giant with his glaring Red Spot.

The mysterious beam of force had transported me to the surface of one of the twelve moons of Jupiter.

Suddenly, a hissing snarl arrested my attention. The bestial sound had come from the edge of the jungle. Although I could see nothing but gnarled, ebon trees and crimson, fanged foliage, I knew that they concealed a prowling predator. I felt the pressure of unseen, burning eyes upon me.

And it came to me that I was in deadly danger. I had been acting like a fool—wandering about this enchanted landscape like an awestruck dreamer, when I would have been far wiser to have sought to return to my own world at once.

That dislike stone that lay amid the ring of columns like some great altar—was it not fashioned of the same sleek, lucent jade as the mouth of the mysterious well in far-off Arangkôr? The transporter beam, or whatever it was, must be a link between this strange world and that lost city in the jungles of Cambodia. If I were to stand in the center of that circle of monoliths, would I not make the return journey to the world of my birth?

I turned and began to run for the Gate Between The Worlds, but it was too late.

Again the air resounded to that terrible hissing cry, and now a fantastic beast out of nightmare came crashing through the crimson foliage directly towards me.

Imagine a saber-toothed tiger crossed with some colossal reptile from prehistoric ages, and you will have an image of the thing that came hurtling from the underbrush with eyes of blazing yellow flame. It had a lithe, catlike body that rippled with steely strength. But instead of the striped fur of a jungle cat its sinewy length was clad in serpent scales. Bright emerald green was this scaly hide, paling to tawny yellow at the belly plates. Its feet were armed with bird claws, and a jagged line of sharp-edged spikes ran down its spine to the very tip of the lashing snakelike tail.

The monster's head was a snarling mask of fanged horror. Fierce cold eyes of lambent yellow flame were riveted upon my running figure. Giving voice to another hissing roar, the incredible thing flashed after me. And I was running for my life!

Strange unlikely thoughts pass through a man's mind

when he stands on the brink of eternity. The thought that passed through mine was that that fanged horror, that sinewy engine of destruction, armed with that bladed, whiplike tail and saw-toothed spine, must be a predator of dread and all-but-invincible ferocity. Yet how cleverly nature had given a measure of protection to her weaker children on this strange and awful world, for that glittering scaly hide of emerald mail could not well slink hidden through the underbrush of the jungle, whose crimson foliage would clash with the green-scaled cat-thing! Thus the monster must depend, not upon camouflage, but the speed of an irresistible charge to secure its meat.

I later learned that the thing at my heels was the fearsome *yathrib*, the savage dragon-cat of the Thanatorian jungles—deadlier by far even than the prehistoric sabertooth of my native world.

I ran like the wind, but the yathrib was almost upon me before I had covered half the distance to the circle of stone pillars and the jade disk of the Gate. I could feel the hot breath panting against my bare legs as I ran. Another few yards, and my adventures on this amazing world would come to an abrupt and gory finish—

And then, charging up the slope of the hill along whose crest I raced for the haven of the Gate stone came a party of even more incredible beings!

At first, so swiftly were events moving, I had no time to look at them clearly. I cast a hasty glance at strange, pale, attenuated figures clad in some glistening armor and mounted upon weird steeds like wingless and gigantic birds—then the foremost of the gaunt riders reined up in my path and loosed an arrow from the great war bow it held in lean, glistening arms.

Behind me I heard a choking grunt, Then, as I swerved

aside to avoid running full into the mounted figures, I struck a root with my bare foot and fell on the crimson turf. At any second I expected to feel the claws of that fanged horror at my heels ripping my flesh. But nothing happened.

I rolled over, sprang nimbly to my feet, and saw the yathrib squirming and wriggling amid the grasses, clawing with its hind legs at a terrible black arrow that thrust from the very base of its soft unprotected throat!

The pale attenuated rider had slain the beast even as it had reared erect to pull me down!

The grim shaft was all of a yard long—hewn, no doubt, from the same black wood as formed the gnarled and twisted trees of the jungle behind me. With incredible skill, the armored rider had struck the yathrib in what I later learned to be its only vulnerable spot—the soft tissues at the base of the throat, where the tough emerald mail did not protect the vital organs.

Even as I watched, the dragon-cat belched a fetid flood of black gore from between its fanged jaws, twitched once or twice, and stiffened in death.

Shakily, I turned to thank my rescuers. And as I did so, something like a lasso settled about my shoulders, slid-down my upper arms, and was tightened with a jerk. The leader of the mounted band had flung it from a slim tube. Now he tightened his grip on the cord and pulled. I was flung prone on the crimson grass, my arms held helplessly at my sides.

Grim irony. I had been rescued from the yathrib's slavering jaws—only to be taken prisoner by my very rescuer!

Dismounting, he bent over me, uttering harsh metallic words in some unknown tongue. I caught a vague glimpse of an inhuman visage—an expressionless mask of glistening silver-gray horn, like the shell of a gigantic crab—huge eyes like flashing black jewels—and a strange, sharp, medicinal odor that seemed vaguely familiar came to my nostrils from his slender form.

He seemed struck with the color of my hair and eyes, for although I could not understand the words of his clacking, guttural speech, his horny hand touched my hair again and again, and one horny finger lightly touched my eyelid.

The next moment I was swung up into the air and found myself face downward behind the saddle, dangling over the feathery cruppers of the strange bird-horse he rode. Then my captor swung astride, jerked the reins about, and the whole party went cantering off.

I cast one despairing glance behind as the jade disk and ring of pillars that represented my only hope of returning to my own world receded and were lost in the distance.

CHAPTER IV
KOJA OF THE YATHOON HORDE

Now I entered the first period of my captivity upon Thanator. For two months I was a prisoner among the strange beings who had saved me from the attack of the yathrib. The days passed slowly and without incident, as I learned the curious ways of this jungle world. To relate a day-by-day chronicle of my imprisonment would occupy far too many pages of this manuscript; hence I shall speak only of the discoveries I made in the camp of the Yathoon Horde.

When I got a closer look at the weird creatures who had captured me, I saw they were in no respect human. If anything, they resembled in their tall attenuated forms and jerking, many-jointed stride, gigantic insects like the praying mantis. Whether or not they were true insects, according to the technical definition of the word, I must leave to whatever scientists may one day peruse this document I now inscribe. Suffice it to say, they more closely resembled insects than any other form of life I could think of.

They stood about seven feet tall and were impossibly slim and skeletal. Like many true arthropods, their lean bodies were clad in an external horny coating like chitin. This segmented exoskeleton was a uniform silver-gray and exuded a sharp but not unpleasant scent which I eventually identified as the harsh metallic odor of ants—formic acid, I believe it is called.

Like many terrene insect forms, the Thanatorian arthropod has a body composed of three major sections.

First, the head, which is a horny and all but featureless ovoid like a slightly elongated egg, sharply pointed at the smaller end. These heads have neither nose nor nostril, insofar as I have been able to observe, and the mechanism of the mouth and jaw is concealed on the underside of this casque-like ovoid and too complicated for me to accurately picture in words.

They have two eyes, one on each side of the head, and much larger than the human, but without whites. These do not seem to be the usual faceted, compound eye structures I have seen in magnified drawings of insects. They are black, glittering, and devoid of any expressiveness. In order to blink, the arthropod uses two horny translucent membranes, one descending from the upper rim of the eye case and one rising from the lower, both covering the eye completely.

The insect creatures have no ears, or at least no external ears, and I have never been able to understand just how they manage to detect sounds. But they do have two long, slender, tapering and jointed antennae or feelers which extend from just above either eye, curving backwards gracefully over the skull. For all I know, these may be sensitive to the vibrations of sound.

Instead of necks, they have a jointed tubular structure composed of two rings, wherewith their heads are fastened to the second portion of their bodies, the thorax, which is a smooth, glistening, upright ovoid larger than the head, and shoulderless. From this two long arms with multiple joints extend. Their arms are twice as long as human arms and have an extra joint, like a secondary elbow. Slim and tapering shafts of chitin, these arms look like bare bones, ending in very long, thin, splayed, segmented fingers. There are four of these fingers, the central pair being about four inches longer than the outermost and innermost fingers, which are also of equal length. They have no thumb, but as the fingers have six joints each and are capable of extreme flexibility, they are able to handle objects at least as easily as do our human hands with their opposing thumbs.

The thorax of the arthropod—the upper chest, you might call it—is joined by a narrow banded waist to the abdomen, a long tapering spindle-shaped structure which thrusts out behind the legs. These hind limbs also have an extra joint like those of the forelimbs, and end in four-toed, or- clawed, splayed feet. In the case of the feet, three widely separated toes are thrust out in front and the fourth toe, like the spur on a bird's foot, extends to the rear. These multiple-jointed hind limbs are oddly constructed. The first segment (you might call it the thigh) thrusts forward from the hip joint, ending in a knee joint; the second segment, the lower leg, thrusts sharply backwards, ending in an ankle joint, from which a third segment thrusts forward again, ending in yet another ankle joint, to which is affixed the enormous, splayed, clawlike toes.

These hind limbs, with their multiple joints and odd articulations, strongly resemble the structure of a dog's hind leg. The arthropods run with incredible swiftness; their great hind limbs send them bounding along in springing leaps. They also use these limbs most peculiarly in war. The Yathoon warriors go armed with most unusual swords, in addition to the great black war bows. These whip swords, as they are called, are not unlike the fencing épée, but are of amazing length—a good sixty inches of finger-thin, very flexible steel, ending not in a point but in a bladed barb like an arrowhead. They use these swords very much like whips, and the wound inflicted by the lashing blow of that bladed barb is a terrible one. In battle, the arthropods leap suddenly into the air like great grasshoppers, their long ungainly arms bringing the whip-sword down in swift, lashing strokes that are very difficult to parry and can best be avoided by hopping backwards or to one side. A duel between two Yathoon warriors—and I saw many such during my internment among them—is a bewildering scene of leaping, agile figures bounding several yards into the air, the whipping needle of their swords whistling through the air shrilly.

Yet for all their height, agility, and speed, the arthropods are less strong than a human being. This is due to the nature of their musculature. In human anatomy, our inner skeletons serve as a solid structure against which our muscles are anchored, giving leverage. But the insect creatures *have* no internal skeletons—their external crust of horn serving to hold them rigid. The muscles of the arthropods, then, are anchored rather flimsily to the inner walls of this exoskeletal crust, which gives them nowhere near the muscular leverage or, thus, the strength of men.

Whether or not they are truly evolved from insects I cannot say. But, if I recall correctly, terrene insects have no lungs, their under-thorax containing small perforations through which oxygen enters their system. The arthropods of Thanator have genuine lungs, for the segmented plates of the thorax expand and contract rhythmically, held together by a hard but flexible gummy substance like cartilage, and their thoraxes swell and diminish to the breathing of inner lungs. It might well be they are not insects at all, but that some form of crustacean life acted as their evolutionary ancestors. I can but give the data I observe—I lack the knowledge to interpret it scientifically.*

For the duration of my captivity I remained in the possession of the warrior who had captured me—the same male who had led the hunting party and whose bow had slain the yathrib there on the slope of that hill. I soon learned that the insect creatures had a language, and that my owner was known to them as Koja.

My position among the warriors of the Yathoon (as they call themselves) was difficult to explain. I was a prisoner, but not exactly a slave; I was permitted to wander where I would in the camp but not allowed to leave its perimeter, which was constantly guarded.

Koja was a *komor* or chieftain among the Horde. His rank was earned by his prowess in war rather than by any nobility of birth. His position in the hierarchy of his clan was very high, and his retinue was princely.

This retinue, or household, to which I now belonged consisted of a dozen young cadet warriors and twice that number of servitors. The cadets were not his offspring, but youthful warriors of the clan who were in his service to learn from a warrior of the greatest distinction the arts of combat and hunting. It was not unlike the system used in the terrene Middle Ages, whereby the younger sons of a noble house would

---

*Captain Dark's description of the arthropods of Thanator make them, indeed, most peculiar "insects." Dr. Edmund Bailey of Columbia University, a renowned expert in the study of insects, informs me that with very few exceptions all true insects have, not four, but six limbs; and lungs have never been observed in genuine insects. The Thanatorian arthropods also seem to lack even vestigial wings or wing cases, which throws them into a dubious classification. No true insect has anything remotely resembling fingered digits or birdlike feet. Dr. Bailey is at a loss to find a species of terrene life to which such creatures could belong, but they seem to bear only superficial resemblance to insects as we on Earth know them.—L. C.

enter the service of another lord, thereby receiving knightly training and schooling in the gentle arts of courtesy, chivalry, and honor. The cadets lived with Koja, served him, assisted in his hunting parties, and wore his markings.

The camp area reserved for the retinue of Koja consisted of some twenty tents of black felt, arranged in a double circle with the largest tent in the very center. Koja himself dwelt in the central tent, together with his hoard, or treasure. As to my position in the band of Koja's retinue, I think I was considered more a possession than a captive, and in this connection I should explain that, among the Yathoon, rank and position were recognized not only on fighting skill but also on the basis of wealth. The arthropods use no medium of exchange such as coinage, but the retinue of each warrior chieftain protects his hoard of treasures. These are not what we would call treasures—gems or precious metals or ven artworks are valueless to the Yathoon—but what we would consider a collection of curios. Rare shells, oddly shaped or colored stones, weirdly twisted bits of wood, bright feathers, the skulls of beasts—these constitute the "treasure" guarded by a Yathoon chieftain. The tents of his retinue resemble a jackdaw's nest, or the hoard of a packrat. And it was with wry amusement that I came at length to realize my true position, as a prized possession, or *amatar*, of Koja.

I was an exotic curio!

I assumed at this time that all of Thanator was inhabited only by these nomadic tribes of arthropods, and that I was unique. It was not until much later that I discovered that the Yathoon Horde shared their world with at least three other distinctly different races of intelligent human beings, and that *it was the peculiar hues of my yellow hair and blue eyes* that rendered me valuable—a "collector's item."

My first impressions of these ungainly, stalking insect

creatures was, I think naturally, one of revulsion and horror. I have never had a neurotic terror of crawling insects, but the weird, gaunt, faceless arthropods were so completely unlike anything I had ever encountered that my initial reaction was to find them repulsive and loathsome.

My reaction during these opening days of my enslavement was due in part to a fear that I was in imminent danger of being served up as the main course in some sort of disgusting cannibal feast—or at least that I was soon to be tortured to death on the altars of some alien divinity. But no such fate ensued, and in time I learned that I was in no danger of either cannibalism or torment, and would receive decent treatment from my captors.

My first reaction to the arthropods was, as I have said, one of revulsion at what I deemed their hideous and inhuman aspect. Inhuman they certainly were, but "hideous" is a matter of open question. The fact that they differed enormously from Homo sapiens was no reason to find their appearance automatically loathsome. Very soon I found myself admiring them. Slim, stalking figures, they were not without a certain grace—even a certain cold inhuman beauty. With their attenuated limbs and extreme height they came, with familiarity, to assume something of the dignity and impressiveness of the lean gaunt statues of Giacometti or Henry Moore's weird stone figures.

Indeed, they had also something of the sleek, economical efficiency of a well-designed machine. Almost I could picture those stalking, multijointed limbs as smoothly machined pistons. Something of the passionless beauty of the machine was theirs, and something of the grandeur of sculpture.

In short, I no longer found them frightening, having no reason to fear my fate at their hands.

I found that they treated me well, or at least did not mistreat me overtly. They seemed, if anything, to pay very little attention to me, wrapped up as they were in their own unimaginable inner lives and busied with their own affairs.

Indeed, the retinue of Koja's slaves—captive arthropods won in battle with rival clans—fed and cared for me solicitously, if coldly. The arthropods do not know the human emotions—love, kindness, mercy, and friendship are completely alien to their mentality. This is a mixed blessing, at best. But, at least, if they know no kindness they are equally ignorant of cruelty. They neither torture nor mistreat their captives. Ignorant of the nobler sentiments, they are devoid of the more bestial.

Koja interrogated me at length upon our return to the vast war camp of the Horde. He seemed baffled at my inability to understand his harsh metallic language. And he seemed equally puzzled as the sounds of English words came from my lips. I tried Spanish and Portuguese, with which I was intimately familiar from my childhood, and a few phrases of French, German, and Vietnamese. He was equally unfamiliar with all of these. Eventually he stalked out, leaving me in the care of one of his servitors, an arthropod named Sujat. Sujat was personally in charge of caring for my needs, which he did with cold efficiency.

A row of uncouth symbols was painted across my chest— symbols whose meanings I was not to discover until somewhat later. As for the rest of my person, I went as naked as when I had first appeared on this world. The Yathoon, of course, with their chitinous exoskeleton which protects their soft inner parts from harm and from extremes of temperature, have no need of clothing. Lacking external sexual organs, they are devoid of the very concept of bodily modesty, as they are of ornament or fashion.

Their only garment, if it can be dignified with such a

term, is a leather strap worn across the thorax like a baldric, and to which is affixed the long supple length of the whip-sword, held thus scabbarded across what would be their shoulders if they had shoulders, which they do not. The five-foot length of this blade would make it impractical to be worn at the hip. This baldric, and a row of painted symbols across the front of the upper thorax, constitutes their entire raiment. These symbols are not unlike those painted upon my own chest, and I was shortly to learn their meaning.

Although Sujat was in charge of me, it was Koja himself who served as my instructor in the Thanatorian tongue. This was, I suppose, a signal honor, but I think it was prompted purely by Koja's curiosity about his new toy. At any rate, Koja taught me his language with enormous patience and an un-swerving sense of purpose that I would have thought highly admirable in a human being. But I could not, at least at this early date, think of my "owner" in terms of human attributes. His gaunt, alien person still, to some degree at least, seemed repellent to me.

This language was very interesting and, in many aspects, unique. I later discovered that the four races who inhabit Thanator have—incredible as it may seem, in mind of their enormous differences—a common tongue which is identical in all respects save, perhaps, in vocabulary. For the arthro-pods have not, or at least do not use, any words for such purely human conceptions as "love," "friendship," "mother," "father," "wife," or "son."

Such concepts do have a place, I later learned, in the universal language of this planet, but as the arthropods have no use or need for such terms, they are ignorant of them.

No other language than this single universal tongue has ever been known on the jungle moon; indeed, it was with the very greatest difficulty that, in the early days of my captivity, I made my captors grasp the notion that I was totally ignorant of their tongue and required patient instruction therein. The very concept of an intelligent being unfamiliar with the common tongue—to say nothing of the idea of a being who spoke "another" language—seemed incomprehensible to them. I am convinced that, at the beginning at least, Koja believed me mentally deficient; an idiot or at least a low-grade moron. But with some effort I managed to get across the idea that I wished to learn their language, and he taught me with great efficiency.

Since I have spent the greater part of my life knocking about the odd corners of the globe, I have developed an ear for languages and have a nodding acquaintance with a dozen earthly tongues. Hence I really did not find it difficult to master the basics of Thanatorian. At the beginning it was easy. I would point to objects, to parts of the body or of the landscape, to tools, weapons, articles of furniture, and receive from the expressionless Koja the relevant Thanatorian term. To assist in memorizing these words I wrote them down in English letters, a process that seemed greatly to mystify my tutor. Among the jackdaw's nest of curiosities that formed the wealth of Koja, I found an enameled box containing writing implements, rather like a Japanese writing case. This was, by the way, my first inkling that the Yathoon warriors shared their world with a higher civilization. For the arthropods were completely ignorant of writing, and when I suggested with appropriate gestures to Sujat that I would like to use these instruments he stalked from the tent to fetch his master, who came to stand, impassively watching as I displayed the uses to which I wished to put the writing case.

It was obvious to me that Koja had no understanding of

why I wished to make little squiggly marks with the cut end of a *thaptor* feather* dipped in black substance and scrawled upon sheets of brownish paper that looked like coarse papyrus. But as I handled the implements with delicate care, he resolved to permit me to play with them as it seemed I had no intention of harming his "treasures."

Thus, able to compile a vocabulary of Thanatorian terms for my own study, I made quite rapid progress in my mastery of the language. We shortly progressed beyond simple nouns to verbs, and here we must have made a ludicrous spectacle, acting out various actions. I recall in particular one hilarious scene: Koja was giving me a verb which he illustrated by hopping up and down. It took me some little while to figure out whether he was giving me the word for "hop" or "walk" or "up" or what. And all the time the poor fellow, with his solemn and totally expressionless face, stood there on the beaten earth outside my tent, soberly jumping up and down like some ungainly grasshopper!

As I say, we encountered no real difficulty in our language lessons until we passed beyond simple nouns and verbs, colors and numbers, into the more baffling regions of the participles. I suppose this is a common difficulty in learning any language in this manner—how in the world do you *illustrate* such elusive terms as "and," "the," or "of"?—but then I had never before had to master a language without a text or at least a teacher familiar with my own tongue.

In the course of these lessons, which we pursued almost every single day from morning to evening, I picked up an

---

*Captain Dark seems to have forgotten that he has not yet discussed the thaptor, which is the name by which the bird-horses of Thanator are called. The quill pens contained in this writing chest (doubtless of Ku Thad workmanship) probably came either from the manelike ruff of feathers around the base of the thaptor's skull, or from the tail feathers.—L. C.

enormous amount of miscellaneous information. I discovered that the arthropods were a race of warlike nomads, divided into several rival clans who were perpetually at war, each clan against all others. These clans, five of them in all, were—this internecine rivalry notwithstanding—all part of the same Horde, the Yathoon, and all under one common leader, who was known as the Arkon, which I suppose could be defined as "king." The Arkon, whose name was Uthar, lived far away at a certain secret place in the mountains. The various clans of the Horde went forth every few months from this hidden place to hunt for meat (and "treasure"), returning at a certain specific date. When they entered their capital—Koja called it "the Secret Valley of Sargol,"—they were instantly at peace with one another, regardless of the fact they were at each other's throats until they reached the very entrance stone of the Secret Valley!

I never found out the name of the clan that had taken me captive. I do not, in fact, believe the five clans had names to differentiate them—a fact which I found rather remarkable. Koja explained it to me in his usual solemn way.

"We know the clan to which we belong," he said. "And we know that the males of all other clans are our foes. And we know a strange male when we encounter him. What need have we, then, for labels?"

I could find nothing wrong with this statement; for all I knew it was by their different smell that the members of one clan identify a stranger. But I seized this opportunity to ask a question that had been puzzling me for some time.

"What, then, are the colored markings on the upper thorax of all Yathoon warriors?"

I should explain that on the front of the thorax a peculiar series of symbols were painted in bright colors: red, black, green, and gold. These were nothing like alphabetical symbols—for, as I learned from Koja's reaction to my use of the writing case, the arthropods have no conception of writing—but were instead geometrical symbols, lines, curves, and irregular splotches of raw color.

My tutor explained to me that these were—ah, but here I come to an untranslatable concept peculiar to the insect creatures. The glyphs, or whatever they were, served as markings to identify tribal rank, prestige, and the number of enemy kills—a strange combination of army rank insignia with the stickers on the fusilage of a fighter plane, I suppose, which indicate the number of enemy craft one ace has downed. I was glad to have my curiosity on this subject satisfied: hitherto I had assumed them to be in the nature of personal names or heraldic blazons, indicating family alliances. But I had discovered that the Yathoon warriors hold their females in common and have no conception of an individual mate. Indeed, paternity itself is unknown to them; all they know is that at regular intervals their females lay a grublike larva which eventually matures into male or female specimens of their race. Since no Yathoon knows who his father or mother were, and since all of the Yathoon larvae or young are raised in common, the arthropods are completely without anything like a family life. I have often wondered whether this total lack of family, or of mating, or of father- and motherhood, was the reason they lacked the more tender emotions.

Perhaps. Or perhaps not. Since they were not human—or even mammalian—I suppose it would be foolish to expect the warmer emotions from these weird creatures, and vain to feel them somehow lacking in that they know them not. And yet surely they were a stark cold race, devoid of religion, science, art, philosophy, and sentiment. They lived only for war and the hunt. They were an amazing people.

The servitors in a chieftain's retinue bore no such marking

painted upon their thoraxes. I, however, did. Koja, when queried, explained at last my amusing position as an exotic "oddity" in his hoard or curio collection; all of his possessions were marked thus, to render impractical and difficult the theft of his treasures by a rival chieftain.

As I became more familiar with the Thanatorian language, I spent many hours conversing with my "owner." Koja, I learned, was one of the mightiest *komors* in all his clan, a warrior of great renown, a huntsman of enviable skill. The meat taken by the Yathoon on this long foray was salted or somehow pickled in kegs of spiced wood, which would be borne along in the midst of the war party in wains drawn by thaptor teams when at last they came to make their long trek home to the Secret Valley of their race.

This great homeward migration would commence in about three weeks, I learned. I was curious to see under what conditions the Yathoon females lived and how they reared their young, so it was with a certain eagerness that I awaited the signal to decamp.

Before the migration could begin, however, there occurred an unforeseen incident that resulted in my making my first friend among the strange and inhuman inhabitants of this distant world.

Koja had been absent from my language lesson for the greater part of this particular day, and I took the opportunity to roam the enormous camp of the Horde, exploring its peculiar ways.

Returning to the cluster of tents belonging to my owner, I saw the servitors of Koja's retinue in an unwonted agitation. The only one of the servitors whom I knew well enough to recognize—at this stage, frankly, one arthropod looked very much like another to me—I caught his attention. It was Sujat. I asked the reason for the flurry and confusion, and he informed me in his cold harsh voice that our mutual master, Koja, had been on a hunting party that morning and had been attacked by a rival hunting party from another clan nearby. The warriors of our clan had been defeated and driven away.

"And what of Koja?" I asked. His cold unwinking gaze bore no expression as he made reply.

"He is sorely wounded and has been left to die," he informed me.

CHAPTER V
I GAIN MY FREEDOM

It is not difficult for me to analyze my feelings on hearing the news of this disaster. To be candid, a certain amount of personal interest occupied my mind. For were Koja to die, his hoard would fall to the next most powerful chieftain of the Yathoon, an arthropod known as Gamchan. While Koja treated me, if not kindly, at least not unkindly, Gamchan had often loudly remarked in my presence and that of Koja that I was no curiosity but an ugly hybrid—he mentioned two nations or races of which I had not heard—"a by-blow of a Zanadar pirate and a Ku Thad" was how he expressed it.

I had gathered that Gamchan was jealous of Koja and sought by such unsubtle means to "put down" his prime curiosity—myself. Koja took no notice of the bad temper of the envious Gamchan, who was a minor chieftain of inferior rank and prowess, although next to Koja in the hierarchical structure of Horde command. But I had few illusions about the sort of treatment I might expect if ever I were unfortunate enough to fall into the hands of Gamchan.

But beyond the problem of my personal safety there was

the simple matter of my indebtedness to Koja, who had not only saved me from the yathrib but had given me food and shelter in his retinue. So I questioned Sujat as to the nature and extent of Koja's injuries.

To my queries Sujat merely shrugged—or, rather, gave a negligent twitch of his brow antenna—a gesture which was the Yathoon equivalent of a shrug. I gathered that the Yathoon warriors take no care of their injured. Here again I saw the drawbacks of their lack of sentiment, and also the advantage inherent in their lack of innate cruelty. For among terrene barbarians, such as the Mongol horde, for example, the injured are often slain. At least his comrades had not bothered to dispatch the injured Koja: they had merely left him behind to die.

Among the possessions of Koja were a number of thaptors. These are the weird bird-horses the Thanatorians use for steeds. They are the size of terrene stallions, or perhaps a bit larger, and, like their equine counterparts on Earth, they have four legs, an arched neck, are ridden from a saddle and guided by reins and a bit. But there the resemblance to a horse ends. For the thaptor is a quadruped species of wingless bird, with clawed feet spurred like those of a rooster. Around the base of their skulls a stiff ruff of feathers extends, almost like a horse's mane. Their heads are very unhorselike, though, with sharp yellow parrot-beaks and glaring eyes wherein a bright orange pupil, ringed with a black iris, stares forth with fierce malignancy. These bird-horses are broken to the bridle with great difficulty and never become completely tractable, although they come at length to recognize their owners and are resigned to carrying them. But woe to the stranger who attempts to ride one!

Snatching up a clean cloth and a container of water, I

went out into the compound where Koja's thaptors were con-strained in pens. My heart was in my mouth and I confess to an extreme nervousness. I had fed and watered these thaptors many times, and I knew they would recognize me. Whether or not they would permit me astride their backs was another question, and one of considerable dubiety.

Sujat followed me curiously.

"What do you intend to do?" he inquired.

"I am going to help Koja," I said.

"But Koja is wounded," he said. There was a stolid finality behind his words which made them equate to "Koja is dead."

I climbed over the bars of the paddock and made soothing clucking sounds to one of the thaptors who had always seemed less unfriendly than the others.

"Wounds heal," I suggested. Sujat shrugged.

"What does it matter?" he asked indifferently.

"To you, nothing; to me, quite a bit," I said. "It is the difference between your kind and mine, Sujat."

I saddled the thaptor, who sidled restlessly but soon sub-sided at my touch. Then, daring much, I carefully climbed astride the thaptor, speaking quietly to him all the while. He peered about with his wide, round, mad little parrot's eye but did not seem particularly enraged to see me in the saddle. I began to relax.

"Where is Koja?" I asked. Sujat described the place; I thought I could find it without difficulty.

At my request, Sujat opened the paddock gate and I guided the thaptor out and down the narrow lane of beaten earth that ran between two rows of tents towards the south gate of the vast encampment. This being the noon hour, few warriors were abroad, most feeding in the quiet of their quar-ters. But many servitors were about, and these eyed me with stolid indifference, although if they had been human they must have been amazed to see a human riding one of their savage thaptors.

I had expected to have to argue with the guards at the perimeter of the encampment, but such was not the case. One guard hailed me.

"Where are you going, Jandar? You know you are not permitted beyond the encampment."

I should explain that to the vocal apparatus of the Thanatorians my name, Jon Dark, is slightly difficult to pronounce. On their tongues it sounds more like Zhan-dar, or Jandar. After several futile attempts to correct this pronunciation, I have become resigned to it. And I have been Jandar to the inhabitants of Thanator ever since.

"I am going to help the chieftain, Koja," I replied.

"But he is wounded!"

"That's why he needs my help," I returned.

He seemed somewhat nonplussed. He stood there, tall ungainly creature, the daylight glistening on his carapace of silvery gray chitin, fiddling with the hilt of his long whipsword.

"But Koja is likely dead by now," he objected. "And it is his order that you may not venture beyond the perimeter of the camp."

"If Koja is dead then his orders are meaningless, is that not so?" I asked. Then, without waiting for a reply, but also without precipitous haste, I rode past him and left the puzzled guard standing there striving to figure out what to do.

I rode for the better part of an hour until I found where Koja had fallen. Several dead arthropods lay sprawled about, and from the unfamiliar thorax markings they wore I assumed them to have been warriors of the rival clan.

Koja had apparently dragged himself some distance and

now lay partially propped up against the thorny bole of a sorad tree. The sorad is rare among the trees of the Thanatorian jungles in that, instead of having black wood and crimson foliage, it has crimson wood and black foliage. I knew that this rareness lent it a unique interest in the minds of the Yathoon, for they prize that which is unusual and hold almost in superstitious veneration that which is unique. Doubtless the rarity of the sorad tree lent it an aspect of reverence in the eyes of Koja, and hence he must have painfully dragged himself to its foot. Now he lay sluggish and dull-eyed, waiting for death, but sustained and heartened in some fashion by his proximity to the unusual tree.

He unlidded his eyes and turned their black glittering gaze on me as I approached, dismounted, and strode over to where he lay.

"Jandar? Why are you here?" he said faintly as I knelt down by him to examine his wounds.

"To give you assistance," I replied. He had sustained a terrible blow across the thorax. The bladed barb of an enemy's whip sword had laid open the horny covering of his thorax and he was losing his bodily fluids. A bubbling froth of colorless, oily liquid seeped from the edges of this ghastly wound and the sharp, medicinal stench of formic acid hung thickly about him.

Koja was somewhat more quick-witted than the majority of his race. But to his way of thinking it was incredible that one creature should render aid to another in this world where all beings were engaged in a relentless war against all other beings.

"Why should you wish to assist me?" he asked as I began tending to his injuries.

As I cleaned them as best I could with clean cloths soaked in fresh water, I replied absently: "Because you saved me from the fangs of the yathrib. Because you gave me food and shelter and the protection of your retinue in a world where all beings are strangers to me. And because you have not mistreated me."

"These are facts; they are not reasons," he protested.

"Very well, then. If you must have a reason, because I—" And here I was forced to hesitate. The Yathoon vocabulary contains no words for such concepts as "friendship" or "pity." The closest I could come was the word *uhorz*, which means something like "indebtedness."

"Because I feel *uhorz* towards you," I said finally.

"Uhorz?"

"Yes. And now please do not speak. I must draw the edges of your wound together tightly, and bind them thus, if they are to heal."

Somehow or other I got Koja back to the encampment, although we were forced to go very slowly so that the jogging pace of the thaptor would not open his wounds and cause him to lose yet more of his bodily fluids. I went afoot, leading the bird-horse at the end of the reins, while Koja rode upright in the saddle, swaying with weakness. I went as slowly and as carefully as possible so as to spare Koja as much pain as I could; but I believe he fainted at least twice during the journey. I had taken the precaution of strapping him securely in the saddle by means of strips torn from the wet cloths wherewith I had cleansed his wounds.

I found no difficulty in reentering the encampment. The guards stood about staring as I led the thaptor past them, but they made no attempt to interfere with my actions. If Koja lived, he was a chieftain of great power, authority, and prowess; if he died, it was a matter of complete indifference to them. So long as I had returned to camp and had not seized this opportunity to escape, they were vindicated in having permitted me to leave it in the first place.

Sujat and I put Koja to bed. The Yathoon sleep in a sort of nest of cloths: devilishly uncomfortable, to humans at least, but they seem to find the nests adequate. Koja had fallen into a deep trancelike sleep, and I did not attempt to awaken him, even so that he might partake of nourishment.

He slept an unbroken slumber for the next several days. As Sujat seemed indifferent to the condition of his master's health, I tended to the warrior myself. This was a simple matter. As the arthropods have no knowledge of the pharmaceutical arts, there were no salves or medicines or healing unguents with which I could treat his injuries. The most I could do was to change the bandages on his wounds once a day and make certain that fresh water and food were at hand, should he awaken and desire them.

Several times during these days the warrior Gamchan came to the area reserved for Koja's retinue and demanded entrance. Each time I told him my master was asleep and did not wish to be disturbed. He seemed baffled at my taking such unwonted authority upon myself and at a loss as to how to face me down. Repeatedly he asked me if Koja was dead: each time I replied, quite truthfully, that Koja lived. He went away, grumbling and dissatisfied, and each time it was more difficult to persuade him to desist from his attempts to enter.

I was not in the least afraid of Gamchan, for I was by now well aware of the enormous difference in strength between the insect creatures and a human being. But I had no desire to blatantly offend against the clan laws of the Yathoon Horde, or to risk the dangers of open enmity between a lowly possession like myself and a chieftain such as Gamchan.

Eventually, the wound seemed to be healing. Cartilage formed, uniting the lips of the wound, gradually hardening into chitin. Koja awoke and requested food. He was very weak, and famished, but he seemed to be mending. He inquired as to who had been tending him and I explained that I had been doing it myself. He made no reply to this, but after I found him eyeing me in a thoughtful fashion.

It was towards the end of the second month of my sojourn among the warriors of the Yathoon Horde that the orders came down that all should be made ready for the expected departure for the Secret Valley. Koja, who was now up and around and seemed almost entirely to have recovered from his near brush with death, came to me in my tent one night, shortly before the departure of the clan. In one hand he bore a bundle of garments and a whip-sword.

"Put these on, Jandar," he said solemnly.

I examined them curiously: they were the first body coverings of any kind that I had seen among the Yathoon, except for the ever-present baldric and shoulder scabbard. They consisted of a high-necked, open-throated leather tunic with short sleeves, a tunic obviously devised for an anatomy such as my own. The bottom of the tunic extended down to midthigh, and there was a loincloth for an undergarment, and soft supple buskins that laced up the ankles.

"What are these, Koja?"

"They are the raiment worn by creatures such as yourself," he replied calmly. "I have always wondered why such beings covered their bodies with these layers, but since you have been among my hoard possessions, I have observed that your body is softer than my own, and I assume that such coverings are designed to protect such softness against the sharp thorn-edged leaves of the jungle."

"That is thoughtful of you," I said. "Is the clan riding through the jungle, then?"

"The clan takes the hill road to the mountains," he said. "But the safest place for you will be the jungles."

My pulses began to race, as I perceived his meaning.

"You are permitting me to escape?" I asked.

"I am," he said. "Take this sword for your defense. And here is a packet of food. As soon as it is completely dark you can leave the tent and find your way to the perimeter with the least chance of discovery. Should any stop you, tell them that you are obeying a command of the chieftain Koja."

He turned away and opened the tent flap and would have gone without another word had I not halted him.

"Why are you doing this, Koja?" I asked.

He turned and regarded me for a long moment of silence. His black jeweled gaze held utterly no expression; the hard gleaming casque of his ovoid face was not capable of registering emotion, and his harsh metallic voice was able to suggest only a limited range of inflection. But there was a wealth of meaning in his words.

"I do this so that you will know that even a Yathoon warrior can feel-*whorz*," he said simply.

And then he was gone.

And so I left the Yathoon encampment, where I had spent my first two months upon Thanator in captivity.

I found no difficulty in leaving the great camp, for the darkness of the night made visibility poor. Only one moon was aloft, lime-green Orovad, and in the bustle of preparation and the confusion of breaking camp, no one had eyes for the small human figure that slipped silently from shadow to shadow until it was well beyond the camp.

I faced the mysterious terrors of the Thanatorian jungles alone, but I was not afraid. I was clothed and armed, and a knapsack of food was upon my back. I did not know where I was going, but it was sufficient that I was free at last to go wherever I wished. I would have struck out for the Gate Between The Worlds had I known in which direction it lay, but I did not know, and so sudden and unexpected was the decision of Koja to give me my freedom that it had not occurred to me to ask its whereabouts.

I reached the edge of the jungle before the rising of the second moon, rose-red Imavad, and entered therein. For two nights and two days I traveled through the trackless jungles of Thanator, without the slightest idea of where I was going. Or even of my direction. I should explain that here upon Thanator—I did not at this time know which of the twelve moons of Jupiter Thanator was—the sun is so distant that it is but the brightest of the stars. The surface of the jungle moon receives very little direct sunlight. I have never been able to decide the source of the light that bathes Thanator, but I suspect that it is the sunlight reflected from the enormous disk of giant Jupiter, or that reflected from the three huge moons that are almost always in the skies.

But I have also observed a curious phenomenon. The orbits of the major Jovian moons are endlessly complex, and there are times when only one moon is aloft in the skies of Thanator during the day. This, oddly enough, in no way diminishes the amount of daylight. The quantity of the daylight remains constant no matter how many moons are aloft, and whether or not the giant orb of Jupiter is visible. I have often wondered if what seems to be daylight is not some radiant effect of the upper atmosphere; I have mentioned earlier in this account of my adventures the odd appearance of the skies of Thanator—that appearance of a crawling film of golden mists. Perhaps the illumination of the moon's surface is somehow due to the effects of radiation striking that golden mist, which must be a layer of unknown gas high above the breathable air of Thanator. An effect perhaps akin to the light that flares from inert neon gas when an electrical current passes through it. You will of course be familiar with neon signs, that boon to the advertising profession: the inert vapor lies in glass tubes, which, when an electrical current is passed through them, blaze with light. Perhaps the upper layers of the atmosphere of Thanator are composed of neon, or of some comparable gas which, during the hours of daylight, is under the bombardment of electrical forces.

But this was only one of the baffling questions that had puzzled me during the many weeks of my captivity.

I had given considerable thought to the problem of just where I was. Astronomy has always interested me, and as I have a good head for figures and an almost photographic memory, I was able to recall quite a bit of information about the solar system, enough, it seemed, to base a firm opinion.

This, obviously, was one of the twelve moons of Jupiter. It could hardly be either of the two planets nearest to Jupiter, which are Mars and Saturn. Mars is something like three hundred million miles closer to the sun than Jupiter, and surely even that banded and Brobdingnagian giant would not bulk so hugely in its skies. Besides, Mars has only two moons and this world at least four.

Nor could it very easily be Saturn, and for much the same reasons. For Saturn was even farther away from Jupiter than was Mars—somewhere in the neighborhood of four hundred million miles distant.

The only bodies close enough to Jupiter for the giant world to bulk so enormously in their skies would be the Jovian satellites themselves. I recalled that some of these are quite large—Io, the second moon counting outwards from Jupiter, is about two thousand miles in diameter, only slightly smaller than Earth's own moon. Europa, the next of the satellites, is slightly smaller than that, while the fourth moon, Ganymede, with its diameter of more than three thousand miles, is perhaps the largest of all the moons in the solar system. The fifth moon, Callisto, has a diameter of about two thousand seven hundred miles. The moons beyond the orbit of Callisto, Hestia, Hera, Demeter, are all extremely small, with a diameter of eighty to ten miles each. These three I could safely eliminate from consideration. And the four outermost of the Jovian moons—Adrastea, Pan, Poseidon, and Hades—could also safely be eliminated because of their very small size, as well as their retrograde orbits. My conclusion, then, was easy and obvious. Three large moons and one very small one were visible in the night sky between this world of Thanator and its titanic primary; they must be the four innermost of the Jovian satellites, the first moon, Amalthea, and the three larger ones, Io, Europa, and Ganymede. Hence I decided, to my own satisfaction, at least, that Thanator was Callisto!*

But if this is true, how can the gravity of Callisto be so very similar to that of Earth? Earth's diameter at the equator is 7,927 miles, almost three times larger than Callisto. It would seem natural for Callisto to have a gravity one third that of Earth, but such is not the case.

And how can a world so small hold an atmosphere? Earth's moon is only a little smaller than Callisto, and its gravity is insufficient to hold anything like this thick rich air

---

*I have not bothered to correct Captain Dark's figures in these four paragraphs, for they are approximately correct. For the benefit of the reader, however, I provide the following more accurate data on Callisto. One of the largest moons in the solar system, it has a diameter of 2,770 miles, is 8,700 miles in circumference, and revolves about the planet Jupiter at a distance of 1,171,000 miles. It was discovered by Galileo in the seventeenth century. It is the fifth of the Jovian moons.—L. C.

that I had been breathing now for two months. Would I ever find the answer to these mysteries?

During the entire period of my stay on Thanator, I have never ceased to puzzle over the curious and baffling anomalies between what I knew the surface of a Jovian satellite *should* be like, and the living reality through which I moved.

Everything that the terrene astronomers had ever discovered about the conditions on other worlds made it clear that Callisto should be a dead, frozen, airless world of jagged peaks and ammonia snow. Yet I walked through a jungle landscape of weird, terrific grandeur, limned in vivid and unlikely hues, and teeming with exotic life.

To this day I have not discovered the answer to this riddle.

On the third day of my freedom, I was suddenly arrested by the sounds of a battle some distance ahead of me.

I had been remarkably fortunate in that my journey through the black and crimson jungles had thus far brought me into no dangerous encounter with any of the ferocious predators wherewith this planet swarmed. In part this was due, I suppose, to blind chance or luck; but to some degree it was the result of a certain oily cream prepared by the arthropods. This substance, the distillation of an herbal sap, had the peculiar property of protecting the traveler who smeared himself therewith from the attack of a yathrib. For, although odorless to my nostrils at least, the substance is extremely offensive to the yathrib.

The Yathoon hunters use it to drive the yathrib from their proximity while engaged in rounding up a beast called the *vastodon*, which they hunt for its succulent meat. The yathrib is a predator who does not scruple to attack even a Yathoon hunter, and when one of the tribal hunts are in session the fearsome dragon-cat of the Thanatorian jungle has the annoying habit of lying low while the hunters round up their meat-beasts, and then charging in to carry off a prize for itself. The offensive cream, therefore, is a valuable adjunct to these meat-gathering expeditions, and I had taken the precaution to carry off a jar and kept my bare arms and legs liberally smeared with the oily stuff.

I burst through a wall of foliage into a small glade or clearing, and an astounding tableau met my eyes.

At one end of the clearing a snarling, hulking brute crouched, about to charge.

Facing him, her back against a tree trunk, her hands empty of any weapon, a young and beautiful woman faced the predator . . . and at last I knew for certain that the jungle moon of Thanator *was* inhabited by humans like me!

CHAPTER VI

DARLOONA, WARRIOR PRINCESS OF THE KU THAD

I had long suspected that the insect creatures of the Ya-thoon Horde were not the only intelligent inhabitants of Thanator. The fact that Koja and his kind found me re-markable for my coloring rather than my physical being in-dicated that they were not unfamiliar with races akin to mine. And that slighting remark the jealous Gamchan had let fall, when he suggested I was some sort of a hybrid born of a mating between "the Zanadar pirates" and "the Ku Thad," re-inforced my suspicion. And then the fact of that writing case I had found among Koja's possessions: a race ignorant of letters does not bother to invent writing cases.

Now, as I stared across the clearing at the first human being I had seen on Thanator, I found my pulse quickening, as much from the beauty of the young woman as from the surprise of the encounter.

She was perhaps twenty, tall and slender and superbly feminine. She wore a high-necked, open-throated leather tu-nic identical with the one Koja had given me, a tunic which extended down over her rounded hips, leaving her long and graceful legs bare save for soft buskins laced high on the instep. A wide girdle heavy with ornaments of precious metals cinched in her small waist, and from this depended a small pouch, an empty dagger scabbard, and a large medallion of some bright metal I could not at once identify.

Her skin was softly golden, clear and pale. Her small, heart-shaped face was radiantly beautiful, with large expressive eyes, slightly slanted and colored a bright flashing emerald. Her hair was a magnificent torrent of fiery red-gold which flowed over her small shoulders and down to her waist. Her mouth was soft, full-lipped, ripely crimson. Even now, in the extremity of her peril, she retained a cool poise and what I sensed to be her natural dignity.

There was an empty quiver between her shoulders, clipped to a baldric that passed over one shoulder, down between her ripe, panting young breasts, to the side of her girdle. I saw no bow, so I assumed that this quiver had held javelins, now expended, as had been her dagger.

The beast she faced was hulking and monstrous, less fearsome in appearance than the yathrib, but heavier and more massive. It looked for all the world like a miniature elephant, the same barrel of a body, the same squat, thick, columnar legs ending in flat pads, the same leathery hide, slate gray in coloring. But its head bore a closer resemblance to a wild boar: little piglike eyes glaring madly, coarse black bristles clothing an unlovely snout, vicious tusks showing the gleam of yellow ivory, bared to view as the thing voiced its thick, throaty, snarling cry. But the piglike snout of the creature was a yard long and furthered the resemblance to an elephant.

I had recognized the beast as a vastodon; it stood six feet high at the shoulder and must have weighed two or three tons. My respect for the courage and prowess of the Yathoon warriors who hunted this hulking menace of the jungle for its meat rose considerably.

The girl, who had not yet seen me, had cast her javelins at the vastodon, seemingly missing the brute. One slender spear protruded from the crimson turf a few yards from where I stood. A vagrant beam of daylight caught the gemmy twinkle of a dagger hilt buried in the beast's burly chest. She had wounded the brute at least, but I could see that this was one monster that would take a lot of killing.

And I was armed only with a whip-sword.

The frozen tableau broke suddenly as the beast charged. If it struck the girl, she would be crushed against the knobby black bole of the tree.

Almost without thought, I sprang from the foliage with a loud shout, waving my arms to attract the vastodon's attention. The girl cast me one astonished glance, and in the next moment I was too busy to look or to think about her for the vastodon swerved in its charge and headed straight at me, heavy pads drumming against crimson turf.

I had never before used the Yathoon whip-sword, a weapon reserved for the warrior caste and forbidden equally to servitors and possessions. But I had observed several duels between rival arthropods during my months in the camp and understood the uses of the weapon. As the roaring vastodon came rushing at me I sprang high in the air and to one side, sweeping the barbed blade downwards, between my legs, the sword hilt gripped in both hands.

Unfortunately, due to the unusual length of the blade, which is fully five feet long, and the weight of the weapon, considerably heavier than any sword with which I am familiar, I found the Yathoon whip-sword an unwieldy instrument. I had intended to bring the barbed blade lashing down across the face of the vastodon, splitting its skull if possible, or at least blinding it by destroying its eyes. But the barb only caught it a glancing blow on the shoulder, which laid open the tough hide in a foot-long furrow, exposing raw lavender flesh. Instead of incapacitating the vastodon, my blow only goaded it to further heights of rage.

It spun about, squealing madly, little pig-eyes red and flaming with the lust to kill, and charged again like a thunderbolt.

I had landed off balance from my leap, and now I sprawled on the turf, the whip-sword flying from my hand. As the enraged vastodon came at me I grasped the javelin the girl had flung—snatched it from the turf—and drove it into the boar-pachyderm as it came crashing into me. The impact of its charge knocked me flying. My head struck some hard object and my senses swam. Then darkness covered the world.

I was looking up into a beautiful face. Curious emerald eyes looked down at me, and ripe moist lips were parted as if to speak.

"Do you live?" the girl asked, and I was suddenly grateful that Koja had instructed me in the Thanatorian language.

"I live—" I began, trying to sit up. Bright pain lanced through me, and I broke off gasping, adding after a moment "—but as to whether I am still in one piece or not, we shall have to see!"

Something—perhaps the tusk of the vastodon—had slashed my forearm, and I had a long cut which extended from just above the wrist to an inch below the elbow. Blood welled freely from the wound, which was a surface cut. No bone was broken, and I seemed to have come through the ordeal in fairly decent shape.

As for the vastodon, it lay across the clearing dead in a

puddle of purplish gore. I can take little credit for the kill; it was the impact of the brute's own wild charge that drove the javelin deep into its breast, straight through the heart. By sheerest accident, just as the beast struck and impaled itself on the blade, the javelin butt was braced against solid ground.

The girl helped me to my feet. I ached from a few bruises; my head throbbed painfully; my slashed forearm hurt abominably, and I felt a bit shaken and nauseous. But otherwise I was all right.

The girl gazed at me curiously.

"You are not Ku Thad, surely! Nor of Zanadar, either—what manner of man are you?"

"I am—" I began; and again I halted. What use to confuse the situation by relating my incredible story of birth on another world? Koja had never once questioned the manner of my appearance; like all his kind, the Yathoon was stolid and indifferent, and curiosity is a simian trait, and therefore, a human one; the Yathoon are neither human nor simian and rarely seem curious about anything.

"I am from a far country," I said lamely. "My name is Jonathan Dark."

She wrinkled her nose at the uncouth polysyllabic. "Jhonna-than'dar—?"

"Jandar," I said, resigned to the nickname first bestowed upon me by my friend Koja.

"I am Darloona of the Ku Thad, Princess of Shondakor," she said proudly. As I had no idea how a Thanatorian would acknowledge meeting with the native aristocracy, I essayed a sketchy little bow, which seemed to meet with her approval.

Reassured by now that I was all right, the Princess regarded me with slightly aloof coldness. I recalled that among the Yathoon the hand of every warrior is raised against every other, and each clan hold the neighboring clan in deadly enmity. I wondered if this was true among the human inhabitants of Thanator.* If so, I might find this imperious lovely an enemy.

"Never have I seen a vastodon slain in so clumsy a manner," she said.

"What matter, so long as the vastodon be slain?" was my reply. She turned from me without further word and began gathering her javelins and her dagger, which was still in the shoulder of the vastodon. I washed my wound with water from the canister in my knapsack and tried to bind the wound with a bit of clean rag, which I found difficult to do with only one hand.

It occurred to me that the Princess might well have volunteered to cleanse and bind my wound. I had, after all, just saved her life and sustained the injury in doing so.

Striding over to her, I thrust out my arm and asked, rather abruptly: "Do you mind helping with this?"

Her emerald eyes held a shadow of disdain. I did not realize it, but already I had twice offended against the Thanatorian code of honor. Among Darloona's people it is considered polite for a warrior to deprecate his own prowess at the kill. When she had made her candid appraisal of my clumsy method of slaying the vastodon, I should have agreed with her gravely. And a warrior is thought somewhat less than manly if he binds or even tends his wounds. In this much, at least, the Ku Thad were not unlike Koja and his kind.

However, the Princess did not refuse but bound my wound in silence. I was aware of a slight breach between us but I did not quite know how to mend it. Darloona could not know the extent of my unfamiliarity with the customs com

*I learned soon enough that it is.—J. D.

mon to all four human races upon Thanator: hence she could not be blamed for thinking me a bit of a boor.

As she bent near, tying the cloth about my wound, her eyes suddenly dilated with incredulous disbelief and she stood apart from me abruptly. I did not understand what had so forcibly repelled her, and I glanced down, to see that the boar-like tusk of the vastodon had torn open the front of my leather tunic, laying bare my chest and the green, black, and crimson "possession" symbols which still remained upon me, to mark me to every eye as a belonging of the Yathoon.

I was not to understand until much later. Her shock at discovering me to be a slave, or a former slave, of a Yathoon, was not so much an aristocrat's disgust at encountering a servile being as her instant suspicion that I was what you might call a Judas goat. The Yathoon sometimes take servitors from the human races, although as it happened there had been no human servitors in the camp of Koja's clan during the period of my stay. And sometimes these slaves, their markings disguised beneath the tunic of a free warrior, such as I wore, are used to lure unsuspecting humans into entrapment by the arthropods. Had I understood her instant revulsion, had I known of this vile custom and understood the suspicion which she now entertained, I could of course have explained and set her mind at rest. But, not knowing, I did nothing but stare at her.

And in the very next moment it was too late for any explanation.

The foliage parted and a dozen Yathoon warriors stepped into the clearing to confront Darloona and myself. The leader of the party was Koja's rival and enemy, Gamchan. If ever I read the slightest shade of expression in the featureless casque of a Yathoon face, it was then. For Gamchan smirked in an oily, ominous, very self-satisfied way. How his immobile masklike face managed to express this emotion I cannot say. For all I know it was sheer telepathy. But smirk he did, and nastily at that.

He had followed on my track the instant it was learned that he was no longer in the encampment. Koja had a perfect right to set me free if he desired, although his motives for doing so would have been incomprehensible to his brethren. But Gamchan, equally, had a perfect right to pursue and, if possible, recapture me, making me *his* possession, if he wished. And, his former slighting remarks notwithstanding, he had gone after me with a pack of junior warriors with just that purpose in mind. It would have made a splendid coup against the prestige of Koja if he were able to seize me for his own. And now he had done so, and had taken a second prize as well! It was no wonder that Gamchan was pleased with himself.

As far as I was concerned, I would gladly have been his possession voluntarily, if only I could somehow have prevented him from making the remark that he now made.

Of all the conceivable words that could have been uttered, no more damning phrase could have been imagined.

"Well done, Jandar," he grated. "The female will make a splendid possession!"

My heart sank, not so much at again becoming a captive. But if you could have seen the look of icy loathing and utter contempt that the Princess of the Ku Thad turned on me the next instant, you would understand my profound depression.

Her cold, contemptuous eyes traveled over me once, and then lifted away. She disdained the futility of attempting battle against so overwhelming a force of the Yathoon and held out her wrists in cold silence while she was bound and led to the thaptors.

As for myself, I was surrounded with drawn swords; my

own weapon lay many yards distant. And I was so paralyzed by the shock of Gamchan's sudden appearance that I was frozen or I would doubtless have flung myself against the warriors. But before I could think or move, a lasso settled about me, jerked tight, and imprisoned my upper arms.

I have no doubt that the lack of any sound of a battle from the clearing only served to further confirm Darloona in her opinion of me as she was led away.

And thus, for the second time, I became the property of a chieftain of the Yathoon.

Towards evening Gamchan's war party caught up with the main body of the Yathoon host and rejoined it. The Horde was marshaled in order of rank, and Gamchan's place in the hierarchy was directly behind the position held by Koja. Thus Gamchan was able to flaunt his two prized acquisitions directly under Koja's nose, as it were.

Koja made no remark on my recapture. Neither did he attempt to exchange words with me, although I am certain he felt regret that I had not succeeded in making my escape, or at least as much regret as a Yathoon warrior is capable of feeling. The Yathoon have a sort of crude, fatalistic philosophy which they refer to by the phrase *va lu rokka*—"it was destined." They seem to regard the future in a dour, Calvinist light as predetermined. No degree of luck or valor or skill on the part of intelligent beings can in their world view avert a coming catastrophe.

I assume that it was with the pessimism of this belief in *va lu rokka* that Koja observed my imprisonment in the retinue of Gamchan. And I knew that he neither would nor could be of any further assistance to me, *whorz* or no *uhorz*. This fatalism infects the entire Yathoon civilization and probably, in part, accounts for the indifference with which they view a fallen comrade's injuries. If he is destined to die, he will die. If not, he will live. Whatever the outcome, *va lu rokka.*

As a possession of Gamchan I was tied with a noose about my neck and forced to run along behind one of the thaptors ridden by a member of the household of Gamchan. I am not sure whether this grueling punishment was awarded me out of malice alone, or whether it was an attempt on the part of Gamchan to display the slightness of his regard for his new *amatar.* I noticed, however, that the girl, securely trussed, was tossed across the cruppers of one of the thaptors and was not forced to run along behind its heels. That much at least I could be grateful for.

We covered some miles before it became too dark to go any further. I was trembling with exhaustion by the time the order finally was passed down the length of the host to halt and make night camp. The experience had not, in fact, been as terrible as it could have been, for I had envisioned falling and being dragged for miles, or being forced to run for hours at breakneck speed. Actually, as it turned out, since the Horde moved together in strict order, it could progress at no speedier pace than that of its slowest member, which was Pandol himself.

I have not yet mentioned Pandol in this narrative because I had no contact with him whatever during my captivity. Pandol was the leader of the clan, the *akka-komor*, or highest chieftain. He had been a mighty war champion in his youth but now was very old and could not endure hard riding for very long. Hence I found the pace a mild one, wearying but not unendurable.

The night camp was set up in a deep valley ringed about with smooth, rounded knolls. As this was but a temporary camp, set up for the night's rest, it did not boast the elaborate earthworks, the barriers of packed earth that had encircled the semipermanent encampment that had been the clan's home during the months I had been an *amatar* of Koja.*

Once the warriors and servitors of Gamchan's household had set up his circle of tents, Darloona and I were led forward. I did not know exactly what to expect, but I doubted if Gamchan would inflict any punishment on so valuable a possession as I represented in his eyes. At his command, I was stripped of my leathern tunic, baldric, and girdle, although I was permitted to retain my buskins and the strip of cloth wound about my loins. The pictoglyphs on my chest, which specified me as an *amatar* belonging to Koja, were removed with an application of some soapy, slightly acidulous cleanser, and a new group of emblems were painted on my chest in their place. Doubtless they denoted my new owner.

As I was led away, I saw the girl being brought forward, and suddenly I realized what was about to happen.

The servitor who had removed my torn tunic fumbled at the fastening of Darloona's garment. The girl stared straight ahead with a cold, proud expression of disdain on her features, which were, however, paler than usual. Gamchan, impatient at the inability of the fumbling servitor to remove the garment, strode forward and seized the open neck of Darloona's tunic in the grasp of his long segmented fingers.

I realized that in the next instant the girl would be stripped bare and the symbols of her slavery would be painted across her naked breasts!

---

*From this casual reference to the earlier camp, I gather that Captain Dark has forgotten that he neglected, earlier in this narrative, to set down any description of the semipermanent encampment. From his brief mention of earthworks I assume the Yathoon erected a circular mound or wall of soil around the entire perimeter of their camp, packing it down by stamping the loose earth into place. There must have been open spaces in this barrier to permit easy egress, since in the passage where he tells how he rode from the camp to assist the injured Koja he does not describe any difficulties in passing the barrier.—L. C.

My gorge rose at the thought of this young, lovely girl of birth and breeding standing nude before the cold unwinking gaze of these stalking arthropods. Some innate chivalry, whose presence in my character I had not been cognizant of until this moment, arose within me.

Without a moment's hesitation I snapped my bonds, which were tough enough to secure the forelimbs of a Yathoon arthropod but which offered only a feeble restraint against the more powerful leverage of terrene muscles. While the warrior holding my leash stared blankly, I sprang forward and grabbed Gamchan by his upper forelimb, snatching his fingers from the girl and, in the fury of my emotion, whirling him half around and letting him sprawl at full length in the dirt.

I think I could have killed him then. A red haze of fury hung before my eyes and my hands were trembling with rage. Gamchan lay asprawl on the ground, regarding me with astonishment.

I looked around and suddenly laughed. The cadet warriors and servitors likewise stared at me with utter amazement. I had come by this time to understand that the arthropods of Thanator are not quite as emotionless as I had first assumed them to be. I had discovered that Koja was capable of feeling something akin to friendliness; and Gamchan, in the envy he displayed towards my former captor, revealed very human emotion. What I had assumed a total lack of emotion was due to a misunderstanding: humans read emotions by gesture, intonation, facial expression; but the arthropods are all but incapable of facial expressiveness save the twitching of their antennae, and their metallic and monotonous speech mode lacks the human range of tones. They rendered shades of emotion by a different vocabulary of gestures than do terrene humans. I had come, bit by bit, to realize this. Astonishment is registered by a frozen immobility and an erratic jerking of the brow antennae, which the Yathoon about me now displayed.

For I had done an unheard-of thing. With their extreme fatalism, their almost Moslem sense of Kismet, servitors consider it their irrevocable fate to be slaves and would never dream of revolting or of seeking their freedom. The most prestigious warrior, fearless and brave almost beyond human conception, if overcome in battle and taken prisoner, becomes a meek servitor and will endure harsh treatment without a thought of protest, resentment, or anger. For a slave to strike his master is virtually unheard of in the annals of this most unusual people.

But for an *amatar* to do so verges on ultimate blasphemy. For how can a possession, a soulless *thing*, be capable of anger or violence against the chieftain who owns him?

The retinue of Gamchan regarded me incredulously. They could hardly believe what their own eyes had seen; that an *amatar* should lay violent hands on its owner was, to them, a complete impossibility.

I met the amazed eyes of Darloona. Her people, I was later to learn, did not keep slaves as they had achieved a higher and more humane level of civilization than that of the poor arthropods. Hence her astonishment was not at my un-*amatar*-like action, but stemmed from curiosity regarding my motive.

She thought me a Judas, a traitor who acted as bait to entrap my own kind into the slavery of the Horde. The human inhabitants of Thanator regard the arthropods with extreme revulsion and loathing. They are considered the most vile and despicable of all species. To be enslaved in a Yathoon encampment is a doom beyond description; hence, a human who induces his fellows into such slavery is considered beyond all humanity. Since she thought of me in such terms, due to the confusion of my recapture and her seizure, she could not understand why I had torn the claws of my master from her body. Since I had already proved myself a traitor to my species by luring her into a trap—why in the world should I react so violently to her being stripped and painted with the *amatar* symbols?

The moment of paralyzed astonishment was over almost immediately and I was ringed with naked steel. I stood panting and glaring about like a trapped beast while one of Gamchan's cadets, a youth named Duthor, assisted his master to his feet. It was a tense moment. I expected to feel the agony of sword-steel tearing out my life upon the next instant. And I still do not quite understand why Gamchan did not order me killed on the spot. Perhaps he was too dumbfounded by my incomprehensible act of violence to give the command; or possibly the rigorous code of punishments that served the Horde as its law contained no variety of death lingering enough to fittingly reward so blasphemous an act, and he required leisure to dream up a suitable one.

At any rate, instead of being cut down on the spot, I was imprisoned among his other treasures in the innermost tent of his area. The flimsy ropes of braided grass which had proved too weak to hold me were replaced by shackles of steel. Chained to the tent pole, I was left to languish until the manner of my demise could be decided.

I smiled wryly in the darkness. My desperate action had proved futile, for Gamchan assured me that Darloona would nonetheless be stripped and painted. And it was likely to prove fatal, as well.

The second period of my captivity in the Horde would prove much shorter than the first, I believed.

True enough, it came to a rapid end—but not at all the sort of end I had imagined!

The following day I was led forth in chains to face chastisement. The cadet warriors of Gamchan's household led me down an aisle of Horde warriors who regarded me in utter silence. The day was hot and still, the sky clear and bright. As it was likely to be my last day on Thanator, I observed every detail about me with great attentiveness.

I felt the eyes of Darloona upon me and turned my head to catch her gaze. Her face was grave and somber, her eyes sad as they lingered on me. Then, as she caught my glance, she drew herself up haughtily and her expression turned to one of icy contempt. I laughed. The eternal woman! The female of the species was the same on this alien moon as on my own far-distant world.

And then, as I lifted my gaze to the clear golden skies to have one last look at this strange and beautiful and terrible world before I went down into the darkness of a nameless tomb, my eyes widened in disbelief.

That which I gazed upon was, of all the marvels and oddities that thronged this weird world, the most spectacular I had yet encountered.

Cruising silently through the bright morning skies, a group of incredible aircraft were hurtling straight for the camp of the Yathoon Horde.

I could not, for a moment, believe my eyes. Like quaint, ungainly sailing ships of yore they were, with gilded figureheads and ornamental scrollwork about the prow. There were three of the amazing flying ships, which appeared to be built of wood, and which resembled nothing so much as fantastic galleons from the Spanish Armada, outfitted with great flapping batwings.

They came cruising down the wind, casting enormous running shadows over the meadow and the camp, while the arthropods exploded into a frenzy of activity, racing about, clacking commands back and forth, snatching up their war bows and seeking cover.

The Yathoon camp, it seemed, was being attacked.

And, in the confusion, everyone had forgotten about Darloona and myself!

CHAPTER VII

A CRUISE ABOARD
THE FRIGATE *SKYGULL*

Although my arms were chained, my feet were free. So swiftly had the arthropods fled to their battle stations that I was left standing alone and unguarded. The Princess stood a bit beyond me, staring up at the fantastic winged ships which circled slowly and ponderously overhead.

"What in the world are those things?"

"They are scout ornithopters," she said. "Have you never seen one before?"

I assured her that I had not. She looked puzzled. I reminded her that I was a stranger from a far land.

"It must indeed be far distant," she observed, "if you have never heard of the Sky Pirates of Zanadar!"

I had indeed heard mention of the name, but had not dreamed of anything like this.

"Now is our opportunity to escape," I said. "While the Yathoon warriors are engaged in battle, perhaps we can steal a couple of thaptors and be off."

I was half afraid that she would refuse my assistance, and not at all certain that the Ku Thad (the term meant the

"Golden People") did not share the *va lu rokka* fatalism of the Horde. But such was not the case. We made at once for the thaptor pens of Gamchan's retinue and secured two beasts.

The bird-horses were restive and upset by the excitement. Perhaps they smelled blood and war and death on the air. At any rate they clashed their beaks at us and screeched angrily as we threw saddles over them and sought to mount. I cursed under my breath and wished for the tractable mount I had made friends with in Koja's corral. But Darloona was a born thaptorwoman and knew the trick of handling an uncooperative mount: you beat him over the top of the head with a little wooden club called an *olo*, affixed to each saddlebow for just that purpose. It looks very much like a dumbbell.

Thus we mounted and cantered out of the camp.

At the perimeter we encountered, of all people, my former owner, Koja. He did not seem particularly surprised to see me.

"Ride due north, Jandar, and then east along the margin of the jungle. I trust the Princess Darloona is most anxious to return to her people," he said solemnly.

"How did you know my name, Yathoon?" the Princess demanded. He indicated the circular medallion of bright metal affixed to her girdle.

"Unless I am mistaken, that is the Seal of Shondakor, is it not?" he asked rhetorically. "If so, and since only the regnant Princess may bear the sacred Seal, it follows to my mind that you are she."

"Why are you helping us, Yathoon?" she asked suspiciously.

Koja shrugged, or performed a twitch of his antennae equivalent to a shrug.

"Why not? I assume the ornithopters are searching for you. The Sky Pirates have never evinced particular interest in our treasures. And unless my eyes misread the insignia on yonder rudder, that is the flagship of Prince Thuton himself, an ambitious and not overly scrupulous man who might well find a path to power through possession of the Princess of Shondakor."

Squinting against the bright gold sky, I saw that the more sumptuous and ornate of the three flying vessels bore a blue and silver emblem, a winged fist, painted on the vertical rudder fin, a structure ribbed like an enormous fan, which protruded from the poop at the aft of the galleon—or frigate, as a scout ship is more properly termed.

Darloona was still not convinced that Koja meant us well. She glanced at me.

"Can we trust this *capok?*" she demanded, using an impolite colloquialism that can be rendered, bluntly, as "bug."

"We can, Princess. Koja is a great warrior, a mighty chieftain, and my *uhorz*-friend," I said. As I still did not know the Thanatorian word for "friend" I used the English word.

"Come, I will guide you. Make way there, guards!" Koja clacked, waving aside the perimeter watchmen. He sprang into a saddle and cantered off ahead of us, waving aside any who might interfere with our flight.

"Koja, why are you doing this? Will you not get into trouble with your own people?" I asked.

"We have small hope of defeating the ornithopters," he said calmly. "But some small measure of victory can be snatched from the very mandibles of defeat if we can prevent the Sky Pirates from obtaining that which they seek. No more talk now—ride!"

Koja's guess as to the objective of the Sky Pirates was confirmed an instant later. The lead frigate, the one with the royal symbol painted on its rudder fin, floated low over the encampment on lazily beating vans, and a rather flashily dressed and overly handsome young man leaned over the ornately carven balustrade to shout through a gilt-paper meg-aphone to the arthropods below:

"Attention, chieftains of the Yathoon! We covet neither your possessions nor your destruction. We wish only the person of the red-haired Shondakor maiden your warriors seized in the jungle yesterday. Send her out alone and we will take her and leave without causing you harm!"

At that moment a sailor, his bright green stocking cap flapping in the breeze caused by the slowly beating vans, spied Darloona's bright hair as we rode like the wind from the other side of the camp. He was stationed aloft on the observation deck atop the command belvedere in the ship's forecastle, and thus had an excellent view of the surrounding countryside. We could hear him shouting his discovery to Prince Thuton, for such the handsome spokesman at the rail proved to be.

Thuton snapped a series of crisp commands. "Helmsman? Forward at ten knots! Take your mark on the three riders! Bosun! Lassomen to the forward port rail—lively, now!"

The great craft began to move with a creaking and a drumming of beating vans. Like a great shark she came gliding through the air towards us. Casting a glance back over my shoulder, I could see the bright work of her prow, and the frowning face of the vengeful warrior that was her figure-head.

Just as we reached the edge of the jungle her shadow fell over us. I thought the overhanging bough would shield us from the lasso gang, and I also thought we would make better time if we rode along the edge of the jungle rather than pushing into her depths. Both guesses proved somewhat less than inspired. For we came to an open space where no branches afforded protection above, and the flying loops came hurtling down to snap about us.

Squealing and kicking, Darloona was hauled out of her saddle like a hooked mackerel. A second lasso caught Koja around his middle and he went flip-flopping upwards, his face solemn and expressionless.

I, too, was roped and drawn skyward. A smooth hull, every chink tightly caulked with a rubbery gum-like substance, swept past me as I was drawn up. Then the deck rail, its supporters carven into the likeness of winged dolphins, swept under me, and I was dropped with a resounding thud to the deck. I saw then that the lasso was affixed to a tall davit which protruded over the side, something like a gallows.

Prince Thuton strode forward, beaming smiles. He was a young man, rather foppish, dressed in tight bottle-green breeches, floppy-topped skyboots, and a frilly white blouse, trimmed with lace at throat and wrist. A rapier hung from his baldric, which flashed with gems. As I got a close-up look at him, I discovered that the Sky Pirates, although fully human as far as I could see, had distinct racial differences from the Ku Thad.

To be precise, instead of tawny and honey-colored, his skin was papery white; instead of flaming red, his hair, worn long and ringleted, was sleek and black, as were his unslanted eyes. He was a handsome fellow, if a little soft in the face, with a brilliant smile and a smooth voice and charming manners. He looked and acted for all the world like some delicate French privateer of aristocratic birth. His eyes lingered for just a moment on Darloona's naked breasts; in the next, he had whipped a scarlet cloak off the shoulders of his lieutenant and draped it about the girl.

He made a profound bow, clicking his heels together like a Nazi officer in a World War II movie.

"My dear Princess! I bid you welcome to the flag frigate

Skygull: its crew and officers are your servants to command. As for Thuton, Prince of Zanadar, who stands before you, he is—your slave!"

It was, I must admit, a pretty speech. Then why did my blood boil as I saw the half-smile Darloona turned on this smooth-faced Sky Pirate, and the gratitude in her voice as she thanked him for his courtesy?

As for myself, I was fighting mad. I came to my feet, kicking out of the lasso, ready for blood.

"We don't need your help!" I yelled. "We were doing just fine! I am returning Darloona to her people, and can get along on my own."

Prince Thuton elevated a polite eyebrow at me.

"And who is this . . . person?" he inquired.

The girl cast me a reproving look. Then, disdainfully, "Some nameless barbarian, a slave of the Yathoon. Please pay no attention to his hasty words—he is very rude and has no conception of civilized behavior."

"So? A turn at the wheels will teach him better manners. Come, dear Princess: I have prepared a light buffet in my cabin—toasted biscuits and a light wine, spiced meat cubes and a scrap of salad—nothing fancy."

"You are too kind, Prince Thuton," she murmured. He offered his arm and they turned to go, ignoring poor Koja and myself.

"Don't go with him, Darloona!" I fumed. "Don't listen to him! You know what Koja said—he has some political motive in wanting to capture you—"

Thuton turned a stern eye on me. Darloona flushed indignantly.

"Silence, you—you—*amatar!*" she snapped. "If you are not capable of feeling gratitude to a noble gentleman who has just rescued you from the perils of the trackless jungle, at least refrain from the insult of openly impugning his motives."

"Presently this fellow will grow tiresome, and I fear I shall have to teach him his place," Thuton purred, an ominous note in his suave voice.

Koja plucked at my arm, but I shrugged him off bad-temperedly.

"Anytime you feel like giving me a lesson, Prince!"

He stopped, turned, and stood with arms akimbo, looking me up and down. In what seemed a deliberately insulting way, his eyes lingered on the *amatar* glyphs painted across my chest.

"I am hardly accustomed to being insulted on my own deck," he said. "Presently, I fear Thuton of Zanadar must instruct you in the maintenance of your temper, fellow!"

"Jandar of—of—of Thanator is ready whenever you are!" I blustered, chest heaving with the intensity of my emotion. He elevated a polite eyebrow again.

"Really, my dear Princess, this barbarian is absurd! Now he takes all the world for his domain!"

Suddenly he was hard as steel. "Will swords suffice you, my peppery savage?"

"They will indeed!"

I had snatched up one of the whip-swords during my flight from the Yathoon camp. I had slung it across my back. Now I dragged it forth and flourished it, albeit a bit awkwardly, due to the shackles with which my wrists were still bound. Prince Thuton noticed this and called for his black-smith, who swiftly released me from my bonds.

The Princess of Shondakor regarded me doubtfully. "You will not, I trust, kill him, my lord? The lout did, after all, rescue me from the Yathoon camp—for all that he was the cause I was there in the first place!"

The Prince bowed, saluting with a flicker of his blade.

"Dear Princess, his life is yours—I but wish to tutor him in his manners." Then, turning to me: "Ready, barbarian?"

I grunted and set my stance. I was well aware that this was a serious mistake; I was acting foolishly, even dangerously. This suave and agile Pirate was going to do his best to make me look like a buffoon—and I so desperately wanted to correct the bad impression that Darloona had formed of me. I cursed under my breath, and wished I had kept my temper and held my tongue.

But it was too late now. I consoled myself by recalling my prowess with the sword. I had been an excellent fencer at Yale, and there was a good chance my skill with the blade could turn the tables on this wily Prince. With luck, I might make *him* look the fool!

We set to it, blades clicking, steel ringing, feeling each other out. Very soon I was puffing for breath, streaming sweat from every pore, my forearms tense and quivering with strain and fatigue. I had been very, very foolish in stumbling into this quarrel. I had not stopped to think that I had passed the whole of last night standing up, my arms shackled to the tent pole. Not only was I close to exhaustion, but the muscles in my arms and shoulders were lame and aching.

Then again the whip-sword was a weapon with which I lacked training and experience. My battle with the vastodon should have shown me that I was making a dangerous error in attempting to duel with the heavy, cumbersome weapon. The flexive blade was all of five feet long and difficult for me to employ, while Thuton used a light, supple rapier that looked very much like the standard fencing épée. His agile, flickering point was everywhere—teasing my cheek, nicking my shoulder, drawing a crimson scratch first on this arm and then the other. He pranced lightly about the deck, while I shuffled heavy-footed and wearily. His men began to snicker. Koja looked as doleful as it is possible for a Yathoon to look.

Well, I shall not dwell on the scene. The memory is painful enough. Suffice it to say that Thuton made me look like a fumbling clown, an oaf of the dullest water. He played with me like a cat with a mouse, but with amusement, not viciousness. He could have cut me to ribbons, but he was in a great good humor, with a beautiful girl for an admiring audience, and he was content to nick me and scratch me and draw me in blundering circles and, for the final *coup de grâce*, to sever the waistband of my loincloth with a flick of the wrist. I had to drop my sword in order to preserve what little of my dignity was left.

He left me standing there, flushed crimson, furious, ludicrously shielding my nakedness, streaming with smeared blood and sweat.

Tossing his blade to the bosun, delicately wiping his brow with a perfumed bunch of ribbons, he turned, offering his arm to the Princess. She gave me a look of genuine contempt and went with him.

All in all, it had not been a very successful day.

Koja and I were sent to work at the wheels, while Darloona enjoyed the trip in a luxurious cabin.

The Sky Pirates are a rough lot, but not unkindly in a gruff way. A fellow named Gomar was put in charge of us, a bluff and hearty old seadog—or skydog, I suppose—with a scarlet kerchief knotted about his brows and a bush of inky beard that made him look like something out of *The Pirates of Penzance*. He let me sponge off in a trough of cold water, dug out a ragged kilt, clean loincloth, and a sort of open vest of repulsively orange felt adorned with copper disks. I felt like a stage gypsy in this getup, but I did not protest. Koja and I were given food, some sour ale, and I was permitted to rest before taking the wheel.

These wheels are enormous flat gears of hardwood set laterally about three and a half feet from the deck, and they are located in the main belowdecks compartment. There are fifty of them, stacked one above the other, with little catwalks and platforms in layers. The rims of the wheels are studded with handles and there is a slave at every handle. They walk about the outside of their wheel, pushing forward, and it is these wheels that supply the motive power which makes the enormous wings—or vans, more properly—flap.

It took us about a week, this cruise. And I was chained to my wheel for all the world like a galley slave out of some Errol Flynn epic of the Spanish Main. I don't think that Darloona realized Koja and I had been chained to the wheel—I suspect her oily-tongued host glibly said we had been given servile shipboard duties commensurate to our social level, or words to that effect.

The week was extremely educational.

Some of the wheel slaves were captives taken in war; others were native Zanadarians sold into slavery by impecunious parents or condemned to the wheels of the flying navy for some misdemeanor, or because of accumulated debts. The Sky Pirates require an enormous number of wheel slaves, a steady supply of fresh new bodies, as the grueling labor wears men our swiftly. Few wheel slaves last out their first year belowdecks. For this reason, I learned, the civil courts of Zanadar used slavery as a standard punishment for almost everything—murder, theft, embezzlement, adultery, bankruptcy, rape, attempted assassination, fraud, and just about any other crime you could name. And slavery automatically meant the wheel.

We labored in shifts around the clock, four hours at the

wheel and four hours off—a murderous pace. After my first three or four shifts at the wheel I thought I would die. After a few more, I wished that I could die. Never had I realized the body could experience such bone-deep exhaustion. As the saying has it: I discovered muscles I did not know I possessed. But we were fed heartily on good vastodon steaks washed down with a ration of some fierce red wine. And unlike the slaves at the oarlocks of an old-time galley back on Earth, the huge compartment wherein we labored and in whose corners we slept were not black stinking holes. Wide-open louvers in the upper works permitted a bracing flood of cold fresh air to circulate. In time I began to harden; my shoulders toughened and my back, belly, and chest began to develop steely thews.

Between shifts I talked with my fellow slaves. They were a motley crew, about half of them black-haired Zanadarians with paper-white complexions, the rest from every tribe and nation across the breadth of Thanator. There were silver-gray, chitin-clad Yathoon such as Koja, although, as it happened, they came from various of his rival clans and there were none of his own people at the wheels of the frigate. But there were many of the honey-skinned, redheaded Ku Thad with their slanted emerald eyes. Beyond these representatives of the three Thanatorian races I had already encountered during the course of my travels and adventures across the surface of the jungle moon, there were others from peoples I had not yet met, including many from a squat, dour-faced race who had lank, colorless hair, swarthy, greasy skins, and yellow eyes. These, I was told, were members of a bandit army called the Chac Yuul, the Black Legion. I will have quite a bit more to say of them before my tale is told.

We were en route to Zanadar, the city of the Sky Pirates. Scuttlebutt had it that the glib-tongued, wily Pirate Prince

LIN CARTER

had persuaded Darloona that he wished to help her people against their foes, but to do so must first return to the Cloud Kingdom to marshal his forces. Scuttlebutt also had it that Thuton was wooing her for all he was worth, with an eye towards uniting the two realms. I ground my teeth at this information, and entertained some bitter thoughts of what I would like to do to the Sky Pirate when next I had him at sword's point.

Talking to the wheel slaves helped fill in the blanks in my background information. There were enormous areas in which I was completely ignorant.

I learned that the planet, or moon, was largely land surface. Thanator has two inland seas. The larger of these, Corund Laj, the Greater Sea, is in the northern portion of the globe, while Sanmur Laj, the Lesser Sea, is far to the south. The Greater Sea and its coast is dominated by a race of red-skinned, bald-headed men, merchants and traders and shop-keepers, a mercantile civilization like ancient Carthage, but culturally closer to medieval Persia. Their civilization is called, for some reason, the Bright Empire of Perushtar: it is composed of the three cities of Farz, to the north, Narouk in the west, and Soraba to the south; its capital, Glorious Perusht, lies on a large island off the southern coast which has the rare distinction of being the only island on all of Thanator.

The superb metropolis of Shondakor lies on the river Ajand, one hundred *korads** south of the Sea of Corund Laj.

West of the Corund Laj and at approximately the same latitude rise the White Mountains of VaranHkor, upon one of

*The korad is the basic unit of distance upon Callisto. One korad equals approximately seven miles, the average distance a rider can travel in one hour on a fresh thaptor.—J. D.

whose peaks Zanadar, the City in the Clouds, is built. To the south of these mountains, west of Shondakor, and at approximately the latitude of that city, lies a colossal tract of jungle called the Grand Kumala. South of the Grand Kumala the Plains of Haratha stretch for about five hundred korads, from the shores of Sanmur Laj the Lesser Sea in the remote west to the foothills of the Black Mountains of Rhador, towards which the Yathoon Horde had been traveling. The distance between the encampment of the Horde and the city of the Sky Pirates, then, was enormous—three hundred and ten korads, or two thousand one hundred and seventy-five miles.

My readers (if any there be) must forgive me for this dissertation on Thanatorian geography, which may be a bit lengthy. But since the course of this story of my adventures on Callisto will take my reader, as it took me, to most places in this hemisphere of the jungle moon, I felt it advisable to describe the location of these lands and cities, and their relations to each other, in some considerable detail. As to the opposite hemisphere of Thanator, there is little that I can say, as I have never seen it. This modicum of geographical information, incidentally, which I gleaned from conversation with my fellow wheel slaves, proved priceless. For at last I had some notion of where lay that all-important disk of milky jade in its ring of guardian monoliths—the Gate Between The Worlds, to which I must somehow make my way again if ever I hope to return to my own world. I have marked its approximate location on this rough map.*

*Here Captain Dark interrupts his narrative to provide us with a sketch of one hemisphere of Thanator. The illustration, which appears on the reverse side of the twenty-fourth sheet of his handwritten manuscript, I have redrawn for reproduction and you will find it in the front matter of this book. The locations are only approximate and the intervals between them are doubtless only roughly correct, since it is impossible, with any degree of accuracy, to duplicate the convex surface of a planet to a flat sheet of paper without using the more sophisticated technical

I also learned something about the recent events on this world. Some months before my arrival on Thanator, the city of Shondakor had been conquered by a powerful bandit chieftain named Arkola, leader of the Chac Yuul, the Black Legion I mentioned a bit earlier. I know of no precise terrene equivalent by which I can explain the nature of this robber horde. They are, in a sense, nomadic warriors like the Don Cossacks of seventeenth-century Russia; they are also, in a way, something like the wandering *condottiere* of fifteenth-century Italy. Professional warriors, banded together under a commander selected by popular acclaim, they go where they will, living off the land, here attacking a merchant caravan, there seizing a fishing village or a hamlet of farmers, sometimes laying siege to the castle of some reputedly wealthy lord, and at other times selling their swords as a mercenary unit in some war between the cities of Thanator. What had led them to attack one of the most splendid and brilliant of all the great cities no man could say. But they had taken Shondakor by surprise, and seized control of the metropolis in a virtually bloodless coup. Perhaps their warlord, Arkola, had wearied of the nomadic life of camp and march, and sought to carve out a kingdom for himself and his Legionnaires—or, even better, to become the master of a kingdom that already existed, rather than creating one.

At any rate, when the Princess Darloona saw that the dreaded Black Legion was already within her gates and that further resistance was futile, she led the bulk of her people from the city into the jungles of the Grand Kumala. Discretion is, by repute, the better part of valor; doubtless Darloona thought it wiser to avoid the massacre of her people by es-

---

methods of professional cartographers. The map will suffice, however, to give you a rough idea of the locations mentioned in this story—L. C.

caping the Legion with her fighting strength all but unim-
paired. Once hidden in the trackless depths of the Grand
Kumala, she could regroup her forces, lay her plans, and live
in hopes of retaking the city. The Kumala is twenty-five hundred miles from east to west, and one thousand five hundred
miles from north to south at its greatest breadth. You can see
how easily one could conceal an army or two in that enormous wilderness, beyond chances of discovery. With nearly
four million square miles of the densest of jungles at your
disposal, you could tuck several fair-sized empires into the
corners of the Grand Kumala and they might never be found.

I did not until much later learn the circumstances
whereby I came upon Darloona alone in those jungles, battling against the vastodon; but she later told me the story, a
simple one of a hunting party broken up by a pack of yath-
ribs, the members dispersing in all directions and thereby losing track of each other. If I had not come along, and if the
vastodon had been elsewhere, it would only have been a matter of an hour or two before she would have found her way
back to the rest of her party.

I did, however, come along. So did the vastodon. And it
is upon such small happenings as these that the fate of worlds
may hang.

It is hard for me to estimate the number of nights and days I
spent slaving at the wheels of the flying ship. The monotony
of the grinding labor, the bewildering succession of work
shifts and sleep shifts, the cumulative fatigue, all prevented
me from keeping an accurate measure of the passage of time.
But these ungainly flying contraptions, I now know, are capable of making at least three hundred miles cross-country in
a single day, so I was at my wheel for a week at the very
least.

While this speed is not remarkable, compared to the velocity at which a terrene jet liner travels, it's fast enough for a ship propelled by muscle power alone.

The *Skygull* was the personal flagship or yacht of Prince Thuton. The pun in its name, incidentally, exists in both Thanatorian and English. There is a species of small flying reptile on Thanator, found generally in desert regions, called the *zell*. A branch of the same species can be found along the shores of the two Thanatorian seas. To differentiate this branch from the desert-inhabiting zells, the shore branch is known as the sea-zell, or *lajazell*, as *laj* is the Thanatorian word for "sea." *Kaja* is the Thanatorian word for "sky," hence the pun in the name of Thuton's ship, the frigate *Kajazell*.

I call it a frigate for, technically, being a light, speedy scout ship, that is what it was. But it looked more like a heavily ornamented Spanish galleon. The *Skygull* was eighty-seven feet long, very broad in the beam and flat-bottomed. It was built up very high in poop and forecastle: the forecastle rising to about forty-two feet above the keel level and the sterncastle to thirty-five feet. The upper works of the fore-castle bulged out sharply, an exposed belvedere with wide, high windows giving a good view on all three sides, and a flat, balustraded observation deck on top of this. The belvedere served as the pilothouse and from there the frigate was controlled and directed. A bowsprit protruded from the fore of the observation deck just above the curved row of windows, with an elaborate figurehead depicting a winged warrior with a fishtail. Further down the curve of the hull, below the pilothouse and at about what would be the water level on a seagoing ship, were two bulging observation balconies, one on either side of the hull. The sterncastle had a similar belvedere, pointing aft, and a vertical rudder fin, ribbed like an enormous fan, was attached to the rudderstock below this belvedere. The rudderstock was linked to the sternpost and thence to the rear steering gear.

The hinged wings thrust out to either side amidships and belowdecks. The spread must have measured at least one hundred and twenty feet from wingtip to wingtip, fully extended. The portion of the wings, or vans, which were attached to the sides of the ship were fixed rigid; but about one-third of the way out, the vans were hinged in a most ingenious and complicated manner, with enormous pulleys and guy-stays which manipulated the outboard wingsections which actually flapped up and down. The movements of the vans were powered and controlled from betweendecks. The huge wheels we slaves turned communicated kinetic energy through sequential cogwheels, pinion wheels successively engaging with larger cogs, and the whole connecting with the guy-stays, which were thin and strong as nylon cord. There was a ratchet-and-pawl arrangement on the wheels to prevent sudden reversal; for otherwise, a contrary gust of wind could have stripped the gears disastrously. The guy-stays wound about gigantic winches above our level, the stays communicating from the winches to the wing sections through a row of circular ports in the sides of the hull.

The concept of a bird-winged aircraft was not uniquely Thanatorian. I remembered that the Renaissance genius of Leonardo da Vinci, however, had not been able to invent a practical model of such a craft although his notebooks are filled with elaborate drawings of ornithopters. Weight and motive power were the main problems.

I was fascinated by the ingenuity with which the Zanadarians made practical the use of genuine ornithopters. For example, the flying frigates were not, as I had thought at first, made of wood at all, but of specially treated paper. Huge sheets of strong woven-reed papyrus were soaked in glue and stretched over plaster forms, layer after layer. When baked dry in brick ovens and stripped from their forms, the result was something like sections of molded plastic. The glue-impregnated paper hulls were incredibly thin, lighter than plastic or even balsa wood, and tough, strong, and durable.

The entire ship was made of paper wherever possible. The beams and masts and keel, sternpost and stempost, bowsprit and van ribs, werehollow tubes. Even the huge figurehead was a hollow paper mold. The vans, the flapping sections at least, were constructed like the wings of a giant bat, narrow hollow paper tubes, like unsegmented bamboo rods, splayed out from a center rib. Between these ribs, however, silk webbing was used instead of the glue-impregnated paper. Tough silk, tightly stretched and pegged like drumheads, was then soaked in wax for extreme stiffness, the interstices sealed with wax. Paper plates had proved impractical here.

But this use of strong, light paper construction alone would still not have made the eighty-seven-foot-long frigates skyworthy had it not been for the gas compartments. The entire lower deck, the bilge, of the frigates was pumped full of a buoyant natural gas like helium or hydrogen, whose enormous lifting power rendered the ornithopters virtually weightless. Geysers of this gas were found in the White Mountains; they were tapped, and the bilge compartments of the frigates were pumped full of gas under high pressure. The nozzles were unscrewed and detached from the input hoses, then transformed by the addition of a simple snap-on valve to pressure cocks which permitted some of the buoyant gas to be ejected at need, permitting the ship to sink to a lower level. The bilge compartment, once full, was then sealed and caulked until it was airtight. And the ships were skyworthy.

There were two masts amidships, set side by side rather than fore and aft as on a seagoing schooner. Light shrouds stretched from mast to mast, and then to the bowsprit and the poop, for the display of signal pennants and for the use of the sailors who manned the lonely and rather windy top-mast observation cupolas.

The ships had a crew strength of thirty-five officers and men, and eighty wheel slaves. It was the number of wheel slaves required to power the vans that kept the number of the Zanadarian vessels at a minimum. Otherwise, with such an amazing technological advance over the other nations of the jungle moon, they could have controlled a world empire.

And if ever the Zanadarians discover the steam engine, God help Thanator!

CHAPTER VIII
ZANADAR,
THE CITY IN THE CLOUDS

As it happened, our arrival at the city of the Sky Pirates came about during one of my sleep shifts.

For days we had been soaring at two thousand feet above the dark crimson carpet of the Grand Kumala. But yesterday, towards evening, we at last reached the foothills of the Varan-Hkor mountains, and by dawn the towers of Zanadar were in sight.

My wheel gang slept in a cubicle on an upper level, just under the row of ventilation louvers. Thus I had a splendid view of the City in the Clouds, as Zanadar was sometimes called.

Directly ahead of our prow, a few degrees to port, a tall peak soared on the horizon, lifting its castled crest out of the purple gloom and into the brilliance of dawn. The mountains were largely of white marl, like snowy chalk veined with sparkling gray quartz; the peak was jagged, the city built at different levels, various towers or battlements connected by airy bridgeways which spanned the gap between many of the imposing structures, looking from our distance rather like cobwebs entangled in stiff spears of grass, twinkling jeweled in the morning light.

As the frigate drew nearer I could hear the stentorian voice of the First Mate bellowing orders through his megaphones to belay all lines and secure hatches.

"Ahoy the poop!" he bawled in his foghorn voice. "Signal crew stand by the aft lines. Prepare to display colors. Look alive at the sternpost steerage, you lads—"

A fainter voice sounded from the pilothouse and the First Mate relayed it aft. "Starboard your rudder, two points!" he bellowed. Then: "Look alive at those winches! Trim your rear surfaces—hard about on that rudder, men!"

I felt a shudder run through the taut structure and the great winches above me creaked, guy-stays thrumming with tension as the winch gang feathered the aileronlike segments of the vans to turn the ship about to port. The endlessly complex process of flying the *Skygull* I found ceaselessly fascinating. I would have given anything to be abovedecks just then, watching how they did it. I understood that the winch gangs controlled the pitch and pace of the vans, while the rudder gang did the actual steering by shifting that enormous fan-ribbed rudder fin to either port or starboard; the whole operation was coordinated from the pilothouse, the captain's commands relayed from the belvedere observation deck to the first mate, who stood atop a sort of conning tower between the twin masts; he in turn relayed orders to winch or rudder gangs.

Now we were coming about into the wind. The wingbeats were slower now, the great vans almost still, gliding on the air currents, the forward motion gradually slowing as the downwards-tilted aileron surfaces dragged against the thrust. Struts creaked as the frigate tilted to port, lurching a little, and the mate raised his voice in a roar, telling the starboard winch gang to trim their pitch. I shall not translate the sulphurous oaths wherewith his command was peppered.

Zanadar lay dead ahead now, and much nearer. Built atop a mountain, the city of the Sky Pirates had no need of walls or battlements or even a barbican. The structures I could see were built in a characteristic style of architecture that ran to four-sided buildings, with flat roofs and tiered levels shielded by bright striped awnings. The buildings were very massive and solid, with enormously thick walls, and they tapered sharply from base to summit; I suppose this style was dictated by the cold air of this altitude and the constant gale-force winds that whistled about us. The crest of this mountain broke into a number of subsidiary peaks, a dozen of which had been artificially leveled off and converted to landing plazas for the ornithopter fleet. I could just see railed runways on the surface of the nearer plaza towards which we seemed to be heading. At each side of the plaza was a sort of roofless hangar, like a dry dock. Three dry docks were occupied by frigates comparable to ours. The docks rose above the level of the amidships deck and the frigates were hauled into place by dock gangs pulling on deck lines. There must be wheels, perhaps retractable ones, on the underside of the ship, for the vessels obviously were landed in the center of the plaza and were slid down the rails into moorage, then secured by heavy deck cables fastened to mooring posts.

Now the wingtips flapped in a swift, light beat. With each agitation of the ribbed vans, the hollow compartments echoed like a beaten drum. Fantastic vistas of tower and airy span and yawning chasm swept past the open louver. I glimpsed rooftop gardens, bright with colored blossoms, ripening fruits, glossy scarlet leaves, shielded from the bitter cold of the mountain air behind glassed cupolas, as we swung about.

From each spire glowing pennants unrolled on the wind

their heraldic glories. Tiered levels fell away beneath, disclosing glass-domed boulevards where bright-robed throngs strolled between flowering trees, or rode in rickshaws of gilt paper and wood. This higher level, I learned later from Lukor, was called the Upper City; here dwelt the nobles and aristocrats and courtiers, with their attendant satellites—minstrels, clowns, jugglers, mountebanks, perfumers, topiarists, paper sculptors, the composers of masques, the blenders of cosmetics, the leaders of revels. This was the leisurely, affluent class, supported by the second level and its labors.

Now, as we circled lower, riding the updraft, we flew over what Lukor later termed the Middle City. The streets here were unshielded, open to the winds; the houses more squat, the streets lined with inns, wineshops, alehouses, mercantile establishments, drinking booths, houses of gaming or pleasure. Gaudy paper lanterns swung in the wind from long nodding poles: blue, copper, witch-green, lemon—like goblin eyes in the early morning gloom. Here dwelt the great Pirate Captains of the Brotherhood of the Clouds: the lordly privateers who led their own ships, or, in some cases, entire squadrons, in raiding expeditions against the trader caravans that attempted perilous crossings through the mountain passes, or against nearby cities and towns. Swaggering in belled cloaks and swash boots, bedizened wenches leaning on their velvet-clad arms, steel rapiers dangling against bulging purses, they strode the windy streets of the Middle City in drunken and arrogant splendor.

Of the Lower City I saw but little: grubby hovels crouched around the bases of the soaring tiers, grim-faced guards and scurrying, bent figures, shuffling laborers, and grimy urchins. Here dwelt the slaves, the servitors, the thieves and the outcasts, fallen from the glittering heights above to this wallow of squalid poverty.

We hovered on motionless vans. The first mate bellowed. Screws turned, releasing pressure cocks. The squeal of escaping gases. The frigate trembled, sagged, hovered, sagged again, and then her keel ground and grated against the floor of the plaza. I heard the thud of work gangs racing to attach the cables. Then the squeak of oiled bearings and the rumble of the rails as we were towed into moorage and made fast.

Darloona disembarked from an upper-deck gang-plank; I caught only a glimpse of her, laughing, pink-cheeked with excitement, resplendent in drifting silks, leaning on Thuton's arm as he urbanely saluted the port colors.

I trudged out at ground level, one of a bent-backed, shuffling line of lowly slaves.

The slave pens were in the Lower City, behind walls as thick and massive as Sequoia palisades. Here Koja and I received numbered tags, suspended around our necks on stiff wire. We would share a three-man cubicle in the giant structure, and would be on call for the next corsair of the skies who required new blood to man the wheels. In the meanwhile, we had nothing to do but vegetate.

For me, the transition from the barbarism of the Horde camp to an advanced urban civilization was unsettling. How like modern Stockholm or London, I thought wryly. Grubby slums cowering at the foot of soaring mansions and palaces; the distant clamor of laughter and music from bright pleasure gardens far above drifting down to squalid alleys and fetid hovels at their foot.

For Koja, who had known nothing but the life of camp, hunt, and war, it must have been a revelation. But the somber fellow spoke little, keeping to his own thoughts.

Ours was a lethargic existence. Twice a day guards marshaled us into double lines and we shuffled forth to feed at long porcelain troughs filled with a luke-warm greasy stew of odds and ends of meat, pieced out with chunks of some tuberlike vegetable. We had each a wooden cup wherewith to dip our slops out of this common feeding trough. The cracked, dirty plaster of the walls—the greasy, food-splattered floor—the scrape and clatter of cups dipped in the congealing slum-gullion—the blurred, weary, dull-eyed faces—how different from the spacious rooms with waxed glistening floors, where well-groomed officers and aristocrats in immaculate uniforms glittering with gold braid—and the Princess of Shondakor—probably spent these same days!

News filtered down from the lordly heights above. Prince Thuton had vowed to restore Darloona to the throne of Shondakor. The emissaries of Zanadar were meeting with chieftains of the Black Legion to discuss the alternatives of peace and war. The entire armada of ornithopters was being readied for an assault against Darloona's capital, unless the usurper, Arkola, relinquished his hold on the throne.

Rumors whispered a royal wedding was imminent.

I began to reconsider my early opinion of Thuton as perhaps a hasty one. Koja's depiction of Thuton's motives as base, sordid, and political had sounded plausible at the time, and perhaps were still plausible—but was I not swayed in my opinion more by personal grudge than by the evidence? For the tenor of the news was such that it looked as if Thuton was making a genuine effort to drive out the Black Legion and restore Darloona to her capital.

I hated the suave, foppish fellow. But the personal humiliation, the resounding defeat I had received at his hands, and my bitterness at the way he had swept Darloona from my side—these explained my dislike.

Doubtless, I should never see Darloona again. She was

not likely to venture into the squalor of the slave pens, and her contempt and loathing towards me, however founded on misunderstanding, would certainly prevent any future commerce between us.

They said the charming Thuton had swept her off her feet, and would make her his Queen ere Year's End Day.

Perhaps it was time I stopped thinking about her.

She belonged to the glittering world of luxury and privilege, far above me. I could not have helped her, and Thuton could. She felt only loathing for me. Perhaps, I thought, I should turn my mind from her and her high affairs and start thinking about myself.

It was Koja who discovered the broken grating.

There had been a ferocious storm. Howling gale winds shook the thick-walled structures of the mountaintop city. Icy rains deluged the peak and went sluicing through the streets. Much damage had been done, so much that the usual work force of street laborers required considerable reinforcements. Every third slave in the pens was pressed into temporary repair and clean-up work. Koja was chosen from my cubicle.

He returned that evening with curious news.

A section of roof tiles had been torn away from the top of the building where we were immured. While laying new tiles by the roof-edge gutters, Koja had discovered a broken louver grating, loose at one end.

The stench of four thousand men penned up in one colossal warren of dirty cubicles was overpowering. Inadequate sanitary conditions contributed to the pervasive and unhealthy miasma. Men long penned in such close quarters were known to eventually develop diseased lungs and succumb to the spitting sickness.

For this reason, high up under the roof, wide louver-shuttered windows had been cut in the walls. Thick gratings of iron rods, clamped to the stone in brackets, kept the windows from serving as a mode of escape.

One of these gratings had broken. The damp had eaten into the outer plaster facing, corroding the iron bolts which had not been replaced for decades.

Koja solemnly reported that with a bit of luck, perfect timing, and the inattention of the guards, a man could climb out through the grating. But it would take two men to effect the escape—one to hold the heavy grating open, while the other slithered through.

"But once through, then what?" I objected. "How do you climb down the sheer wall?"

"That is not the way," he said, his harsh tones low so that none could overhear. "From the window, a man could climb up to the roof ledge, which is only a few feet above the top of the louver. And the roof of the slave pens connects with other buildings and higher tiers by means of those aerial bridgeways we glimpsed as the frigate descended to moor. It should not be difficult for one as strong as Jandar."

We discussed the notion further; in the end we decided to try it. Even should the attempt result in our demise, such an outcome was preferable to a short, dreary life at the wheel.

We resolved, in fact, to attempt our escape that very night. Delay might well foil our chances, for at any time an ornithopter might require wheel slaves for a voyage.

We slept in flimsy cubicles which extended, one after another, around the succession of balconies which lined the walls of the huge room. Wheel slaves are not chained, and their activities are kept under the most cursory observation. I do not know whether this is because the enervating and monotonous drudgery of wheel labor is believed to break morale and crush spirit to the point at which a wheel slave is incapable of seeking to escape, or whether the deadly *va lu rokka* philosophy is shared by other races of Thanator besides the Yathoon arthropods. However, it is fortunate for Koja and me that such is the case. Guards stroll about the balconies at irregular intervals, but in the hours between midnight and dawn they tend to congregate in the guardhouse, swapping erotic boasts and swigging a potent liquor called *quarra* with their comrades-in-arms, to the neglect of their regular rounds. Hence we selected two o'clock in the morning as the best time for our escape.

When daylight died, the guards lit flickering oil lamps, sealed against tampering and pinned to the wall with iron brackets. Koja and I retired to our pallets, yawning as if overpoweringly sleepy, and stretched out. All about us slaves scratched, grumbled, spat, prepared to retire.

For hours we lay motionless, pretending to sleep. From time to time a guard ambled by, starting on the lowest tier of balconies, circling the huge dim room, ascending by creaking ladders to the next tier, thus passing all cubicles. After the third such complete tour, the rounds became perfunctory, and the upper balconies were unvisited.

At the agreed time, Koja and I slunk silently from our cubicle, and ascended as unobtrusively as possible to the highest level. Here all was dark, and few eyes could have seen us had anyone been awake at this hour. We clambered as quietly as possible to the top of an unoccupied cubicle directly below the louvered window. Koja, whose long arms gave him greater reach, was elected to hold open the heavy grating while I, the more agile of the two, climbed upon his upper thorax and wriggled through the opening. Luckily the Zanadarian mode of architecture uses very thick masonry; and thus the jamb of the window was two feet wide, affording me plenty of room to stand.

I climbed out. Koja lowered the grill back into place, so that I could use the bars of the grating as the rungs of a ladder. It was not difficult to climb up to the roof from the top of the grating, using the slats of the louver for extra footing.

The night was clear and cold. Europa, which the Thanatorians call Ramavad, was aloft, a luminous globe of frosty azure-silver. Neither of the two other large moons had yet ascended the night skies, but Jupiter's smallest and inmost moon, tiny Amalthea, hung like a throbbing flake of gold against the dark. To the natives of Thanator, it is Juruvad, the "Little Moon."

The roof thrust out sharply in an overhanging ledge. Anchoring one arm over this abutment, I bent to assist Koja. I had bound a strip torn from my loin-cloth to the barred grating, and now I pulled on this, opening the grille so that my companion could climb out.

But even as I did so, and as Koja thrust his head and one segmented arm through the opening, the sound of angry cries and thudding feet came to me from within.

And so our escape was discovered. Hanging there above the street, one arm hooked over the edge of the roof, the other holding the barred grating free, my toes braced against the topmost slat of the louver, there was little I could do to aid my comrade. I urged him to hurry, to climb up on the jamb. But guards had seized his lower limbs and in a moment they had dragged him back into the pens.

He turned one last solemn gaze on me before vanishing from my sight. And he spoke one last farewell.

"The Lords of Gordrimator be with you, Jandar! Do not attempt to help me. Now you must seek your own freedom—"

"Koja!" I cried.

His last words were: "Save yourself! And thus I discharge my *uhorz—*"

And then they dragged him from the window.

I hung between earth and heaven, wishing there was something I could do to help him. But then the snarling visage of a guard thrust through the grating, the silver luminance of Ramavad gilding his copper helm while he jabbed a long spear at my legs.

It would do Koja no good if I were slain or captured. I kicked free of the louver and clambered up over the edge of the roof. The grating I let slam back: it caught the guard full in the face and I heard him fall with thump and clatter.

Safe on the roof, I climbed to my feet and looked around me. A feeling of grim despair possessed my heart. Never in all my months on Thanator had I been so completely alone as at this moment.

My only friend in the hands of the guards of Zanadar, I was alone and without a weapon in a strange, unfamiliar city, surrounded by enemies.

CHAPTER IX
I ESCAPE FROM THE SLAVE PENS

The roof was flat and bare. Two of the airy skywalks connected it to adjoining structures. But before I could even begin to make my way towards one of them, I was under attack and fighting for my life.

The strident clamor of an alarm gong sounded within the huge building. And now, racing across the roof to challenge me came a burly guard, his dark cloak floating out behind him like immense wings, the naked glitter of a rapier in his hand.

I was unarmed and nearly naked, but I ducked under his stroke. The sword sang past my ear as I drove my fist into his belly. He doubled over, grunting and I lifted his heels two inches off the roof with a right to the jaw. He fell heavily, his head wobbling loosely, and I saw that I had slain him.

I had known that my muscular strength was far superior to that of the Yathoon arthropods, but I had not realized my superiority to the human natives as well. The gravity of Thanator is somewhat less than that of Earth: not much, but there is a discernible difference. But it would seem that even that slight variance makes a measurable increase of strength in one born and raised under the heavier gravitational pull. For my blow had broken the fellow's neck.

I had no time just then to mourn the guard's demise, even if I had felt the inclination. I am no pacifist, and in fact I am perfectly ready and willing to kill an enemy seeking to strike down an unarmed man with a swordblade, especially when that man is myself. I bent over his body and began stripping him, exchanging my ragged slave clout for his high-necked, open-throated leathern tunic with the blazon of Zanadar on the breast. Where there is one guard there may soon be two, and if I must fight for my life and freedom I prefer doing it clad in fighting harness.

In half a minute I had donned his tunic, buskins, girdle, baldric, helmet, and cloak. Wrapping my old loincloth about his middle, I tipped his corpse over the edge of the roof and heard him thud against the cobbles far below. The discovery of a slave corpse by guards seeking an escaped slave might delay pursuit by an appreciable fraction of time, perhaps permitting me to complete my escape.

In the pallor of moonlight I hoped to pass scrutiny as a Zanadarian. The copper helm would cover my unusual yellow hair and the eye-shield of the helm would hide my blue eyes, and there was nothing I could do about the tan of my skin except hope that no one would notice.

I crossed the roof swiftly and made a remarkable discovery.

The guard had landed here in a two-man flying gig, which was tethered to a mooring post towards the rear of the roof.

I had not seen one of these miniature ornithopters before, and thus I consumed some moments of precious time examining it. It did not bear a very close resemblance to the enormously larger frigates, and of course it was not powered by slaves at the wheel, since it was only twelve feet long. The craft looked for all the world like a kayak, an enclosed canoe. It rose high in prow and poop, with a curved and ornamental bowsprit like that of a Venetian gondola. Instead of having a bilge compartment filled with the levitating gas, it had an airtight double hull that rendered it completely weightless. The wingspan was twenty-two feet from tip to tip, and the gig obviously did not fly by flapping the vans, for, although they were hinged and could be operated by foot pedals which communicated via external cables to a pulley arrangement on the van-tips, mere pedaling action alone could not suffice. I assumed the gig was more of a glider than a true ornithopter, and that it rode the strong updrafts of the mountaintop city.

I suppose it was suicidally foolish of me to attempt to fly the thing. But I climbed in, cast off the blowline, settled my feet against the pedals, and began testing the controls as an updraft whirled me away from the rooftop.

I was in a vile, self-recriminatory mood, and did not hold my life to any great account just then. It proved a good thing that this was so, for before the rooftop vanished beneath me I saw guards come pouring out of a trapdoor to scour the area for me.

Like a leaf caught in a millrace, I was whirled between tall tapering towers. The curved span of airy skywalks flashed past, one of them narrowly missing me. I could well have wrecked the gig during those first few minutes, but luckily I did not.

The controls were simplicity itself. Levers controlled the pitch of the ailerons and the rear vertical rudder fin. The jointed wingtips served to turn the craft in midair as desired. Whatever the nature of the buoyant gas held within the hollow space inside the double hull, it had remarkable lifting power and rendered the gig completely weightless. Never have I had so completely the sensation of flying; it was like a dream, wherein you are unconscious of weight or of effort, but flit about at will.

As soon as I had familiarized myself with the controls, I swung her bowsprit about and headed for the Middle City. If the swiftness with which I mastered the craft seems uncanny, I must confess I have had some experience piloting gliders in Switzerland, and that I fully grasped the principles of glider flight.

Doubtless my decision to quit the Lower City was a wise one. Lukor later heard that my substitution of the guard's body for my own allayed for at least an hour suspicion that I had escaped. It was not until the Slavemaster had been roused from his sodden slumbers, shortly before dawn, that my escape was confirmed. For of course the guard, being a native Zanadarian, lacked my yellow hair, blue eyes, and tan skin. And I also learned that even after it had been discovered that one of the wheel slaves had made a successful escape from the pens, no one dreamed he had made his way up into the Middle City, and the search for my whereabouts was confined to the lower levels on the theory that I had found a hiding place in some hovel. The spans leading to the Middle City are heavily guarded against thieves from the slum regions below, and hence it did not seem possible that I had crossed over undetected. No one knew at first of the theft of the gig.

I achieved the tiers of the Middle City, but only by a hairsbreadth. A chance gust swept me against the carved gryphons and gargoyles on an ornamental balcony with a resounding crash which breached my hull. I did not need the scream of escaping gas to know my craft no longer was airworthy, for she was settling sluggishly and I barely had time to hop out on one of the bridges before she lost buoyancy altogether and fell like a stricken gull into the dark chasms between the huge structures.

It was nearly four o'clock in the morning. I must find some haven in which to hide before daylight exposed my alien coloring to all eyes.

I decided to dump my guard clothing. The first guard I passed might be suspicious of my presence. I was unfamiliar with the ranks in the guards of Zanadar, and I did not know password or salute. I retained the common leather tunic and girdle, which are worn by most Thanatorian warriors, as well as cloak, buskins, and baldric. But I got rid of my copper helmet and the blazon of the city, tossing them into a convenient trashcan. The cloak was a simple, unmarked garment of dark wool, with a cowl which I drew up to hide my hair and shadow my face. Then I set forth to explore the winding ways of the City in the Clouds.

As the skies brightened with dawn, I was passing down a broad avenue, keeping well to the shadows and avoiding the gaze of the chance passerby, when I glimpsed a dramatic tableau.

A dark alley thrust from one side of this broad boulevard, like the tributary of some mighty river. It ended in an enclosed courtyard. And there a lone man battled for his life against a growling circle of oafish opponents.

I have always favored the underdog and I have never avoided a good fight. And besides, I could not in all conscience turn aside and pretend I had not seen a fellow human battling valiantly against impossible odds.

He was an elderly man, thin and slender, of middle height, with a short, neatly trimmed beard of iron gray and a leonine mane still streaked with black. He had cool, thoughtful eyes and a good jaw, and he stood with his back to the wall, not even deigning to cry for help, his agile, flickering blade holding at bay a dozen coarse-faced bullies armed with cutlass and cudgel. His blade had already accounted for four of the bravos, who lay dead at his feet, and as I came on the scene he evaded the backhanded blow of the biggest of his foes, sliding past the other's guard with a supple twist of the wrist, his blade flashing in and through the other's burly chest, and out again with a practiced recovery.

As the hulking bully swayed a moment on his feet, gurgling blood before crashing to the pave, I sprang on the scene with drawn rapier. I must have seemed like some apparition melting out of nothingness, so swift and silent had been my approach. Indeed, the man closest to me turned with a start, eyes goggling, as I sprang from the alley's mouth to drive my steel through his shoulder. His cutlass rang on the cobbles and his hoarse cry of astonishment and pain drew the attention of his fellows to the fact of my presence.

Surprise is always a strong advantage in any battle, and I managed to slay two of the mob before a sufficient number engaged my blade. Unlike my last experience in sword combat—my humiliating defeat at the hands of Prince Thuton—in which I was burdened with an unfamiliar Yathoon whipsword, this time I fought with a slender rapier I had taken from the guard's body—a weapon much more to my liking. I engaged their blades and was soon fighting for my life.

The elderly man to whose aid I had come cast me a merry glance from bright, appraising eyes, and smiled grimly.

"I know not from whence you have sprung, friend, but you are most welcome indeed!" he greeted me.

I grinned recklessly. "My sense of chivalry will doubtlessly be the death of me yet, sir, but I thought you might not be so selfish as to keep this fight all to yourself."

He laughed. "I am unselfish to a fault—so pray help your-self!"

And then we were both too busy for any further jesting. We fought back to back for a while, each accounting for two more of the bullies. Eventually, and just before my arm began to tire, the foemen decided they had had enough, and dis-engaged. We permitted them to flee without pursuit, and then turned to salute each other.

"Your assistance was most timely, indeed, sir, and I thank you for it," my companion said with a smile and a nod of the head.

"Not at all; I have always thought twelve against one most unequal odds, and, besides, I felt the need of a little practice," I replied—having learned by now that on Thanator a warrior always depreciates his own skill and prowess.

"I was returning home from a late performance at the theater and had unwisely bade my companions goodnight, thus proceeding alone through an area not entirely safe. The street gang doubtless mistook me for a man of substance, and I doubt not they would have been heartily disappointed had they succeeded in cutting me down, only to find my purse perhaps leaner than their own," the elderly gentleman ex-plained.

"And no leaner than mine own." I grinned. "Had both of us fallen, they would have had all that work for nothing."

"My home is not far. Will you share the hospitality of a warm hearth and a cup of wine, sir?" he asked in a courtly manner.

"I should be most glad to do so, as the night grows cold and I am far from my home," I said gratefully.

We strode through a passageway into another court where a red and black sorad tree lifted glistening leaves against the first light of dawn. Here my companion unlatched a door and gestured for me to proceed him.

"Be welcome, my friend, to the poor home of Lukor the Swordsmaster, proprietor of the Academy Lukor and its sole tutor in the gentlemanly art of the blade," he said, offering me a comfortable chair before the fire. I introduced myself as Jandar, but did not mention a home city, saying only that I was a traveler from a faroff land. My host was too polite to ask further information.

It was a bare, spartan room, scrupulously neat and of immaculate cleanliness. The few articles of furniture were of the finest quality and the artworks, if inexpensive, were of superior skill. These were obviously the quarters of a gentle-man of bachelor habits, aristocratic breeding, and slender fortunes. The Swordsmaster took my cloak and his own, hung them in a closet, and left the room, inviting me to make myself comfortable before the fire.

In a moment he returned, bearing a wine service of fine if well-worn silver, two tall goblets and a chilled carafe of a light, dry wine of most excellent vintage, as well as a small platter of cold spiced meats, unfamiliar candied fruit, and the most delicious, crusty biscuits—a repast most welcome to one who had scooped greasy stew from a slave trough for the past few days.

We drank to each other's health and relaxed in the flick-ering warmth of the fire. It was a snug, cozy little room, mullioned windows bright with dawn, the air spicy with the scent of some subtle incense. I felt very comfortable and relaxed.

"So you are a swordsmaster, sir? I should have guessed as much from the ease with which you were holding your own against a dozen foes."

"Aye, my friend. My name is not completely unknown

among the masters of the art, I must confess; although the young nobles of this city, alas, regard the finer elements of swordplay as superfluous and frivolous pedantry! But permit me to return the compliment: your own performance was not without agility and adroitness, if a bit soft from lack of practice, if you will pardon the observation—the eye of the professional is too exacting, and I fear I display incivility towards one whom I can only regard as my gallant rescuer!"

I smiled and said something to the effect that I had enjoyed insufficient leisure in recent weeks to keep in practice. "I gather from your words," I continued, "that the Academy Lukor is new to this city, and that Zanadar is not your native homeland?"

"Quite so: I am a Ganatolian," he said, naming a small city between Shondakor and Narouk, in the eastern foothills of the White Mountains. "There are already two schools of the sword in my native city, hence I adjourned to the realm of the warlike Sky Pirates, hoping to find a virgin field for my craft. Alas, my pupils have been few and my earnings insufficient to permit even the hiring of a second instructor."

Then, eyeing me with polite inquiry, he turned the subject of our conversation to me.

"But you, sir; obviously, you are not native to Zanadar either, for never have I met a gentleman of your unique coloring of flesh, hair, and eyes. May one inquire, without offense—?"

"I, too, am a stranger here," I admitted. Then, in a rush of honesty, I went on to say that although born in Rio and tutored at Yale, I had most recently lived in Vietnam before departing for these regions.

These terrene names, of course, were unknown to him. Lukor considered them gravely, then observed: "They must certainly be far distant, these lands whereof I have not heard, I assume the people of your homeland visit these regions but rarely?"

"Most rarely, indeed," I said—truthfully—"in fact, so far as I know, I am the first visitor from my homelands to these parts."

Conversation languished for a bit. I blinked sleepily, lulled by the superb wine and the warmth of the fire. Perhaps I even dozed a bit—after all, I had not slept a wink this night. The next thing I knew, my host was shaking my shoulder.

"The morning is upon us, and I am for my bed; I must be off to the citadel before midday, as I tutor the young lords Marak and Eykor in the sword. Rather than make the long trek to your own quarters, will you not accept the hospitality of my roof?"

I made polite objections, suggested that I was imposing upon him, but nothing would satisfy the Swordsmaster but that I sleep in his house.

And since I did not in fact have other quarters, I accepted his kindness, slid out of my garments, and was soon fast asleep.

Thus calamity led to a fortunate meeting, and I made my first friend in Zanadar. And never again will I question the wisdom of springing to the assistance of a stranger in need, seeing how well the friendship of Lukor was to reward my chivalrous urge.

CHAPTER X

LUKOR THE SWORDMASTER

M y host was an elderly gentleman of about sixty years, but slim and strong, straight as a spear shaft, and he moved with the agility and elastic grace of one in the most perfect health and fitness, as might be expected of one whose craft and art is the blade.

He would not hear of my leaving. Word had gotten about the City in the Clouds of the escape of a wheel slave with tan skin, yellow hair, and blue eyes. I would be seized on sight, and Lukor would not permit the man who had saved his life to fall victim to the first guard that came along. I knew without question that I could trust him, for he was one of those rare individuals whose worthiness and honesty are evident upon the slightest meeting. He bent a sympathetic ear to the tale of my troubles, and vowed that I would have a haven in his house for as long as I desired to stay.

The house of Lukor opened upon a small secluded court to the rear; the front faced on one of the major thoroughfares of the Middle City. It was two stories high, the first story given over to Lukor's living quarters, and the second story, an enormous empty loft, to the fencing school he managed. This was a large high-ceiling room, one wall lined with floor-to-ceiling mirrors, the other covered with pegs and racks from which depended fencing masks, padded gloves and tunics, and a variety of swords. Sabers, foils, rapiers, cutlasses, swords, and daggers of every description hung there, kept in perfect condition. Not a fleck of rust or speck of dust was to be found.

Lukor had few pupils and his academy barely managed to survive. The sons of a few merchants and innkeepers, with pretensions towards gentility, came to him every other day for brief lessons. And twice a week he made the long trek to the royal citadel in the Upper City where he gave private lessons to a couple of lordly young courtiers too proud to descend to the Middle City for tutelage.

As I could not hope to remain invisible to all eyes, my newfound friend prevailed upon his friend Irivor for cosmetics. Irivor worked backstage at one of the theaters in the Middle City, which produced adventure melodramas featuring considerable swordplay and thus required a resident fencing master to train the actors in the art. Through his colleague, Lukor obtained a bleaching cream which turned my skin milk white, and a hair dye with which my yellow locks were transformed to silken black. Naught could be done to disguise the unusual color of my eyes; however, the rest of me could be made over in the likeness of the average citizen of Zanadar.

On days when Lukor had no pupils, he tested my skill in the mirror-walled fencing room. I was interested to see how the art of the blade, as practiced upon the jungle moon, differed from terrene tradition. We stripped to the waist, our features protected by fencing masks, selected slim rapiers with button-guarded tips, and set to.

As I watched Lukor with a sword in his hand, it was difficult to realize that he was sixty years old; his light, spare frame moved with extraordinary grace and elasticity. He had a wrist of supple steel and an arm that never tired. Within moments the room echoed with the click and slither of steel on steel.

I suppose that any two worlds inhabited by human beings using basically the same kind of sword will invent virtually identical modes of swordplay. At any rate, I saw that the Thanatorians knew the *ward of tierce*, the *coupé*, the eight guards, and even the *quinte par dessus les armes*—which have been common in the art of fence on Earth for centuries. One after another I tried all the tricks I knew, only to watch as Lukor disengaged or parried with magical ease. He was immune to double and triple feints, and to the most advanced tactics with which I was familiar.

We broke for a rest period and refreshed ourselves with chilled wine. I, the younger and stronger man, my thews toughened from a week at the slave wheels, found I was covered with a sheen of perspiration and was breathing heavily, while my elderly opponent was calm and unruffled. It was humiliating: I had not touched him once.

As we opened the second bout, I began with a swift *glizade*. For a moment our blades clashed and rang together, a blur of flashing steel, the large empty room resounding to the chiming song of steel on steel. Then from a low engagement in *sixte* I stretched forward to lunge in *tierce*. My blade glided past his parry with a supple twist and I was lucky enough to touch him above the heart.

We disengaged and sprang apart. Lukor was laughing delightedly, his keen eyes sparkling.

"Well played, my young friend! That was superb—my compliments! I had not expected you should be able to touch me at least until the third bout. You have a gift for the fence, and you have obviously studied under a master."

"A lucky stroke, nothing more," I said, attempting to sound modest, although actually I was glowing with satisfaction. He shook his head appraisingly.

" 'Twas luck in part, but only in part. You have a good wrist, a steady arm, and a cool head. You are able to think and plan while engaged, and these are the essentials of a master swordsman. With practice and training you will acquire the only thing you lack at present—which is science. Come—once again?"

I did not manage to touch him in the third bout, and by the fourth I was shaking with exhaustion. We called it a day.

Guards were still combing Zanadar for the runaway slave, and rumor had it that Prince Thuton was particularly anxious that I should be taken. So it was decided that I stay on with my new friend. I felt a trifle uncomfortable at sleeping in his spare bed and eating at his table without being able to repay my debt to him in any way. Lukor, the most tactful and chivalrous of gentlemen, soon became aware of this and so suggested that I lend him assistance with his pupils. There were so few of these that it seemed superfluous to add a second tutor, but he explained that a few novices were always coming in fresh, and while he gave advanced training to his more experienced pupils it would spare him much if he could rely on me to teach the newcomers the rudiments of the art. As my disguise was sufficient to protect me from chance discovery, we decided to pass me off as his nephew, newly come from Ganatol. My new name was Lykon.

One day followed another without incident. Between my training of the novices and my periods of advanced practice under Lukor I was rapidly developing into a brilliant swordsman, as Lukor often remarked himself.

These were happy days—my happiest on Thanator—and I

look back on them fondly. Between work and practice and training, we relaxed at a wineshop frequented by theater people, jugglers, mountebanks, and magicians. Sometimes we spent the evening at the theater, and sometimes we strolled in the pleasure gardens of the Upper City into which Lukor was permitted to pass by virtue of possession of a medallion which gave him entrée to the citadel for his private lessons.

As my plans were vague, I remained at the Academy Lukor for the better part of a month. The fortunes of the Princess of Shondakor were now in hands better equipped than my own to render assistance to her cause; my only other friend, Koja, was doubtless dead. I had no plans for the future save for a dim hope of somehow finding my way back to the Gate Between The Worlds.

And that hope was extremely dim. Two thousand miles of mountain and jungle lay between the City in the Clouds and the circle of monoliths that was my one hope of ever returning to Earth. Alone and on foot it seemed an impossible task.

So I stayed. And, while waiting for some chance to offer itself, I was well on my way to becoming a great swordsman.

My discovery of the secret *botte* came about as follows.

One evening I had gone to the theater as the guest of one of my young pupils, the son of a prominent merchant. Lukor, that night, was host to his friend Irivor; as the play that night was a romantic comedy devoid of swordplay, the fencing master had a night off. The old comrades usually got together at least once a week to drink a few bottles and chuckle over old times.

Returning home alone in the small hours, I found neither my host nor his friend in the living quarters; but from the practice hall above I heard the ring and slither of blades. I went up the stairs and found the two in their cups, stripped to the waist, industriously plying their flickering rapiers and bawling ribald commentary on the other's style.

For a few minutes, grinning, I watched the duel unseen. Then fat, red-faced Irivor made some stinging remark that touched Lukor to momentary rage. As I watched, the Swordmaster executed a very adroit and rapid action which ended with his button-tip tapping the astounded Irivor above the heart.

Never had I seen that deft and dazzlingly swift bit of strategy, and it puzzled me. The next day I asked Lukor about it, and he was shocked and somehow taken aback that I had witnessed the action. When I pressed, he admitted that he should not have used that attack even in playful bout. Indeed, he would not have, had he not been in his cups and had not the boisterous Irivor taunted him until he lost his self-control.

"It is a secret botte, known only to the greatest Swordmasters, and never taught or even demonstrated to ordinary pupils," he confessed shamefacedly. "You will understand, Jandar, that a teacher in the art of fence is forbidden to duel, as to pit his superior professional skill against an ordinary swordsman would be tantamount to murder. Some generations ago a great Swordmaster named Kamad of Tharkol discovered a secret botte that is invincible—the Botte of Kamad, we term it, and it is a secret of the profession. I am forbidden even to discuss the matter, so I will ask you not to press me further."

Of course, as was only good manners, I agreed not to embarrass Lukor further on this point. But I could not help being intrigued by my discovery. I tried to remember the exact sequence of moves that I had seen Lukor make. You will understand that by this time I had been breathing, eating, sleeping, and living swordsmanship for every day of the past month, and I was by now trained in all the finer points of the art. Alone before the mirrors, I practiced what I could recall of Kamad's Botte, and one afternoon Lukor caught me thus engaged. I flushed crimson, but he waved my embarrassment away, saying my curiosity was natural enough. And then, because it was obvious I was not going to forget about the secret attack, he set out to teach it to me.

The art of fence consists of a sequence of attacks and parries, a succession of disengages from one line into another. You attack and your opponent parries the attack; as you recover, he attacks; you parry and make another attack, and so on. Where superior skill comes into the picture is through a higher knowledge of the forms and varieties of attack and parry, and the ability to *think while fighting.*

Lukor patiently instructed me in the secret botte, which was at once staggeringly simple and remarkably sophisticated. As the Thanatorian fencing terms would be meaningless to my reader I shall render his instruction in the comparable terrene terms for the art of fence, insofar as I am able to recall them correctly.

"First, Jandar, you engage in tierce, which your foe will most likely counter with a demi-contre. Next you counter with a thrust in quinte, and when it is parried, you reenter lower—thus—and, as you are parried your foe will be slightly off balance and his arm *here,* his point *there.* As you can see, it is remarkably difficult for him to recover in time to parry your next thrust—and, if you lunge with your point in carte, it is physically impossible."

We practiced the action. It was incredibly beautiful in its simplicity. And it was foolproof. I said as much.

"Quite so. For that reason, the Swordmasters' Guild have kept it a carefully guarded professional secret. Armed with this simple technique, you can overcome any swordsman alive—even another Swordmaster who, however well he knows the trick, is physically unable to counter it. Most masters think it preferable to enter into a series of four passes and then to strike on the fourth disengage. Or, if you like, you can thrust on the fifth, but that is pressing it a bit."

"Master—could not the botte be employed after a double feint just as well?"

Lukor's eyes flashed with approval.

"Ah! Very good. You are thinking, Jandar! Yes, it can follow a double or even a triple feint, if you are pressed for time and doubt if you have leisure for the entire sequence. But now I must enjoin you to secrecy as regards the Botte of Kamad. I do not ask you to promise me that you will never use it in a duel, for when one's life is at stake, such vows are foolish. But I ask on your honor that you will never divulge the botte to another."

Although with my disguise I could come and go as I pleased, Lukor was still my major link with the outside world; especially with the Upper City.

I should perhaps have explained earlier that the old Swordmaster was no friend of Thuton's regime. The Prince had succeeded to his father's throne only a year or two before, and Thuton's father, Gryphar, had himself been a rogue, usurping the throne and slaying the last member of the true Zanadarian dynasty in a palace coup. Lukor had supported the old king of the previous dynasty, and considered himself an enemy of the present family of usurpers, paying only lip service to his Vow of Fealty to Prince Thuton, whom he disliked and distrusted.

To Lukor I had disclosed the whole story of my recent adventures, my enslavement by the Yathoon Horde, my rescue of the Princess Darloona from the attack of the vastodon, our capture by the *komor* Gamchan, our escape and capture anew by the frigate *Skygull*. Indeed, I had withheld nothing from his sympathetic ear save the fact that I was not native to Thanator.

He often returned from his tutorial visits to the Upper City with news concerning the Princess of Shondakor. It was his considered opinion that Thuton was planning to wed the Princess only to have a claim to the throne of Shondakor, which he hoped to tear from the hands of the Chac Yuul warriors on the pretext of being the champion of Darloona's cause. But this was merely Lukor's opinion, as I reluctantly was forced to point out. I tended to disregard my own inclination to distrust the wily Prince, still hoping he was sincere in his avowed purpose of helping Darloona regain her rightful throne.

Lukor relayed certain morsels of palace gossip to me. Thuton, said the wagging tongues of the Upper City, was a thorough villain: he was simultaneously negotiating with Arkola of the Black Legion in secret while, in the open, pretending to raise a force to lay siege to the city of Shondakor.

"Negotiations to what purpose?" I asked Lukor.

"Just this, my overtrustful young friend," he stated firmly. "If Arkola can raise enough gold to buy Darloona, Thuton will sell her without a qualm. If not, he will win her promise of marriage and then invade with his flying fleet, conquer the Black Legion by force of arms, and make himself Lord of Shondakor. The Princess knows nothing of this, of course."

I scoffed. "Where is your proof of all this? No, Lukor, it is too incredible. The Gods know I have no reason to love Thuton, but even he is not capable of such out-and-out dastardly behavior."

He yielded, grumbling. "Someday you will listen to me; I only hope it will not be too late."

Incurable romantic that he was, Lukor was disgruntled that I did not go charging off, sword waving, to rescue my princess from the very stronghold of her enemies single-handedly. I tried to argue that such things happen only in romantic melodramas, and that this was real life. He shrugged eloquently.

"Life, then, could learn a little from a study of the stage," was his rejoinder.

Then it was that we learned of the whereabouts of Koja, and the idyll of my month in the Academy Lukor came to a precipitate end.

Every year the Sky Pirates of Zanadar hold great, week-long gladitorial games in the colossal amphitheater adjoining the citadel of Thuton.

In the main, these games consist of armed contests between champion gladiators. There are also thaptor races, chariot races, and competitions of athletic prowess.

But the feature that most delights the citizens of Zanadar is that which takes place on the last day of the games. For then it is that condemned criminals, those who have committed crimes so great that the usual punishment of slavery at the wheel of the flying galleys is deemed insufficient, are slain.

The prisoners are torn apart by wild beasts in the arena, while thousands of bloodthirsty Zanadarians watch avidly, drinking in the last death throes of the unfortunates.

A list of these criminals, together with their crimes, is on public display for some days before the Day of Blood, as it is called, when these men and sometimes women must battle with bare hands against ferocious jungle monsters.

It was Lukor who saw Koja's name on such a list.

My familiarity with the written script of Thanatorian was

not adequate to puzzle the whole thing out. But Lukor saw and remembered the name of the *komor* of the Yathoon who had become my first friend on this strange world, and he gave the grim news to me.

It was grim indeed. I had thought Koja probably slain when the guards interrupted our escape. Now it seemed that his crime of attempted escape—so very against the rule of *va lu rokka!*—placed him in a rare class of supercriminal, and as such he was decreed a lingering death in the arena on the Day of Blood.

What could I do to help him? For I instantly resolved that I must do whatever I could.

There was just one chance.

It was an enormous gamble, but I was in a mood for such a gamble.

Lukor's medallion gave him the right to unquestioned entry into the Upper City and the royal citadel at any time, night or day. For half a year now he had come and gone in the royal precinct, giving private tutelage to the young nobles who patronized his academy. The citadel guards were well accustomed to seeing the tall, trim, stiff-backed old man with the neat gray beard and quiet, conservative clothing. They would not find it remarkable that he continued to give his tutoring even during the games of Year's End Day. Or so we hoped!

Once within the citadel itself, what could we do to free Koja? Perhaps little, perhaps much. But it was worth a try. Because the pits below the citadel communicated directly with the pens of the arena, which was situated to the rear of the palace.

And Lukor knew of a secret passage through the walls. . . .

CHAPTER XI
THE FACE IN THE CRYSTAL

I t was a cold, windy night.

The cold emerald globe of Io, which the Thanatorians called Orovad, the Green Moon, burned high in the western sky, while the Red Moon, Imavad, which we Earthlings know as Ganymede, hung low athwart the horizon, and the mighty bulk of Jupiter had not yet arisen.

Here in the heights of the Upper City, the wind howled about the tower tops and whistled through the streets that climbed in broad flights of steps from the Middle City below our feet.

Wrapped from head to foot in cowled cloaks of warm dark wool, Lukor and I approached the side entrance to the citadel that the Swordmaster frequently used. The tall arch was brilliantly lit and six or seven guards were posted there. These were not the lowly copper-helmed thugs who patrolled the slums at the foot of the mountaintop city, but the elite, the very cream of the guardsmen of Zanadar. They wore winged helmets of silver and their cloaks were of indigo silk, trimmed with rare white fur.

As we approached into the light, Lukor thrust back his cowl so that the guards could see his face.

"Well, by the Lords of Gordrimator, is it not the old Swordmaster himself!" one of them exclaimed. "Can it be, Master Lukor, that your noble pupils are so avid in their study of the art of the sword that they spend even a festival night under tutelager?"

"So I must assume, Captain Yanthar; at least they have summoned me in the usual way, and I must obey, although I would much rather be emptying a bottle at the wineshop," Lukor said affably. The officer laughed.

"But who is this who accompanies you?"

"My nephew, Lykon of Ganatol, who has recently joined the Academy as an instructor," Lukor replied. "Perhaps you have heard that I now employ another swordsmaster to teach novices. The Lord Marak has been kind enough to express a desire to meet the lad, so, as he has never seen the citadel, I thought I would use this opportunity to slay two zells with a single dart."

"Hmm, yes, I had heard something of the sort. So the sword school prospers, eh? Step forward, lad, and let me see you."

I stepped into the light. For this outing I had taken especial care with the cosmetics. My features, bare arms, and legs, were completely colored with the bleaching agent which rendered them a papery white. My hair had just been redyed inky black, and black paint also disguised my eyebrows. There was, however, nothing I could do to disguise the startling blue of my eyes, so I kept them downcast, as if from timidity. The officer appraised me casually.

"A well set-up lad, surely, Master Lukor, if a bit shy. Well, pass on to your tutorial labors."

Lukor bowed and passed the officer a coin.

"My thanks, and a good festival to you all. Perhaps you will accept this small Year's End gift as a token of my regard. Might I ask you and your men to drink to my health on Year's End Day?"

Captain Yanthar turned the coin in his fingers: it was a gold bice, a coin of considerable worth, stamped to the one side with an idealized portrait of Prince Thuton in full-face, and on the other it bore the clenched fist, with wings springing from the wrist, that was the device of royal Zanadar.

"You are generous, Master Lukor! Evidently, the Academy prospers in very truth! We shall drink to your health with pleasure—a gay festival to you both!" The captain smiled, waving us by. And I began to breath again.

"Your friend Irivor will be surprised when I tell him you have an unexpected gift for the theater," I grinned in a quiet aside to Lukor. He flushed and snorted through his nostrils.

"Nonsense, my boy!" But I could see he was pleased. A romantic to the heart, the old Swordmaster was enjoying himself vastly. For this was the very stuff of melodrama! An entrance into the palace under disguise—a daring midnight rescue—why, he was happy as a boy.

The palace, even at this late hour, was bustling. Lordly gentlemen in court robes charged with heraldic devices swept past us. Beautiful women in bizarre costumes were continuously streaming up and down spiral staircases of glistening marble. Gold statuettes and silver urns throbbed in the light of crystal chandeliers. The silken carpets under my buskins were deep and soft as the finest plush. Thousands of milky candles cast a wavering, romantic glow, faintly golden. Splendid tapestries displayed scenes of the hunt, the battlefield, and the bedchanmber to every aside. The odor of perfume and incense and candle wax and fresh-cut flowers filled the air.

Lukor nodded and smiled and bowed and paused to exchange snippets of gossip with half the personages who swept so grandly past. The Swordmaster was well known here from the days of the previous dynasty, and I reflected with an inward qualm that it would be dreadful if his complicity in my rash attempt to free Koja from the dungeon pits should become known, to the detriment of his reputation if not, indeed, of his freedom.

We progressed at a leisurely and unobtrusive pace to a lower level of the palace. I was in a constant sweat over the possibility of encountering Darloona in one of these sumptuous rooms; however, I saw her not.

At length we came to a side corridor that was seemingly deserted. Lukor pulled aside an old tapestry adorned with a scene from the life of Prince Maradol, a monarch of the former royal line. Then he felt about, fingers probing. He gave an exclamation—there sounded a distinct click—and a black opening yawned before us, into which we plunged without a moment's hesitation.

For a considerable period of time we went forth through utter blackness, edging along sideways between close walls of rough stone. This was not as difficult as it might have been— at least we were walking at a level, however dark the going was. But when at length we began descending a winding coil of stone stairs and I had stumbled three times, and had almost fallen once, I began to wish the technological ingenuity of the Zanadarians had extended to the invention of the flashlight.

After an eternity of stumbling and tripping on narrow

spiral stairs we came into an open corridor. Here, Lukor said, we were safe from scrutiny and were free at last to make a light. While he fumbled, cursing eloquently, with flint and steel, he explained that spyholes were set in the walls of the passages through which we had thus far come, and that a light might well have been visible to any persons in the corridors or apartments into which these spyholes gave view, had they chanced to be looking in the right direction at the right time.

My companion soon had a small oil lamp lit, and from here on we were able to go forward with ease. He went first to light the way, and I followed close upon his heels.

"What are these passages?" I asked. "It's a regular labyrinth—I'd be afraid to live in this place myself, for fear of assassins lurking in the dark!"

"A labyrinth in very truth, my friend," he replied. "You will by now have noticed the characteristic feature of Zanadarian architecture is very thick walls. This is partly for warmth, for the mountain winds can be very cold, and partly for strength, for the winds can also be very powerful. But the custom affords a perfect opportunity for the construction of secret passages and tunnels. These were, I believe, constructed during the third dynasty of the Zanadarian kings, in the reign of Warlak the Mad. This peculiar monarch had the fancy that his life was in constant danger and that a hundred plots were constantly being spun to catch him in their toils. When he rebuilt this portion of the citadel, he had this elaborate network of secret passages built, and he employed a veritable army of spies to keep those he suspected of being his enemies under constant scrutiny. I learned of the existence of this network through an old friend, the former archivist, now deceased. The present dynasty of usurpers do not even dream of the existence of such a spider web of secret tunnels within their very walls."

"That's interesting," I said. "But whatever happened to old Warlak the Mad?"

My companion chuckled gruffly. "His constant suspicion and lack of trust in his own lords and nobles eventually aroused fear in them. They suborned several of his own spies and Warlak was murdered in his own bed—by assassins using the network of secret tunnels he had invented for his protection against just such an eventuality!"

We went forward for a very long time. The tunnels twisted and turned, branching into side tunnels, crisscrossing yet other tunnels, until I was hopelessly lost. Lukor knew his way, or, at least, he could follow the cryptic markings wherewith the turns and intersections of the passageways were emblazoned.

The royal citadel clung to the utmost peak of the mountain. On a somewhat lower level, it adjoined the Arena of the Games, and the network of secret passages communicated with the slave pits beneath the arena. I suppose it sounds easy enough on paper, but it certainly involved a lot of walking. My legs were growing weary and I was getting rather warm— the tunnels had the poorest ventilation imaginable, and I was muffled to the ears in a dark woolen cloak which served to hide the fact that a long Yathoon whip-sword was strapped to my back. I had my own rapier at my hip, of course, but I had taken the precaution of bringing along a weapon for Koja. It would be somewhat presumptuous of me to have expected the poor fellow to fight his way out of the pits without a sword. Luckily the Academy Lukor had several fine whip-swords in its collection of foreign weaponry.

Everything had gone so splendidly up to this point, that I should have expected trouble. However, I assumed that Lukor possessed a greater familiarity with these secret passages than was actually the fact.

Our first inkling of this came when suddenly Lukor cried out and vanished and I fell face forward into a wall.

The barrier had certainly not been there a moment before. Lukor had been plodding along ahead of me, the light of his lamp casting his shadow huge and black over the walls to either side. But now he and the lamp had vanished and a stone wall stood before me. I called out his name but heard no answer. I began to sweat. Only Lukor knew the secret code symbols that made it possible to thread a path through this tangled maze of passageways. Without him I was completely lost.

I thumped both fists against the obstruction but it was solid and immovable. Again I called his name, but there was only an unbroken and ominous silence for reply.

What had happened? Had Mad King Warlak set traps and deadfalls along his secret tunnels? Had we accidentally tripped or triggered one, springing into place a sliding barrier of solid stone? I did not know; nor did I ever learn precisely what had happened to part the old Swordmaster and myself. As far as I knew I was buried alive beneath a mountain of solid stone.

At length I turned back and retraced my path to the last intersection we had passed, noting the code symbols—a row of blue disks. I took a side branch, hoping it would run parallel with the interrupted passage, and rejoin it further on.

The passage, however, curved sinuously around unseen obstructions, and seemed to run on before it intersected another tunnel. When such occurred, I took the new tunnel and went back along its length, hoping to find Lukor. But instead

I became lost in a perfect maze of crisscrossing passages until I had to give up all hopes of ever finding my way along the route we had been following.

At each intersection, luminous code symbols glowed through the murky gloom, but instead of three blue disks the new symbols were two red arrowheads, one above the other.

I resolved to follow these for a while and see where they led me.

Hours later, or so it seemed, I became aware of a dim illumination. It was only the ghost of light, but anything was better than the unrelieved blackness through which I had been wearily stumbling for endless stretches of time.

At length I ascertained the source of the faint luminance. The light leaked from small dime-sized orifices set along one wall of the passage at intervals of about twenty paces.

My pulses quickened at this exciting discovery!

These must be the spyholes of which Lukor had spoken. Their presence meant I had somehow retraced my steps and was back in one of the inhabited portions of the citadel again. Which meant, in turn, that I might well find a secret door or a sliding panel which would let me escape from this gloomy labyrinth into the lighted halls of the palace.

I set my eye to one of these minute openings and received a shock.

I stared into a luxurious apartment whose stone walls were hung with sumptuous tapestries. The floor was buried under heavy silken carpets of subtly contrasting colors, indigo, lavender, puce, old rose, dull silver. Instead of furniture, nests of gorgeous gold and orange cushions lay heaped about.

In the center of the room, directly opposite me, stood a most extraordinary device. A tripod of twinkling brass supported a huge orb of cloudy crystal whose interior structure was fractured into a thousand shining planes. From the axis of this crystal sphere, copper electrodes protruded, and to these were attached heavily insulated coils of wire. The instrument resembled nothing so much as a bizarre version of a television receiver.

Seated before the tripod sat none other than Prince Thuton himself.

The suave and handsome ruler of the City in the Clouds was adorned as if for carnival. His close-fitting garments were patterned with gilt and crimson and jade green. Gems flashed at earlobe and brow, throat and wrist. A half-mask of jet beads lay discarded at his feet. His hands were busily manipulating the control verniers at the base of the tripod as I gazed into the room.

A shrill and piercing whine arose from within the mechanism. Whirling lights spun within the inner planes of the crystal orb. These lights resolved into the heavy features of a man. I had not seen that face before.

The face was powerfully molded, with a square jaw and a heavy brow. The thick neck was sunk between burly shoulders which were wrapped in a heavy cloak of some shining, crinkly-surfaced black cloth I could not identify. Beneath this cloak I glimpsed a deep and powerful chest in a warrior's leathern tunic. There was a symbol emblazoned on the breast of the tunic which meant nothing to me—a grim device, like a black, horned skull with fanged and grinning jaws and eyes of ruby flame.

The man's features were coarse, blunt, brutal, commanding. He had a greasy, swarthy complexion, his bullet head covered with lank colorless hair of a peculiar consistency. Gold baubles twinkled in his earlobes. Under scowling black brows, eyes of fierce yellow blazed with somber and wrathful fires, like the burning gaze of lions.

There was an aura of cold authority and command about this heavy, swarthy, impassive face, with its cold burning eyes and cruel lips. I wondered who the man could be. My question was answered for me almost as soon as it sprang into my consciousness.

In a suave, laughing voice, Thuton addressed the face in the globe.

"Again we converse, Arkola, and again to no point or purpose—unless you have increased the price you are willing to pay for the person of the Princess Darloona," he said.

I tensed with astonishment. So Lukor had been right—and my own convictions had been correct all along! The suave, mocking Prince of the Cloud Kingdom was indeed willing to trade the Princess of Shondakor for hard gold! My blood heated at the oily cynicism and cold mockery in Thuton's tones, and I itched to have him at the point of a sword. The outcome of our next encounter would be very different from that of our previous duel!

In a harsh grating voice, with an odd lisping accent, the personage Thuton addressed as Arkola made reply.

"I say again, Zanadarian, that one hundred thousand gold bice is the limit of my resources. And I repeat that possession of the girl is a luxury to the Chac Yuul, and far from being a necessity. For, look you, I hold the city of Shondakor with ten thousand warriors of the Black Legion—what need have I of the girl, save as a means whereby to impose my authority upon her captive people, using her as a puppet for my wishes? You ask too high a price, Prince, for something I do not really need. I am the conqueror here, and I am secure in my conquest."

Thuton laughed, a vile snigger. "Boast not too loudly of conquest, O Lord of the Black Legion," he advised silkily. "For I seem to have heard that the city of Shondakor fell to the

Chac Yuul through the cunning of a certain priest named Ool and not through the warcraft of the chieftain Arkola. But doubtless this is a misapprehension on my part, and you will correct me in my error."

The grim, impassive face in the crystal flushed angrily. I recalled that I had heard something of this Black Legion priest, Ool, who seemed to be the spiritual leader of the bandit legion. Lukor had mentioned him, but I had paid little attention.

This mention of a priest reminded me of something I had found a bit puzzling about the civilizations of Thanator. For a planet, or moon, rather, inhabited by races hardly advanced above the Bronze Age level (with the exception of the sophisticated Sky Pirates, of course), the Callistans have precious little to do with gods and temples and priests. In this, I believe, they are strikingly different from similar barbarian cultures in Earth's own history who were to a high extent dominated by superstitious veneration for one or another pantheon of divinities. The Thanatorians have gods, of course, but they hardly ever think about them or speak of them, or so it seems to a stranger. The Callistan gods are referred to as "the Lords of Gordrimator," which is the name the Callistans have for their primary, Jupiter. And while they make occasional reference to these Lords of Jupiter by way of a casual oath, that seems to be about the extent of their dealings with the Divine. I have yet to see a temple or a shrine, or to meet a priest, in all my wanderings across the face of Thanator. It is but another of the many baffling mysteries of Callisto.

While my thoughts had strayed into these channels, the conversation between Thuton of Zanadar and Arkola of the Black Legion had continued, and I had missed a few words. They had been arguing over the price the Prince of the Sky

Pirates had set upon the Princess of Shondakor, and as my attention returned to the confrontation, their argument came to an abrupt end as Arkola turned off his transmission. His face faded from the crystal and it became blank again. Thuton turned from the globe with a cold, mirthless chuckle and strode from the room.

And I knew that I must rescue Darloona from the clutches of this treacherous and mercenary Prince who would sell her to the conquerors of her city if her enemies could meet his price!

I forced a rather mirthless smile of my own.

That made *two* people I had determined to rescue—and I, myself, was a prisoner in this secret labyrinth of stone!

If any sliding panel or secret exit existed by which I could escape the passageways into the inhabited portion of the citadel, I failed to find it. Doubtless Lukor knew of the whereabouts of such, but he was either lost himself, or imprisoned, or very possibly dead—slain in the trap of rising stone that had come between us.

I soon was lost in the lightless labyrinth again.

I roamed the winding narrow corridors of stone for hours. It must have been near dawn by this time—and at dawn began the last day of the festival, when the condemned prisoners were to be driven forth blinking into the light of day to face swift and terrible death at the fangs of ravening beasts.

After endless hours of wandering, I came at last into a little room with no exit.

In the wall facing me was a barred window, the first I had seen in this maze. As I saw it, my hopes lifted.

Shrugging off the cloak of leaden despair that bowed my shoulders and made every step heavy, I strode forward into the little cell. This might be the one means of egress I sought—

the mode by which I could come to the aid of my friend Koja, who was otherwise doomed.

As I strode into the room, my foot struck some slight obstruction on the floor and I pitched forward off balance and struck my head against the floor.

I had botched everything.

I had come charging into the citadel like some hero out of romantic melodrama—charging single-handedly to the rescue of a doomed and imprisoned friend.

First I had become separated from Lukor. Then I had forgotten myself thoroughly lost. And now, finally, I had knocked myself unconscious.

I fell into welling blackness, and even as consciousness left me, I felt the bitter taste of failure and defeat upon my tongue.

Koja had come to face death in the arena because of me. And now, in the hour of his greatest need, I had failed him yet again.

For a brief instant I felt despair, knowing myself helpless to save from his doom the first living creature on Thanator who had offered me the gift of friendship.

And then I struck the wall and knew nothing more.

CHAPTER XII

THE DAY OF BLOOD

I t was a sound that aroused me, whether moments or hours later I never knew.

A thunderous swell of sound, rising and falling like the sea—a booming surf of clamorous noise.

I sat up stiffly, and clutched my head. Throbbing waves of pain went through my skull, in rhythm to the rise and fall of those waves of sound.

At first I could not think where I was. I blinked about me in the dimness, seeing the small square room of rough stone. And then the memories came crowding back into my consciousness—Lukor, the trap, the endless hours of stumbling through the black labyrinth.

But this was not blackness, this dimness that lay about me—it was light! *The light of day!*

And that dull roar, rising and falling like ocean surf, I could identify it now. The applause of many hundreds of human voices!

Where *was* I?

I sprang to my feet, ignoring the throb of pain from my

gashed brow, and stared out of the small barred window into a dazzling scene of circling stone tiers of seats crowded by a brilliantly clothed throng of Zanadarians—with a sandy floor at their feet, whereupon men struggled with their bare hands against enormous beasts.

This stone cell overlooked the arena itself! Irony of ironies—I could not aid Koja, but I was forced to look on helplessly as he went forward into the jaws of death!

I raved and wept and hurled myself against that barred grille that covered the small window, but it was too strong even for my earthly muscles to force. I was, indeed, helpless.

How had I come into this tiny room? I strove to recall, and it came back to me. I had glimpsed the window and strode carelessly over to it, and my feet had struck some obstruction in the floor, which had pitched me forward into the wall.

I bent my gaze downwards, and my heart leaped within me as my eyes discovered an iron ring in the floor.

The iron ring was the obstruction which had tripped me.

And it might prove, as well, the key to my escape from this dungeon of despair. For on Earth, at least, such rings indicate the presence of trapdoors.

Crouching on the floor, I closely examined the stone floor about the iron ring. The amount of daylight which filtered through the bars of the narrow window was not sufficient to give much illumination, so I used my sense of touch, running my sensitive fingertips over the dusty surface of the floor.

It was true—my fingers traced the rectangular outline of a trapdoor!

I caught the ring and strained to pull it open, while the roar of the distant throng pounded dimly through the small dusty room. Sweat broke out on my brow and I heaved at that iron ring until my muscles ached from the strain, but to no avail.

I released the ring and squatted there on my heels, resting for a moment and gathering my strength.

Then I hurled every ounce of force in my back, chest, arms, and shoulders into one great heave.

Was it my imagination, or was the crack in the floor wider?

Again and again I strove to lift that square of solid stone, my face black with effort, the blood roaring in my ears, my thews taut and cracking with the strain.

At last I heard a splintering sound—startlingly loud in the stone box of my cell—and whatever had been restraining the trapdoor gave way, and a black opening yawned in the floor at my feet. The stone trapdoor fell backwards with a room-shaking crash and I could see what had resisted my efforts—the undersurface of the trap had been coated in thick plaster. Doubtless the corridor or chamber below—whatever was there—had been newly plastered by workmen ignorant of the fact that a door existed in the roof.

I threw myself face downward and peered into the black opening, but in the gloom my eyes could discern nothing. The rise and fall of distant applause continued to beat against the silence, and I knew that I could not delay my next move for very long. Even now my brave and faithful Koja might be facing the slavering jaws of some monster of the arena with bare hands while I lingered, debating!

I slid through the opening and dropped feet first into darkness—

—And landed astride something enormous, and—alive!

It bucked and writhed under my unexpected weight. By instinct alone, I clamped my legs around its barrel, locking my heels together under its belly. And hung on for all I was worth. It was pitch black; as the saying goes, I could not see my hand before my face. But the hot musky smell of pent-up beasts was heavy and rank in my nostrils, and I guessed that I had fallen into the beast pens, where the wild and monstrous predators of the jungle were kept, awaiting their chance to rip and ravage the helpless and unarmed condemned prisoners in the arena beyond.

How I managed to keep my seat on the back of the unknown monster is something I shall never know. It jumped and writhed, striving to unseat me. The clash of snapping jaws and the acrid fetor of its hot breath told me the invisible thing was craning back over its shoulder, seeking to get its fangs into me. If I permitted this to happen, I would be ripped from the relative safety of my place astride its shoulders and torn and trampled underfoot.

There was little enough I could do to prevent this, in the black darkness, but what little there was I did. The jungle thing had a mane of coarse bristling hair about its neck, and I dug my fists into this and hung on for dear life while my savage steed leaped and snarled, hurling itself from side to side in its frantic efforts to dislodge me.

How long I could have held my seat I do not know. But after only a few moments of this, the sudden blaze of brilliant day struck me blind. Hinges groaned—a huge door swung suddenly open—bare sands lay beyond, baking under the clear light—and my savage steed catapulted to freedom, soaring over the doorsill to land like a great cat upon the hot sands of the arena.

I caught a swift, kaleidoscope impression of things around me: rising oval tiers of stone benches on all sides, lined with throngs of gaping, astounded faces—blazing dome of golden sky overhead, where three huge moons hung—level plain of yellow sand, trampled and torn and splashed with blood—and a cluster of perhaps fifty men, naked save for buskin and loincloth, gathered in the center. In the next moment my beast went absolutely wild in its efforts to shake me from my seat.

First he charged like a thunderbolt straight for the pitiful cluster of unarmed slaves. Then, enraged by my weight, he sprang straight up into the air, landing on his hind legs, his body almost vertical to the ground. Somehow or other I managed to cling to his back through even the worst of his contortions. One hand buried in the coarse ruff of his mane, my other sought the hilt of my rapier. If it occurred to him to roll in the sand, I was lost, for he must have weighed a couple of tons. I would surely have been crushed under all that meat and muscle. But his tiny brain was inflamed with red roaring rage, to the detriment of his natural feline cunning, and he continued leaping madly, like some bucking bronco out of a cowboy's worst nightmare.

A horde of other beasts had been penned in the same black pit, and they poured in a howling, hissing, growling flood of savagery over the sill at our heels. The unexpected appearance of myself, riding the largest beast of the herd, must have struck the throng of carnival-goers dumb with astonishment, for an enormous hushed silence hung over the brilliantly lit scene. What would have happened had I not interrupted the proceedings was that the horde of beast would have charged the small band of the condemned, overwhelming them in an instant and rending them asunder with fang and claw. But my arrival on the scene changed things considerably. For one thing, my beast was so wildly enraged by the unexpected indignity of having a rider that he ignored the very presence of the condemned, and went racing about the oval arena in wild leaps and bounds seeking a way to dislodge me. As well, his actions unnerved the lesser beasts who had followed us from the pits. They were a collection of oddly shaped creatures—scaled reptilian predators with long snakelike necks, who bounded about on huge hind legs in fantastic leaps like midget tyrannosaurs crossed in some unlikely mating with giant kangaroos. In his fantastic contortions, my enraged steed went blundering among them, knocking them about with resounding buffets from his heavy paws. One got in his path and my brute ripped out his throat with a savage sidewise slash of fanged jaws.

The scent of the blood of one of their own kind drove the remainder of the herd wild. Obviously they had been starved for days or weeks in preparation for this event. Ignoring the huddled men, they fell upon the corpse of their fallen brother and tore him to gobbets.

Then they turned on each other, rending and tearing, long snaky necks writhing, fanged jaws agape, filling the air with hissing cries like steam whistles.

I had my sword out at last and was futilely hacking at my enraged steed. It was vaguely akin to a colossal tiger, but nearly twenty feet long, with a lashing whiplike tail with jagged serrations of horny blades down the length which turned it into a terrible instrument of death. Tigerlike, too, was the snarling, wrinkled mask of its face, the wrinkled snout, the blazing eyes. But there the resemblance ended. For the brute was covered with shaggy scarlet fur and two fantastic curling horns sprouted from its flat, low, wedge-shaped brow. These features, together with the stiff ruff of fur that stood out behind its head for all the world like the starched ruff worn by Elizabethan gentlemen, transformed it into a thing of nightmare. From descriptions I had heard, I knew the beast for a *deltagar*, one of the most terrible and dreaded predators of the jungle.

My sword ripped and tore at neck and shoulders, inflicting long raw slashing cuts, but the thickness of its fur, and the steely rippling muscles which clothed its bulk, effectively prevented me from dealing it a killing blow. Indeed, these wounds only served to infuriate it more. Foam dripped from its slavering jaws, bedewing its throat fur, and its hissing roars rose to a screaming crescendo of madness.

In its frenzy, the brute sprang at the top of the wall that enclosed the arena on all sides. Claws scraped and scrabbled along the top of the wall as the great scarlet cat clung for an instant. The arena-goers who had been sitting in these seats for the best view fled screaming, trampling weaker or slower members of the crowd underfoot. Obviously they expected the deltagar to land among them in the next instant. But he fell back with a bone-shaking thump to the packed sands of the arena.

The thronged stands were full of mobs of screaming, people scurrying to every exit. Amid the chaotic uproar, I saw grim-faced guards pelting down the stairs, and some of the braver sort came over the walls on knotted ropes to catch the enraged deltagar in weighted nets manipulated at the end of long claw-tipped poles. I caught a flying glimpse of the royal box. There, his pale, handsome face a picture of mingled astonishment and fury, sat Prince Thuton, throned beneath a canopy blazoned with the royal insignia of Zanadar.

And at his side, staring at me, eyes wide with amazement, Darloona reclined, arrayed in silken robes, jewels twinkling in the crimson splendor of her flowing mane.

But just then I was too busy fighting to notice more.

A lucky stroke of my rapier had at last found the brute's vitals. A straight, sure thrust through the base of the skull, at the place where the spinal cord entered the brain, brought it down.

It crashed to its full length on the trampled arena sands. I sprang clear just in time to avoid being crushed beneath its ponderous weight. Coming to my feet again, I got, for the first time, a good look at the monster I had been riding, and if I had not already a fit of the shakes I might have fainted dead away. The deltagar was enormous—frightful! Imagine three full-grown Bengal tigers rolled into one and armed with fangs the size of machetes, and you will have a fairly good idea of the thing on whose back I had landed in the dark.

The condemned prisoners were hastening across the sands toward me. In their forefront stalked the tall glistening figure of my old friend, Koja. Now I tore off my cloak and tossed him the Yathoon whip-sword I had been carrying scabbarded on my back all this while.

He tested the blade, making it whistle through the hot dusty air which reeked with blood and sweat and the musky stench of the deltagar. We had no time just then to exchange words—even if we could have heard one another over the uproar from the stands and the squealing fury of the battling beasts. But he wrung my hand in his own supple-fingered grip in silent thanks.

And then we turned to view an amazing sight.

The prisoners condemned to death with Koja were a motley crowd. There were papery-skinned, black-haired Zanadarians among them, and a few swarthy Chac Yuul bandits with lambent eyes and colorless hair, and even a couple of the hairless, crimson-skinned men of the Bright Empire of Perushtar. They were a dull-eyed, dilapidated, dispirited-looking lot, and from the looks of them they had been starved, beaten, and sorely mistreated in the slave pits. But now they had a fighting chance for freedom, and they were eagerly striving for it!

Taking advantage of the confusion they sprang from behind upon the Zanadarian guards who were fighting to calm or kill the rampaging beasts. In a second three of four guards were down, and half-naked prisoners turned on the others with stolen steel glittering in their hands. I exchanged a de-lighted glance with Koja, and we wasted no time in joining the unequal battle.

The guards were better fed, better trained, and better armed than the half-starved slaves. But it didn't really matter. The slaves had seen nothing but a grisly death ahead of them, to be crunched and mangled in the jaws of jungle predators in the sands of the arena for the entertainment of the cruel Zanadarians—hence they fought wildly, recklessly, taking in-sane chances no ordinary warrior would dream of taking.

And there was another factor here. The guards were fight-ing merely to protect themselves. But the prisoners fought for that one thing that is even more precious than life itself—*their freedom.* Hence it was a foregone conclusion from the first that they should triumph, and they did. In less time than it would take me to tell of it, half the guards were slain or trampled underfoot or sorely injured and the others, tossing aside sword and helmet in their flight, were running for the knotted ropes which still dangled over the walls of the arena and by which they had descended to our level. Few—very few—made it alive. But the victorious prisoners, now well armed indeed with the guards' cast-aside weapons, went swarming up those ropes themselves. As the arena seats were a turmoil of running, shouting men, they easily mingled with the panic-stricken crowd and I have no doubt that many of them found their way at length to secure havens in the Lower City.

But as for me—I had another goal.

I climbed hand over hand up the rope to the top of the wall and advanced up the rising tier of stone benches, with Koja following at my heels. Straight for the royal box I made my way. For Thuton and Darloona still stood there, unable to flee amidst the press of the mob.

Here at last was my chance to rescue the flame-haired Princess of Shondakor from the treacherous swine she thought a friend! And there, too, was my long-awaited opportunity to confront the wily Prince of the City in the Clouds, and to take my revenge for the cruel humiliation I had suffered at his hands when last we had crossed swords.

Then I had been exhausted, injured, and armed with a weapon with which I was completely unfamiliar. He had whipped me soundly, but what was much worse, he had mocked me and humiliated me and made me look ridiculous in the eyes of the woman an I—of a woman whose friendship I esteemed and whose respect I desired to earn.

Through the weary hours at the slave wheel of the frigate *Skygull*, in the squalor of the slave pens of Zanadar, and during my enforced weeks as the guest of Lukor the Swordmaster, I had hungered to face him again, sword in hand.

And that time had come.

CHAPTER XIII
AT SWORD'S POINT

As I sprang over the low partition and into the royal box, I heard Darloona gasp with astonishment. Turning, I smiled at her amazement and saluted with the naked sword.

"We meet again, Princess," I observed. She regarded me with a mingling of amazement and outrage—and perhaps there was just a hint of joyful relief mixed therein as well, for I had no reason to assume that she meant me ill.

"Jandar—*you?*" she asked puzzledly. "It was you who slew the deltagar and set the slaves in revolt?"

I smiled and nodded. It was even as I had expected. With my flesh disguised with the bleaching agent supplied by Lukor's theatrical friend, my yellow locks dyed jet-black, the Princess had not known for sure that it was I until she had looked me full in the face. For my blue eyes, unique among the races native to this world of Thanator, alone gave me away. And I sensed the reason for the bewilderment that gripped her. From our past experiences, and the various misunderstandings between us, she thought me either a cunning and treacherous rogue, or an arrant coward.

Yet here I was, for once cast in the role of a hero!

It must have seemed a baffling contradiction to her. But her companion in the royal box felt different emotions. Thuton's drawling, silken voice sounded from behind me, and I turned from my Princess to face his mocking smile with a level stare.

"So, the barbarian returns, eh?" he sneered. "I had thought you safely consigned to servile labors more fitting to one of your lowly rank and savage ways than mingling with your betters!"

Beneath his condescending sneers I sensed a red rage trembling for release. I resolved to needle him a little before we crossed swords at last.

"Save for the Princess Darloona and a certain gentleman, I have not yet encountered any in this city better than myself," I replied calmly. "And surely the treachery involved in seeking to sell your royal guest into the hands of her greatest enemies, the Black Legion, puts yourself forever beyond the comparison."

His eyes narrowed and a dull flush stained his paper-white cheeks. I could see from the sidewise glance he directed at Darloona's startled face that he had of course kept all knowledge of his secret dealings with Arkola of the Chac Yuul from her. He bent a coldly furious gaze on me and his purring voice lost its sleekness and became harsh with menace.

"Mind your tongue, fellow, in the presence of the Princess, and cease spewing these despicable lies, or—" and here one strong white hand strayed suggestively to the hilt of his sword "—perhaps the lesson in civilized behavior I gave you when last we met was inadequate and you require a bit of further tutoring!"

I laughed easily. "Yes, I recall how soundly you defeated me when last we stood at sword's point," I remarked casually. "But do not bank on our last bout too much, Thuton. Then my arms were weary from a night spent with them chained above my head, and I was moreover weakened from a wound in the forearm dealt by the tusk of a vastodon, whom I slew, rescuing the Princess from certain death."

My gaze became cool and insolent, raking him from head to foot, lingering on the slight suggestion of a paunch that was visible above his jeweled girdle, on the dark circles dissipation had traced beneath his bloodshot eyes, and on his foppish and almost feminine elegance of dress.

"Today you may find me in somewhat better condition for swordplay," I hinted. "Indeed, I might succeed in teaching you a lesson or two in—manners."

His face went hard and ugly, and his hand went to the hilt of his sword. But behind me I heard an exclamation from Darloona.

"What insolence!" she said, and her tones were scathing. My heart sank just a trifle: I had hoped to restore myself somewhat in her esteem. But I had forgotten the code of gentlemanly behavior which was almost religiously observed by the warriors of Thanator. And I had offended against its prime tenet—a gentleman of Callisto does not boast of his prowess, but remains silent, letting his actions speak for him.

Noting her reaction, Thuton smirked.

"Shall I teach this crude buffoon another lesson, my lady?" he inquired. Darloona raked me with a haughty eye and nodded. He made me a mocking half-bow, and drew his sword with a flourish. We exchanged no salutes, but engaged at once.

All about us was raging turmoil, shouting guards, screaming and milling throngs of hysterical arenagoers, and battling

slaves seeking freedom. But I soon forgot about them, concentrating on the smiling face of Thuton. The universe narrowed and shrank, until the three of us—the Princess, the Sky
Pirate, and myself—were inclosed in a private little world of
our own, insulated from everything that was going on around
us. All we could hear was the click and clang of our blades,
feeling each other out, the rasp of our buskins on the stone
floor, the sound of heavy breathing. I focused my concentra-
tion on that smiling white face that floated before me beyond
the flicker of our blades. I yearned and hungered to wipe that
smirk away, to bring sweat to that smooth ironic brow, and
the gleam of fear to those mocking eyes.

At first, Thuton engaged my point negligently, carelessly.
Obviously he thought he was facing a rank novice hardly
capable of knowing one end of a sword from the other. I held
myself in check, content for the moment merely to turn aside
his point whenever it came near me, playing a purely defensive role.

But before long, as he watched me parry every thrust, he
became irked at the course of our duel, and pressed me back
before a shower of gliding strokes, any one of which could
have disemboweled me had I not turned aside each stroke
with a practiced twist of the wrist. He glared at me as we
disengaged, and I smiled quietly and stood waiting his next
attack.

He sprang to engage my point in tierce. I countered easily
with a demi-contre, and, as I parried, my point glided past
his guard to nick him slightly just above the heart, slicing
through his tunic.

Darloona gasped, and Thuton's face went all loose with
shock. I merely smiled, and stood waiting for the next engagement.

He entered with a thrust in quinte, which I turned aside

effortlessly—and again my point slid through his guard, this time to draw a line of crimson down one cheek. He sprang backwards with remarkable agility, staring at me with utter astonishment. I elevated one eyebrow ironically, and stood waiting for his next attack.

It was blatantly obvious that my superb and almost effortless competence had disconcerted him mightily. And he must have been baffled that I had turned neither of my thrusts into a killing or disabling wound. He engaged my point cautiously a third time, and the air rang with the clang and slither of steel on steel as he felt me out.

I was delighted to see the flushed, congested appearance of his face and the puzzlement in his eyes. And particularly pleased to see a trickle of perspiration slide down his face from his hairline, to mingle with the blood from the slight scratch I had given him on the left cheek.

He was now playing a cautious, defensive bout, even as I had been earlier. Hence, I disengaged and reentered in sixte, and as he parried that—and failed to make a counterthrust—I extended my arm lithely and gave him a similar scratch on the *right* cheek!

Thuton cried out with astonishment and alarm, disengaged awkwardly, stumbling backwards in his haste to elude my dancing point. And, as I turned to face him again, I caught the expression in Darloona's eyes as she watched my swordplay.

Was it—admiration?

Now Thuton threw all caution to the winds and hurled a storm of ringing steel against my slender blade. He pressed me back with a swift glizade, a dazzling blur of steel, and I gave way before him, but not without a chuckle at his manner of fighting. I know not in which school of the fence the Prince of the City in the Clouds had learned the art, but he fought in a flashy, noisy manner—with much floor-stamping and hand-flourishing, sharp little cries and barked comments, screwing his face up in the most fearsome grimaces—all very impressive to an audience, I suppose, but a little showy for my tastes. I, by way of contrast, fought in a quiet, easy, re-strained manner, with a minimum of movement or gesture, content merely to give way before his stamping lunges, and to turn each aside with an adroit twist of the wrist.

We circled the box twice, kicking the chairs out of the way. I let him press me back because I knew he could not keep up this intensity for long. And I was right. Ere long he began to get winded and his wrist and arm were wearying fast, for his blade began to tremble in his grip. He sought to disengage and rest, but now it was my turn to press him, and I slid past his guard and gave him another nick above the heart. Again I extended it into a scratch, drawing a parallel line across the breast of his tunic, slitting the material to the bare skin.

I continued to press him and a few moments later I slit his tunic at the shoulder, and next at the *other* shoulder—and all the time, blowing like a beached whale, his face black with effort, he was trying to disengage. When I finally had him virtually helpless, I had cut away the whole front of his tunic, laying him naked to the navel. His sword arm was trembling with exhaustion by this time and the glint of fear shone in his eyes at long last.

Thuton was a fine swordsman and he had learned from a master of the art. It was not that I was by very much his superior. But for many hours every day for the past month I had practised with novice after novice, ending each day with a bout against one of the finest Swordmasters this planet had ever produced. Naturally my arm was tougher than Thuton's and my swordsmanship, honed and whetted through exhausting hours of continuous practice, was better than his.

Now that I had laid him naked to the waist, I proceeded to cover his torso—which glistened with perspiration—with scratches. I marked him on both shoulders, and drew a scarlet line down his ribs to either side, and I was carefully attempting to write "Jandar" across the breadth of his chest between the nipples, when his nerve broke and he suddenly gave way to rank cowardice.

Squealing like a panic-stricken woman, he literally *threw* his sword in my face and sprang clumsily out of the box, falling down several steps, to stumble to safety amid the milling throng. It was an act of almost unheard-of cowardice, and even I was amazed. One swordsman just simply does not elude a foeman's blade in such a manner—not on Thanator, at least! Even if you are outmatched hopelessly, the Callistan code of honor demands that you stand and die, if need be, before running away from a duel. Nevertheless, I had broken Thuton's nerve, and he had showed the yellow streak. I had erased my previous humiliation, vindicating myself gloriously, my only regret being that I had not killed him.

To tell the truth my own sword arm was a bit wearied, for the duel had been a prolonged game of cat-and-mouse, and I had not enjoyed much sleep the night before. So I leaned on my blade and caught my breath, watching him run into the safety of the mob. And I wondered if, after all, I would have been able to write my name in the Thanatorian script upon his naked chest even if he had not fled in so cowardly a manner.

The Thanatorian language is written in a cursive hand in a script made up of many hooked, swash-tailed characters, not unlike a simplified version of Arabic, and very hard to write with a sword point. It would not have been difficult to write "Jandar" in Roman capitals, but it might well have proven impossible to inscribe Thuton's breast with my cognomen, limited as I was by the intricate nature of the native alphabet. Ah, well, perhaps Thuton and I would meet again, at some later date. At which time I might again attempt to complete the little love note I had been carving on his breast.

As my blade was somewhat sticky with Thuton's gore, I bent and used his thrown-aside cloak to wipe it clean, whereupon I returned it to my scabbard.

All the while Darloona was regarding me with an unreadable expression on her lovely features.

Such was my rather high opinion of the way I had conducted myself in the bit of swordplay just past, I rather naturally interpreted this expression as denoting intense admiration on her part.

Of this incorrect notion I was, ere long, soundly disabused. While I had acquitted myself with the sword well enough, and had doubtless corrected her earlier misapprehension of my manhood, courage, and swordsmanship, I failed, as seemed always to be the case, to read the psychology of the female. For she fixed me with a searing glare of outrage and contempt.

"I know not for what reason you dog my heels, barbarian," she said levelly, her voice shaking with fury, "but I would that I could be rid of you."

The world swung around me dizzily, and I fear I stared at her slack-jawed. I do not recall just what sort of a reaction I had expected her to display towards my recent battle, but it surely was not rage and contempt.

"What—why—" I fumbled for words.

"The Lords of Gordrimator have surely cursed me for my

sins," she continued, now almost tearfully. "Why must you continually be bursting in upon my affairs, to their eternal detriment?"

I was baffled in the face of her tearful fury. I had expected praise, perhaps, even admiration—but not a storm of tears!

"My Princess, why do you—"

She stamped her small foot furiously, tossing her crimson mane like a spirited mare.

"Stop calling me that, you—you *horeb!*" she wailed, naming a particularly repulsive Thanatorian scavenger—something like a pink, naked rat the size of a small dog, whose accustomed habit is to feed on garbage.

Before I could think of anything to say, she blazed at me: "I am *not* 'your Princess'! I want nothing to do with you—*nothing*, do you hear?"

"I—I hear well enough," I stammered witlessly, "but I—I do not understand. What have I done to offend you?"

She burst into tears, turning to solemn-eyed Koja who had stood quietly through all this, blinking curiously on the scene and doubtless reflecting on the odd mating habits of the human race, so unlike the placid and practical methods enjoyed by his own people.

"Listen to him!" she raged. "Here I am, a guest in the citadel of the powerful Prince of Zanadar, whom I have at length consented to marry, and whom I have persuaded to lend me the uses of his magnificent flying navy—the mightiest fighting force on all of the world—with which I had hoped to wrest my kingdom from the hands of the Black Legion—and along comes this annoying oaf yet once again, to meddle into my affairs, and ruin all my plans," she stormed amidst a rain of tears.

I was considerably taken aback. But now I understood! I had, for the moment, forgotten that only Lukor and myself knew the truth of this matter—that is, that Thuton was treacherously seeking behind Darloona's back to sell her into the very hands of the same bandit legion he was pretending to be willing to battle against! Naturally, she had misinterpreted my actions. I tried to explain the real situation to her, but she stamped her small foot furiously and shook her head until her hair flew about in a flaming cloud and refused to listen to my "clumsy lies," as she called them.

Just then Koja drew my attention to an unfortunate development.

While I had been busied, first with cutting up Thuton and then with countering the enraged accusations of Darloona, the hard-faced Zanadarian guards had at length restored the throng to a semblance of order and were now advancing in a heavily armed squad on the royal box, doubtless with the intentions of capturing Koja, as an escaped prisoner, and me, as the ringleader of the slave revolt.

All of Koja's fellow slaves had, by now, either made their escape by successfully mingling with the crowd, or had been recaptured or slain. Thus there were only he and I to face twenty men armed with swords, bill-hooks, and crossbows—and mailed in full armor, protected by helmet and long kite-shaped Norman-type shields.

And they would be upon us in a minute or two.

I cursed my foolhardy hunger for revenge which had made me draw out my duel with Thuton to such inordinate length. Had I simply run him through when first I had him at sword's point, we could all three of us have been out of the arena and halfway to the Middle City by now, where doubtless we could have found a haven of safety in the Academy Lukor, to which I possessed a key.

But, no! I must play at cat-and-mouse, and dawdle out the duel, so as to show off my newly perfected swordsmanship before the woman I—before Darloona of Shondakor—instead of doing the smart thing, and making an escape while I still had the opportunity.

I choked back a guilty curse, bitterly reflecting on the self-evident fact that while my intentions were usually of the noblest, the most admirable, to the point of the heroic. I somehow or other managed to fumble my every chance to do something worthwhile.

Attempting against impossible odds to set free my friend Koja and the Princess Darloona, I had only bungled the whole matter and thrust both them and myself into even worse danger than before.

But there was no hope for it. Koja and I must stand and fight against twenty armed men. It was hopeless, but there was no other course open to us.

I bitterly cursed my own self-pride and arrogance, wishing I was dead . . . knowing I soon would be.

CHAPTER XIV
RIDERS OF THE WINDS

T he guards were almost upon us. I could see the grim expressions on their hard faces clearly, and the cold fury of vengeance in their eyes. Koja and I stood with drawn steel, ready to defend the Princess of Shondakor to the last, but that last, I knew, would not be long in coming. For, however much mastery in the gentle art of swordsmanship I had imbibed from the tutelage of Lukor, it would not long suffice to hold at bay twenty fresh and well-armed soldiers.

And then a weird shadow fell over the canopied booth, and all of us looked up with astonishment at a fantastic flying monster!

For a moment—so completely unfamiliar was the aerial contraption to me—my eyes simply could not resolve the thing. But then I saw it was an ornithopter. Not one of the eighty-foot monstrosities, like the frigate that had flown us here, but more on the order of the small flying gig wherein I had made my escape from the slave pens to the Middle City.

This particular style of ornithopter was something new to my experience. It was a four-man scout, some twenty-five feet long, with four cockpits, like a king-sized kayak. And it resembled nothing so much as an ungainly aerial version of a Polynesian outrigger canoe. I use this handy comparison because the helium-like gas which rendered the contraption airworthy was contained in two long pontoons below the keel and to either side of the hull, braced apart with struts. This lower structure looked rather like the runners on a sled.

The fantastic flying machine may have looked fairly ridiculous, but it very obviously flew.

And, equally important, it was a way out of our present dilemma.

For there, grinning down at me from the left front cockpit was—*Lukor*!

Only the Lords of Gordrimator know what happened to him after we became separated in the labyrinth of secret passages beneath the royal citadel. I had thought him either slain in a deadfall trap, or lost somewhere and still within the maze of tunnels. If I had stopped to think about it, I should have realized that if I, who was unable to read the coded markings that showed directions within the maze, had somehow been lucky enough to stumble on a way out, Lukor, who *could* read them, must have made his exit long before I.

Such, apparently, had been the case. The gallant old Swordmaster had escaped from the maze and had somehow bluffed his way out of the citadel and had been waiting near the arena for an appropriate moment to help Koja and me escape. Somewhere he had found the ornithopter—probably at one of the rooftop guard stations, such as the one atop the slave prison where I had found my ill-fated gig a month ago. At any rate, I would be able to hear the tale of his adventures later, and from his own lips. What was important now was that he had provided us with a means of escape.

The four-man flying craft hovered on throbbing wings

directly above the royal box. While Lukor held it steady above us with one hand on the controls, he tossed overside a rope ladder with the other. The end of the ladder brushed the top of the canopy.

I turned to Darloona.

"Swiftly now, Princess," I said. "You ascend the ladder first. Koja and I will hold the guards at bay until you are safely aboard and we may follow you ourselves."

She stared at me, her slanted emerald eyes filled with contemptuous astonishment.

"Are you completely mad, Jandar?" she demanded hotly. "Why should I wish to escape from the city of my friends? I have already told you that Prince Thuton and I are to wed, and that he has pledged his aerial navy to make war against the Black Legion who hold my city—you may escape, if you wish, but I intend to remain here and regain my throne."

Impatience made me rather curt.

"That is all nonsense, Darloona! Thuton is a treacherous liar. He has been lulling you with false promises, while behind your back he has offered you for sale to Arkola of the Chac Yuul for two hundred thousand gold bice!"

"That is a filthy and despicable lie!"

I know not how long we would have argued back and forth, but solemn Koja intervened.

"Cannot this controversy be continued when we are all in safety?" he inquired in his clacking metallic voice. "For, look, Jandar, the guards are almost upon us."

He was right. I had no time to continue my arguments with the hotheaded girl, which were futile anyway as she simply did not believe me. So I did something that perhaps was unwise, but seemed the only thing to do at the time.

I knocked her cold with a right to the jaw!

She folded limply, and I caught her in my arms and tossed

her over my shoulders and sprang up on the wall of the box, found a foothold among the ornamental carvings of the posts that supported the canopy, and thus clambered to the roof of the box from which height I could grab the lowest rung of the ladder.

In a moment I was climbing up the ladder to safety.

I doubt if it would have been possible for anyone except a professional acrobat or a strong man to have performed a similar stunt on Earth. It was only possible for me to do so because of the slight difference between the gravitational fields of Earth and Thanator, and because my muscles, accustomed to the slightly greater gravity of my home world, gave me a strength that was quite beyond the human norm on Thanator.

Still and all, it was not a feat that I would care to attempt again. Dangling between ground and sky on a swaying rope ladder; the hovering ornithopter above me looking too flimsy to support my weight, the girl's dangling arms and legs impeding my movements, expecting at any second to receive a bolt in my back from one of those miniature Zandarian crossbows—I was never so relieved in my life as when I eventually gained the top rung of the ladder and looked into Lukor's grinning face.

"Lukor!" I exclaimed. "I have never been more delighted to see anyone in my life! Here—take the girl, can you?"

He dragged her from my shoulders and flopped her down unceremoniously into the other front cockpit beside his own. Then he lent me an arm while I climbed over the gunwales and took a seat in the rear behind him. I was puffing and blowing from the exertions of climbing that swaying rope ladder, encumbered by the weight of the girl draped about my shoulders, and it took me a moment or two to catch my breath.

But the old Swordmaster was in grand spirits, burbling with good humor. He was chattering away at a great rate, lifting his voice so as to be audible above the hubbub from below and the thunder of our throbbing wings.

"Ho, there, my boy!" he chortled. "I was not sure whether you were alive or slain, but I should have known that you would be able to find your way out of that cursed labyrinth. You have the luck of a born hero!"

He was obviously having the time of his life, the old rascal. His cheeks were ruddy, flushed with excitement, and his sharp old eyes flashed with gusto and delight, gray locks tousled and flying in the wind of the beating wings. He looked twenty years younger, and I was so happy to see him alive and safe I could have kissed the old fellow on the spot. His almost Gallic sense of chivalry and romance lent vast enjoyment to the escapade— this was the sort of thing he craved, last-minute rescues from certain death, the heroine torn from the grip of fiends, valiant warriors battling against hopeless odds!

"When we were separated by the deadfall trap, I followed the passageway to the nearest exit and lied my way to a rooftop landing stage," he continued. "Reasoning that you might well be hopelessly lost in the maze, I thought that the least I could do was rescue your Yathoon comrade and hide him safely away in the Academy, thinking that the two of us might be able to find you later in the secret passages."

I thanked him fervently for this rescue, which had come in the proverbial nick of time, and peered over the side to see how faithful Koja was doing.

He was doing superbly, holding twenty warriors at bay with the deadly flail of his Yathoon whipsword. Less than twenty, to be precise, for that flying lash of razory steel had already accounted for no less than seven of the guardsmen.

Lukor peered down at the battle with lively interest, bellowing encouragement and praise. The whipsword was the one bladed weapon of Thanator which the old Swordmaster was not adept in using, for the ungainly length and weight of the whiplike steel blade makes it difficult and awkward for any but one of the stalking arthropods to fight with.

While Lukor loudly applauded Koja's dazzling prowess with the whip-sword, I yelled at him to hurry it up. From the vantage of our height I could see guards gathering from all over the arena, and many of them were armed with the deadly little crossbows—whose bulletlike steel darts might well puncture our balloon pontoons or wreck one of our ponderously flapping wings, bringing the aerial contraption down.

But Koja knew what he was doing. Spinning about, he lashed out with the steely flail, clearing a wide area about him as guardsmen ducked away from his singing steel. Then, folding his gaunt and triple-jointed legs, he catapulted into the air. It was a fantastic leap—he must have bounded a good eleven feet straight up. His segmented fingers closed over the middle rungs of the ladder and in a moment his lower limbs had found rungs of their own, and he came up hand over hand to join the rest of us in the cockpits.

"Koja, that was magnificent! I have never seen the whip-sword used so splendidly." I laughed as he settled into place beside me, folding his ungainly limbs awkwardly in the tight, enclosed seat. He blinked at me solemnly.

"I might return the compliment, Jandar," he clacked in his monotonous and metallic tones, "by observing that when you set out to rescue a comrade, you do so in the most spectacular manner conceivable!" And he gestured eloquently with a quirk of his long antennae at the turmoil below, the screaming mob in panic-stricken flight, the battling beasts, the escaping slaves, and the infuriated guards shaking their fists at us in helpless frustration far below. I grinned.

"But who is this human whose flying machine offers us an unexpected mode of escape?" he inquired.

I introduced Lukor and Koja in a perfunctory manner, for just then we had little time for words. Thuton had returned with a squadron of crossbow-men and steel darts were flickering through the air in our direction.

"Hold on, my friends—here we go!" crowed Lukor, and he gripped the controls, sending the craft dipping away to one side. We rose in a dizzy spiral, circling the arena. Tiers of stone seats swept past underneath and then the fabric of the flying machine shuddered beneath to the shattering impact of some unseen obstacle. A jagged rain of thick fragments of clear glass showered our shoulders and then we were caught in the grip of a howling gale whose rushing winds were bitterly cold.

It had not occurred to me, so hectic had the past half-hour been, to wonder why the arena was so hot, baking under dayglare, when the open streets and forums of the mountain-top city were generally swept by frigid winds because of our height. But now I saw that the whole arena was roofed with glass—a gigantic dome shielded the amphitheater from the cold air and the howling winds, and acted like a colossal greenhouse, concentrating the light of day into baking warmth so that the arena-goers could sit on the exposed stone tiers in comfort. Through one of the gigantic panes of glass which formed this greenhouse dome our aerial contraption had just shattered its way to the freedom of the outer air.

"Where now, Swordmaster?" I shouted, gasping as the bitter cold wind struck the sweaty surface of my bare arms and legs. Lukor lifted his voice above the bellow of the winds.

"I suggest we adjourn to a friendlier clime," he yelled.

"My native city of Ganatol would afford a less hostile haven than we may expect from Zanadar, after all this uproar and rescuing!"

I was smitten by a sudden sense of guilt.

"But, Lukor! Your home—your Academy! I cannot expect you to give up everything you have, just to help me and my friends out of a difficult spot!"

He grinned like a mischievous boy, gray mane flying in the wintry blast.

"Nonsense! With what I have here—and here—I can reestablish the Academy Lukor wherever I go," he said, indicating his sword arm and tapping his brow.

"But your house, and all your possessions!" I protested helplessly, unwilling that he should sacrifice everything for my cause.

"*Poh*! Mortgaged to the hilt, my boy—the Academy never really brought in sufficient funds to be a paying concern. As for my belongings, well, I shall regret a painting or two, perhaps a statuette, but there is nothing else that cannot be replaced in time. I shall regret that old Irivor and I shall never again share a bottle and boast about the good old days, but that's about it. And now, no more arguments. I shall need my wits about me to get out of these cursed updrafts."

The spires of the Upper City swung about us as Lukor manipulated the controls with finesse. At this altitude the air was biting and thin, but the winds were furious and gusty, screaming like so many banshees. I ducked down behind the cowling of my cockpit, shivering and wishing I had not so recklessly tossed aside my warm woolen cloak.

After a bit Lukor found a steady downdraft and rode it in wide circles. The tiers of the Middle City swung below our hurtling keel and I caught a flying glimpse of the slums and squalid alleys of the Lower City before they were whipped from sight. One swift look and I recognized the slave pens where the wheel slaves were immured and remembered the dreary days Koja and I had spent behind those beetling walls.

How strange a thing is a man's life! A twist of fate, a turn of the balance, and he is thrust from one situation to the next, with very little say in the matter. Never had I thought to escape that frowning fortress—but, once out of it, wandering the windy streets of the Middle City in garments stolen from the man I had killed, I had wondered where I should find a haven of safety. And then I had seen an unknown gentleman fighting for his life against a gang of street thugs!

Had I not impulsively—even rashly—sprang to his side to set my blade with his, I should not at this hour be hurtling through the wind in this flying contraption, on my way to new adventures in strange lands.

Cause and effect rule the universe, say the philosophers. Well, that may be. But I would cast my vote for blind Chance as the most significant factor in human affairs, if not in the very cosmos itself. For it was Chance that I stumbled upon the Lost City there in the trackless jungles of Cambodia, Chance that Koja spared my life because of the unusual color of my hair and eyes, Chance that I should have encountered the Princess battling against the vastodon when I was escaping from the Yathoon camp through the jungles, and Chance that I had made a friend of Lukor the Swordmaster.

Before long we left the City in the Clouds behind us and were flying through the White Mountains. It was with a curious mingling of nostalgia and relief that I watched the turrets of Zanadar fall away behind our stern. There I had known not only the grim squalor of slavery and the terror of being a hunted fugitive, but also the snug safety of a home and the kindness of a friend. But now that chapter in my adventures was fading behind me.

To either side lay some of the most spectacular scenic wonders imaginable: soaring cliffs and jagged peaks of snowy marl, crumbling plains and boulder-strewn plateaus, riven weirdly with the clefts of terrific ravines and gorges. We were traveling at truly fantastic velocity now, riding a gale that blew due south towards the foothills and the black and crimson carpet of the Grand Kumala that lay beyond.

We had descended a couple of thousand feet by now, but the screaming winds were still as biting cold as the edge of a knife. I huddled low in the cockpit, clutching my shoulders in an effort to keep warm. But despite the cold, this was certainly a better way to travel than on foot. It would have taken us days, perhaps weeks, to make our way through the desolate mountains of Varan-Hkor. And here we were coasting far above them in style, if not exactly in comfort.

I paused to reflect on the marvels I had seen. Such a fantastic flying contraption as this aerial outrigger canoe denoted an extraordinary technology. The civilization of the Zanadarians was the highest I had seen or heard of in all my months on Thanator. How could it be that one people, like the Sky Pirates, possessed stone cities, flying ships—even that tripod-like television crystal I had seen when Prince Thuton had conversed with Arkola of the Black Legion—while another, like the Yathoon Horde, were so far down the scale of culture that they could not even read or write?

Such enormous cultural differences were common enough on Earth, I reflected, where supersonic jet liners hurtled over the jungles of New Guinea, whose inhabitants are still scarcely out of the Stone Age. But this is due, in part, to the enormous distances involved. On Earth, vast oceans and entire continents separate such widely different cultures, but such is not the case on Thanator, which as a moon is much smaller than a planet. Indeed, Thanator measures only four thousand three hundred and fifty-one miles from pole to pole. The Zanadarians and the Yathoon are virtually neighbors— why then are they so vastly apart in the scale of cultural development?

And these ruminations brought me to another mystery. How was it possible a people such a Koja's, obviously evolved from some species of insect, probably one of the so-called "social insects" like ant, termite, or bee, could have grown to the rudiments of civilization on the same world with human inhabitants—the Sky Pirates, the Ku Thad, and the Perushtarians?

On Earth the insects evolved to a certain level and stopped, entering a stage of cultural stasis millions of years ago. Terrene insects were not truly intelligent beings, were not self-aware, but possessed a rudimentary intelligence called "the hive mind." Man alone had fully evolved into a rational being, and yet both species shared all those millions of square miles, surely room enough for both to develop intelligence!

Yet here on Thanator, which was only a fraction of Earth's size, two completely independent civilizations had come into being, and two widely different species had evolved to rationality side by side.

Apart, and yet close.

Dwelling only two thousand miles from each other in spatial terms—yet millions of years apart, culturally.

The arthropods had learned nothing from the Zanadarians, not even the rudiments of technology, the use of the alphabet, or the simplest of humane emotions.

Yet both races spoke the same language!

It was a mystery, all right. And a baffling one.

And I had a hunch that when at last I found the answer it would prove an astounding one!

Darloona swam groggily back to consciousness while we were still flying out of the White Mountains.

As might have seemed natural, she was wildly furious at me, and at my companions as well. Her anger at me was understandable—after all, I had knocked her unconscious in order to get her into the flying machine, which was an action hardly conducive to bettering our personal relations. But her rancor towards the gallant old Swordmaster was also virulent, and with less cause.

"I beseech you, sir, as you are a gentleman, to give over this attempt to flee and return to Zanadar. If you will take me back to the citadel, I will intercede with Prince Thuton on your behalf, and I can assure you that you will not be punished for your crimes," she vowed.

Lukor fixed her with a courteous gaze, but firmly shook his head.

"My lady," he said gently, "you are suffering from a most extreme misapprehension. Prince Thuton is not your friend, but one of your most active enemies—and we here with you are truly your friends."

"How can it be a friendly action to kidnap me from the company of a powerful prince who has vowed to lend his forces to assist me in regaining my throne?" she demanded.

Lukor again shook his head. "No, my lady, that, too, is a misapprehension. For, while Thuton may be suave and charming, his charm lies entirely on the surface—underneath he is wily, scheming, and treacherous. Regardless of what he may vow to you, I know it for a fact that behind your back he was negotiating with your arch foe, the Lord of the Black Legion."

She stared at him incredulously.

"Yes! This 'friend,' as you are pleased to call him, coldly and callously offered to *sell* you to the Chac Yuul—if they could meet his price!"

Her eyes flew to me as Lukor enunciated this last item of information. It was exactly what I had told her below in the royal box, when I was attempting to persuade her to mount the rope ladder and enter the flying machine. Now I nodded and added my affirmation to Lukor's avowal.

"He is right, Princess. It's true—I know it, for, while I was lost and wandering through the maze of secret passages that lies within the walls of the royal citadel, I overheard Thuton discussing the matter of the price he had set on you with none other than Arkola himself."

"But that is absurd," she protested weakly. "What would Arkola be doing in Zanadar? Surely he is in my city of Shondakor, almost three hundred *korads* to the southeast!"

I explained, as best I could within the technological limits of my Thanatorian vocabulary, about the television crystal atop the tripod. Lukor had heard of such instruments—he called them *palungordra*, which means "far-seeing eyes"—but they were not known to Darloona, and she was somewhat sceptical. However, she did not argue the point and made no further attempts to persuade Lukor to turn back; instead, she fell into a meditative silence, obviously mulling over our words. My own beliefs she could doubtless discount as the result of prejudice and ignorance, for, although I do not believe she any longer regarded me with contempt as a vile and treacherous *amatar*, devoid of honesty or honor, I had still not fully redeemed myself in her eyes. But Lukor, as I have noted before, was the sort of decent and honorable gentleman you instinctively trusted on first meeting, and his stout, unwavering, firm, and sincere statements on Thuton's villainy she could not so easily disregard.

By this time it must have been late afternoon. The canopy of golden vapor that is the sky of Callisto was still bright with day; two moons were aloft, the frosted azure globe of Ramavad and tiny golden Amalthea, or Juruvad, as the Thanatorians call it. The mighty bulk of Gordrimator, that banded colossus of the skies, hove into view ere long.*

We flew for hours.

I was becoming rather weary of the enforced inactivity, and, to tell the truth, the seat in my cockpit was rather hard and by now it had become most uncomfortable. I could not recall just when I had last had anything to eat and or drink, but my belly was clamoring for attention.

We were traveling along at a frightful clip, fairly zipping along. The wind was terrific over the foothills. At this rate we

---

*To my recollection, nowhere in the manuscript does Captain Dark explain the meaning of the Thanatorians' name for the planet Jupiter—Gordrimator. But, thus far into the story, we have learned enough of the universal language spoken on the jungle moon to attempt an interpretation. At various places in the manuscript, the author names the Jovian moons, as in the opening of Chapter 11, where he tells us that the Thanatorian name for Ganymede is Imavad, which means "Red Moon." From the common endings we can safely assume that *vad* in Thanatorian means "moon." But the native name for Callisto, Thanator, has a different ending. It would only be natural for the Callistans to regard their world as a planet, not a moon, hence we can assume the ending *tor* means "world." Since Gordrimator has the same word ending, I hazard the guess that its enormous size is so impressive as to persuade the Callistans that it, too, is a *tor*, a "world," otherwise they would name it Gordrimavad. Since *ima* means "red" in Thanatorian, and considering the above translation of *palungordra* as "the far-seeing eyes," I think we can probably interpret the name Gordrimator as *gordra ima tor*, "world of the red eye." Not an extraordinary appellation when you consider how impressive Jupiter's most prominent feature, the famous "Red Spot," must look to one standing on the surface of her fifth moon!—L. C.

would be out of them in no time, and could perhaps land and seek game and make camp for the night.

Ahead to the south stretched the vast black and crimson carpet of the Grand Kumala, which extended from horizon to horizon. It occurred to me after a time that Lukor should begin veering away to the east, for in that direction lay the city of Ganatol, his homeland, and thence we were bound. I leaned forward, tapped the Swordmaster on the shoulder, and shouted into his ear something to that effect. He turned a rather grim and worried face to me.

"I quite agree with you, my young friend," he said brusquely. "And, believe me, I would turn east if I could."

"What do you mean? What's gone wrong?"

He forced a laugh.

"I have been complimenting myself on my luck in finding an air current to ride," he confessed wryly, "but now that luck has turned, alas! The current has grown steadily more powerful. So long as it carried us in the direction in which we wished to travel, I made no objection and did not bother my mind with the increasing force of the wind. But some little time ago I decided it was about time to start curving away to the east—and found I could not!"

I stared at him blankly.

"You mean the wind is too strong?"

He nodded. "It is very strong. It is almost a hurricane. But that is not the trouble! The vans of the ornithopter are equipped with ailerons for just such a condition: by varying the pitch and angle of our movable surfaces, we should be able to veer even in a gale. But we cannot—look—can you see?"

I followed his pointing arm and studied our port wing. The ailerons, or whatever the movable rear surfaces on the aft side of the wing are properly called, were manipulated by foot pedals in the pilot's cockpit which Lukor occupied. These pedals communicate with the movable surfaces by means of wires and pulleys, the wires exiting from the hull through a row of small ports just above wing level.

I looked.

We had not made our escape from the City in the Clouds unscathed!

A steel dart from a guard's crossbow had lodged in our port aileron, fouling the guy-wire.

I tightened my jaw grimly, as the import of this discovery sank in slowly. Without the use of that aileron, we could not turn. We had lost our control of the flying machine, and the rapidly growing gale in whose grip we were now helpless would sweep us many leagues off our course ... on and on over the trackless jungles of the Grand Kumala.

And night was coming.

CHAPTER XV
THE HAND OF FATE

Helpless in the grip of gale-force winds, we were driven farther and farther off course, flying ever further south over the trackless maze of jungles known as the Grand Kumala.

Night was upon us now, the magically swift, sudden nightfall of Thanator. I do not believe I have yet in this narrative described the strange and almost supernatural nature of daybreak and nightfall on the jungle moon.

Day and night would seem to have no connection with the presence or even the number of Thanator's moons in her skies. Those strange skies of drifting golden vapor, like curdled flame of amber and yellow, remain constantly brilliant and evenly luminous for a period of something that seems like twelve hours. Then they dim and darken, without any apparent cause, to darkness which lasts for an equal period.

At this colossal distance, of course, the sun is far too small to have any important effect as far as illuminating the surface of Callisto is concerned.*

I have noticed, time and again, that the daylight sky of Thanator remains uniformly brilliant when no moons are aloft, as it does when all four of the inner moons and even the titanic sphere of Jupiter are in the heavens. From this I can only suppose that, at periodic intervals, Thanator is bathed in some unknown radiation which sparks a luminiferous effect in the golden vapor of her upper atmosphere, which is probably a layer of some inert gas like neon which becomes incandescent when subjected to electrical current. Perhaps at regular intervals Jupiter gives off a storm of electrical particles which interact with the inert gas of Callisto's stratosphere. Or perhaps the luminous periods are due to the actions of some completely unknown force or phenomenon. I cannot say with any degree of certainty; I can but report the phenomenon as I have personally observed it.

At daybreak, then, the *entire* dome of the sky flushes with soft brilliant radiance which takes about seven or eight minutes to go the full cycle from a velvety brown gloom to full noontide luminance. The experience is most startling when you are first exposed to it—it is almost as if the entire heavens are illuminated by some colossal explosion. The luminosity remains constant, unvarying, a sourceless glow, until the hour of nightfall, when the phenomenon is reversed. Again; it takes about seven to eight minutes, as nearly as I can calculate the time without a watch, for full daylight to be replaced by brown velvet darkness.

The only effect this cycle has on the appearance of the moons is that, of course, they seem more brilliant at night,

*Callisto is four hundred and eighty million, nine hundred and thirty thousand miles from the sun. The Earth is only ninety-three million miles from the sun; hence, Callisto is slightly more than five times farther away from the sun than our planet, and thus receives only a fraction of the amount of sunlight we enjoy.— L. C.

when they are not in competition with the radiance cast by that dome of glowing golden vapors.

Hence night was suddenly upon us. It was as if some cosmic magician cast his spell over an entire world, darkening its sun. I groaned a bitter curse.

It would be difficult enough to unsnarl or repair the vital control wires by day; by night it might well prove impossible.

"Is there nothing you can do, Lukor, to free the wire?"

He shook his head grimly.

"I have been working the pedals, hoping to dislodge the quarrel, but to no avail," he said.

"What is it? What has gone wrong?" Darloona asked suddenly. We had been conversing, Lukor and I, in terse whispers, to avoid spreading panic. The girl, sunk in a brooding melancholy, had not been aware of our dangerous plight. But she must have overhead us talking, for now she turned a questioning gaze on our pilot, the old Swordmaster. He explained the problem in swift, economical terms.

"Every second is carrying us farther south at a frightful speed," he concluded. "We are many *korads* into the Grand Kumala by now, and traveling yet deeper with every moment that passes. Unless I can somehow free the aileron and turn the flying contraption about and to the east, we shall end up at the pole!"

"Is there nothing you can do?" solemn-faced Koja inquired in his harsh, expressionless voice.

"Nothing," Lukor said with grim finality. "I fear to use the pedals again, for any further attempt may snap them. The quarrel from the crossbow has them snarled and they may well be frayed by this time, from rubbing against its edges. But they are most certainly not broken. Neither does the aileron seem to have been pierced by the bolt. The shaft seems merely to have lodged itself in the slit between the inner surface of the aileron and the rear surface of the wing. But unless we can manage to remove the obstruction, we are helpless, and will be carried hundreds of *korads* off course, for my city of Ganatol is far behind us by now, and to the east."

I bitterly regretted the untimely arrival of darkness in that it would make all the more difficult the feat I knew I must now attempt.

With a swift word to Lukor, advising him to adjust the balance of the ornithopter as best he could in order to compensate for the shift in weight, I climbed out of the cockpit and put one leg over the side.

"Jandar—what are you trying to do?" Darloona shrieked as the flying machine swung giddily to port under my weight. I forced a careless laugh, although it was somewhat difficult to do as my heart was in my mouth at the time.

"Tut, Princess," I said gaily. "If the aileron control wire is fouled there is nothing to be done but to clear it. Steady as you go, now, Lukor—"

And I climbed out onto the wing.

I am not really a particularly brave man, although the necessities of chance and fate have occasionally forced me into the role of one. Hence, in all candor, I must admit I was frightened. I was acutely aware that we were hurtling through the night at something under a hundred miles an hour in a flimsy craft made of baked and compressed *paper*.

I was also terribly conscious of the fact that we were flying at something like fifteen hundred feet above one of the thickest of all jungles, and that the slightest misstep would hurl me to a swift and certain death.

The wind whipped past me, clutching at my body with invisible fingers. My eyes teared from the blast of stinging air until I was almost blind. My hair and my garments whipped about me with such force that it was all that I could do to keep my hold on the edge of the cockpit.

If I lost my grip I would be torn loose like a leaf in a hurricane, and the wind would whip me away to hurl me like a human bomb down through the thick branches far below. I recall once reading an adventure story by Lin Carter in which his hero is marooned on the narrow ledge of a mountain peak, high above a deep lake. When at length the hero could retain his balance no longer and sprang into the air, he fell like a stone into the lake—but lived, because he fell at just the precisely correct angle so that his body met the surface of the lake with a minimum impact.* But there was no lake below me, and, alas, I had no solicitous Author watching over my fortunes, ready to bring a bit of aerodynamic hocus-pocus to my rescue, had I fallen!

Bracing myself against the terrific force of the gale, I strove to reach the tightly lodged crossbow bolt. But my arms were not long enough—my fingers brushed the hullward edge of the aileron but fell several inches short of where the quarrel was wedged.

There was nothing else to do, then, but to climb outside the wing, and stand on the pontoon-like undercarriage. This undercarriage, which I mentioned somewhat earlier, consisted of two long pontoons, one to either side of the hull, filled with the compressed levitant gas that rendered the contraption airworthy. Had it not been for them, there would have been no way I could have reached the snarled wire, for of course the wing itself could not bear my weight.

---

*The story to which Captain Dark refers is a novel entitled *Thongor Against the Gods*, the third of my Lemurian books, which was published in November, 1967. Captain Dark recalls the scene correctly, save that it was the *heroine*, not the hero, who was saved by a fortunate aerodynamic factor.—L. C.

With infinite care, still clinging with both hands to the cowling of my cockpit, I lowered first one leg and then the other, until at last I was standing on the portside pontoon. It was braced by narrow struts to the pontoon on the starboard side, and both were attached to keel and to the base of the wings by yet more struts. I sincerely hoped that these members were strong enough to bear my weight. If they were not, then we were in *real* trouble!

Now, standing sidewise on the gas-filled pontoon, I removed my grip from the cowling of my cockpit, and transferred my grip to the edge of the wing itself. This I did in agonizing slow motion, because I was terribly afraid that the wind would tear me loose and whirl me away into the night.

Looking up, I caught a glance at Darloona. She was staring at me with awe and terror in her enormous eyes. Her face was pale, and one hand lifted so that her knuckles were pressed tightly against her lips.

Suddenly I felt recklessly heroic! It was delightful to discover that someone aboard this flying deathtrap was even more frightened than I!

I wondered if the beautiful Princess of Shondakor still considered me a weakling and a coward. Doubtless she was convinced by this death-defying feat that I was a lionhearted hero. I could have laughed out loud at the thought. Actually, I was so terrified my knees were trembling.

Now I was clinging with both hands to the edge of the wing, my feet resting one in front of the other on the pontoon. Again I strove to reach the lodged bolt, but I simply could not.

Well, there was nothing else to do, so I sat down on the pontoon, straddling it uncomfortably, my legs hanging over either side, my hands above me, holding onto the edge of the wing.

Now, slowly and with enormous care, I transferred the grip of each hand from wing edge to the struts which held the pontoon fastened beneath the portside wing.

I breathed a silent prayer that the Sky Pirates of Zanadar had built the *strongest* paper airplanes known to the universe!

Now I released the strut with my left hand, and leaned far out to the side, groping for the underside of the aileron.

By tilting myself at a sickening forty-five-degree angle, I finally managed to reach the damned crossbow bolt. My fingers were numb with the cold wind, but I could feel the pointed tip of the quarrel where it was thrust through the slit between aileron and wing surface.

Gripping it between the tips of my fingers, hanging almost face down over the jungles that rushed by at a nauseating velocity beneath me, I began working the head of the quarrel back and forth, back and forth, gradually working it loose.

When, after an infinity of time that was probably only two minutes in duration, I had worked it so loose that it trembled at a touch, I reached up around the aileron and felt along the shaft of the quarrel to see if it was entangled with the guy-wire.

To do this I had to stretch from my place until most of my body was hanging over empty space. I retained hold of the pontoon with my right leg alone, which was hooked over it, while my left leg hung free.

My fingers were trembling with the strain. My wrist and forearm were numb and taut. With infinite care I felt the tangle of the wires and, wriggling the crossbow bolt between my fingers, I managed to draw it free of the wire a fraction of an inch at a time.

Thanks to whatever Almighty God or Gods rule this world, the crossbowmen of Zanadar use smooth-headed bolts!

For if this article had been barbed with a hooked arrowhead I could never in a million years have worked it free from the tangle of wires in my precarious position, hanging head down over the abyss, holding on with my right arm alone, and unable to see what the hell my left hand was doing!

With a *twangg* of suddenly-drawn-taut wires the quarrel came free and flew away, and I felt as glad as the inhabitant of Death Row whose local governor has had a change of heart just as they were strapping him in the chair.

Wires creaked as Lukor tested his pedals.

The aileron flapped up and down.

Everything was fine again, and I could begin drawing my aching, ice-cold, and exhausted body back to a more secure seat on that pontoon. Taking it very slowly I retraced my former actions until I was standing erect on the pontoon. Then, moving my hands an inch at a time—my whole arm from wrist to shoulder trembling with strain and fatigue—I inched my hold along the wing until I was facing the cockpit again. Darloona, Lukor, and Koja were staring at me.

I got the feeling none of them had been breathing while I had been out on the wing.

From the ache in my lungs I suddenly realized I had been holding my breath, too.

I hooked one half-frozen arm over the side of the cowling, and hauled my left knee up onto the edge of the wing. Then I levered my weight up, until my right foot was off the pontoon.

And then it was that the hand of Fate played an amusing little trick—

My right arm, numb from the strain, slipped sickeningly, hurling me backwards.

My right leg, which was still stiffly extended, came crashing down with all my weight on the heel.

Directly onto the hollow pontoon of stressed paper which was filled with the levitating gas—

And punched a hole right through it!

We sagged, our aerial contraption floundering from side to side as the precious gas went screaming out through that horrible rent in the balloon-pontoon.

The flying machine veered suddenly to port, hanging at a steep angle.

Obviously both pontoon held the same amount of gas, thus perfectly balancing the weight of the craft.

And it was equally obvious that, with one pontoon breached, we were no longer airworthy.

I tried to plug the hole with a bunch of cloth, with the palm of my hand, with my foot—it was no good. The gas was escaping rapidly. The pontoon was almost half empty by this time, and we were losing altitude very fast.

Lukor played on the controls like a virtuoso on the keyboard, striving to right our sickening tilt, striving to bring the flying machine into a smooth glide, but it could not be done.

The gale was too powerful.

As we lost flying trim, sagging drunkenly to port, the flat of the wing swung about—caught the full force of the howling gale—and was torn to rags in an instant.

I was almost flung loose as half the wing fabric sheared away and slapped me violently in the side of the head.

We fell in a long wobbling curve towards the treetops far below.

In mere moments we would hit those upper branches, and at the speed we were traveling our craft would be torn apart and we would be slammed with killing force to the ground below.

My mind was working now with incredible rapidity.

Suddenly, the most audacious plan sprang full-blown into my head. It had about one chance in a thousand of working—but, unless we tried it, we wouldn't have even that one chance.

Yelling like a madman I told my companions what to do.

They must have thought me insane, but the urgency and the note of command in my voice must have been so completely compelling that they sprang almost instantly to obey my directions.

It was probably that instantaneous obedience on the part of Darloona, Lukor, and Koja that saved all our lives.

It was a crazy gamble but there was simply nothing else to do.

They climbed out of their cockpits onto the starboard pontoon, which was still, thank the Gods, airtight!

The moment they were all out on the pontoon, I swung underneath the hurtling keel like an acrobat, swung along a strut until I, too, clung on that last pontoon.

Then, hacking away with our swords flying, like crazy men, we cut loose the pontoon!

All was a tumbling fall through whirling darkness—the treetops horribly close—wind blinding us—it was a miracle we managed to cut the pontoon clear of the hull and wing in time.

But we did.

Now a dead weight, the hulk of the flying craft was swept away from us. It struck the treetops with a sickening impact that tore it apart, smashing it into a spray of flying fragments. It must have been traveling at close to a hundred miles an hour when it suddenly lost *all* buoyancy at once, and swerved into collision with the trees beneath us.

As for we four mad mariners of the sky, we dangled with our hands alone clinging to the stubs of the severed struts.

The sole remaining pontoon floated above us like a weightless log. With the dead weight of the wings, hull, and empty portside pontoon cleared away, the amount of gas in the remaining pontoon was just barely sufficient to hold us aloft.

Our brush with death had been so miraculously close that I was tempted to ascribe the whole affair to some unseen Jovian Providence. A few seconds delay would have been fatal—we would still have been hacking away at the struts when the craft collided with the treetops.

It was the narrowest escape I have ever experienced, or have ever heard of, for that matter.

We spent the rest of that night on the ground. Not even up in the crotch of one of the soaring *borath* trees, which would have afforded us safety from the predators who prowled the jungle aisles at night. No—we had, all of us, had enough of aerial high jinks to last a lifetime. I, for one, would be delighted to try my luck against any creature aprowl in the jungle rather than leave the safe flatness of solid ground.

Our levitating pontoon, of course, was not enough to hold the four of us aloft for long. But the blessed thing did indeed suffice to break our speed of descent so that we floated down, buffeted by the winds, and climbed off onto big solid branches. It took us a long time to climb down to the ground from there; we were all shaking with fatigue and nervous exhaustion from our narrow brush with destruction. But reach the good old terra firma (or Callista firma, as you prefer) we did at last.

We were just too bone-weary to worry about anything else right then, so we decided to camp right where we were. Lukor still had the flint-and-steel in his girdle wherewith he had lit his oil lamp when he and I had been exploring the

secret passages within the walls of the royal citadel of Zanadar, so we managed to make a good bonfire with dead leaves
and dry branches. Then we curled up and slept the heavy
dreamless sleep of the completely exhausted.

The next day we found a jungle stream from which to
drink our fill of cold, clear, deliciously pure water. And Koja,
the hunter, spotted a game trail beaten to the water's edge.
While we hid he watched the trail, and before very long a
family of vastodons, the elephant boars of the Thanatorian
jungles, came down the trail for a drink. He rose out of hiding,
flailing away with his whip-sword, and managed to kill a cow
vastodon.

Hacking boar steaks off the kill with our blades and roast-
ing the dripping red meat over a fire, we feasted gloriously.
I have eaten in the finest restaurants in my world, from An-
toine's in New Orleans to Luk Chow's in Hong Kong, but never
have I enjoyed a meal more than that half-raw, half-charred
chunk of bloody vastodon steak chewed down without ten-
derizer, spices, or even salt and pepper.

Of course, this was the first food I had eaten in the past
two days, which may have lent savor to the entree!

It was about three days later that Fate again took a hand in
our affairs.

We had been working our way due east, or as due east
as we could ascertain, for it was difficult to tell directions on
a world in which no sun lights the sky, arcing from east to
west like a natural compass needle. According to what we
could tell, the nearest settlement of men should be a dozen
korads in that direction.

We covered quite a bit of territory in three days—the bulk
of the Grand Kumala, in fact. Our progress through the jungle

country was greatly facilitated by the discovery of a swift-flowing river which poured out of the mountains and curved away east, probably joining with the Ajand further on.

It had not been difficult to cut supple lianas, lash together fallen logs into a crude and flimsy raft, and set ourselves adrift. The rushing current carried us many leagues, and we traveled faster and easier than had we been forced to hack a path through the dense jungle underbrush on foot. Poling our way past obstructions, battling off the attacks of nameless river creatures—I shall not bore my reader with a drawn-out account of our struggle downriver, for it is easily told in summary.

We were forced, towards the close of the third day, to leave the river and press forward on foot, for here it angled away sharply to the south.

Towards nightfall disaster struck.

Without the slightest warning, as we were making our way across an open glade, a gigantic beast sprang roaring from the underbrush right into our midst, scattering us to all sides.

It was a full-grown deltagar, a horned, scarlet, tiger-like beast such as the one I had ridden to its death in the arena of Zanadar, as big as four tigers rolled into one, armed with claws like steel hooks and glistening bared fangs like naked scimitars—a fearsome opponent even for a heavily armed hunting party to encounter. And we were but three men and a girl, and armed but lightly.

The monster charged Koja and me. The arthropod snatched me up under one arm and leaped out of he way, his grasshopper-like lower limbs carrying the two of us halfway across the jungle clearing with a single bound.

Baffled, snarling, the deltagar whirled to charge Darloona, who was on the other side of the glade from our position. She turned on her heel and ran into the shelter of the thick underbrush to avoid its charge. The beast went crashing after her but gallant Lukor sprang in its path, brandishing his rapier and yelling to capture its attention.

Alas, the brute was in no mood for a challenge. Hunting must have been poor in the sector of the Kumala, for the deltagar looked half-starved, ribs thrusting like curved struts through the scarlet fur of its sides. So it did not swerve to engage Lukor but merely clouted him aside with a terrific buffet from one mighty paw, and sprang after the fleeing girl. In an instant the jungle had swallowed it up, but we could hear it crashing and floundering through the bushes, getting further and further away.

The savage blow of the deltagar's forepaw had knocked the old Swordmaster reeling. He lay sprawled some distance away, white-faced, scarlet leaking from his scalp. Koja sprang after the deltagar, in search of Darloona, while I paused to see what I could do for Lukor. As soon as I ascertained that the old man was not seriously harmed—merely unconscious and bleeding freely from a light scalp wound—I followed Koja to help in the search. But I met Koja returning to the clearing: neither Darloona nor the deltagar were to be found. She must have fled far into the depths of the jungle to avoid the hungry predator.

The next two days were consumed in a grim and desperate search for the lost Princess of Shondakor. We searched day and night for any sign of the missing girl, but we found nothing.

The deltagar, however, left a clear track due to its enormous size and weight. Acting on the assumption that the beast was also tracking the Princess, we tracked the beast. I was in a restless fever of impatience, for I was horribly conscious of the fact that Darloona was completely unarmed.

Towards dawn on the third day of her disappearance we burst suddenly through a screen of trees and gazed in amazement at an incredible sight.

At first my heart lifted with buoyant hope. But ere long those hopes were dashed into despair.

For the sight upon which we stared in grim silence was more terrible than words can express.

I shall never exorcise from my memory the profound horror of what I saw as we stepped through the fringes of the jungle and stared at that which lay before us on the broad plain under the golden skies of morn . . .

CHAPTER XVI
DARLOONA—FAREWELL!

As I sit here in my tent, day after day, laboriously inscribing this account of my adventures on the weird and marvelous world called Thanator, I am possessed of a curious sense of futility and of hoplessness.

I watch as the brilliant and varicolored moons of Thanator one by one ascend her strange skies of golden vapor. They are familiar to me now, those gorgeous orbs of colored fire—tiny Juruvad, a disk of bright gold, lime-green Orovad, the immense frosty azure sphere of mighty Ramavad, and the rose-red globe of glorious Imavad, the nearest of the four moons.

Like goblin lanterns they fill the world with rich and marvelous hues, casting weird multiple shadows from the gnarled black trunks of the many trees along the edge of the Grand Kumala. Like the glaring eyes of a host of Cyclops they stare down at me as they drift through the dim skies of this jungle moon.

They are old friends, by now. No longer do I miss the wrinkled, pitted, gray-silver face of Earth's own satellite.

But then the colossal arc of the Jupiter thrusts above the dark and distant horizon. Bit by bit the Lord of the Sky lifts his titanic globe to fill the heavens. A vast surface of luminous yellow and ocher is his shining face, banded with horizontal zones of darker sulphur and curdled brown and gloomy puce. And in the southern hemisphere, the great Red Spot blazes like an angry crimson eye—vast—dwarfing even the moons.

And in the presence of that banded giant of the skies, suddenly I am a stranger to this world again and crave to return to dwell under skies that are blue and not golden, and where but one moon rides the tides of darkness.

For the rising of mighty Gordrimator brings back to me the fact that I am farther from my home than any man who has ever lived. For I am three hundred and ninety million miles from the planet whereon I was born—and three hundred and ninety million is a lot of miles.

Although I have lived for months on Thanator, and made good friends, and found a life for myself, a cause and a mission, it still is not home to me. Nor will it, perhaps, ever be....

My hands are weary from writing. With a sigh I put down the pen I have cut from a thaptor quill, set aside the neat stack of coarse fibrous brown papyrus, and step forth from my tent onto the lawn of crimson grass that slopes down from the edge of the jungle.

Like exiled Lucifer staring at the locked gates of Heaven, I stare down through the gloaming at that which stands, an eternal enigma, on the slope below me.

A ring of monoliths, encircling a thick broad disk of milky substance like pallid Soochow jade.

The Gate Between The Worlds....

It is the irony of all ironies that I have found it at last—

now that I can never use it to return again to the world where I was born!

Perhaps I am an obstinate fool. For, indeed, the way lays open before me—in two nights, the Ku Thad tell me, the flickering shaft of throbbing light that is the mode of travel between the worlds will thrust up from the disk of lambent jade amidst the ring of standing stones.

I could enter there, naked as first I came, and after that timeless interval of flashing speed, of cruel cold, of absolute darkness, find myself yet again within that Lost City in the jungles of Cambodia. Or such, at least, is my assumption; for whether the Gate links together yet other worlds than Callisto and the Earth, I cannot be certain.

And, indeed, why should I not go? This world is strange to me, and every man desires at last, however far he has traveled, to go home.

What, then, is there to keep me here? Koja and I have long since discharged our debts of *whorz* in service to each other—he set me free and provided me with a thaptor, twice, as I recall; and I rescued him from death in the great arena of Zanadar at peril of my own life. We are quits; or, rather, say that we are friends now, with all debts canceled.

And I do not think I owe anything to Lukor, although I will always be grateful to him for his hospitality and his friendship. But I feel no guilt at being the cause for which he fled from the City in the Clouds, leaving behind his home, his work, and everything he possessed. For in truth he did it gladly, willingly, of his own volition, the act prompted more by his romantic love of adventure and derring-do, I think, than for me.

Yes . . . I could step between those pillars of carven stone the day after tomorrow, and return again to my home and the planet of my birth.

But I cannot!

Instead, after I add a few final touches to this manuscript, and bundle it securely, with a covering sheet that requests the finder to deliver it to my old friend Major Gary Hoyt in Saigon and claim a reward, I shall toss the bundle of closely written pages within that lambent shaft of occult radiance. Old Zastro, the wise man of the Ku Thad, who has studied the weird phenomenon of the Gate Between The Worlds, assures me that only organic material can be carried from one world to the next within the beam. That explains why I materialized on the surface of Thanator as naked as in the hour of my birth . . . my clothing, boots, everything, even my identity tags and my wristwatch, were of nonorganic substances like metal or plastic or synthetic cloth. Thus they were left behind in the Lost City of Arangkôr, while I flew through space as a cloud of dematerialized force.

But the manuscript is completely organic in nature, the paper a crude reed papyrus, the ink a distillation of the fluidic secretions of a squidlike river beast. Hence the manuscript should be transported successfully to Earth. It may molder undiscovered and unread for years, until rain and sun and decay render it forever undecipherable. I only hope that such is not the case, for it seems to me that I have undergone the most remarkable series of adventures within the span of human knowledge, and I feel it my duty to pass along some account of the mysteries and marvels I have discovered here upon this strangest, most terrible, and yet most beautiful of all worlds.

I shall watch the disappearance of my manuscript with a mingling of emotions my reader, if any, can doubtless imagine for himself.

For while my written account of my months upon Thanator voyages between the worlds, eventually, I hope, to re-materialize on the Earth—I cannot!

For one debt remains undischarged. One obligation yet holds me its helpless prisoner.

The knowledge that I could never turn aside from this quest came to me, weeks ago, there at the eastern borders of the black and crimson jungles, when with Koja and Lukor I stared at a sight of nameless and profound horror.

And in all the days since then, to this very hour, I have not been able to forget that terrible vision.

Nothing that has happened since then is worthy of much in the way of recording. Hopelessly, my comrades and I turned aside from the sight that we had seen, to reenter the Grand Kumala. Days later we encountered a hunting party of Darloona's people, the Ku Thad. At first we were in danger of imminent death, for upon this jungle moon the hand of every man is lifted in eternal enmity against every other man. But when we divulged that we had accompanied the Princess of Shondakor out of captivity and had made ourselves her friends and protectors, we found ourselves very welcome among the Golden People, whose leader, the Lord Yarrak, Darloona's uncle, had long since thought his niece the Princess slain by some jungle beast.

And so we joined forces with the exiled Ku Thad. Learning of my desire to find again in the Gate Between The Worlds, they escorted me to it, for they know it well, as they know all the paths and byways of this mighty jungle. And so, ironically, I found that for which I had yearned so long, now that I could no longer use it!

Yarrak himself suffers from a deep and personal sorrow; yet is he gentle with me for cause of mine own. He drew from me gently my account of the terrible thing we had seen—the thing I have been so reluctant to describe in cold words. Knowing now what I know, he too understands why I cannot again retrace my weird and magical flight between the worlds to the planet of my birth.

For I am chained to this world until such time as I shall know the truth. Until at last I have learned of the ultimate fate of the Princess Darloona, whether she be yet alive or whether her young and lovely body is cold and stark in the grip of death.

Never shall I forget that terrible moment when, with Koja and Lukor at my side, I peered through the edges of the jungle and looked upon a broad and fertile plain in whose midst arose the mighty ramparts of a walled city of stone.

"It is Shondakor itself," Koja said in his expressionless metallic voice. *Shondakor—*!

I gazed upon the splendid metropolis with amazement ... upon the lofty towers, the splendid mansions and palaces, the broad and level boulevards, the soaring structures of intricate and heavily ornamented architecture, worked with snarling masks and carven pediments and spiral columns and long arcades. Pale golden shone Shondakor under the brilliant skies of dawn, its great structures mirrored in the broad river that flowed beneath its mighty walls, a river I knew to be the Ajand.

One narrow bridge of carven stone spanned the breadth of this broad river, ending at the bastion gate of the walled city.

Lukor seized my arm with a stifled cry.

"Look!" he exclaimed. "Is it nor—?"

I looked—and felt my heart lift with a tremendous joy. For *she was not dead*, slain in the trackless jungles by some slavering reptile, some savage predator—*she lived!*

I watched as Darloona, her glorious flaming hair fluttering like a scarlet banner, rode across that bridge to the frowning gates amid a mounted escort of small, swarthy soldiers clad in leathern tunics blazoned on chest and back with the emblem of a horned black skull with eyes of red flame.

And then my heart, which had lifted on the wings of joyous hope, sank into the darkness of profound depression.

For these were warriors of the Chac Yuul—the Black Legion!

And I watched hopelessly as the woman I suddenly knew I loved more than my life itself was borne, a helpless captive, into the gates of the very stronghold of her deadliest enemies!

The gates closed behind her with a clang of ominous finality. And I never saw her again.

And it is here, at this unfinished point, without any further note, that the curious manuscript of Jonathan Andrew Dark comes to an abrupt end. Shall we ever learn the rest of his amazing story? Somehow, I doubt it. For in all these months, no further word has come from that distant, mysterious world of unknown terrors

—Lin Carter

PART TWO

BLACK LEGION
OF CALLISTO

CONTENTS

A FEW WORDS OF
INTRODUCTION

The morning of January 5, 1970—a Monday—I went into the city to discuss a new contract with Henry Morrison, my agent, and to visit one of my publishers. Since I had gotten an early start, I concluded my business shortly after lunch and returned to my home on Long Island a little before three o'clock in the afternoon. My wife Noël met me at the door.

"Guess who called while you were out," she said, with an air of suppressed excitement in her voice.

"Sprague?"

"No—Gary Hoyt."

"Gary Hoyt!" I exclaimed in amazement. "Where did he call from? I didn't even know he was in the country!"

Noël grinned. "As a matter of fact, he hasn't been in the country for more than an hour or so," she explained. "He phoned about two, saying he had just arrived at Kennedy. I knew you'd be anxious to talk to him, so I invited him to dinner."

Frankly, there were very few human beings alive on the

face of the globe that Monday afternoon with whom I was more interested in conversing. Gary Hoyt! He was my only link with a gallant young soldier of fortune named Jonathan Andrew Dark who had vanished in the jungles of Cambodia early in March of 1969. Hoyt, a major in the Air Force stationed in Saigon, had been Jon Dark's closest friend, and from his hands the previous November I had received a thick bundle of manuscript which purported to be the first-person narrative of Jon Dark's amazing adventures following his disappearance in the Cambodian jungles.

"Swell. But what'll he be doing between now and dinner? Why couldn't we put him up in the Chinese room? How long is he going to be in town?"

"Just a day or two," my wife said. "He had already made a reservation at the Chelsea in Manhattan. I took down the number. . . ."

Writers usually have a lot of friends they have never met—people who like their books so much that they write a letter to the author, care of his publisher. Sometimes a correspondence springs up, and author and reader become friends without ever actually meeting in person. This was how I knew Major Hoyt. His friend, Jon Dark, was serving as commander of a helicopter squadron flying mercy missions for the International Red Cross in South Vietnam. Billeted together, the two had become close friends. Dark disappeared from human knowledge almost a year before when his copter was forced down across the Cambodian border while his squadron was flying food, medics, and supplies from a temporary field near Hon Quan, which is about sixty-five miles north of Saigon and only about ten miles from the border, to a small village in the north which had been hard hit by Viet Cong terrorists. The jungle area in which he disappeared is one of the densest and least explored jungles on Earth, and routine search flights had discovered neither the gallant young pilot nor the wreckage of his helicopter.

But early in August of last year, Cambodian natives had discovered a bundle of dilapidated manuscript somewhere in the interior; a covering note had requested the finder to deliver the manuscript to Hoyt and assured that a reward would be paid. This manuscript, which was handwritten in some sort of homemade ink and inscribed with a quill pen on a crude brownish paper resembling ancient papyrus, told an incredible story . . . and it was, if the word of its author can be accepted, a *true* story.

Captain Dark told of being forced down by engine troubles on a jungle river, of finding a ruined city and therein stumbling upon a mysterious well lined with strange milky translucent stone like Soochow jade. From the mouth of this well a beam of sparkling force thrust up against the star-jeweled jungle night. Accidentally coming into contact with this weird beam of radiance, Dark found himself miraculously transported to the surface of another world which the natives called "Thanator" but which he believed to be Callisto, the fifth moon of the planet Jupiter. The manuscript consisted of a narrative of his adventures and travels on the moon Callisto, and if we can accept the veracity of that account, it is the most fantastic true adventure in the annals of human experience.

Hoyt had forwarded the narrative to me on sheer whim. Dark, it seemed, had no family had no heirs to dispute this literary property, which the Major cautiously assumed to be a venture into fantastic fiction. Since both Jon Dark and Gary Hoyt had a mutual interest in sword and sorcery, and had enjoyed several of my own novels in the genre, Hoyt reasonably assumed I might be willing to pass judgment on the worthiness of this "novel," if that was all it was. In a covering letter, Gary Hoyt remarked that Dark, then missing in action a good five months and presumed dead, left no heirs and that I might do what I wished with the novel—keep it as a rather unique souvenir or even have it published. I found the novel splendidly exciting and well worthy of print, edited it into a typescript, and delivered it to Gail Morrison, my editress at Dell Books, who waxed enthusiastic over the story, purchased it, but insisted on using my name as author. I suspect that Gail did not and does not believe my account of receiving the manuscript anything more than an elaborate hoax. However, if the story be a hoax, it is not of my doing, and if Captain Jon Dark ever returns to this world he will find that I have banked the royalties in an escrow account under his name.

To the edited version of Captain Dark's manuscript I have given the title *Jandar of Callisto*—"Jandar" being the way the Callistan natives pronounced his name, Jon Dark.

The annoying and baffling thing about *Jandar of Callisto* is that Captain Dark left his story unfinished, its plot unresolved. Dell made no comment on this, assuming, I suppose, that I intended to follow it up with a sequel. The story breaks off at a suspenseful point. Jandar, who had rescued the Princess Darloona of Shondakor from a thousand perils, was struggling through a dense tract of Callistan jungle known as the Grand Kumala, attempting to make contact with Darloona's people, the Ku Thad, driven from their city by a bandit army known as the Black Legion. During the excitement of attack by a ferocious yathrib, a gigantic predator of the Callistan jungles, Jandar and Darloona were separated, and he later watched in helpless anxiety as she was taken, a bound prisoner, into the very stronghold of her foes, the Black Legion. At that point his narrative concluded, despairing of ever seeing again the woman he now realized he loved.

A FEW WORDS OF INTRODUCTION

Frankly, that's a hell of a way to end a novel! It leaves the reader hanging in suspense. I briefly considered writing my own ending to the tale, but eventually decided this would not be proper: it was not so much a matter of believing the narrative to be a true record, for on this point I determined to keep an open mind. It was a question of my right to tamper with another man's work—that was the deciding factor.

Captain Dark explained that amidst the jungles he had encountered Darloona's warrior people and they had led him to the disk of milky jade, encircled by a ring of standing stones, which was the Callistan end of the mysterious "transporter beam" which linked two worlds. After completing the narrative of his adventures, he planned to place the manuscript in the path of that beam of sparkling force, hoping that some account of his remarkable adventures and discoveries on the jungle moon of Thanator would thus be returned to Earth. This would seem to be what had happened, for according to later letters from Major Hoyt, Cambodian hunters found the bundle of papyrus in a ruined city closely resembling the one which Captain Dark had entered, and to which he had given a name, calling it the Lost City of Arangkôr.

I had by this time exchanged several letters with Gary Hoyt, and among other things I had informed him of my intentions of publishing *Jandar of Callisto*. Now, it seemed, we were at last to meet. I was curious to discover just what sort of a man he was.

It was beyond the realm of possibility to prove Dark's narrative either a work of fiction or a truthful account of the most amazing adventure any man ever lived. I had devoted a not inconsiderable amount of effort and research to the solution of this problem, and had, most infuriatingly, found evidence to support *both* answers.

A FEW WORDS OF INTRODUCTION

An afternoon's conversation with astronomers at the Hayden Planetarium disclosed that Callisto could not possibly support the variety of life forms claimed by the manuscript. While it is true that Callisto is one of the larger satellites in our solar system, it could not possibly have the earth-normal gravity and atmosphere Captain Dark describes because it is only a fraction of the size of our planet. The authorities at Hayden Planetarium were most definite on this point, calling my attention to the very slight gravity experienced by the Apollo astronauts on our own Moon whose diameter is only six hundred and seven miles less than that of Callisto. The heroes of Apollo 11 found an arid desert world, virtually devoid of atmosphere save for minute traces of such unbreathable gases as xenon and krypton, baked by the unshielded fury of the sun, frozen in the lunar night, with a gravity only a fraction of earth norm.

Conditions on the moon Callisto should be virtually identical, but much colder, since the fifth satellite of Jupiter is some three hundred and ninety million miles farther distant from the Sun. Frozen in perpetual night, surrounded by a hard vacuum, scoured eternally by life killing space radiation, Callisto could not possibly be the lush, fertile world Captain Dark describes.

It had, of course, occurred to me that the manuscript might actually be the work of Gary Hoyt. This I could neither prove nor disprove, but I could at least ascertain whether "Jon Dark" was an actual person or not. I found conclusive evidence, both from the United States government and the headquarters of the International Red Cross, that a Jonathan Andrew Dark had in fact disappeared on a mercy mission in Vietnam at the time and under the same conditions as the manuscript relates. This still proved little: the Major might well have used a friend as model for his character; hence, as you can imagine, I was very interested to meet him and to form my own opinion of his personality and truthfulness.

For, while there was much in *Jandar of Callisto* that was, if not intrinsically impossible, at least fantastic and unlikely, there was also an intriguing amount of corroborative detail in the manuscript that was, or could be, true. The approximate area of the Cambodian jungle into which he vanished *was* largely unexplored; lost and ruined cities, such as the one Captain Dark claimed to have discovered, *do* in fact exist— such as the colossal edifices of Angkor Vat farther to the north—and in a book called *Unsolved Mysteries of Asia*, written by a British archaeologist and explorer, Sir Malcolm Jerrolds, published in 1964 by Macmillan, I learned that native legends tell of a city in that same area, and that a Southeast Asian saga mentions it by the name of Arangkôr—the identical name which Dark used! With these facts in mind, I looked forward with eager anticipation to that evening and my first meeting with Gary Hoyt.

He was a tall, lean man in his early forties, tanned and fit and most distinguished in his Air Force blues, with steady gray eyes, a firm handshake, and a quiet, precise way of speaking. He apologized to my wife for any inconvenience his visit might have caused us, acknowledged the excited, yelping welcome of our five dogs—gravely shaking the huge paw our St. Bernard, Sir Dennis, extended—and dealt manfully with the superb roast beef dinner Noël had prepared, apologizing for the relish with which he tackled a second helping, saying this was the first home-cooked meal he had enjoyed in a long time.

Over coffee and liqueurs, the Major and I talked. His tour of duty in Vietnam was now over and he was en route to his family home in St. Paul, Minnesota. My wife had gone to college at the U of M, so they had common landmarks to discuss. While my wife and the Major talked, I looked him over thoughtfully. Like just about everyone else in the world, I pride myself on my ability to size up a man on first meeting, and everything about Major Hoyt—his quiet deep voice, his clear steady gaze, his gentlemanly manner—told me this was a man I could trust and believe in.

Moreover, he liked my dogs, and they liked him, That was enough for me!

Eventually, of course, we got around to Jon Dark. And here Gary Hoyt had some exciting news to surprise me with.

"Mr. Carter, I don't suppose you've ever heard of a fellow named Jerrolds—an Englishman, traveler and archaeologist, wrote a couple books on Southeast Asia?" he began. I repressed a start, for Jerrolds was the man in whose book I had found corroborative evidence to support Jon Dark's discovery of the Lost City of Arangkôr! I said as much and Gary Hoyt nodded soberly.

"That's good," he said. "He was one of my professors at college, which is how I know of him. Ran into him in Saigon just before Christmas. Well, I told him about Jon's book, although I was careful to point out that it was just a story and nothing more. He got pretty excited when I told him how Jon said it was so close to that jungle river where he crash-landed his chopper—dug out some maps and showed me how the Mekong makes a curve through that neck of the woods. He said nobody ever hunted for the Lost City down in that part of the country, because all of the other ruined cities of the Khmer race were quite a bit to the north, beyond the Tonle-Sap. That's a big lake in central Cambodia, you know."

I nodded. "I've read about it, Major. Supposed to be the last shrinking remnant of a mighty prehistoric sea. Please go on—you've got my imagination working!"

He laughed. "I guess I got the Professor's imagination going, too! Because he said all of this confirmed a theory he had been working up for years. Let me see if I can get this straight, now.... Seems the natives have queer old legends about a ruined city down in the south, around where Jon said he found Arangkôr, and they have some odd stories about it, too, in their sagas. Story goes something like this: way back at the beginning of time there was a great sorcerer-king of the Khmer race, a fellow named Pra-Eun. Well, the 'gods' spoke to him and told him to gather all of his people together and build a mighty city in the jungles, and to set a big square plaza in the middle of it, with a well in the exact center, and a ring of big statues, and all—"

"—just like the scene in Captain Dark's book!" I exclaimed.

He nodded. "They told him how to build this well to certain specifications, and to line it with a certain rare stone. And when everything was finished, just like the gods had said, this Pra-Eun called all of his people together and they prayed, and a ray of light came down from heaven like a golden ladder and all the people marched up that ladder into the country of heaven—and that's what happened to the mysterious lost race we call the Khmer!"

He paused to take another sip of brandy and to ruffle the ears of my little brown dog, Molly, who was pawing his knee for attention.

"Well, to make a long story short, the Professor thought he had a good idea of the exact part of the country Jon was talking about, and he set out for it just a couple days after that. He was in Saigon on his way to Cambodia to join an expedition that was being recruited by some of his people—I guess I should have mentioned earlier on that he had left the U of M years ago, and was now on the staff of the Oriental Institute of Chicago, the people that organized all those expeditions to Egypt and dug up all those tombs. Well, I didn't expect to hear anything from him, and I was just about to get out of the service anyway, and thinking about getting back home, but just before I left, he sent me—"

Here he paused again, to open up the small leather attaché case that had never left his side since he first entered my house. He drew something out and handed it to me.

"—*this!*"

I stared down, with a mixture of delight and astonishment, at a thick sheaf of crude brown papyrus covered with small neat handwriting inscribed with a quill pen in homemade ink. A *manuscript identical in every respect with the first book of Jandar's narrative!*

"He found Arangkôr, then," I breathed.

"He found it. And the plaza, and the ring of statues, and the jade well that Jon calls 'the Gate Between The Worlds.' And in the bottom of the well—this manuscript, just like the other one."

Major Hoyt left the city a day or two later, promising to keep in touch, and I settled down to the exciting task of reading the second installment of Jandar's adventures on the moon Callisto—the same story I have published here.

As before, I have not tampered with the narrative, save to do a little editorial tinkering with the grammar and punctuation, to give titles to the chapters, and to provide a few explanatory footnotes which I have signed with my initials. We have reproduced my redrawn version of the Callisto map which adorned the first Jandar book, since the scenery is the same in this volume of his history.

Also as before, the story breaks off without the full story having resolved itself. Whether or not any further word will arrive from the unknown depths of space is a matter I cannot answer. But I have written to Sir Malcolm Jerrolds, who is still engaged in the work of excavation, cataloging and exploring the ruins of the Lost City of Arangkôr, and he confirms the account of the discovery of the manuscript in every particular.

In a few months, my wife and I had planned to take a short vacation. We had been thinking of England, but right now Noël is looking at some literature from Trans-World Airlines to see what flights they provide to Cambodia. Sir Malcolm has invited us to visit the dig, if we are in that part of the world. And, in all truthfulness, I dream of seeing the aeon-old towers of lost and legended Arangkôr loom up against the mystery of the jungle night, and of seeing with my own eyes that flickering beam of uncanny radiance from within the jade mouth of the well that is the Gate Between The Worlds . . . wherethrough passed many months ago a daring young adventurer, bound on the most fantastic journey known to the annals of exploration, to face ten thousand perils on an unknown world of magic and beauty and terror.

Shall I ever know the truth of the tale? Or will it exploration, to face ten thousand perils on an unsolved mysteries of the Earth?

Time will tell . . .

Lin Carter
Hollis, Long Island, New York
January 20, 1970

BOOK ONE

THE BOOK OF JANDAR

CHAPTER I

YARRAK, LORD OF THE KU THAD

I t is one of the more remarkable of the verities of life that in many circumstances one man can accomplish that which thousands would find impossible.

I refer to the means by which I achieved the solution of my dilemma.

Through the action of a mysterious force, whose nature was still an inexplicable enigma, I had been transported across the tremendous gulf of space which yawns between the planet of my birth and Callisto, moon of Jupiter.

No sooner had I materialized on the surface of that strange and beautiful world of black and crimson jungles, whose queer skies of golden vapor are lit by enormous moons, than I found myself thrust into the midst of adventures beyond parallel in human history.

Alone and friendless in an alien world of curious peoples and ferocious monsters, that I managed to survive unscathed I owe to a mixture of audacity, chance, and accident, rather than courage or wisdom.

I found a primitive world torn by savage antagonisms,

where the hand of every man was lifted in eternal enmity against every other. Three races of sentient beings, each distinctly differing from the other, had I thus far encountered during my wandering adventures across the face of the jungle moon.

Lowest in the scale of civilization was the Yathoon Horde, a primitive nation of warrior clans. The Yathoon are not human beings, are not, in fact, even remotely hominid, but a peculiar species of arthropod. Like tall, jointed insect-men they seem, their gaunt yet not ungraceful limbs clad in sheaths of gray chitin, their faces mere featureless masks of glistening horny substance adorned with quivering antennae, their eyes somber and expressionless orbs of jeweled blackness, their clacking and metallic voices devoid of inflection. Naked, seemingly sexless, the stalking monstrosities live lives of endless warfare and know nothing of the finer sensibilities: love, paternity, friendship, mercy—all the emotions which adorn the human soul are unknown to them.

At first I feared the uncanny arthropods and found them loathsome. But eventually, during the months of my captivity in which I was not mistreated, I came to understand the poor creatures and to sympathize with their cold, lonely lives. I found them no longer ugly or repellent; their stalking, multijointed limbs assumed the functional perfection of a beautifully designed machine, their gaunt skeletal figures the elongated beauty of an attenuated sculpture by Giacometti.

At length I succeeded in making my first friend upon Thanator, which is the name by which the natives of Callisto call their mysterious world. This individual, a chieftain named Koja, to whom I belonged, proved susceptible to the finer emotions once their practical utility was demonstrated to him. I saved his life when the indifference of his fellow warriors would have left him to die, and in so doing I placed him under a certain obligation, for the Yathoon are not without a primitive code of honor and are cognizant of indebtedness (which they call *uhorz*). Ere long he reciprocated my kindness by releasing me from my involuntary servitude.

And thus, in my new freedom, I encountered the second of the higher races of Thanator, for I chanced to rescue from the attack of a savage dragon-cat, or yathrib, a beautiful girl named Darloona. She was the reigning princess of a walled stone city, Shondakor, whose people, the Ku Thad, had but recently been driven into exile by a bandit army. The Ku Thad are fully human and represent a higher level of civilization than that yet achieved by the poor arthropods. In appearance they resemble an unlikely combination of Southeast Asian and Nordic racial features, with their honey-amber skin, slanted emerald eyes, and curly red-gold manes. Seized by a rival Yathoon chieftain, one Gamchan, and condemned to torment, we were freed by my friend Koja, only to fall into the clutches of yet another race.

This race, the Sky Pirates, as they are called, represent the most advanced civilization on all of Thanator. They dwell in a mountaintop city called Zanadar, whose lofty elevation would render it inaccessible save for their remarkable and ingenious flying ships, which are unlike any form of aerial vehicle ever perfected upon Earth and demonstrate an astonishing level of technological ingenuity. The Sky Pirates differ from the Ku Thad in their papery-white flesh, lank black hair, and Caucasoid features.

The cunning and unscrupulous monarch of the Sky Pirates, Prince Thuton, condemned me to slavery while pretending to befriend Darloona. I won freedom, and found a friend among the Zanadarians in the person of Master Lukor, a gallant and gentlemanly master swordsman who taught me the skills and secrets of his craft. Learning that Thuton was secretly negotiating with Darloona's deadliest foe, the bandit chief who had overwhelmed her city, Lukor, Koja, and I effected our escape from the City in the Clouds by means of one of the ingenious flying contraptions.

Injured in a gale, the flying machine crashed in a mighty zone of dense jungles called the Grand Kumala. Although we had escaped the wreck without harm, our party was attacked by one of the savage predators of the jungle and the Princess Darloona became separated from us and was taken prisoner by a bandit patrol. Helpless to render aid, we watched from the margin of the jungle as she was borne a prisoner into her own city of Shondakor.

Wandering in the jungles, we eventually encountered her people, the Ku Thad, and joined forces with them.

Although the Ku Thad were able to direct me to the mysterious Gate Between The Worlds, whereby I had first come to this barbaric world, I elected to remain behind, for I realized at last that I was hopelessly in love with the flame-haired beauty of Darloona. I employ the word "hopeless" to describe my suit, and for excellent reason. Not only did it seem impossible that I should ever see her again, but even were such to occur, she would coldly spurn my affections, for the proud, fiery Princess had conceived a misapprehension concerning me, and deemed me a coward, a weakling, and virtually an enemy.

At an impasse, helpless to rescue the woman I loved from her captivity, I set down an account of my adventures on Thanator, feeling that some narrative of my remarkable discoveries, however crudely composed, should be preserved. This manuscript I placed within the Gate, hoping that it should thus be transported to the far-distant planet of my birth. It was with mixed emotions that I observed it as it disappeared in the weird beam of sparkling force. Whether or not it safely traversed the colossal distances between the worlds, to reach the surface of Earth at last, I shall probably never know.

Shondakor was in the grip of a wandering bandit host known as the Chac Yuul—the Black Legion—who had taken the city by surprise or treachery some months before.

I am at a loss to find any parallel in terrene history for this bandit legion. A large and disciplined force of fighting men, homeless nomads, willing on the one hand to sell their swords as mercenaries in any conflict between opposed cities, and on the other, to seize by force lands or loot, they are uniquely Thanatorian. I suppose the closest parallels could be found in the nomadic warrior clans of seventeenth-century Russia, such as the Don Cossacks. Then again, in certain characteristics the Black Legion resembles the wandering bands of *condottieri* found in fifteenth-century Italy.

Professional warriors, forswearing homeland and family, banded together under a military commander selected by popular acclaim, they go where they will, living off the land, here attacking a merchant caravan, there seizing a fishing village or a farming hamlet, sometimes laying siege to the castle of some wealthy aristocrat, at other times selling their swords as a mercenary unit in some internecine conflict. What had led them to assault one of the most splendid and brilliant of all the great cities of this world was still an unsolved mystery, but they had seized control of the metropolis in a blitzkrieg attack. Perhaps their warlord, Arkola, wearied of the rude nomadic life of camp and march and yearned to wield power over a kingdom of his own.

The enemy already within the gates, the Princess of Shondakor chose a reckless expedient and led many of her people forth to the freedom of the open plains, rather than attempt the defense of the city, which would have resulted in a massacre. The class of warrior nobility which followed her into self-imposed exile did not unanimously favor her decision, but they venerated their gorgeous and high-spirited princess, the descendant of a thousand kings, and at length were persuaded as to the truth of the old adage, "he who fights and runs away, lives to fight another day."

Now bereft of their princess, the leadership of the Ku Thad had devolved upon the stout shoulders of Lord Yarrak, Darloona's uncle. He was a tall, stately, martial leader with a natural ability for command. When Lukor, Koja, and I were first brought before him and he learned of the various assistances we had rendered to his niece and queen, he welcomed us with great honor and hospitality. And thus for weeks we had lived with the Ku Thad warriors amid the trackless jungles of the Grand Kumala.

These jungles covered literally thousands of square miles and in their density and tracklessness afforded the Shondakorians the most perfect hiding place imaginable. The Black Legion warriors had never pursued the exiled nobles, not caring what became of them so long as they presented no menace.

And indeed they did not. Although the Ku Thad were stalwart and courageous fighting men, and although they hungered to free their captive nation from their bandit overlords, they were too few in number to offer the Chac Yuul a challenge. The Shondakorians totaled no more than two or three thousand, and the Black Legion could summon to arms three times their number. Also, the walls of the city were monumental, and their girth immense. So huge a metropolis was Shondakor that it would take an army of no less than ten thousand warriors to effectively lay siege and block all gates and exits. The irony of our situation lay in this trick of fate, that it had been the ancestors of the Ku Thad who had, with infinite labor and over scores of years, raised those strong walls which now formed an impassable barrier to their own descendants.

Night after night around the council fires we discussed the ways and means whereby we might successfully wrest Shondakor from her conquerors. The great many-colored moons of Thanator gazed down on our fruitless arguments and vain discussions, and the problem remained unsolved when the vaporous golden skies paled with the sudden flare of the Thanatorian dawn.

Overwhelming force of arms might have breached the walls, but our numbers were insufficient.

A surprise attack might well gain us entry through one of the less well-guarded gates, but our very smallness of number made it hard to see how we could manage to overcome so great a force as would then oppose us.

Eventually, I conceived of a desperate plan.

It had one chance in a thousand of success.

I would attempt to enter the gates of Shondakor alone!

Yarrak regarded me with an expression generally reserved for the ravings of a madman.

"Jandar, no one doubts your courage or cunning, but what can one man possibly do against so many?"

"He can do one thing alone, which would be impossible to a number," I replied. "He can get in."

"I do not follow your reasoning," he admitted.

"Simply this. The Black Legion guards would hardly permit two thousand armed warriors to enter the gates without a pitched battle. But one man will enter easily and without opposition. Because they will feel the same as you—what can one man do against them?"

My old friend, Lukor the Swordmaster, instantly realized the truth of my observation.

"And, once within, you will have considerable freedom and an opportunity, at least, to see what can be done towards freeing the Princess!" he suggested.

"Even so," I nodded.

Lord Yarrak considered the matter in silence. "But why should they admit you at all?" he asked at length.

I shrugged. "Why not? I am not of the Ku Thad race, as my tan skin, yellow hair, and blue eyes freely attest. A Ku Thad seeking entry would arouse suspicions, but I will not. I will present myself in disguise as a wandering mercenary seeking entry into their ranks. The Chac Yuul are not a race, a nation, or a clan, but a free association of fighting men from every corner of Thanator, brought together through a common desire for loot. A solitary warrior should have no great difficulty in gaining access to their host."

Yarrak smiled, his troubled face clearing.

"I must confess myself reluctantly persuaded to the strength of your plan," he said, "although I still question whether one man behind the city walls can aid our plans in any way."

"One agent within the walls can do more than *no* agent within the walls, my lord," Lukor pointedly observed.

Yarrak laughed and admitted the truth of that statement.

"I shall wear the simple leather tunic of a common warrior," I said, "and bear unmarked steel. The most they can do is turn me away. But if they do not, then I have a fighting chance of winning a place in their army, and, in time, perhaps of affording the Princess some opportunity of escape."

"You will need a covering story, to account for yourself," mused Lord Yarrak, falling in with my plan. "You could say you had been a mercenary swordsman in the service of Soraba, which is a city of the north. The Chac Yuul have not been in the north for ten years, so you will run no danger of having the details of your account brought into question."

"My lord, Jandar may find some difficulty because of his unusual coloring," spoke up wise old Zastro, a sage elder of the Ku Thad who had been listening to our discussion.

"I shall tell them simply that I am a traveler from a far distant land," I said, "which is nothing more than the truth."

They smiled at this, for of course they knew my story, and my remark, although true, was something of an understatement. For my homeland was three hundred and eighty-seven million, nine hundred and thirty thousand miles away—"far distant" indeed!

"I do not think you should go into this danger alone, Jandar," said Koja in his solemn way. The gallant old Swordmaster nodded in vigorous assent.

"I could not agree with friend Koja more," he said. "Together, the two of us—"

"The *three* of us—" added Koja.

"Thanks, but I think one man has a better chance of getting in, than three," I said firmly.

"But—"

"I am young enough, and a fair-enough swordsman, to pass myself off as a landless, penniless mercenary," I pointed out. "But you, Lukor, are a master in the art of fence, and a most distinguished gentleman in your appearance, taste, and manner. It would be hard going to convince the suspicious Chac Yuul that any gentleman of your evident sophistication and sense of honor is a wandering sell-sword rogue. And, Koja, when have the noble chieftains of the Yathoon clans enlisted with the Black Legion bandits? No, friends, I thank you. But this adventure is mine alone."

There were several further arguments to be thrashed out, but in the end it was decided to my satisfaction. I would leave at dawn.

CHAPTER II
TO THE GATES OF SHONDAKOR

T he dawns of Callisto—or Thanator, as I should accustom myself to thinking of this jungle world—are a unique experience. They have to be seen to be believed.

Thanator, the fifth moon of Jupiter, literally has no sun. In common with the rest of the twelve moons of the giant planet, it is so very distant from the central luminary of our solar system that the sun seems but the brightest of the stars visible in its skies.

By all rights, I suppose that the surface of Callisto should be a cold and airless waste of dead, frozen stone, drenched in perpetual gloom, illuminated only by the dim reflected glory of the Jove-light, for that mightiest of the planets bulks enormous in its skies. The above description doubtless tallies with the sober and considered pronouncements of terrene science.* But in fact, Callisto enjoys a gravity only fractionally

*Captain Dark is quite correct in making this assumption. I have consulted with astronomers at New York's Hayden Planetarium, and they have assured me that Callisto cannot possibly support any indigenous life forms above the level of certain hardy lichens. The satellite, which is more than five times farther away from

less than that of my home world; and however impossible it may be, according to the currently accepted dogmas of science, Thanator is a warm and even tropic world, teeming with fecund life.

The skies of this jungle moon are composed of breathable vapors whose composition seems to me identical with that of Earth's own atmosphere (if this were not so, then how could I breathe it and continue to live?) with just one rather peculiar difference.

And that difference is the sky itself.

For high in the stratosphere of the Thanatorian atmosphere a layer of strange golden mist may be seen. Indeed, the skies of jungle-clad Thanator are not *azure*, but a glowing amber!

Dawn on Thanator is a sudden, sourceless brightening of this dome of golden vapor, which changes from complete darkness to a full and noonlike brilliance in just a matter of minutes.

This peculiar illuminative effect extends uniformly across the entire dome of the heavens, and it does not "rise" in the east and "set" in the west. I have never found a satisfactory answer to this phenomenon, but many are the mysteries of Thanator, and this is but one more.

All night we had traveled north through the Kumala, until shortly before dawn we were some distance north of Shondakor. Here I bade my comrades an affectionate farewell.

---

the sun than is our own Earth, receives a correspondingly diminished fraction of the solar warmth and illumination which makes life on our planet a possibility. This would seem to definitely rule out the chances of Captain Dark's narrative being a factual rather than a fictional document. I inquired if it were not possible that Callisto had a molten core of temperature such as to render the surface tolerable to life, and learned that the authorities consider the moon far too small for this to be possible.—L. C.

From this point I must go forward alone in the face of whatever perils the unknown future held for me.

I traversed the plains to the shores of the river Ajand, forded the river, and came to a stone-paved highway which Lord Yarrak had called to my attention; from thence I turned south and rode for Shondakor. Since my story would have it that I came from Soraba, which is on the southern shore of the inland sea of Corund Laj, it would not do were I to approach the city from any direction but the north. I rode steadily, while the golden sky flushed suddenly with brilliance above me and bathed all of the level plains round about with noontime light.

My steed was a thaptor, a beast used by the natives of Callisto in place of the horse, which is unknown upon this world. In fact, mammals of any description are exceedingly rare upon Thanator, I have noticed.

Thaptors are wingless, four-legged avians. They resembled nothing so much as an unlikely hybrid of bird and horse, and whenever I see one I am irresistibly reminded of old Earth legends of the hippogriff,* for the thaptor might well have modeled for this fabulous creature. It is about the size of a large horse, but has clawed bird-feet, is clad in feathers, which rise in a manelike ruff just behind its head. Its beaked head and staring eyes bear a marked resemblance to the parrot.

The thaptors are unruly and restive and have never been completely domesticated, which makes riding one of them

*I fear Captain Dark has confused the gryphon with the hippogriff in this comparison. Thaptors are beaked, wingless but feathered, quadrupeds. The gryphon, described by classical authors such as Pliny, is a hybrid of eagle and lion, beaked and feathered. But the hippogriff is merely a winged horse, and beyond its feathered pinions bears no relation to the bird. At any rate, the hippogriff is not correctly termed a "legendary" beast, as it was an invention of the Italian poet, Ludovico Aristo, and first appears in world literature in his heroic romance, the *Orlando. Furioso*, a production of the Renaissance.—L. C.

partake of the element of an adventure. Indeed, a mounted Thanatorian warrior habitually carries, strapped to his saddle, a small wooden club called an *olo* wherewith to crack his mount soundly atop the head should it seek to dislodge him from his place, or strive to crane its neck around and bite out a portion of his leg. This last habit of the thaptor makes me puzzle that the Thanatorians seem never to have invented the riding boot.

In their jungle home, the Ku Thad have little use for thaptors, but retain a few whereby their messengers can travel more rapidly than on foot. Thus it was that Yarrak was able to lend me a mount: it would have aroused needless suspicions in the breasts of the Black Legion had I arrived before their gates unmounted, claiming to have traversed the many miles of road from Soraba on foot.

After an hour of hard riding I came within sight of Shondakor.

The great city of the Ku Thad rose amidst the Plains of Haratha, on the eastern shore of the river. It was a splendid metropolis. The massive ramparts of its mighty wall encircled the city; tall spires rose in the brilliant morning light, and I could see the domes of palaces and mansions. All was built of stone, and the outer walls were faced with plaster that gleamed pale golden—hence its appellation, the "Golden City."

As I rode down to the gates of the walled stone city, I could not help feeling like some heroic warrior in a Sword and Sorcery novel. I'm sure I straightened my back, threw out my shoulders, and let my hand rest on the pommel of my sword in a swashbuckling manner.

Somewhat to my surprise, the gates were open and a number of farmers were passing through, leading carts and wagons filled with bags of grain, sides of meat, sacks of vegetables, and the like. This, I soon realized, was market day and the farmers from the surrounding countryside were bringing their goods to the bazaar. Ahead of me, as I joined the line filing through the gates, I saw warriors of the Chac Yuul negligently waving the peasants through the portals. Wheels creaked, dust swirled, and the heavy wagons clattered over the stone pavement. They were drawn by a species of draft animals unfamiliar to me—a heavy, lumbering beast with a thick short tail and a massive head, beaked, and horned, which looked like some ungainly cross between rhinoceros and triceratops.

I observed with a touch of wry humor that evidently life must go on, even in a conquered city which lay in the grip of its enemies. Farmers must sell their produce at market, housewives must purchase them, and men must eat, the rise and fall of dynasties notwithstanding.

I joined the end of the line and rode slowly towards the moment of decision. Would I be permitted to enter the city of the Chac Yuul, or would I be challenged?

As I approached the gates I felt the eyes of the guards upon me. One of them, a flat-faced, Mongol-like little warrior with bandy legs and long, apelike arms, gestured me to a halt.

"You, there! Where do you think you are going?"

I looked down at him from the height of my saddle.

"Since this path leads only within the city, you should be able to figure out the answer to that question yourself," I replied calmly. Some urge of inner deviltry inspired the mocking insolence of my manner. I do not know whether or not it was wise, but it aroused a chorus of laughter from the bow-legged guard's comrades. His swarthy cheeks flushed and his eyes went cold.

"Get down off that thaptor," he snarled.

"Certainly. But I will still be taller than you, even when dismounted," I smiled. He flushed again, and again the hooting mockery of his comrades stung him. He turned on them.

"You—Calcan! Fetch the komad," he snarled. Then, displaying a vicious little hooked dagger, he said in a cold, level warning voice: "The next one of you *horeb* to laugh will kiss this."

They fell silent.

A horeb is a repulsive, wriggling rodent, a scavenger of loathsome habits, not the least of which is that it feeds off rotting garbage.

I waited, standing quietly, ready for anything. My hands swung easily at my sides, only a fingerbreadth from the pommel of sword and dagger. The bandy-legged little guard eyed me with cold malevolence and spat into the road dust eloquently.

"What's the trouble here?" a deep voice boomed.

A burly-shouldered, hulking Black Legion warrior strode through the gates, to look over our little tableau.

"It's this fellow here, Captain Bluto," the bandy-legged little guard who had challenged me at the gate whined, cocking a thumb in my general direction. "He wants to get in the city, but he wears weapons, which is against the rule."

Bluto looked me up and down with a squinting eye. He was truly enormous, one of the tallest men I have ever seen, and he literally towered over the other Chac Yuul guardsmen, who tended to shortness on the average. And he looked to be every bit as tough and as strong as he was big. I felt an inward qualm.

Then I caught the look in the little bandy-legged guard's eye. It was a smirk. I could read his thought clearly: let's see you crack wise in front of Bluto, he was thinking. I straightened my shoulders. In for a penny, in for a pound.

"So you want to get in the city," Bluto grunted. He rubbed a black-stubbled jaw with one hand the size of a ham. Truly he was an enormous specimen of manhood, although, I suspected, an abnormal specimen. I thought I detected in his underslung, prognathous jaw and the swollen muscles of his broad shoulders, deep chest, and heavy legs the signs of a glandular malfunction.

"That's right," I agreed. "Why all this? If a bunch of mere peasants can troop in, who is to stop a trained and experienced fighting man?"

Bluto grinned nastily, and a hot eager glint came into his eyes. Instantly I had him pegged for a bully. Most big men I have known were extraordinarily gentle; it was as if with their unusual size and strength went an obligation not to swagger it before less burly men than themselves. Not so with Bluto, I guessed. He delighted in crushing a man smaller than himself.

"So, he's a fighting man, is he?" he chuckled coarsely. And he began striding around me, looking me up and down with mock admiration. Then he looked a trifle disgruntled. His broad humor would have been more appropriate if I had been a lesser man myself, but I am considered rather tall and I believe I may truthfully state that the past months of action and adventure I had come through amidst the thousand perils of this jungle world had developed my musculature to a superb degree.

"In this city there are no fighting men but warriors of the Chac Yuul," he growled. I nodded amicably.

"So I have been given to understand. It is for that reason that I am here—to join forces with the Black Legion," I said.

He gave a belch of crude laughter. "The Black Legion! So, you think you are worthy to stand and fight by our side, eh? A little fellow like you?"

His men chuckled, but their humor was forced. For, in all truth, I must have looked rather prepossessing to men of their dwarfed stature, even when standing beside Bluto.

He slapped his arms and thumped his chest. "You think men like me need you to defend them?" he demanded, obviously working himself up into a fighting rage. Doubtless the poor lout's single pleasure lay in showing off his prowess before his warriors.

"I may not be as tall a man as yourself," I said with a cool, level glance, "but I have a long arm," and here I indicated the rapier that swung at my side.

"Give it to him, Komad," the bandy-legged little guard leered. "Show him how a Chac Yuul swordsman deals with braggarts!"

Bluto was breathing heavily now, his dark face flushed, his brows congested. "You want to fight Bluto? You want to see what it takes to measure up to a Black Legion warrior?"

"I would prefer to save my fighting for the enemies of the Chac Yuul," I said. "To whom should I apply for enlistment?" And I made as if to step past him. He let loose with a bull-like roar and, reaching out, seized me by the upper arm and swung me about so that I faced him again.

"Stand still little man, when Bluto is talking to you—*uhh!*"

That gasp with which his bellow ended is easily explained. I dislike being handled, so I broke his hold with a karate chop that must have numbed him from elbow to wrist.

With an inarticulate roar, he struck me across the face!

I staggered—more shaken by surprise and astonishment than actually hurt by the clumsy blow.

My foot slipped and I went down on one knee.

A deathly silence had fallen over, the thronged guards.

I felt my heart sink within me. Not that this noisy braggart worried me, for I was well aware that my skills with the sword were superior to anything this oafish bully could bring against me. But it had been my hope to enter the city of Shondakor without attracting any attention to myself. And nothing was more likely to bring me to the attention of the Lords of the Black Legion than a display of superb swordsmanship before their very gates, by one who pretended to be nothing more than just another ordinary mercenary!

Those hopes were dashed now, for it was unlikely that I would be able to get past this Bluto without a fight.

Cursing the luck, I rose to my feet again and brushed the road dust from my garments while my mind raced furiously, striving to think of a way out of this dilemma.

CHAPTER III

I WIN A FIGHT AND MAKE A FRIEND

There was no way to avoid the conflict, for a blow had been given and heated words had been exchanged.

Bluto stood there before me, legs spread, one hand hanging by the pommel of his sword. He was breathing heavily, his coarse features flushed, his little piglike eyes gleaming with fury.

"Draw your steel, man," he growled. "Let Bluto see what sort of a man you are and what your guts are made of."

I kept my hand well away from my blade, and with some difficulty I retained a calm smile.

A flash of excitement lit his little glinting eyes. I think he thought he faced a coward, and the bully within him heated to excitement at the thought. But this, also, was not the way out—for a coward would not be welcome in the ranks of the Black Legion.

Suddenly an inspiration occurred to me. I relaxed, breathing easily. For there was after all one mode of combat in which I could display superior prowess without arousing suspicion in those who were soon to be my superior officers.

"Well? What are you waiting for, you horeb?" he snarled.

I smiled and stood calmly, letting all see that I was at my ease.

"I presume even a band of ruffians such as yourselves has some conception of warriors' honor, and that a man struck in the face has the right to defend himself without charge of treason, riot, or insurrection," I remarked.

Bluto nodded, grunting. "Draw steel," he growled. "No man will speak against you. This is between the two of us."

"Very well," I said evenly. "If this is between we two alone, then it is a duel, and, being such, is under the code of honor. As the challenged, I have the right to choose weapons, and, as I prefer not to sully my steel with the vile gore of a bully and a coward, I choose—*fists!*"

Balling a fist, I swung a firm right and caught him in the pit of the stomach with every ounce of strength in arm, shoulder, and back. He was not anticipating such a blow, and the muscles of his abdomen were slack. Thus my balled fist struck his middle with an audible smack, like a butcher's mallet smacking a side of meat. My fist sank into his guts a good two inches.

His mouth drooped slackly; his face went sallow; he swayed, the heavy sword dropping from loose fingers to clang against the stony pave. He regarded me with a look of blank astonishment in his little piglike eyes.

Then I followed with a right to the jaw that must have broken a tooth or two. He bounced backwards, lifted a couple of inches off the ground by the impact of my blow, and fell with his back in the dust with a terrific thump and clatter of accouterments. And he did not get up again. He was out cold.

The fine art of fisticuffs, I should perhaps note here, is all but unknown on Thanator. It is not that pugilism is despised as an ungentlemanly mode of combat. It is, simply, that it has yet to be invented. And a man who knows how to use his fists is never without a weapon on this world.

Thus my conquest of their bully must have seemed almost magical in the eyes of the other guards. They gaped in amazement as I dusted my fingers together, and stepped across the prone Bluto, and led my steed through the gates of the city.

Not a man among them raised his voice in protest. And thus, at last, I entered the city of my princess.

The quiet voice of a tall, gentlemanly young man accosted me as I passed the gates.

"That was indeed well done, stranger," he smiled. "I believe I heard you express a desire to join the Chac Yuul. If that still holds true, permit me to guide you to the man to whom you should speak. For, in my estimate, the Black Legion has a place within its ranks for any warrior who can lay out the likes of Bluto with his bare hands!"

I laughed. "In my country, friend, we have a saying, which holds true, it seems, even in Shondakor. 'The bigger they are, the harder they fall.'"

He was amused by my quotation and offered me his hand. "I am Valkar of Ganatol, a *komor* of the third cohort," he said.

A *komor* is a chieftain, the leader of a cohort of warriors, which meant that my new-found friend was an officer of some importance in the Black Legion. I looked him over and liked what I saw. He was tall and trimly built, with dark skin, black hair, and green eyes—an odd combination I had not before come across during my adventures on Thanator; doubtless a half-breed, although he had the bearing of a noble or at least a gentleman of good family. His features were regular without being handsome to the point of prettiness, and he had a strong jaw, a good smile, and frank eyes. I liked him on sight.

I have discovered that I possess the unusual ability to measure a man's qualities almost on first meeting, and I can make up my mind on a man's honor and trustworthiness in moments after meeting him. This rare ability has saved my life ere now, and I have come to trust it. Hence I extended my hand to Valkar and we were friends from that moment to this, and will be friends, I trust, until Death, the great Dissolver of Companionships, comes between us at the end.

"I thank you for your friendly words," I said, clasping his hand in a firm grip. "My name is Jandar."

He eyed my blond hair, tan skin, and blue eyes with frank curiosity.

"Never have I seen a man with your coloring," he admitted. "May I ask of what nation you are a citizen?"

"The United States of America, a far-distant land," I said, and this was no more than the truth, as my country was at that moment distant by some nearly four hundred million miles, which I believe qualifies as "far."

Valkar repeated the name, stumbling a little over the unfamiliar sounds. Then he shook his head. "It must be on the other side of Thanator, for never have I heard of it before, nor met a man from there."

"That is quite understandable," I said. "For it is my belief that I am the first of my people to travel in these lands." This also, of course, was no more than the truth.

My new friend guided me through the streets of Shondakor to the citadel of the Black Legion. And as we conversed I took the opportunity to familiarize myself with the city. While Shondakor had been conquered by the Chac Yuul some months before, their new rulers seemed to reign with a light hand over the people of the city, for I saw citizens going about their business, opening their shops, conversing in the forum, purchasing goods in the bazaar, with a freedom of movement that denoted that the occupation of alien troops had imposed few limitations upon the natives.

The city was large and impressive, the buildings imposing and splendid edifices. Broad avenues lined with flowering trees were busy with traffic. Chariots clattered by, drawn by matched teams of finely bred thaptors. Wealthy merchants and their women went by in veiled palanquins supported on the shoulders of husky slaves. Urchins played and squabbled shrilly in the mouths of alleys, tattered and noisome beggars whined from doorways, Chac Yuul warriors spent their off-duty hours lounging in wineshops. The daily life of the city obviously went forward undisturbed, despite the change of dynasty.

The commandant of recruits—I shall not bore my readers, if any, with the title of this officer, in the original Thanato-rian—was a busy man, and since the *komor* Valkar vouched for me, I was signed up and sworn in without delay or undue questioning. I gave my most recent place of service as the city of Soraba on the shores of Corund Laj, and gave as the reason for my leaving the service of the Quraan of Soraba a quite natural disgruntlement at the preference given to nobles of family connection over common-born warriors of superior command and combat ability, such as myself. This may have seemed a trifle immodest of me, but I guessed that among a bandit horde such as the Chac Yuul the usual gentlemanly code of self-depreciation, common to the other fighting men of Thanator, would be absent and that a man would be taken more or less at his own estimate.

This seemed to have been an accurate guess on my part. At any rate, within the hour I was a full-fledged warrior of the Black Legion, assigned, at my own request, to the cohort that lay under the command of my new friend, Valkar of Ganatol.

And thus I had accomplished the first part of my plan, and had managed to enter the city and join the forces of my enemy.

As for the remainder of my plan, only time would tell if luck and accident would conspire to permit me the opportunity of rescuing the woman to whom I had given my heart.

CHAPTER IV
I JOIN THE BLACK LEGION

And it was thus that I, Jandar of Callisto, entered upon my new career as a lowly warrior in the Black Legion, under the command of my newest friend, Valkar of Ganatol.

The third cohort, over which my friend was commander, was housed in a crude barracks along the southern side of a broad square or plaza which was called the Forum of Zeltadar. I later learned that the forum derived its name from the king of some remote era, an ancestor of Darloona's dynasty.

The common warriors, myself among them, slept in one enormous room upon flat, hard pallets which, during the hours of daylight, were rolled up and hung out of the way on hooks riveted to the wooden walls of the building.

We customarily arose at dawn, and upon those days when guard duty was not assigned to our cohort, we trained in the great Forum under the sharp eye of our commander, Valkar. And I soon came to understand that there is much, oh very much more to being a soldier than merely the ability to wield a sword.

In brief, we marched. We drilled. We practiced maneuvers, some of them quite sophisticated. I began to discover a healthy respect for the martial prowess of the Chac Yuul; they were as well-trained a body of fighting men as any I had ever encountered, on this world of Thanator or on my own Earth, and they were under an iron discipline that never faltered.

And I began to realize why the folk of Thanator spoke of them in fear and trembling. They must have been the most splendid body of warriors on all this planet.

In the days that followed my entering the third cohort, I learned many tricks of warfare that I had never previously had reason to study.

For example, I mastered the technique of sword fighting while mounted on thaptor-back, which is a very different art from dueling on foot.

I became practised in the various tactics of using a Thanatorian weapon called the longspear, which, insofar as I know, is unique to the Thanatorians; at least, I have never heard of any such weapon ever being used by an earthly army. The longspear is just that, a long slender shaft of wood, measuring about twenty feet from heft to tip, ending in a steel claw or hook. The Thanatorian warriors use it on foot to dismount thaptormen in battle.

As well, Valkar and his lieutenants trained us in the use of the short throwing javelin which I had seen used ere this, in the lasso, a favorite weapon of the Thanatorians and in whose use they are amazingly adept, and with the hand axe and the war bow as well. I found myself tackling my meals with a ferocious appetite and slept each night the deep slumber of the bone-weary.

Valkar was an excellent officer: firm but restrained, utterly fair, and a man of his word. Each warrior under his command was given to know exactly what limits were set over his actions, beyond which he would stray at peril of punishment. The rules—which, incidentally, were original with Valkar himself, and were not the general orders obeyed throughout the rest of the Legion, as I later learned—were very precise. The women of the city were not to be molested, neither were the homes of the Shondakorians to be entered, on penalty of twenty lashes. Fighting with other warriors, drunkenness, and leaving the barracks during the night were punishable by ten lashes. To be caught sleeping on sentry duty was rewarded with death.

While most of my fellow warriors in the cohort of Valkar were an unruly lot, mere surly oafs for the most part, even the most brutish of them responded favorably to the just discipline of their commander. No man was ever punished on whim, and every man who was punished was made aware of the exact reasons for his culpability. Valkar explained that the Shondakorian citizens vastly outnumbered the occupying forces, and that while the presence of the Black Legion was tolerated, any abuse of the native women, or robbery of a native home, might well touch off the tinderbox and rouse the citizens to resistance. As well, he pointed out that a man who became drunk or who fell asleep on guard duty might well be responsible for the death of his comrades and the defeat of the Legion, were foes to creep past his post. The men came to reward Valkar with a grudging respect and, eventually, with a doglike devotion that was a testimonial to Valkar's ability to lead and to command.

Although Valkar and I were good friends, he gave me to understand that it would be detrimental to discipline were he to be seen to have a favorite among his own troops, hence I saw little of him in private during this early period of my service

under his command. I, of course, understood the very good
reasons for this, and my estimate of him grew. But we never
met without a friendly word or look or smile and I was well
aware that he kept a close eye on my progress. Indeed, ere
long, once I had gained a certain proficiency in the martial
arts, I was awarded a minor role in the training of the less
intelligent and more awkward warriors, and from this I soon
rose to the rank of squad leader, a rank equivalent to that of
a second lieutenant.

As a minor officer, I had a semiprivate room near the
front of the barracks, which I shared with five or six other
men of similar rank, and I ate in the officers' mess, in which
Valkar himself dined. He found occasion to compliment me
on my rise in the ranks, and we occasionally exchanged a
friendly word.

Once my own training was over, and once the squadron
under my command had completed their training in the finer
arts of war, my duties slackened off. We were on duty one
full day and off duty the next, which gave me frequent op-
portunities to explore the byways of the city and to discern
something of its structure.

The fifteen men under my command were a brutal and
oafish lot, but, bearing in mind the methods of command I
had observed Valkar to use with such excellent results, I took
to treating my men with utter fairness and utter firmness. I
believe I won their respect quite early, when my authority
was questioned and I was challenged by a hulking bully or
two, whom I promptly and soundly whipped with the same
sort of pugilistic display which had lowered Bluto in the dust.
This small trial-by-combat was performed in privacy, and my
superior officers never learned of it. If they had, the men I
had fought and beaten would have been whipped until they
were unconscious, a fact of which the men themselves were

fully cognizant, and I believe they came to respect me all the more for the fact that I was willing to settle with them on my own without invoking the superior authority of the hierarchy of command.

At any rate, the general appearance and performance of my squadron was of an obviously superior degree, which earned us the commendation of our commander, and I found myself elevated to a full lieutenantcy and put in charge of two additional squadrons as well as my original command.

Weeks had passed, however, and I was nowhere nearer to finding the Princess Darloona than on the day I had entered the city.

I consoled myself grimly with the fact that at least I had a career in the military service if I desired it!

My new rank threw me quite often into close proximity with Valkar, for which I was grateful. For among the warriors of my command, or even among my fellow officers, I had found none of my own sort with whom to establish friendly intimacy. I think that Valkar, too, felt the loneliness of command, for his fellow *komors* were a brutal lot, given to gaming and drinking rather than to intelligent conversation. Hence he now rather frequently paid me the compliment of asking me to dine at his table, and not infrequently we went down into the city together on our off-duty days. I came to know him quite well, and, if anything, my respect and trust of him grew.

It was so obvious that he was of a finer sort than his fellow commanders, that I puzzled myself over the mystery of why a well-bred gentleman of good family such as he could have desired a place in the Chac Yuul, for by now I had learned that he had joined the *Black Legion* only a few months before my arrival. His rise through the ranks had been the mirror image of my own, for while the Chac Yuul are a band of coarse ruffians for the most part, the senior commanders of the host have a keen eye for a gifted and intelligent commander, be he of whatever race, and do not hesitate to promote such a man whenever they find one. But, all this notwithstanding, he seemed *very* out of place in their ranks, and more than once I mused curiously over the mystery he represented.

In all honesty, it never once occurred to me that his presence here might be accounted to much the same reason as that which had motivated my own.

The mystery deepened one evening some weeks after my rise to command. As our off-duty day had fallen on the same time, Valkar suggested we attend the theater together, and I readily agreed.

Dressed in our best, the medallions of our rank pinned to our leathern tunics, we found a box in a lower tier of the King Gamelion, a theater of supreme prominence in Shondakor; indeed, the Gamelion was virtually a national shrine of the arts, and its position was not unlike that of the Comédie Française in Paris, or the National Theatre of Great Britain. The highest families of Shondakor attend its performance of the national classics, and although most of the warrior nobility of the realm had fled into exile with Darloona and Lord Yarrak, her uncle, there were of course certain nobles or aristocrats unable to leave due to age, illness, or infirmity. Hence the cream of that which remained of Shondakorian society attended the Gamelion, as well as the upper crust of the Chac Yuul command, who were themselves now the dominant social class.

The play that night was unknown to me, a verse tragedy called *Parkand and Ylidore* by the renowned poet, Sorasto, of an earlier generation. My acquaintance with Thanatorian literature was rudimentary, hence I was all the more eager to repair that lack, and greeted Valkar's suggestion with enthusiasm.

I found the play an admirable work, not unlike some of the lesser dramas of Shakespeare, although the stilted dramatic vocabulary of an earlier epoch was somewhat difficult to follow.

Halfway during the first act, a stir went over the audience, and people turned to whisper to their companions, while casting a curious gaze at one of the boxes above. I turned to look, nudging Valkar, and froze with astonishment.

For there sat *Darloona*—my lost, loved Darloona!

She was pale but composed, and gorgeous in a gown of creamy lace with gems blazing at her throat. Accompanying her was a dark-faced, sardonic young man I had not seen before. He had a hard, mean look to his eyes, which were quick and cold and clever, and a thin-lipped mouth I did not like. His skin had the swarthiness of a pure-bred Chac Yuul, but his hair was sleek and black, inherited (I later learned) from his mother, a Zanadarian. He wore the most splendid uniform imaginable. It was a blaze of glittering decorations and gilt.

I paled, gasped, and bit my lip, glancing at my companion to see if he had noticed my sudden start.

To my utter amazement I saw that Valkar, too, had paled, going white to the lips, and that a strange emotion flamed in his grim cold eyes as he stared aloft at the Princess and her unknown escort.

The mystery deepened! And it was soon to deepen even more.

Busy with my thoughts, my mind a turmoil, I fear I paid scant attention to the remainder of the drama that evening, and to this hour I do not know whether the Masked Prince disclosed his identity to the magician Zarakandus in time to prevent Ylidore from marrying the wealthy merchant who had betrayed her intimacy with the landless warrior to the choleric baron into whose hands at all costs the mysterious letter must be prevented from falling.

But I suspect my own inattention went unnoticed, for Valkar himself seemed preoccupied with his own thoughts that evening.

After the theater we repaired to a better-class wine-shop in the neighborhood to share a bottle. And there occurred an accident that only served to increase my curiosity regarding my friend. For the mystery of his background took a wholly new twist.

A serving girl by accident stumbled, spilling a goblet of wine on Valkar, splashing his face.

It was a trivial accident and he laughed aside the girl's apologies, wiping the wine from his face with his scarf.

The accident would have gone unnoticed, had it not been for one small detail. I chanced to notice the kerchief as Valkar replaced it within his tunic: a smudge of dark tan substance discolored it.

Glancing at my friend, I noticed that the side of his face from which he had wiped the spilled wine now showed clear golden amber where before it had been dark tan.

A moment later, Valkar excused himself and left our booth to seek the sanitary facilities. Upon his return a moment later, the patch of clear golden skin was no longer evident.

I was intrigued, but kept my silence and made no comment, nor did I presume upon our friendship to pass a perhaps embarrassing question.

But I began to wonder why Valkar held a command in the Black Legion *in disguise*!

For he was no outcast half-breed as he had claimed.

The swarthy skin, which indicated Chac Yuul blood, and the black hair, which suggested Zanadarian parentage, had gone curiously with the emerald eyes of Shondakorian ancestry.

Now I suspected that beneath the false coloring of skin and hair, Valkar of Ganatol was a full-blooded Shondakorian.

But why the masquerade?

Who *was* Valkar?

BOOK TWO

THE BOOK OF VASPIAN

CHAPTER V

I AM BEFRIENDED BY A PRINCE

Two days after I made the remarkable discovery that my friend Valkar was in reality a pure-bred Shonda-Korian in disguise, events took a new turn.

Strolling down one of the broad, tree-lined avenues of the Golden City of the Ku Thad, I heard cries of distress.

Gazing ahead, I perceived a chariot with a single passenger. The team of matched thaptors drawing the chariot were out of control, hurtling and careening down the boulevard at breakneck speed. At any instant, the chariot might overturn as its wheel caught an irregularity in the pave, thus hurling the chariot's occupant to the pave and dealing him a serious injury.

The thaptors might have stampeded from any one of a number of causes—a chance noise, a sudden movement, a flick of the whip on some tender portion of their anatomy, or sheer cantankerousness alone. For the weird bird-horses of Thanator have never been fully domesticated and are restive and unruly, and quite likely to bolt or to turn upon their rider on chance whim or the slightest provocation.

What I did was not a matter of conscious decision, or even of thought. It was purely instinctive. As the madly careening chariot approached the place where I stood, I sprang out into the street, full in its path, and waved my arms above my head with a sudden shout. I could have been trampled and maimed in the very next instant, but frankly the thought did not even occur to me.

The thaptor team came to a sudden halt and reared up in panic, slashing at empty air with their birdlike claws.

I leaped forward and seized their bridles and forced them down again. It was all over in an instant, but I must confess that I found myself shaking like a leaf, and drenched in cold perspiration from head to foot.

The lone passenger of the chariot sprang to the ground, pale and shaken as myself.

"My thanks, warrior," he gasped. "The Lords of Gordrimator alone know what made those empty-headed animals bolt like that. But had you not chanced along when you did, I might be a dead man at this moment!"

He wrung my hand in a grateful grip and I found myself staring in amazement at the lean, dark-faced, hard-eyed young man who had been Darloona's escort at the theater on that memorable evening!

Evidently he mistook my surprised expression for awe at his rank, for he smiled in a rather complacent manner. Frankly, I did not have even the slightest idea of who he was, for I had decided not to query Valkar on that point for fear of revealing my unusual interest in the Princess. But his next words disclosed the identity with which he naturally presumed me to be familiar.

"Yes, warrior, you have saved the life of your Prince!" he said. "And think not that the son of Arkola shall not remember and reward the heroic bravery of your deed. Your name and cohort?"

"Jandar, *kojat* of the third," I said rather dazedly. He nodded, smiled, accepted my salute, and vanished in the throng.

That evening as I returned to the barracks, I was told to report to the commander at once. I entered his office and saluted Valkar, who returned my salute absently, his gaze bent upon me and an expression of some perplexity visible in his features.

"Jandar, I was not aware that you were acquainted with Prince Vaspian," he remarked.

"Indeed, I am not," I replied. "To the best of my knowledge, I have only seen him twice; the first time at the theater the other night, and the second time was this morning, when I chanced to halt his runaway chariot by seizing the reins of the thaptors."

His brow cleared. "Ah, that explains the riddle! For I have received a note from the palace, commanding that you be detached from my command and assigned to the retinue of the Prince in recognition of your 'loyalty, bravery, self-sacrifice, and service to the crown.' It was this last that baffled me, as well it might."

I was elated at this opportunity to get inside the palace, but somewhat puzzled at the Prince's impulsive request.

"Do you mean to say that merely because I chanced along at just the right time to halt his runaways, I have been elevated to some sort of bodyguard of the Prince?" I asked.

He shook his head. "No, not just for that alone. Prince Vaspian inquired into your full record in the Black Legion, including a report on the way you handled that bully, Bluto, at the city gate, and your remarkable record in service, your rise to command, and so forth. He seems quite pleased with your career thus far."

"What sort of a person is this Prince?"

Valkar shrugged. "It is hard to say: I have had no personal contact with him, myself. But you must understand, Jandar, that the high councils of the Chac Yuul are ridden with rivalry and factionalism. The information that you are a veritable newcomer to the Legion seemed to delight His Highness most. You have no clan allegiances within the Black Legion, you see, and you have been with us for too brief a time to make very many close friends. Hence Prince Vaspian can trust in you to a considerable extent, where in another man he might fear a spy or even a carefully planted assassin. At any rate, he has fixed on you to join his retinue, and you are thus immediately detached from service to the third and reassigned to the palace. I shall be sorry to have you leave us."

This remarkable accident afforded me entrance into the palace and a chance to be near Darloona, hence I was tremendously excited by my good fortune. But I strove to conceal my elation, for I perceived that Valkar was somewhat saddened that we should see no more of each other and that our paths should part here.

"I shall regret leaving the cohort," I confessed, "and even more, I shall be sorry not to see you again. But perhaps my new assignment need not sever our friendship entirely, for surely we can continue to meet and to share our off-duty hours together, even as before."

He smiled, but shook his head reluctantly.

"I fear not, Jandar, for a mere *komor* has no business in the high circles of the Chac Yuul. But I shall not forget our friendship, and perhaps after all we shall meet again at a later time."

We bade each other farewell, and within the hour I was on the way to the palace compound with my few possessions bundled into the saddlebags of my thaptor.

*   *   *

At the very center of the city of Shondakor lies a square plaza, and on the northern side of this central plaza rises the ancient palace of the kings.

This palace has three main wings, and it is surrounded by parks and gardens which are themselves enclosed in a high wall, smaller, but no less strong and well guarded than the wall that encircles the vast metropolis itself. This inner enclosure forms the fortress citadel of the city and is designed to serve as the last defensive area in case the rest of the capital is overwhelmed in siege. These things I had learned from conversations with Lord Yarrak before setting forth on my mission to rescue the Princess Darloona from the stronghold of the Black Legion.

A pass, signed with the medallion of the Prince, gave me entry into the palace enclosure, and a chamberlain led me through endless suites and corridors, anterooms and apartments, meeting chambers and feasting halls, to the north wing where the retinue of Prince Vaspian was housed.

All about me lay scenes of vivid splendor and regal luxury. No expense had been spared in decorating the sumptuous apartments of the palace. Rare woods, exquisite tapestries, precious gems and noble metals, had been lavished on the ornamentation. Pierced lamps of burnished silver shed an even glow over silken carpets and carved ivory screens. Vases of sculptured jade, amber, and gleaming onyx bore fresh-cut flowers. Standing globes of perforated brass exuded coiling threads of priceless incense to sweeten the air. Superb statues of marble or bronze were enshrined in niches along the high-roofed corridors. Gems flashed in the folds of gorgeous tapestries. The masterworks of painter, sculptor, and mosaicist adorned every room. The luxury, the opulence, the beauty of the palace decor was overwhelming. I recalled my brief tour of the citadel of Zanadar, months before, that time Lukor the Swordmaster had smuggled me within the palace of Prince Thuton in a last-moment effort to free our Yathoon comrade, Koja, from death in the arena. Even the kingly citadel of the City in the Clouds could not outshine the sumptuous splendors of Shondakor.

Prince Vaspian met me in a glorious room whose walls were hung with heavy folds of shining cloth. The Prince was clothed in glistening white silks, diamonds flashing from lobe, brow, throat, wrist, and girdle. He acknowledged my salute with a casual wave of a glittering hand and gestured for my attention.

"The servitors will take your belongings to your new quarters," he said in a low voice. "I require your immediate services. In a short time I will attend a council meeting with my royal father and certain other lords of the Chac Yuul, here in this very chamber. I desire you to guard my person, for among the lords of the Legion are certain enemies who wish nothing so much as the chance to injure me. Do you understand?"

"I shall do whatever the Prince requires," I answered. "Precisely what are my instructions?"

He strode across the room and pointed to a low ottoman, one of a half circle of such.

"I will be seated here," he said. Then, striding behind the ottoman, he drew aside the curtains with a flourish, disclosing the yawning mouth of a black unlit passage.

"You will station yourself here," he said. "All you have to do is keep your eyes open and watch for treachery. If anyone makes a move towards me, strike to defend my person. Here you will be unseen, for the curtains are opaque unless one stands very close to their folds, in which case the fabric can be seen to be transparent. Remain completely silent, regardless of what may happen—and do not let anyone know you are there unless there is an attempt upon my life. Is this clear?"

"Perfectly," I nodded. "And what do I do later on?"

"At the conclusion of the council, we will all file out. It would not be wise for you to emerge from your hiding place in order to accompany me, for that would give away the fact that I suspect treason and am guarding myself accordingly. Therefore, once all have left the chamber, you may withdraw. At the end of this passage you will find a secret door which leads out into a corridor. Go out into the open and ask directions of whomever you should meet. Go at once to my suite and my servitors will show you to the room set aside for yourself; remain there until I call for you. My servitors will bring you wine or food or whatever else you may require. You may sleep, if you like."

"I understand," I said.

"Very good. Now take your position behind the curtains, and be careful not to give away your presence by a word or a sound!"

I stepped through the shining curtains to stand in the unlit doorway of the secret passage. Standing close to the curtains I saw that it was indeed easy to see through them, for at intervals in the heavier weave, gauze-thin patches of a lighter fabric of identical hue were set, as if for this very purpose.

Vaspian withdrew swiftly from the room and I settled down to await whatever should happen.

After a few minutes, several Chac Yuul guards filed into the room and took up positions on either side of the door, holding long spears, the light from bright-paned windows sparkling off their helmets of burnished copper adorned with small cubes of silver.

Then several men entered, one by one. They were squat, burly, and heavy-thewed, obviously warriors, although no longer young men. Probably high-ranking officers of the Black Legion. They had a swaggering, piratical look about them—men accustomed to power, command, authority—men who had led the bandit legion in many battles, sieges, and forays.

Next followed my "patron," Prince Vaspian, a haughty look on his dark, lean, and not-unhandsome face. He disdained to notice the courteous manner in which the senior officers of the Legion rose to salute him. He stalked across the room to the low ottoman he had indicated to me earlier, and seated himself directly in front of the place where I was standing.

No sooner had he taken his seat than another individual entered, and the Prince struggled reluctantly to his feet again to stand in the presence of Arkola the Usurper himself, the all-powerful Warlord of the Black Legion.

He was a remarkable personage: a most impressive man; the almost tangible aura of supreme power radiated from his powerful frame and heavyset features. Of course, he was no stranger to me, for I had seen him once before, or his image, mirrored in the *palungordra** I had seen in operation weeks before, in Zanadar, at which time I had overheard a conversation between Arkola and Prince Thuton of the Sky Pirates from a concealed passageway in the walls of the royal citadel.

The face of the Usurper was powerfully molded, with a square jaw and a heavy, scowling brow. His thick neck was sunk between burly shoulders, and his long, massive arms and deep chest were banded with thick sinews like heavy cables.

*These ingenious television crystals are among the more amazing instruments perfected by Thanatorian science. The term translates as "the far-seeing eyes," and the incident to which Captain Dark alludes may be found in the first volume of these adventures, *Jandar of Callisto*, Chapter 11.—L. C.

He was no bandy-legged dwarf, like so many of the Chac Yuul, but a veritable Hercules of a man, no taller than myself, but much heavier and stronger.

His features—coarse, blunt, brutal—caught and held your attention. He had a swarthy complexion and a bullet-head covered with lank colorless hair of a peculiar consistency, unlike his son's black hair. Gold baubles flashed in his earlobes and a chain of fire-rubies smoldered about his thickly corded neck. Under scowling black brows, his eyes were fierce yellow pits of somber, lion-like flame. This was no man to trifle with. This was a man born to command others. He wore simple warrior's leather—the familiar high-necked tunic worn all over Thanator—open at the throat and displaying a thatch of body fur and the curve of heavy pectoral muscles. Emblazoned on the breast of his tunic was the dread emblem of the Black Legion, a black horned and fanged grinning skull with eyes of scarlet flame.

Flung loosely about his massive shoulders were magnificent robes of emerald and saffron velvet, heavily embroidered with stiff gold wire, falling to swish around his booted ankles.

Amid utter silence the Lord of the Black Legion took his place at the center of the half circle of ottomans, on a dais slightly raised above the level of the rest. His son, the Prince Vaspian, sat on his left hand. The ottoman to his right was unoccupied.

Now there entered into the chamber the last member of the high council of the Chac Yuul.

I had heard of him, but had never seen him before. Nevertheless, I recognized him the instant he entered the room. Ool the Uncanny, they called him, and among the conquering lords of the Black Legion he was a power to be reckoned with.

A fat, placid-faced little man in gray robes, his hands

muffled in the long sleeves, came shuffling into the council chamber. A certain stillness came over the other occupants of the room.

The little man was bald as an egg, his face butter-yellow, his slitted eyes black and cold as frozen ink. A gentle smile hovered perpetually on his features. He looked as peaceful and harmless as a man could look. Why, then, did my nape hairs stiffen and a prickle of awe roughen the surface of my skin?

From the awkward silence of the others, I knew that my own almost instinctive loathing and fear of the harmless-looking little fat man was shared by them as well. About him, it seemed, blew a cold, ghastly wind from the hidden places of nature. The chill, dank breath of the Unknown . . . an icy, nameless wind from the dark abyss of the Ultimate Pit. . . .

Who he was, this little man who called himself Ool, and from whence he had come, was cloaked in mystery. No man knew his heart, and only the shadow gods he worshipped knew the secret recesses of his soul.

Some men called him wizard; others called him priest; and there were yet others, and they were not few in number, who called him a black-hearted devil in mortal flesh.

Such a being was Ool the Uncanny, warlock of the Chac Yuul, priest of the Dark Powers, servant of the Unknown.

CHAPTER VI
THE SECRET COUNCIL

Now that the seven lords of the Black Legion were assembled, the council began.

Arkola spoke in a deep, strong voice.

"Lords, you have all seen the ultimatum delivered by the messenger of the Zanadarians, and you are all familiar with our present position. What say you to the threats of Prince Thuton?"

One of the senior commanders, a grizzled, scarfaced old warrior, growled: "I say let us cast his insolent demands back in his teeth!"

One or two of the other commanders added guttural agreements to this position. Arkola cleared his throat and silence fell.

"True enough. After all, when have the warriors of the Chac Yuul shrunk from war? Yet consider: the flying contraptions of Zanadar are powerful weapons. We have no defense against attack from the skies, for all the power our fighting men display on the land."

My patron, Prince Vaspian, spoke up, silkily.

"Surely, my father, you do not intend paying the price I had almost said, the tribute—demanded by this affrontive Lord of the Sky Pirates?"

Arkola's scowl deepened.

"Someday, if he lives long enough, it may be that the Prince, my son, will learn that gold may be given away without loss or harm to a man, and that more gold may be gotten to replace it. Whereas a man's life, once he has parted with it, cannot be replaced. What is a few thousand pieces of gold to us? We shall wring many times that sum from the fat-gutted merchants of Shondakor before the year is out. And, I say again, we have no defense against the flying machines of the City in the Clouds!"

"All this is true, Arkola, but never yet has any foe forced the Black Legion to pay tribute to escape from the danger of battle," growled the grizzled old warrior who had spoken up before—his name, I later learned, was Murrak. "How will the men take it? What will it do to their morale, and to the degree of confidence they place in us, their commanders? And will not the payment of one tribute without quarrel but spur this wily Thuton to demand yet further tribute at a later date? Perhaps we should take a firm stand now; and fight it we must, for later, when we are wrung dry, we shall have to fight after all!"

Arkola permitted his grim face to relax in a grin.

"Now, those are wise, shrewd arguments, and there is much good sense behind them," he nodded. "If the Prince, my son, had but half the wits of my lord commanders of the Legion, he would make his father proud of him. Alas, I fear the hand of a woman has softened his manhood and be-clouded his mind."

A chuckle ran around the semicircle and the dark face of Prince Vaspian flushed angrily, but he wisely refrained from making a reply. I began to get the notion that the "enemy" Vaspian fancied he had among the council was his own father.

Flushed, sullen, Prince Vaspian made no reply. His father smiled, a cold hard smile.

"And since the root and cause of our present dilemma is that same love which has somewhat softened his manly strength, it behooves my son to think twice ere he impute the warriors of the Black Legion and slander their honor. Know that if we do indeed make payment, as demanded, it will not be 'tribute' but a calculated investment which will buy us valuable time."

Then one of the warrior lords, a balding but burly-shouldered old commander spoke up, and his words froze me with a shock of unbelieving astonishment.

"Since my lord has already raised the matter, may I ask when we shall celebrate the nuptials of the Prince Vaspian and the Lady Darloona?" he asked.

I started involuntarily. For a moment I could hardly believe my ears. Darloona and this puny Prince? It did not seem possible. I strained my every sense, following the conversation.

"The Princess demands that it be very soon," Vaspian said, and he smirked a trifle as he said it, and at the suggestion of a sniggering leer in his tones I could cheerfully have strangled him on the spot.

Arkola snorted. "Never shall I understand how the Prince my son has managed to win the affections of so strong-willed and womanly a bride-to-be," he said with a mocking half-smile. "However, this marriage will give the seal of legitimacy to our possession of the throne, and I oppose it not."

"She is mad with love for me," the Prince said loudly,

almost boastingly. "Every day that passes seems to her an unendurable delay!"

"Ah? Well, let us pass to more significant matters," Arkola said.

Turning from the boastful Prince, Arkola directed his attentions to the one member of this council who had yet to speak. The little wizard-priest, Ool, had sat quietly through all this, plump soft hands folded in the deep sleeves of his robe, his bald, buttery face placid and unreadable. Like a cold, malignant little Buddha he squatted, clever slitted eyes roving from face to face, listening to every word, but never permitting the slightest shadow of a reaction to mar the calm indifference of his impenetrable serenity.

"What says the Uncanny One to these dangers that now confront us?" demanded Arkola. The little priest put his head on one side, considering. Then he spoke, and his voice was mild and gentle, soft and high of pitch.

"Like all mighty men of valor, my lord, you reduce the range of possible actions to the simple alternatives of battle or surrender. However, there remain other avenues open to us."

"And what are they?" Arkola growled. "I confess I can see no other choice but to either pay the price the Zanadarians ask, or refuse to pay it and face a battle."

The priest nodded, candlelight glistening on his round bald pate.

"Yet other solutions do exist," he said mildly. "Let me call them to your attention, and to the attention of my lords. Suppose—" a sweet smile hovered about his lips and benevolence beamed in his cherubic expression "—suppose we refuse to acknowledge our debt, and yet Thuton is *unable* to attack us."

Murrak, the grizzled old war leader, stared at the calm little priest in puzzlement.

"How 'unable'?" he rumbled.

"From illness, perchance," Ool purred, his face placid and his voice gentle. "There are ways, you know, my lords! A letter from this council to his hands—a letter imbued with a toxic venom—or a gift of nubile female slaves, each infected with a virulent fever—or a jeweled gaud, some precious bauble, with a sharp edge calculated to cut his fingers, an edge steeped in some poisonous decoction. . . ."

I have heard the voice of evil in my time, but I must confess that my blood ran cold as I listened to the soft, mild voice of this smiling little priest as he discussed the ways and means of poisoning a man without his knowledge. And I consider it much to the credit of the lords of the Black Legion, simple, hard, practical war veterans all, and no subtle Borgias, that they were almost as revolted as I at the oily, purring suggestions proffered by Ool the Uncanny.

"My Lord!" Murrak appealed to Arkola. "Never would a Black Legion warrior sully his honor by stooping to such vileness! Surely, you cannot consider—will not consider—"

Arkola pondered the priest's words, jaw resting on one scarred fist, his cold eyes thoughtful. I could see his mind exploring, however reluctantly, the possible avenues of action opened up by such a plan. But his grim mouth was puckered with distaste and sour disapproval was stamped into his features.

His reply temporized without actually giving a firm answer to the little priest's proposal. Then the conversation turned to a more general discussion of fighting strength and military preparations. I gathered from the following converse that Prince Thuton of the Sky Pirates demanded payment for the person of Darloona. Some while before she had been captured by the Chac Yuul, Darloona had been a guest or prisoner of the Zanadarian monarch; our escape from the City in the

Clouds had been occasioned by my chance discovery that the treacherous Thuton, while pretending to espouse her cause, had actually been negotiating secretly with Arkola over her person. He had demanded a heavy price for her, but had been willing to sell the Princess of Shondakor to her enemies.

Now that her escape from Zanadar had brought her so swiftly into the clutches of the Chac Yuul, Thuton evidently believed that Arkola had somehow had a hand in that escape—which was completely untrue. But it seemed he now demanded full payment of the ransom, on the threat of all-out war. This was the dilemma in which the conquering legions of Arkola now found themselves.

Little of the conversation that ensued registered on my mind. My brain was a whirling turmoil of consternation, caused by the incredible discovery that the woman I loved would soon wed the sly, foppish Prince of the Black Legion—*and by her own desire*, or so it was given out. I could not and would not believe this terrible news to be true. Doubtless a helpless prisoner of the Prince, Darloona was being forced into this wedding.

Whatever the true reason for her acceptance of Vaspian's proposal, I must know it. I must hear from her own lips that she truly desired to wed the Black Legion Prince, or I would never believe it.

A thousand thoughts went through my dazed mind. That I loved the proud and beautiful Princess with every atom of manhood in my body, mind, and soul, was known only to me. She knew nothing of my love, for never had I dared to speak of it—indeed, the full realization of my love had only burst upon me when she had been taken from my side, and hence the opportunity to speak of it had never arisen.

I know not what she thought of me. Surely, by now, her

first contempt had been allayed. Through a series of confusions and accidents, Darloona had become persuaded that I was a coward and an honorless weakling. My labors in her behalf, my striving to rescue her from the grip of her wily and treacherous enemy, Thuton, must have proved to her that her original opinions of me were inaccurate. At any rate, I must hear the truth from her own lips.

And I dreaded the moment when I should learn the truth!

Not long after this, the Black Legion council broke up and the lords departed their several ways. My patron, Prince Vaspian, rose languidly to his feet, drawing about his slender shoulders a hooded cloak of dark green velvet, and left the chamber after directing a secret glance of dismissal at the hidden position where I stood, concealed from all eyes by the draperies.

In obedience to his command, I retreated from the opening and made my own exit from the chamber by means of the secret passageway whose presence he had indicated to me.

This passage, I noted, connected with yet others. The walls of the royal palace of Shondakor were thick, and it seemed they contained a maze of secret tunnels and sliding panels and spyholes even as had the mighty citadel of Zanadar.

Whim directed me to explore these passageways a bit before going to my quarters in the Prince's suite. I had no way of knowing but what a working knowledge of this secret network of hidden passages might someday soon become valuable to me.

The walls of the tunnels were at intervals pierced with spyholes. Small shields masked these eyeholes. Sliding them aside I saw that the passageways had carried me deep within the royal precincts of the palace.

I vowed to explore just a bit farther before turning back and going about my business.

The sound of muffled voices conversing in low tones drew me to one particular eyehole. I slid the shield aside, set my eye to the tiny aperture, and found myself gazing into a sumptuously appointed apartment. From the delicacy and luxuriousness of the decorations, I assumed it was a lady's boudoir.

I had but slender opportunity to observe the decor, however, as my attention was seized by the two figures who stood within the center of the room. They were a man and a woman, but I could not see their faces and from the faint murmur of their voices I could not even make out what they were saying to each other, except that the woman seemed to be pleading tenderly and the man giving quiet refusal.

With a shock of amazement I saw that the man was none other than my princely patron, Vaspian himself!

Or—as his back was turned to me and I could see nothing of his features—I assumed that the figure was that of Prince Vaspian. At least he wore a green cowled cloak like the one I had observed the son of Arkola to don before leaving the council chamber some little while before.

And now as he embraced the woman passionately, his hood fell back as the movement of his arms dislodged it, and I saw that he had the same sleek, black hair as the Prince.

And the next moment I made a discovery that drove the breath from my body in a gasp of astonishment . . . a discovery which plunged my spirits into profound depression . . . a discovery at which I turned silently away with averted face and bowed shoulders, and left the maze of secret tunnels for the quiet of my room.

For in the intensity of their emotions, the man swung the woman he was embracing about so that from my secret hiding place I could see her features perfectly.

That rippling glory of red-gold hair—that tawny amber

skin—that full, ripe, passionate mouth and those slanted, glorious eyes of deep emerald mystery—there could be no mistake.

It was Darloona of Shondakor, the woman I loved!

Darloona, clasped in a close embrace, her tear-wet cheeks
and quivering ripe lips giving clear evidence of the intensity
of her emotion, with—*Prince Vaspian!*

CHAPTER VII
MARUD'S MISSION

The apartments that formed the suite of Prince Vaspian were superb. Glistening floors of marble tile, walls of fretted stone hung with beautiful old tapestries, lit by hanging lamps of pierced silver. There were, surprisingly, very few servants. I suppose this reflected the all but neurotic suspicions the Prince held towards nearly everyone around him. There were few that he felt he could trust, least of all, his servants.

The apartments were in a far corner of one wing of the royal palace, quite secluded and separated by many rooms from the main corridors. I was given a small but comfortably furnished room situated between the Prince's living quarters and the main palace. I suppose that Vaspian figured any foes or spies or assassins dispatched by his enemies would have to manage to get past me before they could do him whatever harm they contemplated. The whole situation would have been rather amusing if it had not been so depressing.

During my first few days as chief bodyguard in the retinue of the Prince I had little enough to do. The Chac Yuul were still, in many ways, an occupying force—a conquering horde, holding the territories they had seized and momentarily expecting to have to do battle for them. Hence there was little in the way of court functions, balls, or masquerades. Arkola held court each day towards the hour of noon, signing proclamations, judging disputes, settling quarrels. The afternoon he spent training with his warriors or reviewing them.

Prince Vaspian had little interest in either of these matters. He was a very spoiled young man, vain and suspicious, idle and without any particular interests that I could see. He was certainly no warrior, hence mingling with the Black Legion soldiers was distasteful to him. Nor did he seem interested in the internal administration of the Legion and kept well away from his father's court of justice. It was the shadowy subworld of plot and counterplot, political maneuvering and rivalry, that consumed him. Those of the lords of the Black Legion that I had observed thus far were, with the single exception of Ool the Uncanny, and perhaps with the exception of the Usurper himself, simple war leaders, hard, strong men of camp and field, totally disinterested in the court intrigues of the Byzantine variety favored by Prince Vaspian. I have no doubt that Murrak and the other war leaders disliked Vaspian, for he was not at all their sort, and his sharp tongue, furtive eyes, and clever words would earn him few friends in any circle. But I could hardly conceive that they were plotting against him. For the most part, they simply left him alone.

As for Arkola, he seemed alternately amused and disgusted by his son. He seemed an able administrator and a powerful leader of men, with enormous charisma and an almost total lack of scruples. The oily intrigues, the cunning hints, the psychotic aura of suspicion and deceit and fear and envy that hung constantly about his son roused him to contempt.

While Vaspian seldom showed himself at what few court functions there were, he insisted on my being present. I was supposed to report back to him the words and actions of his "enemies." And thus I suffered through endless tribal disputes, property settlements, arguments over new laws, and the like. Upon my return to the Prince's quarters each day I was endlessly questioned about every conceivable detail of what had taken place. In what tone of voice had this or that *komor* argued for his clan? To whom did this or that lord glance when a certain question was raised? Had I seen this captain of the Chac Yuul whispering to that Captain? Were any notes passed at the tribal court? Endless, reiterative, and boring were these sessions with the Prince my patron; and were it not for the fact that my service in his retinue had gained me entrance into the palace where Darloona was held, I cannot but think I should long since have somehow severed relations.

As for Darloona, I hardly ever saw her, and never close enough to speak to or even close enough for her to see me. A couple of times she appeared at the evening banquet, usually on the Prince's arm, and since I was stationed immediately behind the cushioned seat where Vaspian sat at table, the first time she made her appearance I was seized with fear that she would recognize me. But it seems that it is not the custom of the Chac Yuul to mingle with their women at table, and hence she was seated some distance from the lords of the Black Legion.

I devoured her with my eyes, being careful to cast my own gaze downwards whenever she chanced to look my way.

But the eyes of the Princess invariably passed over me without lingering for a single moment or displaying the slightest flicker of either interest or recognition.

But it seems that my surreptitious gaze had caught the attention of at least one of the Lords of the Black Legion.

For, turning my eyes from Darloona, I found the cold, slitted gaze of Ool the Uncanny fixed upon me with speculative curiosity. A slight smile hovered over the placid features of the little wizard-priest, and I turned my eyes away with a semblance of indifference, trying to convey the impression that my attention to the Princess had merely been curiosity or some other idle emotion, and that I had not really noticed that my actions were under the scrutiny of Ool.

During my tenure in the ranks of the Black Legion I had set about to learn something of its recent history.

I had heard a few puzzling and cryptic hints as to the mode whereby the Chac Yuul had taken the walled city of Shondakor on the banks of the river Ajand. It was a bit curious that the city should have fallen so swiftly and so easily to its enemies. Generally, a city so walled about with strong masonry and so closely guarded, as from its gates and portcullises and barbicans and guard towers Shondakor seemed to have been, would have been able to stand against a siege for a very considerable length of time. I had heard, ere now, some reference to the fact that Shondakor had fallen virtually without siege—that the Black Legion warriors had been within the walls in force even before the first alarm was given.

I became friendly with some officers of my own rank who were also attached to palace duty, although I was careful not to form any relationship with a member of the retinue of any of the other lords, for fear of arousing the suspicions of my patron. Plying them with liquor on our off-duty hours, I learned much of the conquest of Shondakor.

Rather than bore my reader with a lengthy account of these conversations, I shall give the gist of what I gleaned from hours of desultory talk.

It seems that there was a secret entrance into the city

known to but a few. Shondakor was very ancient and many kings had held sway over the Golden City of the Ku Thad. During the long-ago days of some remote dynasty, a hidden entrance had been built whereby the main gates could be circumvented. Even the present royal house was not in possession of this secret, but the arts of Ool the Uncanny had, it seemed, discovered the whereabouts of the hidden door and by its means the Black Legion had gained entry into the city in numbers sufficient to take it before an adequate defense could be mounted.

As my reader can imagine, this news I found most exciting. If such a route could be made known to the Ku Thad force hiding in the jungles of the Grand Kumala, they might make very good use of this information to retake the city themselves. It would indeed be ironic if the secret entrance which had permitted the Black Legion to gain entry into Shondakor were to prove the very method of their undoing.

The secret entrance was not exactly a secret after all, as many hundreds of the Chac Yuul had gone through it before the gates were seized and the main body of the Legion entered the city.

Ere long I found one of the squat little warriors who had been among the advance guard into the city, and luckily he had a weakness for a certain strong liquor called *quarra*. From him I learned that the hidden route was not a secret gate in the walls, but a passageway tunneled beneath the walls and beneath the river itself! An astounding engineering feat, to be sure; and now that I knew the secret it was vital that I somehow pass it along to Lord Yarrak and his warriors. But I could hardly ride out of the city and into the jungles without arousing the suspicions of the Chac Yuul.

Fortunately, before parting from Lord Yarrak, he had envisioned the possibility that I should require a method of communication with him, and he had given me the name of a certain innkeeper in Shondakor who was friendly to the royal cause and who acted in the capacity of a secret agent, smuggling out information to the Ku Thad whenever it became needful to do so.

On one of my off-duty hours I found occasion to enter this inn, which was called The Nine Flagons, and drawing the innkeeper aside I exchanged with him the secret password which Yarrak had taught me. I entrusted to him a letter to Lord Yarrak wherein I divulged the hidden entrance to the tunnel. In that letter I also counseled Lord Yarrak to be patient and not to use the secret tunnel until such time as I gave the word, for I had yet to arrange with the Princess our escape.

The innkeeper, a large, red-faced man named Marud, promised to convey the message that very night.

"Gods, Captain," he wheezed, for Vaspian had elevated me to the rank of *komad* upon entering his service. "I have kept my eyes and ears open for months, strivin' to learn how these bandy-legged little horebs whelmed the city so sudden-like, and naught did I get for all my pains. You should only know how much free wine I ha' poured down Chac Yuul gullets trying to loosen a few tongues!" He chuckled, his vast paunch quivering with seismic ripples of humor.

"They be a close-mouthed lot, yet you ha' pried some valuable matters out," he said.

"You will have no difficulty in getting through the secret tunnel, will you?" I asked. "I have not been able to discover if it is guarded or not, but if it is, at least no guards are stationed out in the open."

He winked, grinning with irrepressible humor.

"Never you mind your heart about *that*, Captain! Old Marud has a trick er two in his old head. You just get along back to your place in th' palace, and leave the rest of it to me. I'll get yer letter into the hands of my Lord Yarrak, never you fear!"

And wiping his red hands on a filthy apron, the bald, fat little old innkeeper went waddling off to tend to the needs of his customers. I stood and watched him go with a bemused eye.

Vast of paunch, red of face, short of breath, the wheezing old fellow certainly did not have about him the air of a hero—he looked more the buffoon, if anything. But this very night would try his qualities to the utmost, and we should see if he had the stuff of heroes in him.

Rarely had so much ridden upon the shoulders of a single man.

Darloona's fate, and my own, and that of all Shondakor, lay in that letter old Marud had so carelessly stuffed into his leathern girdle. Well . . . we should see what happened. . . .

I returned to the palace without incident and made my way to the remote corner of that wing wherein the Prince's suite of rooms was found. I disrobed and sought my pallet, but sleep did not come to me for a long time. For I was baffled by this priest they called Ool the Uncanny, and I marveled that he, and outsider, should have known of the secret tunnel under the walls of Shondakor when even the ruling dynasty of the city knew it not. (For had they known it existed, surely they would have had it guarded heavily or sealed up.)

What strange powers did this little man possess? And what role was he to play in this adventure?

At length, despite the tension and turmoil in my mind, the urge to sleep overcame me and I slumbered.

The skies of Thanator, those strange, shifting skies of golden vapor, lit suddenly with the sourceless glory of the dawn.

I became aware of running feet thudding down the corridor beyond my chamber. The shouts of distant voices came to me, and there was urgency in them although I could not make out any words. On sudden impulse I rose, drew on my leathern tunic, slung the baldric, scabbard, and sword about my shoulders, laced on my buskins, and went out to learn, if I could, the nature of this unwarranted excitement.

I intercepted a guard captain whom I knew slightly.

"What is all the disturbance, Narga? Is the palace being attacked?" I asked, laying my hand on his shoulder as he hurried by me.

"No, Jandar, nothing like that. But they have taken a spy!" he said curtly.

"Who has?"

"They who serve the Lord Ool," was his rejoinder. "The spy was attempting to use the secret passage under the river and the walls, but was seized by the guards which the Lord Ool had commanded to be posted at that place."

The chill breath of presentiment was blowing upon my nape.

"Is the name of the spy known?" I asked, with whatever semblance of casualness I could summon.

He nodded. "It is one Marud, a fat innkeeper of the city," he grunted. "It seems he was attempting to convey some sort of message to the rebels in the jungle, but the Uncanny One, with his shadowy arts, gained forewarning of the plot."

"I see," I said, and I fear my face went pale at this dire news, although so dim was the illumination at this hour that I doubt if my acquaintance noticed.

"Was he taken with the message on him?" I asked.

"No; or so I have been told. They seized him and carried him before Arkola the Warlord, but. . . ."

"But?"

"But he snatched a dagger from one of the guards escorting him and slew himself before he could be questioned," he said. And then, saying he was called to his post, he bid me good-day and went on down the corridor, leaving me to my thoughts.

Alas, brave, loyal Marud! Obviously, he had slain himself rather than betray my part in this business. I felt a qualm of conscience. A man had killed himself to save me. Or, rather, to save me that I might yet serve the Princess Darloona.

Well, he was not the first patriot to die in the service of a worthy cause, and he would not be the last. But I determined then and there that, once this dire business was resolved, and all our present dangers at an end, Marud's sacrifice should not be forgotten nor his name go unremembered.

But one overwhelming question soon filled my mind to the exclusion of all other matters. Had Marud been seized *before* delivering my letter to Lord Yarrak—or *after* doing so?

During that morning I made inquiry as best I could, but none could answer me this riddle. Marud had been arrested in the entrance to the tunnel, but he could either have been about to leave the city or about to reenter it at the time he was seized. And no one knew which!

Unless it was Ool the Uncanny!

CHAPTER VIII
OOL THE UNCANNY

For the next couple of days I walked cautiously, expecting at almost any time to be arrested. But nothing of that nature came to pass, nor was I under surveillance, so far as I could judge, or even under suspicion. Gradually, I relaxed, thinking myself safe and my role in the unfortunate martyrdom of Marud unknown.

My patron had dispatched me on an errand of small importance, which took me into a portion of the palace I had never visited till now.

Delivering his message, I was on my way back to Prince Vaspian's apartments when suddenly a soft voice from behind me halted me in my tracks.

I turned to look into the cold, glinting eyes of Ool the Uncanny!

The fat little man smiled at the involuntary expression of surprise that must have shown on my features.

"Ah, it is the *komad* Jandar," he purred in his silky voice. "We have not yet had the opportunity to meet, *komad*, although I have followed your rise in the ranks with considerable interest."

"I am surprised that the Lord Ool has any interest at all in a mere warrior such as myself," I said. He laughed in a most peculiar way without making a sound.

"Ah, but I am interested in everything which touches upon the safety of my Lord Prince Vaspian," he said. "Come— you have a moment, surely—there is chilled wine in my quarters here—indulge me for a moment."

I accepted his invitation after some little hesitation. I was in no way afraid of this fat, buttery little priest, and I was very curious to know more about him. So I permitted him to usher me into a large chamber where he evidently dwelt.

It was a spacious, sunny room, very comfortably furnished, with thick carpets and gorgeous wall hangings and cushioned chairs. He poured me an excellent yellow wine in frosted goblets of silver and set beside me a platter of small pastries and cold sliced meats. I observed to myself that this priest obviously did not live in stark poverty but liked his bodily comforts.

I also resolved not to sample aught of food and drink in his presence, lest it be embued with some narcotic of a tongue-loosening nature. So I but moistened my lips with the wine and politely refused the pastries, saying I had just eaten, which was true enough.

Ool seated himself across from me and folded his plump soft hands across his belly, regarding me with cunning, observant eyes and a slight smile which did nothing to warm the coldness of his reptilian gaze. And I became aware that he had seated me so that I faced the windows and my face was clearly illuminated, while he himself had his back to them and was in shadow.

"Now, then, *komad*, we can gossip for a breath in comfort.... I believe you were last in service to the Lord of Soraba?"

I replied that this was true.

"And was my Lord Kaamurath still regnant in that city when you were there?" he inquired, which rather surprised me, for when we had chosen Soraba to be my fictitious last place of mercenary service we did so on the knowledge that the Black Legion had been far distant from that city on the shores of the Corund Laj for years, and hence there was little likelihood of my having to answer any embarrassing questions about a city which I had never seen in my life.

"Why, yes," I replied, "although somewhat aged."

This was true, or so Lord Yarrak had assured me. For he had carefully primed me with certain items of information about Soraba in case I *did* have to answer any queries about my service in that city.

Ool nodded thoughtfully, and then inquired after the health of someone called Lord Urush. I had never heard of this personage, and decided to temporize. So I laughed and said that I had been a mere swordsman in the city guard and had come into only the smallest contact with the great lords.

Ool's smile deepened. I did not like the way he smiled. Nor the cold glitter of his black eyes as they peered cunningly at me.

"Naturally, that would be so," he purred. "Yet is it not odd that with only a few weeks service here in Shondakor you have risen to a high rank and a place beside the Prince Vaspian himself, while for all the length of your service in Soraba you remained a mere swordsman?"

I shrugged with seeming casualness, although perspiration was running down my ribs under my leather tunic.

"No, not odd at all, my lord. My commander in Soraba was a self-seeking man who sought to curry favor with the great houses of that city by promoting only their younger sons, and passing over deserving but less well-attached warriors like myself. And as you must know, my lord, it was not my military honors which attracted the favor of my Lord Prince Vaspian to elevate me to his retinue, but a lucky chance whereby I was able to rescue him from danger by halting a runaway thaptor."

"Ah, yes, somewhat of that story I have heard ere now—a most fortunate accident indeed, as the Prince was unharmed by it, and as you rose to good fortune by this same accident. From what land do you hail, *komad?* Never have I met a man with eyes and hair the color of yours."

"A country called the United States of America," I replied.

"What an odd name! I do not believe that I have ever heard of that city. Where is it?" he inquired lazily, and still that smile hovered about his full lips.

I felt that I was being played with, but there was nothing that I could do about it. Now I knew what it was like to be a small mouse at the pleasure of a smiling, lazy, fat, and very well-fed cat.

"It lies a very great distance from these parts," I said, and truthfully enough. "I am uncertain of the direction, for I have been long from my homeland and have visited many lands since leaving it."

"It must indeed be very distant," Ool said lazily, "for I have never heard of it, and geography has long been a hobby of mine. Tell me, *komad*, do all of your fellow citizens in that land have eyes of such a rare color?"

"No, not all. We are a nation made up of several peoples who have long interbred. A considerable number of my fellow countrymen have blue eyes, however. They seem to be the most rare here."

"Indeed they are, most rare, most rare indeed!" he said,

and once again he gave that soundless laugh which made my skin crawl, although for the life of me, I could not say why. But there was something about this fat, soft, mild-seeming little wizard-priest that instinctively put me on the alert. I had the feeling that he was about as harmless as a cobra.

I brought the interview to a close at this point, pleading that I dared not be too long absent from the side of my patron.

"Ah, yes, the Lord Prince is somewhat, shall we say—oversuspicious?" he purred, rubbing his fat little hands together. "He has the strange feeling that he is surrounded by unfriendly persons with great secrets—an odd thing to fear, is it not? Tell me, *komad*, have you secrets which you hold to yourself?"

I forced an awkward laugh. "Of course, my lord! Does not every man have a secret or two?"

He laughed again, rising to usher me out of his silken little nest.

"Oh, yes—but some of us have the most astounding secrets!" he chuckled, and I did not like the sound of that remark at all.

I bowed my farewell and made my way off down the corridor. And all the way I felt his cold, glittering little eyes on me until I had turned the corner and was out of sight.

And thus concluded my private interview with Ool the Uncanny. I had the feeling that he either knew or suspected that there was something about me which I did not wish known. But he did not thereafter interfere with my actions nor make any report of me to those who were my superiors, so I could not be certain.

But thereafter I avoided him as best I could. And, luckily, Prince Vaspian did not again send me into that portion of the royal palace.

*　　*　　*

The following evening and for several nights thereafter I attended my patron at these court feasts I have ere now spoken of, so I had frequently the opportunity of seeing Darloona and of observing her in public.

Ool the Uncanny was often present on these occasions, so I was careful not to let myself seem overly interested in the Princess. I felt he was already suspicious of me for some reason, and I was anxious not to attract his attentions any more than I could help. Luckily for my peace of mind, Prince Vaspian had an unholy horror of the fat little wizard and a marked aversion to his presence, and whenever they were thrown2Ointo close proximity, as during a council meeting or one of these royal feasts, he avoided the presence of Ool in a very obvious manner. Ool did not seem to take any affront at this, but merely smiled his placid, Buddha-like smile.

Hence, although we did speak and she took no notice of me whatever, I saw quite a bit of my princess during the course of these long state dinners.

Her demeanor at these feasts was proud and reserved. Although splendidly robed and adorned with flashing gems and plates of precious metals, she seemed more of a helpless prisoner than a reigning queen-to-be. She spoke little to the other women at her table. They were mostly women of the Chac Yuul, the wives or daughters or mistresses of the Black Legion chieftains, bold-eyed, barbaric, and quarrelsome. Constantly they made slighting remarks about her apparel or deportment, and went off into gales of nasty laughter at almost everything she did, until my hands ached where they gripped tightly the hilts of my sword and dagger, and I yearned to spring down among them and scatter them left and right. But I said nothing, holding my peace, sometimes with very great effort, and I do not think that any at the feast observed anything out of the way in my manner.

When she would enter or leave the hall, always on the arm of the smirking Prince, they talked in low voices. She did not hesitate to accept his arm; neither did she greet him with any perceptible animation or enthusiasm. For the life of me, I could not figure out her true feelings for Prince Vaspian. Surely, they did not act like lovers, for all that the Prince lingered over her hand, kissing it and whispering to her in a semblance of intimacy. Her features remained pale, her expression reserved, and if she did not decline speech with him, neither did she seem to welcome it with any marked pleasure.

I began to wonder if the Prince did not perhaps have some hold over her. Had he seized some advantage over her so that she did not dare openly affront him or rebuff his fawning attentions before the chieftains of the Black Legion?

For it did not seem possible that she could love him. I have no doubt but what the proud and fiery Princess of Shondakor was capable of a strong and passionate devotion, but she was too much the woman, and he too little the man, for him to have earned her love without some manner of coercion.

You can see the dilemma that confronted me.

I had gained my entrance into the city in disguise for the sole purpose of effecting her rescue. But now—how could I be certain that Darloona, in truth, *wanted* to be rescued?

And I could not help remembering how, many weeks ago, when Koja and Darloona and I were all prisoners of the wily and unscrupulous but handsome and charming Prince Thuton of Zanadar, she had willingly accepted the smoothly spoken Prince as her friend and ally and, almost, her betrothed. When Lukor and I had forcibly rescued her from his clutches, at first she was violently angry with me and denounced my assistance as unwanted. Was this adventure to be a repetition of that earlier fiasco? I could not be sure, but one thing was certain: before I attempted to free her from the hands of the Black Legion, I must hear from her own lips whether or not she was in love with Prince Vaspian.

And always before my mind's eye I saw again that terrible scene in her boudoir when she had stood, clasped in the cloaked arms of one I was convinced was none other than Vaspian, pleading passionately with him, her tear-wet cheeks and shining emerald eyes lifted to scan his visage, concealed from me by the angle at which he stood.

Had it been a love scene I had spied upon unwittingly?

If so, how could I reconcile the subdued and reserved manner of her public meetings with him, against the tempestuous emotions she had displayed when clasped in his arms in privacy?

There was simply no other course for me to follow.

I *must* have words with Darloona—and soon!

As my luck would have it, that very night an opportunity to speak privately with Darloona occurred.

Vaspian's one vice, insofar as I had yet discovered, was a fondness for a certain substance called Dream Lotus.

This was a powerful narcotic which dulled the senses and set the mind whirling free amidst a thousand gorgeous but substanceless dreams. In moments of despondency or boredom, my patron would lock himself within his private quarters, imbibe heavily of the noxious fumes of the Dream Lotus, and spend the remainder of the night sunk deep in a drugged slumber.

This night, seething with fury over some fancied slight, or perhaps due to a neurotic conviction that his faceless, and as yet unknown, foes had gained a slim ascendancy, he slunk, snarling and cursing, into his den, loudly calling for his pipe and canister of the Lotus. I was satisfied that he would not stir the remainder of the night, and thus could make no un-expected call upon my presence. Since my quarters were the outermost of all his suite, I could pretty much come or go as I pleased, and so, wrapping myself in a dark cloak, tossing my baldric over my shoulders, I set off for my long-delayed interview with Darloona.

I selected a poorly lit and seldom used corridor that wound into a virtually abandoned portion of the palace. There, in a dusty, neglected chamber, I scanned the wall for the secret sign which I had discovered to mark the sliding panels which gave one entry into the network of hidden passages wherewith these walls were tunneled.

I stifled an exclamation as the dim light of my flickering lanthorn showed the small cryptic symbol. In a moment my fingers had probed for and found the secret spring. There was a click, a grating of hidden gimbals, and a black opening yawned before me, into which I plunged without a moment's hesitation, letting the heavy arras fall behind me.

I strode with rapid yet silent steps through the winding passages within the walls of the palace. On many previous tours I had familiarized myself with the small painted signs that gave indication of direction. Thus oriented, I made my way by the shortest route to the area of the palace wherein the apartments of the Princess were situated.

My heart was in my mouth as I strode through the dark-ness, and I must confess my mouth was dry, my brow damp with moisture, and my heart pounding to the hurried rhythm of my throbbing pulse. It was not inconceivable that the words I would soon hear from the lips of the Princess would forever change the future of my life. For—what if she truly loved Prince Vaspian of the Black Legion? What if her impending nuptials were indeed of her own free choosing, and were not somehow being forced upon her by threats of some dire punishment?

My heart turned to lead within my breast. If such were to prove the case, then the words I should hear from the lips of the incomparable Princess I loved would be tantamount to a death sentence.

For although never yet had I spoken of my love to Darloona, and although the gap between my own lowly station and her exalted rank would likely prove an insurmountable obstacle, still in the secret places of my heart there burned, clear and pure and brilliant, the small flame of hope.

That love which is completely without hope is not love at all, but a black and bitter canker eating at the heart. Would this prove to be my doom? Did she—*could* she—love the Prince of the Black Legion?

The answer to this enormous question I would perhaps learn in the next few moments.

And so, with what inward trepidation I give my reader freedom to imagine for himself, I approached the passages that led to the secret spyhole and sliding panel in the wall of Darloona's apartments.

All was impenetrable gloom, yet here I must douse my lamp, for the slightest bit of light might well be visible through some crack or cranny of the walls, and it would never do to give advance warning of my presence. I could not know for certain that the Princess was alone.

Hooding my lantern under a dark cloth which I had carried for that very purpose, I went forward into utter blackness on wary, silent feet.

And froze with astonishment!

For ahead of me, limned with dim radiance against the gloom, I glimpsed the face of an unknown man.

His features were masked behind a black vizor and all that was visible was the glitter of his eyes, which were set against the spyhole in the wall. Lights from the apartment beyond dimly illuminated his profile.

Another had come to spy upon Darloona in the dark!

I drew back in mingled consternation and alarm, and I fear I stumbled slightly in the blackness, for my foot dislodged some bit of loose stone. The clatter of the stone seemed horribly loud in the utter stillness of the black passageway, and at the sound the unseen watcher snatched his face away from the peephole and, thus, vanished completely.

With drumming pulses, my breath coming in quick short gasps, I stood silent, searching the blackness with every sense for the slightest sign of my opponent's position. I could not see or hear him, but I sensed his presence. My flesh prickled and my nape hairs stirred, as if with some sixth sense I registered the pressure of invisible eyes.

Then a beam of blinding light struck me full in the eyes—a naked steel blade flashed for my heart—and in the next instant I found myself fighting for my life.

BOOK THREE

THE BOOK OF VALKAR

CHAPTER IX
A FIGHT IN THE DARK

This was far from being the first time I had ever fought for my life, and it was not likely to be the last. But I sincerely pray to whatever gods may be that never again shall I find myself in so hopeless and desperate a situation.

A battle in the narrow confines of a secret passage is bound to be a difficult one, but when both you and your opponent are totally invisible to each other, the result is chaos.

I could hear the sound of his heavy breathing, the rasp of his buskins against the stone floor, the cling and click and slither of our swords—but in the complete darkness, I could see nothing, nothing at all!

My own sword was clear of its scabbard in a trice and I managed to engage and parry his blade to one side, but it was so close that his point drew a thread of scarlet agony across my chest, slicing through my leathern tunic. A fraction of an inch deeper and I would not be here to tell the tale.

I fought a purely defensive bout, and it took all of my science to keep that unseen sword tip from my throat. I paced backwards, step by step, yielding to his advance, and all the while I searched my wits for some way to disengage and flee—for at any instant the sound of our combat might arouse the occupants of the suites beyond the wall, and the passage might be filled with guards. My imposture would be revealed, I would be taken prisoner, and all of my hopes of giving succor to the Princess in her peril and her captivity would be dashed into the blackest depths of despair.

But, in the meantime, it was all I could do to defend myself against the attack of my invisible opponent.

Never have I fought so brilliantly as in that hour. If it had not been for the thousand tricks and tactics of advanced swordsmanship I had learned during my tutelage under the guidance of Lukor, one of the greatest swordsmen of all Thanator, I would have been slashed to ribbons or spitted upon my opponent's blade in a trice.

Whoever he was, he was a master swordsman in his own right. And this was, when I later had the leisure to ponder it, a bit puzzling. For doubtless he was some lord or warrior of the Chac Yuul, and the Chac Yuul are by no means schooled in the finer points of the art of fence. They are mounted warriors, for the most part, used to chopping away with heavy cutlass-like cavalry weapons, and far more familiar with the uses of spear, battle-ax, and morning star, than with the rapier. Yet my opponent was a marvelous swordsman of consummate skill and of a degree of science that came near to equaling my own. And, with all due modesty, I may safely claim to be one of the finest swordsmen on all of this jungle world of terror and mystery.

The duel was fast and furious, but it did not occupy very much time. In fact, it was over in a few seconds.

For I had backed by now into the corridor, and yielding before the furious assault of my unseen foe, suddenly I stumbled again—this time over my own lantern—and fell flat on my back.

In falling, my foot tore away the cloth whereby I had shielded the glow of my lantern. The sudden burst of brilliant light must have bedazzled and even temporarily blinded my foeman, for his blade faltered, and although he could probably have put a length of steel through my breast as I sprawled prone and momentarily stunned, he blundered.

In the next instant I sprang to one knee and my own blade flashed in a lucky stroke. So dazzled was he by the sudden flare of illumination that he did not parry the stroke and the tip of my steel caught him in a shallow cut across the cheek, just below the black silken vizor that masked his unknown features.

It was only a slight scratch, but it would nevertheless take some days to heal, and it occurred to me that should I chance to encounter my unknown assailant in the next few days, I should be able to identify him by the wound.

Seizing the opportunity for flight, he sprang backwards, ducked into a side branch of the secret passage, and was gone in an instant.

I sprang to my feet, ready to give pursuit, but the sound of clattering footsteps came to my ears and I heard curt, questioning voices and the clank and clamor of metal accouterments, and knew that someone had heard the sounds of our duel in the dark and had given the alarm, summoning the guards.

Thus it was that I hastily retraced my steps to avoid the chance of discovery. And I did not that night, after all, have the opportunity to hear from the lips of my beloved princess whether or not she had truly given her heart into the keeping of another.

*   *   *

For the next day or two Prince Vaspian kept me busy to such an extent that it was impossible for me to contrive a private interview with the Princess.

The morning following my duel in the dark against a mysterious foe I scrutinized the Prince's features closely, without appearing to do so, and was curiously relieved to discover his face innocent of the slightest scratch. I say "relieved," but actually my emotions were somewhat more mixed. I knew the Prince knew little of the art of fence, and thus it did not seem likely that it was the son of Arkola with whom I had battled in the black gloom of the secret passage, for whoever my unknown opponent had been, he was a brilliant swordsman of superb skills.

And yet, since it had been the Prince who had instructed me in my first knowledge of the secret passages, I knew that he was well aware of them; and as Darloona had once been mistress of all this palace, and presumably was privy to a knowledge of the network of passages within her own walls, and since I believed the two of them were lovers, he was the most likely candidate to have been my nameless foe. For I had yet to encounter another person in my explorations of the secret passages.

Two days after my duel in the dark Prince Vaspian required me to attend him at a court function of such importance that his presence was commanded by the Usurper. Certain officers of the Black Legion were to receive acclamation for their bravery or ability at command, and all the lords of the Chac Yuul were required to be present.

The function took place in a mighty hall, high-ceilinged and lit by a thousand tapers. The hall was thronged with barbaric warriors and splendid chieftains adorned in all their wealth of savage finery, and among them all the Prince my patron shone in the jeweled splendor of his raiment. Nodding plumes crowned his burnished helm, gems glittered from the hilt of his sword, and badges and honors of precious metals encrusted his tunic and girdle.

As he circled the hall, I paced silently behind him, a pace or two to the rear. My stay in the Black Legion had not yet covered a sufficient interval of time for me to have made the acquaintance of any of these chieftains, and thus it was with some surprise that I felt a hand clap me on the shoulder and turned about to meet a friendly smile in a familiar face.

"Ah, Jandar, it is a pleasure to greet you again!" cried a warm voice, and I realized that it was my former comrade and commander, Valkar of Ganatol.

"How do you like palace duty?" he inquired. "Somewhat different, I am certain, from the hard life of barracks and practice field, eh?" He laughed and I forced a smile, but ere we could exchange more than a few words my Prince shrilly demanded my presence, darting a suspicious glance at Valkar, and I was forced to bid the *komor* a hasty adieu.

"Some night when you can get free, meet me at the wineshop beside the forum—do you recall the place where we shared a bottle after the theater that night?" he called. I smiled and nodded, but had to turn away for the Prince's hand was on my arm and his jealous eyes were taking in every detail of my chance acquaintance.

"Who is that fellow to whom you spoke?" he hissed.

"It is the chieftain Valkar under whom I served in the third cohort, Lord—surely you recall questioning him about my record of service, after I was lucky enough to halt your runaway thaptors?"

"Ah, yes; I remember him now," he muttered, and the light of jealousy and suspicion died from his pinched, sharp features; however he retained his clutch on my arm. "Do not stray away from my side again, Jandar; I require your constant attendance, for here I am virtually surrounded by those who call themselves my friends but who secretly plot behind my back."

I nodded and obediently fell into place behind him, and it was all that I could do to keep a wooden expression on my features. Shock, astonishment, and surprise whirled through my brain.

For it would have been indeed a pleasure to renew my friendship with the gallant, gentlemanly Valkar, had it not been for the scratch on his cheek—*the scratch my sword had made two nights before, when we had battled in the dark!*

The remainder of that festive evening is but a blur to me. Strive as I may, I can recall but a giddy panorama of plumed warriors and beautiful women. Resounding speeches were made and toasts were drunk, but I recall neither the speeches nor those whom the toasts saluted.

For I could not expunge from my mind that it was Valkar whom I had battled in the darkness of the secret passage—Valkar whom I had surprised in the very act of spying upon the apartment of the Princess Darloona—Valkar who had been prowling the secret passages, masked and cloaked, in the darkness of the night!

After returning to my quarters following the close of the festivities, I disrobed and stretched out on my bed, but sleep came not easily to me. My mind was a bewildered turmoil of unanswered questions and unsolved mysteries.

I remember that night at the theater to which Valkar had made reference, and I recalled the strange intensity of his gaze and the pallor of his features as he gazed upon Darloona, seated at the side of Prince Vaspian in the royal box.

At the time his tension and the alertness of his gaze had puzzled me, but only slightly, and in the flow of events I had all but forgotten the incident, which seemed in retrospect of little importance. But now I was no longer certain just how important it might have been.

And I recalled, as well, an incident in that wineshop to which Valkar had also referred, the wineshop to which we had repaired after the play. The chance stumbling of a servant wench had spilled wine upon the features of my companion, and in wiping his face he had accidentally wiped away some of the swarthy hue of his features. And thus it seemed that Valkar, even as I, was an impostor.

Tossing and turning on my bed, unable to slumber, I puzzled over these baffling mysteries and wondered exactly who and what my friend Valkar really was, and what was his true reason for joining the Black Legion?

And even more important—was he my friend, or my foe?

Long had I anticipated a private interview with Darloona and the opportunity came about at last, but in the most unexpected manner possible.

The impending nuptials of Vaspian and Darloona were now very close. Only a week remained before they would solemnize their vows before the idol of the dark god worshiped by the Chac Yuul barbarians.

And yet another deadline was drawing close, as well. For the ultimatum delivered by Prince Thuton to the Black Legion was almost due for its answer. Thuton demanded a mighty ransom for surrendering his interests in the person of the Princess of Shondakor, and in default of the prompt payment of that price he had sworn to bring the awesome aerial navy of Zanadar down upon the city in war. Soon, very soon, the lords of the Black Legion must decide upon a course of action.

And so must I. For I could not plan any rescue of Darloona until I had heard from her own lips whether she was being forced into marriage with Prince Vaspian, or whether she truly had given him her heart and hand. But how could I get to see her?

The solution to my dilemma came from, of all persons, Prince Vaspian, himself!

He hailed me, a day or so after my chance encounter with Valkar, and bade me attend him.

"Soon, as you know, the Princess Darloona and I shall be wed," he said, and I inwardly writhed in revulsion at the oily, self-satisfied smirk wherewith he accompanied his words. "I have a small gift for my bride-to-be; generally, my tokens are delivered by the hand of my confidential valet, Golar, as you must know; alas, he is busy on another errand this evening, so I entrust the task to you."

I suppressed, with some difficulty, the exclamation of delight which rose to my lips. I do not think that so much as a flicker of surprise or eagerness crossed my features, although within my heart I was shaken by this sudden flash of good fortune. And I am positive that Prince Vaspian observed nothing of my feelings.

"As my prince commands," I said quietly.

He smirked. "There's a good fellow!" Then he pressed into my hands a gorgeous ornament that blazed with precious gems unknown to me and gave me minute directions so that I might find my way to the secluded chambers wherein the Princess dwelt, and a note from his hand that would get me past the guards.

I should explain that while Darloona was not technically a prisoner, she was kept under the closest possible watch and no one might gain entrance into her presence without passing the examination of those watchers assigned to guard her. This surveillance aside, she was permitted the greatest latitude and could command whatever she wished.

*   *   *

Without delay I made my way to her suite by the shortest possible route. As I approached her quarters my heart was thumping like that of a foolish school-boy on his first date, my mouth was dry, and I was mentally composing my speech to her.

The guards stationed at her door halted me, examined the Prince's sign manual which I carried, and became extremely uncomfortable.

"*Komad*, we mean no affront to our lord the Prince, but the Lady Darloona has given us express instruction that she be not disturbed this evening. Since the Warlord, Arkola, has commanded us to obey the Princess in all things, save permitting her to elude surveillance, we thus cannot allow you to pass."

"But it is a message from her betrothed!" I protested. "And surely the Princess cannot have retired to her couch so early in the evening as this. Can you not—"

The officer shook his head with reluctant firmness.

"We are not permitted to transgress against her wishes in such matters," he said. "It is the command of the Lord Arkola that she be given the illusion of freedom and that her privacy be not intruded upon, save in matters of the most dire necessity. We must, therefore, refuse to let you pass."

My face reddened. "But I am expressly commanded by Prince Vaspian to deliver this gift—"

"And I am expressly commanded by the Lord of the Black Legion to obey the wishes of the Princess," he said curtly. Then, misunderstanding my distress as a rather natural fear of returning to my patron with his commands unfulfilled, he softened: "You can, of course, leave the gift with me and I shall see that it is delivered into the hands of the Princess personally. Or you may simply return tomorrow morning and deliver it yourself."

I was seized by a fury of impatience and frustration, but I could not afford to argue. For how could I explain that if I waited till tomorrow, the Prince's confidential valet, Golar, would be back on duty and since a task of this nature was usually assigned to him, I would thus lose my one opportunity to seek a private interview with Darloona without risk of arousing the suspicions of the Chac Yuul?

As there was no recourse, I nodded and turned away, but the turmoil in my breast was such that I did not go far. It was perfectly infuriating to be this close to my goal and unable to progress a single step further.

On sudden impulse I turned aside into certain seldomused side passages and followed them, searching for the unobtrusive sign which I knew denoted a sliding panel which would give me entrance into the system of secret passages within the palace walls.

Ere I had gone far I found that for which I sought. A swift glance revealed I was alone and unobserved. My fingers found and depressed a spring concealed in the carven detail of the wall. A panel slid ajar and I stepped into the darkness.

Without difficulty, so familiar had I become with the system of secret passages by this time, I made my way to the apartments of the Princess. My hand was upon the spring that would open a panel and give me entrance into her boudoir, but a sudden flash of caution bade me survey the room before entering it so abruptly. I found the nearest spyhole, slid aside its cover, and set my eye thereto, peering into the room.

To my astonishment, once more I found myself gazing upon my beloved in the arms of another. A tall man, cloaked and hooded in dark green—surely, it was the same man whom once before I had discovered thus engaged in a tender embrace with the Princess Darloona—a man whom I felt certain was none other than my patron, Prince Vaspian, himself.

But this was most peculiar indeed! Why on earth—or on Thanator, for that matter—would Vaspian have gone out of his way to send me to the Princess with his gift when he was en route to her quarters himself and could easily have delivered the jewelry in person? It simply did not make sense!

Alas, while I stood paralyzed with astonishment at this most puzzling and unexpected development, the hooded man turned swiftly from the embrace of Darloona, bade her farewell, thumbed the spring, and opened the sliding panel.

Before I could rouse myself to action—before I could move away into the dark recesses of the passage or even think of so doing, the secret door opened, bathing me in the light of the room and the cloaked and hooded figure stepped into the passage where I stood frozen and confronted me face to face.

For a moment we both stood motionless, gripped by the surprise of this sudden and unexpected encounter.

Then Darloona's lover forced an unsteady laugh, and said, "Doubtless, friend, you are thinking the same thing, but—whatever are *you* doing here, Jandar?"

CHAPTER X
VALKAR UNMASKED!

I t was not Prince Vaspian at all, but *Valkar!* By the light
of the small lantern he carried I could see him quite
clearly, the guarded expression of his face, and the way
his right hand hovered rather near the hilt of his rapier.

It should not have come as such a surprise as it did. I
should really have been prepared for this discovery. After all,
had I not encountered Valkar, masked, peering into the Princess' suite some days earlier? Had I not marked his face with
my sword during that terrible duel in the dark, and had I not
identified him as my unknown assailant at the court function,
when I saw the fresh scar on his unmasked face?

However, I had by now convinced myself that the cloaked
man I had seen holding Darloona in his arms was my patron,
Prince Vaspian; and such is the power of self-conviction that
it had not even entered my mind that her lover might be
someone else. Now that I began to see things in their true
light, I realized that the Prince and Valkar were about the
same height and build, and that they wore cloaks of identical
design and hue, which was not surprising, as most warriors

of the Chac Yuul wore cloaks of this design—I had one, my-self—and the hair of both was sleek and black.

Valkar saw the blank expression of surprise on my face, and the tension left his handsome features. He laughed and clapped me on the shoulder. "But we cannot converse here, where the guards beyond Darloona's door may hear the muf-fled tones of conversation and become alarmed. Indeed, it is surprising that they did not become earlier alarmed at our recent sword duel—for now I believe that it was you, Jandar, who surprised me peering into the apartments of the Princess to see if she was alone, and who gave me this small scar on the face! Come, I know a place nearby where we can be alone and where no one is likely to overhear us."

He led me to a secluded chamber which, from the accu-mulated dust and other tokens of neglect, was very seldom visited. There he lit a half-consumed candle in a silver holder, threw off his cloak, and turned to regard me with a half se-rious and half humorous gaze.

"I suspect, old friend, that you are here for much the same reason as I—to effect the escape of the Princess Darloona," he said.

"I am. It was for that reason alone that I entered Shon-dakor and sought a place in the fighting forces of the Chac Yuul," I admitted. He nodded.

"It is the same with me. But I do not recognize you as a defender of the cause of the rightful queen of Shondakor," he mused. "Never do I recall having seen you at the court of the Princess, nor even as being among the warrior nobles who fled into the Grand Kumala with the Princess when the treacherous arts of Ool the Uncanny permitted the Black Le-gion to enter and seize the city. Why, then, this desperate mission? Who *are* you, Jandar?"

"I am not a Shondakorian, but a stranger from a far-off

land," I admitted. "I am the man who assisted the Princess to escape from the clutches of the Yathoon Horde when they took her prisoner in the jungle country; and, still later, when she was held captive by Prince Thuton of Zanadar, it was I, together with a friendly renegade Yathoon chieftain named Koja and a gallant old Swordmaster from Ganatol named Lukor, who rescued her from the Cloud City of the Sky Pirates, only to lose her to a patrol of Black Legion warriors. Since her present captivity by the Chac Yuul is in part my own fault, I resolved to gain a place in the Legion and see if I could not undo my failure to adequately protect her by yet once again effecting her freedom and returning her to her people. Thus I disguised my identity with a false history even as you, Valkar, are disguised with cosmetics! For I know that you are truly a Shondakorian, a man of the Ku Thad, and that the color of your skin and hair is false."

This fact that I knew he was disguised came as a bit of a shock to Valkar, and I think that it was this, that I had known for some time of his disguise and had not ever revealed it to the authorities, that convinced him that I was a friend and a defender of the Princess. He blinked, his expression sobering.

"How long have you known this?" he asked slowly.

"Ever since that night in the wineshop when the serving wench spilled wine on you, erasing some of your false skin-coloring," I said. He nodded grimly.

"Against such accidents no man can adequately guard," he admitted. "I recall the incident well; since you made no remark, and gave no sign of having noticed, I assumed that I had managed to repair the damage to my makeup before you observed."

Then his eyes grew thoughtful and he laughed.

"Is it not odd how fate plays small tricks upon we mortals? You and I, I think, instinctively liked and trusted each

LIN CARTER

other and soon became fast friends—both of us spies, infiltrating the ranks of the Black Legion for the same purpose, but neither aware that the other was here for the same reason as himself! It is almost as if our secret sympathy and common cause communicated by some sixth sense, finding a kindred soul to which it felt drawn for unknown reasons." Then he shrugged and a friendly smile warmed his sober features.

"For all these months I have been here in Shondakor, unable to effect Darloona's rescue, although I did manage to win a high rank among the host of the Chac Yuul. Whereas you, Jandar, enter the Legion and almost at once attract the patronage of that sneaking *horeb*,* Prince Vaspian, and are able to come and go in the palace as you please, where I can gain entrance only by the most extraordinary use of caution and agility. I congratulate you on your good fortune! Between the two of us, we may be able to render aid to our Princess."

"If she truly desires our aid," said I, gloomily. He asked my meaning with some surprise, and I recounted to him something of my own suspicions regarding Darloona—suspicions that had been roused by her ambiguous behavior with Prince Vaspian and by her seemingly willing acceptance of his suit. I pointed out reluctantly that I could see no reason why a woman so fiercely proud as Darloona should accept the cowardly and psychotic Vaspian as her consort-to-be unless, by some incredible chance, she had actually fallen in love with the son of Arkola.

"Darloona," I concluded glumly, "is no tender maiden to be frightened into a marriage by threats of punishment. She is strong-willed, a warrior princess if ever there was one, and

*In another place, Captain Dark explains that a *horeb* is a repulsive scavenger of disgusting appearance and even more disgusting habits. It is, in fact, the Thanatorian equivalent of a "rat," and like the terrene rodent it so closely resembles, its name has become a derogatory synonym for a skulking, treacherous person.—L. C.

322

I cannot believe that she would permit any threatened danger to force her into a marriage where love was not. Indeed, I can hardly imagine any threat that could coerce the Princess of the Ku Thad into a wedding with that whining little monster. Unlikely as it seems, she must truly love him!"

He listened to my suspicions with a meditative mien. My reasoning was now somewhat shaken, you will perceive, by the discovery that it was not Vaspian I had surprised in a clandestine embrace with the Princess of Shondakor in the seclusion of her boudoir, but Valkar himself: yet it was true that she had accepted him as her betrothed and that she did not publicly repulse the affections of the Prince. So her behavior in this regard was still a mystery to me.

When I had finished, Valkar wasted no time in setting me to rights on this point.

"Let me relieve your mind on this question, Jandar, my friend," he said vigorously. "The Princess loathes and despises Prince Vaspian as any proud and noble woman of her high birth and breeding could. She has told me that she would rather sheathe a dagger in her heart than accept the hand of Vaspian before the dark altars of the Chac Yuul."

I looked at him with some surprise.

"If this be so," I mused, "why then does she not repudiate her promise to wed the Prince?"

His voice was somber and his eyes smoldered with repressed fires as he explained the puzzle.

"She *dares* not. For Vaspian holds the key to the safety of her people. You see, the policies of the Black Legion are decided by a consensus of the high council of the Lords of the Legion, one of whom is Prince Vaspian."

"So I have been given to understand." I nodded.

"And, hitherto, whenever the question arose of whether it would not be wise for the Legion to protect its rather shaky and insecure control over the citizens of Shondakor by mass executions and imprisonment—a logical, if cold-blooded, course of action which Arkola himself approves most heartily—Prince Vaspian holds the deciding vote, for the council is neatly divided upon this question."

"But why should Vaspian object? Surely, not from any humanitarian considerations, for he is as cold-blooded as the rest of them."

"True." Valkar smiled grimly. "But Vaspian hates his father and wherever possible opposes him in public measures out of sheer spitefulness. Hence he has always cast his vote against the measure in the past, whenever it has come up on the agenda of the council meetings. But he has threatened Darloona in secret that if she does not agree to become his bride, he will raise the matter again and this time cast his vote upon his father's side. It is virtually the only way the Prince can injure his father, whom he hates for being more of a man than himself, and he takes great delight form openly frustrating Arkola's will. And against this sort of rebellion, of course, even so powerful a leader as the Warlord is helpless, due to the very laws of the Black Legion, and their customs and traditions."*

I nodded, remembering the open hostility I had observed

---

*If my reader finds it difficult to understand why so strongly willed and supremely powerful a man as Arkola could be completely helpless in this situation, let me call your attention to what Captain Dark said earlier about the unique traditions of the Chac Yuul. Arkola is an elected leader, chosen from among the various clans and tribes of the free Black Legion warriors to lead them, and his will is unquestioned and his commands obeyed, but only so long as a majority vote of the high council of the Legion supports him. Were a majority of the council members to oppose him, he could be voted from his high office and another chosen in his place. Neither hereditary monarch born to power nor a general commanding by virtue of seniority, Arkola rules only so long as the clan chiefs desire him to do so. This is why Vaspian is able to openly defy his father's wishes, and why Arkola is helpless to discipline the Prince.—L. C.

between Vaspian and Arkola at the council meeting I had attended some days ago.

Valkar continued: "As for Darloona, the only thing the unhappy girl can do to prevent the mass slaughter of her helpless people is to promise to wed the slimy little monster. Thus she dares not repulse his attentions in public."

Why had I never thought of this logical answer to the mystery of her behavior? As the true realization of Darloona's ghastly plight burst upon me, cold sweat bedewed my brow and I tasted the metallic, bitterness of dread.

Of course it was impossible that Darloona could have given her love to the cowardly, whining Prince!

But it was equally impossible that, even with the aid of my newfound ally, Valkar, I could ever persuade Darloona to escape the city with me. For the vengeful and malicious Vaspian would punish her betrayal of him by bringing about the mass execution of the unarmed and captive populace—and she knew it!

Was there ever a dilemma so completely hopeless?

There was utterly nothing that I could do to prevent the woman I loved from marrying the man she loathed and despised from the very bottom of her proud heart.

After a time I roused myself from these grim thoughts and queried my friend Valkar, asking if he had any ideas as to how we could help Darloona resolve her problems.

He shrugged gloomily.

"None whatsoever," he admitted. "Ever since I managed to locate the secret entrance into the palace, whereby to effect my secret interviews with the Princess, I have begged her to flee the city by my side, but to no avail. It is impossible for her to consider such an action, for to do so would mean that she dooms to death the very people who love and trust her, and whom she has sworn to protect. Alas, my poor cousin! She is helpless in such a situation."

"Cousin?" I asked.

"Why, yes. I thought you knew—how stupid of me not to explain who I am. My name really is Valkar, but as you know I am not a Ganatolian, but a prince of the Ku Thad. My father is Lord Yarrak, the Uncle of the Princess, and the leader of the Ku Thad during her captivity."

"I see; yes, I know Lord Yarrak well, he has been my host for some weeks, prior to my joining the Black Legion. Odd that he never mentioned a son—especially a son who had infiltrated the Black Legion in disguise—when he knew I was planning the same sort of thing myself!"

"Not at all, Jandar. My father doubtless believes that I am dead, long since slain in the street fighting when the Chac Yuul first entered the city months ago. We became separated in the confusion, and when the warrior nobles escaped from the city, bearing the Princess away to the safety of the jungles, I remained behind. I was protected by friends among the common folk and stayed in hiding for some time, until matters quieted down. Before I managed to make my escape, the Princess had been captured, and so I remained here without seeking to join my father and my people. Friends in the city helped me disguise my golden skin and flame-red hair, and as a Ganatolian mercenary I gained a place in the ranks of the conquerors, hoping to assist the Princess, my betrothed, to escape later on—"

I fear some involuntary exclamation must have escaped my lips as Valkar spoke these words.

He broke off, staring at me.

"Why, what is it, Jandar? What is the matter? What have I said to disturb you? Why, man, you are white to the lips!"

I forced my features into a semblance of calm and steadied my voice with a considerable effort of will.

"Your—*betrothed?*" I repeated in a low voice.

He shrugged a little and laughed in a self-deprecating way.

"Why—yes. The Princess and I have been betrothed since our childhood. A formal alliance of the two major branches of the blood royal—you understand; that sort of thing."

"I did not know," I said faintly. I felt exactly like a man who had just been kicked in the stomach. And I hope it did not show.

"In Shondakorian custom," he went on idly, "a prince or a princess of the royal house will very often be pledged to marry his or her cousin from earliest ages. Darloona and I would most likely have been married by now had not the Chac Yuul invasion somewhat disrupted the normal flow of events." He chuckled ruefully at this enormous understatement.

"But whatever is it, Jandar? Didn't you know that Darloona and I were to wed?"

"In all truth, no."

He laughed helplessly. "But, surely you must realize that only the fact that Darloona is to be my queen would force me to this dangerous extremity! Only to save my bride-to-be would I take such enormous risks as trying to maintain this masquerade and walk in disguise among the very ranks of they who are my enemies and the enemies of my house."

I nodded wordlessly. I knew exactly what he meant.

And thus was I struck down into the very depths of despair, as must any man be, when he discovers that his best friend also loves the woman whom *he* loves, and has, in fact, already won her love and her promise of marriage!

All these long months of being hopelessly in love with a woman who despised me, who considered me a coward, a fumbler, and a fool—I thought I knew by now what hell was like.

But I had yet to learn what hell could *really* be!

CHAPTER XI

IN THE DEPTHS OF DESPAIR

Yes, I knew what Valkar meant when he said that only his great love for the Princess would have driven him to take such a desperate risk as venturing into the very ranks of the Black Legion in disguise.

I knew it all too well! For I, too, loved Darloona with a hopeless and consuming passion. My devotion to her was almost beyond the ability of words to describe. And only the fact that the woman I loved, the peerless Princess to whom I had given my heart, was in terrible danger would have driven me to the desperate extremity of penetrating the conquered city as an impostor.

Of course I knew exactly what Valkar meant! For I had been driven by the same emotion to risk precisely the same dangers as had he.

I thank God that the parallel did not occur to him, but of course he could have no reason to suspect that my devotion to Darloona was spurred by a passion identical to his own. Had he known this, I think I would have died of shame.

Neither he nor Darloona must ever have reason to suspect

that I love her. Never by word or deed, by look or glance, must I permit either my best friend or the woman I love to guess the depths of my adoration.

It is a foolish passion, I admitted, that I, a homeless and wandering adventurer, a stranger come by chance or accident from another world, a lowly born member of an alien race, dared to love the splendid Princess of Shondakor—what a mockery!

I had known that my love was a hopeless one, of course; known it even before discovering that Darloona had sworn to wed Prince Vaspian of the Black Legion. Her contempt for me, freely expressed upon many occasions; her unfortunate experiences at my bungling and incompetent hands; these and many other factors had given an indication to me that I had been most foolish to admit my love, even to myself!

And so my position had long been a hopeless one. But worse was yet to come!

For the hopelessness of my situation was only increased by a feeling of horror and dread, when I came to realize that the woman I loved was being forced into a marriage with a man she despised—a marriage which she dared not oppose or avoid.

But now I had truly descended into the depths of despair.

For if Valkar and Darloona were in love, and sworn to each other, how could I hope to win the woman of my dreams, even if by some miracle I managed to free her from her vows to Vaspian and from the captivity of the Chac Yuul?

Black, bitter depression filled my aching heart. For I remembered that glimpse through the spyhole. I had seen Valkar with Darloona clasped in a passionate embrace, I had seen her shining eyes lifted to his, her tear-wet cheeks, and had heard the soft warmth of her pleading voice.

I had thought that my only friend in the city of Shondakor was now my accomplice and ally in the task of freeing the woman I loved from those that held her prisoner. And now it seemed that he was my rival for her heart. Nay, no rival, but already the victor in the unequal contest, for he had long since won her love.

And I wished that I had never set foot on the jungled surface of this strange and terrible and beautiful world, and that I had never looked upon Darloona, Warrior Princess of the Ku Thad!

The next day or two passed by without any occurrence of note. I fear I went about my duties like a mindless automaton, or a somnambulist. I hardly managed to pay attention to the things which went on around me. So deeply was I plunged into a black mood of utter despair that my drugged condition and leaden mood must have been obvious to everyone who encountered me. I responded with dull monosyllabic replies whenever anyone chanced to speak to me. I must have looked like a man stricken by some horrible discovery, some overwhelming calamity.

And that is precisely what I was.

But fortunately the Prince my patron dwelt secluded from the more populous sectors of the palace, and as my duties were few and I remained in my room most of the time, few if any could have noticed my depression.

Concluding my secret meeting with Prince Valkar of Shondakor, and without seeking an interview with the Princess Darloona, since it was now futile even to hope, I returned to Vaspian's suite.

The Prince was greatly annoyed that I had not been able to obey his wishes and deliver the trinket to his betrothed, but it was a matter of the smallest importance, and the following morning, when Golar had returned to his duties, he dispatched his confidential valet with the ornament and that was that.

Usually alert and sensitive to the slightest moods of those around him, because of his psychotic fears of plots and spies and his consuming suspicions of the motives of everyone he encountered, the Prince was so caught up in the last-minute preparations for his impending nuptials, now mere days in the future, that I strongly doubt if even he noticed anything out of the way in my behavior. At any rate I saw little of him and spent most of the time in my room, busy with my doleful thoughts.

I believe there can hardly be a more terrible situation in the human condition than to discover that your closest friend has wooed and won the heart of the woman you secretly love. I, at least, have never before tasted such black bitterness, and I pray to the known Lords of Gordrimator, whom the Thanatorians call gods, that I never taste such again.

Valkar and I parted on pledges of mutual assistance, and we arranged to meet secretly a few days before the wedding of Darloona and Prince Vaspian.

What this meeting was supposed to accomplish, I do not believe either of us knew. But as a last-minute attempt to rescue the woman we both loved from the grim results of her folly, we hoped to arrive at some solution to the dark dilemma in which we were immersed.

It may well be that Prince Valkar had thought of the same possible solution to our mutual problem which had also occurred to me. For there was *one* way out of this corner.

Prince Vaspian could—die.

Never have I slain a man in cold blood, and I did not face the prospect with any particular joy. Although the Prince disgusted me, and the manner in which he smirked and strutted and preened himself over his so-called "conquest" of the most

beautiful woman of all Thanator stung me to a fury of loathing, he was personally weak and vain, frivolous and ineffec-
tual—and I could not consider the slaying of such a weakling
as anything more noble than sheer murder.

I have always considered myself a man of honor. But like all
men, I have once or twice in my life done something of which I
was not proud. To strike down this smirking fool in cold blood,
to pit my vastly superior skill with the sword against his feeble
arm and uncertain hand, would be rank cowardice.

Yet I must do it, if I wished to save Darloona from his
unclean lust.

I wrestled with my conscience during those black, bitter
hours. Just how much did I owe this woman, who did not
return my love and was to wed my friend? Must I stain my
honor with cold-blooded and cowardly murder for a woman
who, after all, despised me?

To this torrent of doubts, there was only one answer possible.

I owed Darloona everything that I could give her, even
the sacrifice of my unstained honor, or my very life, if she
should require it. And I did not have the right to demand so
much as the favor of a single smile in return.

For when a man loves, he loves wholly, he withholds
nothing of himself, or it is not truly love. This sort of chivalry
may sound old-fashioned, and perhaps it is, but my love for
her was beyond any question of payment or price.

And thus I agonized for days. My situation rapidly became
all but intolerable. Valkar was my closest friend, my confi-
dant, my coconspirator. That he had won the love of my peerless Princess should not have caused me pain, for whom better
should Darloona marry than a man like Valkar?

He was brave, intelligent, noble, and strong. He was a brilliant officer, a mighty prince, and his mission here in entering the city of the Chac Yuul in disguise, in a desperate one-man attempt to rescue the woman he loved from the very stronghold of her enemies, was heroic almost to the point of madness.

Why, then, should I begrudge him the love of the most beautiful woman of two worlds? Because of my own selfish passion?

It was absurd! My own love for Darloona was strong and deep and sincere, and it would endure to my last heartbeat. I would adore Darloona and fight for her while a single breath remained in my body, while a single drop of blood remained to animate my flesh.

But I was not even nobly born, much less a powerful prince, heir to a kingly house and a great fortune. My passion for her was hopeless. Darloona needed a man beside her on the throne who had been trained since childhood to rule. Such a man, of course, was Valkar. I could just imagine what kind of a prince consort I would make! Why, what did I know about being a king? The only thing I knew how to do was pilot a helicopter—and get myself into trouble: I had a real talent for doing that.

But I am as human as the next fellow, and I fear that I was often rather curt, sullen, and incommunicative with Valkar whenever we met to consider the various possible ways we could rescue Darloona from her impending marriage.

I did not mention the possibility of slaying Prince Vaspian. The onus for such a crime must rest on me alone; Valkar must know nothing of it in advance. When the time came, when it became necessary—I should simply do it.

*　　*　　*

Thus things went on for some days and the time of the marriage came near.

And then the most extraordinary accident occurred. To this hour I can remember the lift of my spirits, and the amazement which accompanied this resurgence. Valkar, I am sure, knew nothing of what was happening within me, although my depression and sullen spirits must have been obvious to all.

We were sitting in a corner table sharing a bottle of wine. Such was my preoccupation that I had thoughtlessly let fall some reference to Darloona's love for Valkar, and of the strength of his emotion for her.

He looked surprised for just a moment, and then voiced a rather apologetic laugh.

"I fear that you have misconstrued my words, Jandar," he said awkwardly.

"How is that?"

"Why—all this talk of how much Darloona loves me. We are, of course, the very best of friends, and have been ever since our childhood. But, alas, we do not *love* each other."

He laughed, a trifle sadly.

"Ours is, as I thought you must surely understand, a marriage of political alliance. As far as I know, Darloona has never yet been in love with me, or anyone else."

"And you—?"

He grinned a bit wearily.

"Oh, I shall make her the finest husband possible, and I admire and like her enormously, but I have never been in love with her."

"But I saw you clasped in each other's arms—I saw her lift tear-stained cheeks and pleading eyes to your face!"

"That must have been when she was begging me to flee from the city and get out before my imposture was discovered," he said idly. "She was in an agony of apprehension lest I be found out and punished, on her account. But here, Jandar! You have turned white as death again! Are you all right, old friend?"

I suppose the shock of this wonderful discovery must have been visible on my features, but I know that Valkar could not have know the depth of joy in my heart.

The woman I loved was yet heart-free-and I could hope, at least!

CHAPTER XII
AN UNEXPECTED MEETING

The next day or two Prince Vaspian kept me busy in the palace and I had no time for any further meetings with my fellow conspirator. But we had arranged a last-minute rendezvous at the wineshop, to take place just a couple of hours before the wedding, which was to be solemnized at the hour of midday.

At this last meeting we planned to coordinate our efforts to rescue Darloona, and, although I feel certain that Valkar did not suspect it, part of my own plans for that fateful hour included the cold-blooded murder of Prince Vaspian.

The day arrived.

The palace was a bustle of preparations; Vaspian preened and strutted like a peacock, leered and smirked over his impending nuptials until I grimly realized that it would be not at all unpleasant to put a yard of steel through his despicable heart.

The time for my rendezvous approached. Vaspian had no particular need of me until the hour of the ceremony arrived, and so I did not find it difficult to make my way through the palace to the nearest exit.

Whatever Valkar and I should decide to do, my own plans were fixed and certain. The task of playing the assassin was mine; it could only be mine, for only I could come and go freely in the private apartments of the Prince; only I had the opportunity to request a private audience with him immediately prior to our departure for the Hall of Hoom, as the devil god of the Chac Yuul was known, before whose high altar the nuptials would be celebrated by Ool the wizard-priest.

And at that private audience I would accomplish the murder and be gone; such was to be my lonely fate.

Or so I thought at the time!

But *va lu rokka*, as the fatalistic philosophy of the Yathoon hordesmen has it. That which is destined shall come to pass, whatever your plans may be.

And, as things turned out, it was not after all my destiny to meet with Valkar at the wineshop that morning.

Fate had a few surprises in store for Jandar of Callisto!

It was my plan to leave the royal citadel by a side entrance which, while well guarded, was rather neglected. Few used it, as most of the lords and chieftains of the Black Legion preferred the more accessible main gate. But as my mission was of a somewhat surreptitious nature, and I did not desire to attract any more attention than I could help, I chose to leave by this side gate. And it is upon just such small matters as these, the passing whims of a moment, that the fate of empires and the destiny of worlds sometimes hang.

For as I strode through the gate, nodding at the guards who knew me for Prince Vaspian's man, I encountered a Chac Yuul war party entering the palace with two prisoners in tow.

When I glanced with casual curiosity at the two captives, I got the surprise of my life.

For they were my old comrades, Koja and Lukor!

Koja, the towering Yathoon, loomed above the squat Black Legion warriors by head, shoulders, and upper thorax. His bare, glistening, chitinous forelimbs were bound behind him with tough leather thongs. His bald, ovoid head, crowned with segmented feelers, bore only the slightest resemblance to a human visage. His horny, immobile face and huge solemn eyes were physiologically incapable of registering changes of emotion, and he regarded me with an unfathomable gaze.

As for Lukor, the peppery little Swordmaster of Zanadar was somewhat the worse for wear. His somber-colored garments were torn, dirtied, and disheveled. His shock of snowy hair was disarranged. He was bleeding from a number of small scratches and minor cuts, and I have no doubt that those who had captured him had not done so without discovering that it is not an easy thing to disarm a swordsman of such masterly skill. His face was stiff and expressionless as he saw me, but from the flash of excitement in his eyes I knew that he had instantly recognized me despite the unexpectedness of our meeting.

As for myself, I fear I retained less composure than did my two old friends. I believe I paled, and an expression of shocked surprise doubtless crossed my features at this unexpected meeting.

The *komad* in charge of the war party saw the expression of astonishment that crossed my features. But, luckily, he did not identify my expression as one of recognition: had he done so I would have been hard put to explain how a warrior of the Black Legion could have known a Ganatolian swordmaster and a Yathoon hordesman.

Instead, he misinterpreted my surprise as mere startlement

at seeing a Yathoon warrior in the city of the Ku Thad. For while the various human races of Thanator frequently take service in alien cities, and while it is not at all rare to encounter a Perushtarian tradesman in Zanadar, a Ganatolian warrior serving in the ranks of the Chac Yuul, or a Ku Thad dwelling in Ganatol, the great, solemn-faced, stalk-limbed arthropods of the Horde stay with their own kind and are not ever found in service with the forces of the human nations of this world.

Proud of his capture, the squat, bandy-legged little *komad* grinned hugely, hooked his thumbs in his girdle, and nodded at the two silent prisoners.

"Fresh bodies for the Games, eh, friend?" he chuckled. "The Warlord will be pleased with them. Why, we have not taken a *capok** prisoner in years. 'Twill be a pleasure to see this one stand against a yathrib for the Nuptial Games. I have always wanted to see one of them in action with those ungainly whip-swords of theirs."

I had gained control of my features by now and permitted them to register slight curiosity.

"Aye, true enough, *komad*," I said indifferently. It came to me suddenly that, in honor of the marriage of Prince Vaspian and Darloona, the Chac Yuul would hold one of their bloody gladitorial festivals in the great arena of the palace compound that very afternoon. My blood ran cold at the thought. How could I free my friends, while attempting to save Darloona from the arms of the Son of Arkola? I did not think it possible to accomplish both; and yet I could hardly abandon Koja and Lukor to so horrible a fate as death in the

---

*Capok is a rude colloquialism for the Yathoon insectoids. It can bluntly be translated as "bug," or so Captain Dark notes in the first manuscript of narrative of his adventures, the book which I have edited for publication under the title *Jandar of Callisto*, and to which the present book is a sequel.—L. C.

arena. Both had saved my life ere this, at the hazard of their own.

"You are the *komad* Jandar, are you not?" the little officer inquired. "I believe I have seen you in Prince Vaspian's retinue ere now."

I nodded, and he identified himself as one Loguar, an officer in the fourth cohort of the Legion.

"Where did you get these two?" I asked, with what I hoped would sound like idle curiosity. Loguar was happy to swagger his triumph and needed no spur to his loquacity.

"Caught them in the lower city," he said, meaning the slums of Shondakor, a dilapidated area of old tenements down by the river docks. "Sneaking along in the shadows, they were, and up to no good, that was obvious. The old one put up a terrific battle, for all his white hair. A devil with the sword, that one! Five of my lads will be months in the mending, and three others will fight for the Legion never again, for they are gone to Gordrimator."

By this, Loguar meant they had been killed, or so I surmise. Oddly enough, for a barbaric world of walled cities and tribal monarchs, the various nations of Thanator have only the most rudimentary kind of a religion. They worship a pantheon of divinities called "The Lords of Gordrimator," by which name they term the planet Jupiter, to which this world of Thanator is the fifth satellite; but the word "worship" may be too strong, for never yet have I met with a priest of this religion or nor have I seen anything that could be described as a cathedral or a temple.

Indeed, the only priest of any description I have heard of on Thanator is that inscrutable little being, Ool the Uncanny, and he is more wizard or enchanter than priest. But I had vaguely heard of the Thanatorian belief that the souls or spirits of the warrior dead travel to Gordrimator, which seems to be envisioned as a sort of paradise or afterlife, so I understood what he meant.

"Odd to see a Yathoon hordesman in the city," I commented. "Where are you taking them, if I may ask?"

"To the Pits," shrugged Loguar, meaning the dungeons beneath the royal citadel. "There they will be safe and secure until the Games."

"Very good. Doubtless someone will wish to question them as to their reasons for being in the city?"

He grunted and spat. "The Warlord generally questions prisoners, but on this day of days I doubt he would be interested. Well, I must be off with my prizes." He grinned, and tossed me a companionable salute. Then he strode off into the palace with his war party and the two captives.

I stood aside as they went past me, and as tall gaunt Koja went by he clacked out one word in his harsh metallic tones.

"Horaj," he said.

He spoke in a low voice and I doubt if any heard him, or if they did, they paid him no notice. The more ignorant of the humans of Thanator, among which the Chac Yuul must certainly be numbered, consider the great stalking warriors of the Yathoon Horde as little more than monsters, and certainly they do not count them as intelligent beings on a par with mankind. Hence if any of the members of Loguar's war party heard the single word which Koja enunciated, they put it down to a bestial grunting. But I have dwelled in the war camps of the Horde and I know that while the arthropods are degraded and cruel and belong to the lowest rung of civilization, being merely nomad warrior clans devoid of the nobler sentiments and immune to the beauties of the arts, they are nonetheless as fully intelligent as men.

What did Koja mean by that single word *horaj*, which he doubtless spoke for my ears alone? *Horaj* means "urgent."

By this enigmatic term, did he mean to communicate that he possessed vital information for my ears alone? I could put no other construction on his remark. And surely Koja and Lukor had not run the risk of entering the city of Shondakor for any other reason than to communicate with me.

I paused in the entranceway for a few moments, indecisively.

The forced marriage of Darloona was but hours away. And if Valkar and I were to attempt any sort of rescue, we must lay our plans at once. And even now he awaited my coming in our wineshop rendezvous.

But I must forgo that meeting, for all its urgency.

I turned on my heel and reentered the palace.

Despite the fact that time was running out, I could not delay having speech with Koja and Lukor. Some mission of overwhelming importance had caused them to dare the risk of entering the city of the Ku Thad.

And I must find out what it was.

BOOK FOUR

THE BOOK OF OOL

CHAPTER XIII
AT SWORD'S POINT

The Pits lay beneath the lowest levels of the palace, and although I had never had cause to visit them during my tenure in the service of Prince Vaspian, I was well enough aware of their location to find them without difficulty.

Getting in to see Koja and the gallant old Sword-master would be another problem. But it seemed likely that my rank as a member of the retinue of the Prince would be sufficient to get me past the guards.

If it did not work, well, frankly, I did not know what I should do. If the secret network of passages within the palace walls continued into the depths of the dungeons, I was not aware of the fact. And I had no time to go exploring. Time, as I have already observed, was running out; and to employ yet another cliché, matters were coming swiftly to a head.

I had a hunch that the masquerade was about over. My imposture had escaped detection up to now, and my false history had survived scrutiny. But things were moving too fast for me now, and, as my reader will observe, I was begin-

ning to take risky chances. I had no valid reason to be in the
Pits at all, and if queried by Vaspian or Arkola, I would not
be able to satisfactorily explain my curiosity regarding these
prisoners. But my friends were in danger, and that justified
my taking even the most enormous chances—I was willing to
risk even the disclosure of my true identity—willing to risk
even to jeopardize my entire mission.

I could do no less for those who had done so much
for me.

And thus I descended into the Pits.

Luckily for me, they were not heavily guarded. Since the
entire palace was in the hands of the Chac Yuul, how could
an enemy of the Chac Yuul penetrate to this place? Such, at
least, was the thinking that had decreed the Pits need not be
heavily guarded. Were it not so, I could not have gotten as
far as I did before a guard confronted me.

Down a long stone corridor I went, striding rapidly, my cloak
tossed back from my right shoulder so that it would not im-
pede the use of my right arm, my fingers brushing the pommel of my rapier.

Grim walls of rough stone lay about me; the air was chill
and dank, and it reeked of the fetor of men held in long
imprisonment with but the rudest of sanitary facilities.

What light there was, and there was but little, came from
oil-soaked torches of black jaruka wood clamped with brackets of rust-eaten iron against the moldering stone masonry.
These crude attempts at illumination cast a wavering orange
glare and painted huge black shadows upon the walls. To me
it seemed momentarily unreal. All of this scene through which
I moved was like a movie set; I felt that I myself was unreal,
a mere actor playing a role in some historical epic; even my
garments, cloak and buskins and the slim rapier that slapped

against my bare thigh with every step, added to this feeling of unreality.

Suddenly I turned a corner and found myself facing a large and nearly empty room paved with stone which was bestrewn with moldy straw.

In one corner of this large open area stood a rough wooden table, its top surface marked with rings of dried wine and ale, hacked with knives, as if generations of bored and idle guards had carved their initials upon it. A bucket of water and a dipper stood beneath the table, and upon it stood a candelabra of brass with three guttering candles. A wooden stool was drawn up to this table, and sprawled dozing thereon a burly guard could be seen. Only one guard! That was a stroke of fortune.

Opening off this large room were several cells. I could not, at first glance, tell what persons were immured within, for the shadows were deep and thick. But even if my friends were not imprisoned in one of these cells, it seemed likely that the dozing guard could tell me where they were being held.

The guard—his head was turned away from me, resting on his folded arms, so that I could not see his face—was a *komad*, as I could tell from the emblems clipped to the shoulders of his leather tunic. In other words, he was of the same rank as myself. This meant I could not use my position as a superior officer to bid him answer my queries; but my favored place in the retinue of the Crown Prince of the Black Legion would doubtless suffice to wring cooperation from him, as few officers of the Chac Yuul would be so foolish as to willingly go against the wishes of the man who would, with luck, someday stand in the highest place of the Legion.

"Sleeping on duty, *komad?*" I asked sharply, as I entered the room. It seemed at the time a good idea to put the fellow in the wrong at the beginning; that it was not at all a wise notion became evident almost immediately.

He started away from his nap and raised his face to look at me, with apprehension and anger mingling in his expression. He was a coarse, crude-looking oaf, with fleshy, unshaven jowls and mean little piggish eyes—eyes which narrowed the moment they rested upon my features.

His snarled curse broke off as delighted recognition dawned upon him. A gloating smile crossed his coarse visage, and my heart sank into my boots, for I had recognized him almost in the same instant, and I knew I should get no cooperation from this particular officer.

For it was Bluto, the swaggering bully I had beaten and humiliated at the city gate when first I entered the walls of Shondakor!

Silently, I cursed my vile luck. Of all the officers in the Black Legion who might have been assigned to this particular post at this particular hour, it had to be the one man in all the Legion least likely to cooperate with my wishes.

"And if I am, what is it to you, little man," he grunted, rising to his feet and laying one huge hairy hand on the pommel of his cutlass. "What be your business here, and where be your authorization?"

I have stated earlier in this narrative that this hulking brute was one of the biggest men I have ever faced, and it was truly so. He was a colossus, towering above me almost as much as Koja did. He was not in the best of fighting trim, for a swag-belly hung over his girdle and there was soft flab in his jowls and upper arms, and he looked somewhat the worse for drink. But the rest of him was solid beef and he had the advantage on me as far as weight and reach went. He would make a dangerous opponent.

I touched the medallion of precious metal on my baldric,

the insignia which denoted me as a member of the court of Prince Vaspian.

"Here is all the authority I need to examine a prisoner, *komad*," I said levelly. "I want a look at the two strangers who were brought down here within the hour. You know the ones, the *capok* and the white-haired outlander in black. Loguar, a *komad* of the fourth, brought them in."

He grinned nastily, eying me from his height. "What do you want with them?"

I shrugged. "It is not what I want, Bluto, but what the Prince my patron wants. They are to do battle in the Nuptial Game following the royal wedding, and he wishes me to see that they are in good shape for fighting and have fed. If they are injured or have been mistreated, I am to inform him of the fact. Now, if you will be good enough to tell me where they are being held, I will be about my business—"

He lifted one great hand, stilling me.

"Bluto has his business too," he growled. "Also his orders! No one gets in to see any prisoner without a note from the Lord of the Pits."

"But the Prince has expressly ordered—"

"No *one* gets past Bluto," he said heavily. And he drew his cutlass with a rasp of steel on worn leather, and held it ready in his hand, watching me from cold little eyes buried in rolls of unhealthy fat. A predatory expression crossed his face; he licked his thick lips with the tip of his tongue.

I stood there, struggling to think. Had the guard been any other except this bully, who hated me for making him look ridiculous in front of his men, I could perhaps have bluffed my way past him through the sheer weight of Prince Vaspian's name. But Bluto was happy to be able to refuse me what I wanted.

I could not, of course, go to the Lord of the Pits, as the

officer in charge of the dungeon guards was called. He would be a senior officer and he would not be swayed by important names; he would want to see my authorization from the Prince in writing. And, even if I could bribe or bully the commandant into giving me a pass, there simply was no time. Minute by minute sped swiftly by, and every passing second brought the woman I loved closer and closer to a forced marriage with a smirking villain she loathed.

If I fought with Bluto, my false identity was exposed. For the duel might arouse guards housed nearby, and I ran the risk of being taken into custody as it was forbidden that Chac Yuul warriors fight among themselves. And how could I explain a corpse, if my skill with the blade were sufficient to strike Bluto down?

In this matter, as frequently in my past career, Fate took the decision out of my hand entirely.

For Bluto lifted his blade and set its point against my heart. A leer of sadistic mirth distorted his coarse features and his voice was thick and hoarse with gloating menace.

"Bluto could kill you now," he growled, "and say you tried to force your way in. No one would ever know—"

I struck his blade aside with my arm.

"I am an officer of the Chac Yuul," I protested. "It would be an act of treason!"

He spat. "Treason, eh? You dirty little *horeb*, you call Bluto a traitor? You made Bluto look like a fool. You dared not face Bluto with steel. You fought with your hands, like a wench!"

I watched the red glare of fury in his cold little pit-eyes, and my heart sank. There was no hope for it—I must fight the man. I must duel here in the Pits, while every racing moment brought my beloved nearer to a horrible doom.

He was panting heavily now, working himself up to a

berserk rage, as he had done that time I beat him at the gates. I tried to reason with him but there was no arguing with the man.

He roared out a string of filthy epithets and swung his great cutlass at my head.

I sprang backwards nimbly, avoiding the whistling blade.

He advanced, towering over me, growling curses.

There was no other way. I slid my blade free of the scabbard, and in the next instant we were at sword's point there in the black dungeons of Shondakor.

CHAPTER XIV
TO THE DEATH!

B arely did I manage to lift my sword to parry his blow. The impact jarred along the blade and numbed my arm. Bluto was immensely strong, and he had worked himself up into a bloodthirsty rage.

I backed away and let him come after me, snarling and spitting ugly curses, his face working. He swung at me, great lusty swipes, his heavy cutlass whistling through the air, and each blow I turned aside, but with great care, for his blade was much weightier than mine, and if I parried in such a way that the full force of his blow met my rapier squarely, he might snap my blade in two.

He fought like a madman, swearing wildly and hacking away with enormous energy. He had little or no science, but his giant strength and endurance, his superior weight and reach, were powerful advantages and for a time I was hard put to keep his edge from slashing my flesh.

As we fought, he taunted me.

"You—too proud to fight with Bluto at gate—too proud to face Bluto with sword, like a gentleman—use your hands on

Bluto, will you, you filthy *horeb!* Now you fight Bluto, steel against steel—how do you like it?" he growled, his red eyes blazing with berserk fury, and whitish foam gathering at the corners of his mouth.

I saved my breath for the duel and did not deign to answer his foul-mouthed raving. I resolved to kill him as quickly as I could, as I soon discovered, it is not all that easy to duel with a man who fights like a maniac, swinging great blows with untiring strength. So I continued backing away from his roundhouse swing, while looking for an opening.

If I had been fighting an ordinary swordsman, armed with a weapon similar to my own, I could have killed him within minutes, if such had been my wish. For I could have caught his blade and turned it aside with a deft twist of the wrist, allowing my blade to glide through his guard and my point to sink in his breast. But Bluto was an entirely different sort of opponent, swinging wildly as if armed with a club, and I continued to retreat warily before his advance, for if any one of those blows had connected I would be weaponless.

He began cursing at me to stand still and fight him like a man, rather than to retreat like a coward. But I paid no attention to his raving, watching his bladework for an opening.

Suddenly, one came—a wide swing that left his burly chest unguarded for a moment. This was the opportunity I had been hoping for and I lunged, my point sinking into the fleshy part of his shoulder just above the heart.

To my astonishment, it failed to stop him, or even to slow him down!

He squealed like a stuck pig, but it was more from blind rage than pain. And instantly he redoubled his assault, whacking away with lusty blows which knocked my blade from side to side like the slender steel needle it was.

Obviously, his berserk fury was such that he was virtually insensible to pain. It would take nothing less than a direct thrust through the heart to fell the roaring maniac.

Around and around the room we went, as I backed away from his advance. The stone room rang like an iron foundry with the clang of steel on steel. I felt my way with caution, fearful of tripping over an unseen obstacle, for I could not see what was behind me and I dared not turn my attention from Bluto for a second to snatch a glance over my shoulder.

I managed to pink him on the throat and on the upper arm, but these were mere slicing cuts, minor wounds, which gushed with blood and must have stung him but were not sufficient to disable him or even to slow him down.

By now he was streaming with blood and sweat, and foam slavered from his grinning jaws, but he still came on, showing no signs of exhaustion.

And then, very suddenly, the duel was over.

One wild, awkward blow had caught me unawares and my slim blade snapped off short, just beyond the hilt. A thrill of alarm ran through me as I realized I was now unarmed.

Murder flamed in his piggish little eyes and a triumphant note entered his hoarse, bestial howl as he raised his nicked cutlass for the kill.

Instead of jumping to one side, as he might have expected, I took a great risk—and sprang forward, to close with him!

Sometimes, in moments of great peril, when all seems utterly lost, it has been my experience that to do the completely unexpected can often snatch victory from between the slavering jaws of defeat. And never was this more ably proven than when I sprang into the embrace of the maddened colossus.

He was dumbfounded, caught with both arms and the

heavy blade raised above his head, and as my body jammed against him he staggered off balance and fell stumbling to the rush-strewn stone pave.

And I was upon him like a striking jungle cat.

The broken sword hilt in my hand was all but useless. The blade had snapped off near the hilt, but where the steel blade had fractured was a sharp, jagged point.

This point I sank into the thick flesh of Bluto's neck—and ripped, tearing his throat out!

As I staggered, panting, to my feet, he died on the stone pave in a gush of reeking gore. To the last, an expression of blank astonishment filled his eyes with dazed incomprehension. I do not believe he understood that he was slain until his eyes glazed in death and his heaving breast gave one last shudder and was stilled forever.

I had not wanted to slay the poor fool, but he would have it so. A fight to the death, sword against sword, but it had been his death, after all.

I left him lying there in a pool of blood.

Taking up his sword in the place of my own, and borrowing the candelabra from the table, I set forth to search the Pits of Shondakor to find my friends.

It probably took no more than a few minutes, but in my state of anxiety it seemed like the better part of an hour. Even now, Darloona might be standing before the hideous idol of the Black Legion while Ool sealed her life forever to that of the oily weakling I once had served!

Most of the cells were empty, mere dim, noisome cubicles which bore a rude wooden bench and a heap of moldy straw. But some were tenanted—by the dead.

I paced swiftly down the first corridor, pausing before

each cell and lifting my candelabra to illuminate the dark recesses within, before striding on.

Repulsive, naked *horebs*—the verminous rodents of Thanator, which sometimes attain the size of small dogs—fled wriggling and squealing from the light. One glance at that which served them for a banquet and I hastily averted my eyes, as nausea clutched at my throat.

But ere very much time had elapsed the flickering illumination of the candles showed a welcome sight—Lukor, looking pale and disheveled, chained to one wall of a filthy cubicle, and gaunt, solemn-faced old Koja blinking his great black eyes, chained to the other.

"Ho! Jandar, is it you?" the old Swordmaster chortled with delight. "My boy, never have these eyes looked upon a more welcome sight!"

I had prudently taken a ring of keys from Bluto's girdle, and after a little fumbling I found the right one, unlocked the cell door and went in to relieve my comrades of their chains.

"I'm glad I could get here before you were interrogated," I said as I helped them remove their shackles. "Are either of you hurt? The Legion sometimes plays mighty rough."

Lukor sniffed, straightening his sober raiment and smoothing his small white beard into something resembling its customary neatness.

"Not at all, my boy, not at all! Oh, there was a trifle of a flurry before we were disarmed, but Koja there dispatched a few of the bandy-legged little wretches with his blade and I gave a couple of the others a brief lesson in swordplay; but neither of us sustained anything more serious than a few scratches," he said complacently.

Koja blinked his huge eyes solemnly at me as I unfastened his chains.

"It is good to see you again, Jandar," he said in his monotonous voice. I clapped him affectionately on the upper thorax and said I was happy to see him, too.

"But what in the world are you two fools thinking of, trying to get into Shondakor like this? Didn't you know you'd be spotted and seized before you got halfway?" I demanded.

Lukor sobered. "We had to do it, lad. Word of the Princess Darloona's impending nuptials to this Black Legion princeling leaked out and the Ku Thad got wind of it. Your friend, Marud, I fear, was responsible for that!"

My pulses quickened.

"Marud—the innkeeper? You mean he got through after all—with my message about the secret tunnel under the river and the city walls?"

Lukor looked surprised.

"Of course," he said. "How did you think Koja and I got inside Shondakor, if not by the hidden tunnel of which your letter apprised Lord Yarrak?"

I had not really thought things out. I guess I had assumed that Koja and Lukor had somehow sought to gain entry through the city gates and were taken prisoner. But now this surprising news changed everything. Marud must have been seized by the warriors of Ool the Uncanny on his way back into the city, instead of on his way out. I had not been sure which had been the case, but for some reason or other I had assumed he had been seized en route to the *entrance* of the tunnel.

I thought rapidly.

"Then this means the Ku Thad warriors are ready to attempt to retake the city by means of the underground passage?"

"That is true, and they are growing restive!" said Lukor, his merry eyes going grim. "Koja and I begged them to wait for some further news from you before charging into the middle of things, but the thought that their beloved Princess was being forced to wed the Prince of the Chac Yuul has maddened them to the point of throwing off all restraints. They will wait no longer, so we came on ahead, desperately hoping to locate you and to gain some word of your own plans in time to coordinate them with the attack of the Ku Thad. Jandar—Jandar! Why in the name of the Lords of Gordrimator did you never communicate with us again, after that first message?"

"It was impossible," I said. "The only man I could trust was the fat innkeeper, Marud—and the guards seized him as he was reentering Shondakor after delivering that first note from me. They were planning to interrogate him, probably under torture, for I am certain that Arkola the Warlord would not scruple over the matter of a little pain!"

"And did they? Get anything out of Marud, I mean?" Lukor asked. I shook my head somberly.

"There was a real man behind that fat belly and that foolish face," I said softly. "For he killed himself rather than yield my name to those who were to interrogate him."

Lukor cleared his throat.

"A very gallant gentleman," he said quietly. "I shall be proud to drink to his memory, when there is a drop of wine and a bit of leisure. But now—"

"But now we must get out of here—and fast, for every moment counts! Darloona will be wed to Arkola's son this very day—almost at any moment! We must get swords and do what we can do to interrupt the ceremonies."

And I cursed the low technology of the Thanatorians that they had not yet invented the wristwatch. For I had lost all sense of time by now and would have given my left hand to know what was the hour.

Koja gathered up the loose length of chain and passed it thoughtfully through his many-jointed, claw-like fingers, swinging it to assess the weight.

"As for Koja," he said, blinking owlishly, "he shall require no weapon but this heavy length of iron chain, for the small blades used by the members of your race do not fit his hand. But this length of chain will serve well enough."

"Then let us be going!"

Lukor led the way out of the cell, peering about through the dimness.

"Which way?" he inquired. I jerked my thumb toward the square stone room where Bluto's corpse lay in a puddle of congealing gore. We sprinted off down the corridor, our footsteps raising echoes.

"Is this not foolhardy?" Koja asked, thudding along at my side, his ungainly strides carrying him along at a rapid pace. "How can such as we hope to traverse the place unmolested? Surely the first Chac Yuul warrior to spy us will raise the alarm."

"There is a network of secret passages hidden within the walls," I said. "We can travel far by means of them, and without being discovered. There should be a panel leading into the labyrinth of hidden passages in the hall beyond the entrance to the Pits—"

And then a pang of despair ripped through my heart! For even above the noise of our running feet and over the thudding of my own heartbeat, I could faintly hear a distant bell tolling the hour!

And Darloona was being married—*right now!*

"But—" Koja began. I cut him off with a curt word.

"Save your breath for running," I panted, and we raced down the echoing hall and burst into the stone room.

And stopped short!

Eyeing the corpse, old Lukor voiced a snort of laughter.

"I see you had time for a bit of practice ere coming to seek us out, my boy!"

I did not reply. I hefted the heavy cutlass in my hands and wondered what the next few moments would bring.

For there in the doorway that led to this chamber from the upper level stood a fat, smiling little man with gleaming, amused eyes.

"I told you that we would have another little talk, O Jandar," the man said in a high, breathy voice.

It was Ool the Uncanny.

CHAPTER XV
IN THE HALL OF HOOM

These things I, Jandar, did not see happen, for I was not there. But much later, when all was over, the fighting was ended, and Darloona taken from me, I heard how they had chanced to occur. And I tell them to you now; just as I heard them from the lips of Valkar, Prince of the Ku Thad.

Valkar waited long in the wineshop, but Jandar did not come. Minute by minute, time ticked past, the hour appointed for their rendezvous came and went, and still there was no sign of Jandar.

What had happened to prevent their meeting? Valkar grimly counted over the possibilities, and none of them were pleasant ones. Jandar's imposture might have been discovered—his true identity revealed—his mission of rescue unveiled.

If this were so, every passing moment might bring danger closer to Valkar. For the *komor* well knew how pain can wring truth from the lips of even the bravest and most stubborn of men. Every minute he remained waiting here in the tavern might draw their plans closer to the brink of disaster. Even now, a contingent of guards might be clanking through the streets of Shondakor, bound for this inn.

The longer he waited here, the more likely was the chance that he would be arrested.

At length it was so close to the time of the marriage ceremony that Valkar dared wait no longer for his friend. If Jandar had not come by now, he was not coming. Some unforeseen happening had occurred to shatter their plan. The gnawing unease, the feeling that something had gone wrong, grew stronger.

Abruptly, Valkar rose from the wine-stained table, tossed a glittering coin at the sallow-faced innkeeper, and strode out of the wineshop, peering up towards the towers of the royal palace where it rose beside the plaza in the heart of the great city.

It was up to Valkar to come to the aid of his princess *and he must do it alone.*

Valkar had entered the palace and its maze of hidden passages within the walls only a few times before, and always by the dark of night, when few were abroad and the chances of being seen were slender.

Never before had he dared to enter the closely guarded citadel by broad light of day. And, under ordinary circumstance, he would never think of making the attempt with the palace crowded with warriors and officers, every corridor thronged with wedding guests, a thousand scurrying servants making last-minute preparations for the impending royal nuptials.

Under such circumstances, the chances of discovery were vastly greater. However, Valkar had no alternative but to try it. For within the hour, unless he found some means of in-

tervening and bearing off the Princess to safety, Darloona
would be married before the hideous stone idol of the Chac
Yuul devil-god, Hoom.

Under his cloak, Valkar was dressed in his most resplendent decorations, for this was a festival day and all the chieftains of the Black Legion had been commanded to clothe
themselves in all their finery as if for parade.

Tossing aside his cloak, Valkar found it not difficult to
mingle with the other officers thronged before a side gate,
and to enter in their midst. His decorations and ornaments
were no less glittering than their own, and thus he gained
entry into the palace without detection or even being noticed.

Striding through the hallways, he thanked the mysterious
Lords of Gordrimator for this small stroke of fortune! On previous secret visits to the palace of the Kings of Shondakor,
he had entered the walls by a small door in the outer circuit
of the walls, a door concealed behind a heavy growth of
shrubbery. But in the broad light of day it was impossible to
use that route without being seen.

Now that he was actually within the palace, he must find
one of the sliding panels that would give him entry into the
hidden passageways behind the thick walls. And this he found
most difficult.

The trouble was, simply, that the palace was bustling with
guests and visitors. Every room and corridor he passed, every
rotunda and antechamber, was filled with people. On the rare
nights when he had visited Darloona in secret to urge her to
permit him to assist her in an escape, he had chosen a late
hour when certain side passages were untenanted. Now, every
passage was filled with busy people. Perspiration started on
his brow; he had the horrible feeling one experiences sometimes in a nightmare, of racing against the clock, of struggling to avert some hideous doom, and of finding that every

step is slowed and encumbered by an unseen impediment, so that one battles forward in slow motion while doom races nearer with every madly ticking second!

Straining to keep the tension from being visible on his features, Valkar turned aside and ascended a staircase to the second level, hoping to find a momentarily empty suite wherein to make his entrance through one of the hidden panels.

At last, after an agonized eternity of strolling past crowded rooms, he found a chamber empty of all occupants and wasted no time in striding to a further wall covered with a richly brocaded wall hanging.

The swordsman stepped behind the hanging and in a moment his searching gaze found one of the minute and unnoticeable signs that marked a hidden door. In another moment his fingers had found and depressed a secret spring.

With a faint clashing of hidden counterweights, the door slid open and a black hole yawned before him. Without hesitation he stepped within and sealed the panel shut behind him.

He had brought no candle or lantern into the dark maze of passageways, for it would have looked odd for an officer to be strolling through the brightly lit palace carrying a lantern when it was broad daylight. And it took his eyes a few moments to adjust to the dimness.

But ere long he could see well enough to make his way down the narrow passage to a side branch where coded markings would direct him to his easiest route. Valkar had spent many hours studying the code wherewith the secret labyrinth was marked, and he could find his way through the winding maze with ease.

It was quite different here inside the secret passages by

day. By night the narrow tunnels are drenched in impenetrable gloom, and without a candle or some other means of illumination it is almost impossible to find your way. But during the daylight hours a sufficient amount of light leaks into the passages through cracks and crannies in the walls to spread a dim, vague illuminance by which, if one goes with care, one can make one's way without great difficulty.

Before long Valkar found the right passage and followed it to its end, striding as swiftly as he dared in the half-gloom.

He came at length to a spyhole and slid its covering aside to peer through the small aperture at a scene of astounding magnificence.

The temple of the devil-god of the Chac Yuul lay before him.

Before the conquest by the Black Legion, the Ku Thad had used the immense hall for a throne room. But now a hideous stone idol stood on the topmost tier of a vast flight of low, broad marble steps where once the Kings of Shondakor had sat in state.

The idol was very old, black with age, and grimy with the stain of splattered blood—for the horror of human sacrifice was not unknown to the savage warriors of the Black Legion.*

*To this passage in Chapter 15 Captain Dark has attached a footnote to the effect that this is the only god, or near-god, he had ever encountered in all his wanderings and adventures upon the face of the jungle world.

Elsewhere, in this volume and in *Jandar of Callisto*, its predecessor, he has mentioned on occasion the puzzling absence of any formal or hierarchical religion among the various nations of Thanator. It would seem natural, from an anthropological point of view, for the barbaric peoples of Callisto—who, with the single exception of the Sky Pirates of Zanadar, seem to belong to a level of civilization approximately that of our own Bronze Age—to have elevated a pantheon of savage divinities comparable to those of the Greeks, the Romans, the ancient Egyptians, or the old Norse. But, oddly enough, such does not seem to have been the case. Save for a nebulous and never-defined reverence for "the Lords of Gordrimator," (Jupiter), the Thanatorians seem to worship no gods, seem to have nothing in the

Half again as tall as a man, the stone image squatted atop the uppermost tier, its legs folded tailor-fashion beneath it, its bulging paunch sagging down in an obscene fashion.

Five arms the idol lifted to its sides and each clawlike stone hand grasped a weapon of war. As for the sixth hand, it was empty, and held out over the top steps as if clutching for human prey.

The face of the god Hoom was indescribably hideous, screwed into a leer of malice, with glaring eyes under scowling brows, and bared fangs. Curling horns sprouted from its bald pate, between the sharp, pointed ears.

A grisly necklace of human skulls dangled about its thick throat.

Such was the demon-god of the Chac Yuul.

Such was the grim divinity whereof Ool the Uncanny was high priest!

On the broad steps below the place where black Hoom squatted, leering and monstrous like some bloated and gigantic toad, a glittering assembly awaited the coming of the priest.

Arkola was there, magnificent in black velvet, his strong face grim and unsmiling. There, too, were the lords of the council and the high chieftains of the horde, in their barbaric finery.

Light streamed through tall tapering windows to flash in mirror-polished shields and burnished helms, to twinkle from

---

way of a priesthood or a system of temples and shrines. It is all very odd.

Save for this monstrous idol, Hoom, and Ool his wizard priest, no other divinities or their priestly servants are mentioned in the two volumes of Captain Dark's narrative. Hoom may well have been an import, for in the next chapter we shall learn something of the origins and background of Ool the Uncanny, and it may well be that the little wizard-priest introduced the idol of his far-off and mysterious homeland when he entered among the ranks of the Black Legion. Such, at least, is my conjecture.—L. C.

the jewels in sword hilt and girdle and the gems that flashed about the throats of the Chac Yuul women.

A step or two below the idol stood Darloona. She was superb in a long gown of golden satin sprinkled with small diamonds, but for all her beauty and the splendor of her gown, Valkar could see the tension and fear in her pale, set features, and in the way her hands gripped and twisted at a small scrap of handkerchief.

Vaspian smirked and lolled at her side, resplendent in silken robes, a gilt coronet upon his brows. From time to time he leaned to whisper in Darloona's ear, and at the way her face tightened with distaste, Valkar could guess the message of his leering whisper, and his hand gripped his sword hilt until the knuckles whitened.

The bell had long since rung the hour, but it seemed that this splendid company yet awaited the coming of Ool. A murmur arose from the throng, as the Chac Yuul whispered. What was keeping the fat little wizard-priest?

Valkar, from his hidden place, searched the audience with a narrow gaze, but not for Ool the Uncanny. He wondered if Jandar was in the crowd, and although he searched for him carefully, he saw him not. For the hundredth time, he wondered what calamity could have prevented his comrade from attending their vital meeting.

Now a stir and rustle went through the throng.

Valkar peered about and saw that at last Ool the Uncanny had entered the hall. The fat little man was muffled in thick robes of a dull, drab hue, and the cowl of that robe was drawn, concealing his face. Head down, hands tucked into his capacious sleeves, the little wizard stumbled across the top of the flight of steps from an entrance on the far side. He was aware of his lateness and had hurried, for he was breathing heavily. Valkar wondered what could have detained him—and again wondered what had become of Jandar.

Now Ool descended the topmost steps to stand between the Prince and the Princess, with the great stone idol towering up behind him.

And now Valkar could delay no longer. With or without Jandar he must act swiftly now, before the nuptials were sealed and Darloona was wed to the man she loathed.

Valkar touched the hidden spring and the panel slid aside.

With a leap he attained the dais whereupon the idol stood. Ripping out his sword, the Prince sprang down the steps, catching a swift glance at the expression of astonishment that crossed the faces of Prince Vaspian and Darloona at his un-expected appearance. Ool still had his back turned and saw nothing.

Daylight flashed on the blade of his rapier as Valkar lifted the sword and sent its point hurtling to cut down Ool from behind before he could speak the doom-fraught words which would seal the marriage.

Ool turned and looked Valkar directly in the eyes!

And Darloona *screamed!*

CHAPTER XVI
THE MIND WIZARD OF KUUR

C old chills went down my back as I stared at the fat little
wizard-priest who lounged in the doorway of the Pits.
"What are you doing here?" I blurted. It was an in-
ane thing to say and it made him laugh, a thin, titter of malicious humor that had no mirth in it.

"Why, I am here for our long-delayed little talk," he
purred, slitted eyes agleam with mischief. "I told you we
would speak together at a later time—and this is it."

He paused, surveying the corpse that lay sprawled in congealing gore amidst the tumbled rushes. His eyes lifted to the
bare cutlass I held, and again that mirthless titter fell from
his fat smiling lips.

"You are a man of action, I see, O Jandar! Alas, you would
not lift cold steel against a fat old man, who hath naught
wherewith to defend himself?" The purring voice trailed off
on a questioning note. I hefted the heavy sword, feeling foolish. Koja and Lukor were watching all this without comprehension.

For some reason the fat little priest gave me pause. I should have simply run by him, but for some reason which I cannot quite explain this seemed not the thing to do. It was, I think, a matter of *presence*.

Whatever else he may have been, Ool the Uncanny was not a man you could easily ignore!

Now he came waddling into the square stone room, hands tucked within capacious sleeves. He wore his usual thick robes of drab hue. His sandals slapped and whispered against the stone pave.

His sharp glance took in the tall somber arthropod and the keen-eyed, white-headed little Swordmaster behind me.

"A warrior lord of the Yathoon people, and a master-swordsman from the City in the Clouds," mused Ool thoughtfully. "How in the name of thirty devils could an ordinary mercenary from Soraba know such as these—so much that he commits mutiny, aye, and murder, too, in the freeing of them! 'Tis a puzzle, indeed: a mystery ... there is much about you, O Jandar, that savors of the mysterious."

Lukor cleared his throat, a little impatient bark of sound.

"I believe you said something about a bell, lad? Why do we stand here talking, when the lass is about to wed that fool of a Prince?" he demanded.

I opened my mouth to speak, but Ool said swiftly: "Rest easy on that point, O Lukor of Ganatol; the Princess Darloona cannot be wed until I arrive in the Hall of Hoom beyond the Throne Chamber. I know, for 'tis I, old fat Ool, who will conduct the nuptials."

"How do you know me, priest?" snapped Lukor. Ool smiled lazily and his eyes drifted from one of us to the other.

"I know you at least as well as you know yourself, O Swordmaster—and the *Komor* Koja of the Yathoon Horde—

and you, as well, O Jandar of—what should I say? 'Tellus' or 'Terra'—or 'Earth'? Aye, Jandar of Tellus—that would be the proper construction."

Jandar of Tellus!

Shock ripped through me, the shock of complete amazement, as I realized this placid little butter-colored Buddha somehow knew my closely guarded secret—knew that I was not native to this world of Thanator, but was a visitor from a far-distant planet! *But how could he have known that?*

Almost as if he read the question in my mind, he smiled again, obviously enjoying my mystification.

"I know many things, O Jandar, which are hidden from other men. You, and all those that dwell within the walls of Shondakor, think me but a priest of Hoom, my god—that, or a wizard of strange gifts and stranger wisdom. You have seen me many times, and each time it has entered your mind that my flesh is yellow and my black eyes aslant, and that I am unlike any people you have yet encountered upon the face of Thanator—but never has it occurred to you to think about this puzzle."

Ool spoke truth. Suddenly it came to me that I knew well the races of Thanator: the Ku Thad of Shondakor, with their amber skin, emerald eyes, and flaming manes—the papery-white Sky Pirates of Zanadar, with their lank black hair—the bald-headed, crimson-skinned men of the Bright Empire of Perushta—the Chac Yuul warriors, with their greasy, swarthy skins and colorless hair—and those cross-breeds, such as the Ganatolians. *And not one of these races had the butter-yellow skin and slant black eyes of Ool the Uncanny!*

Yet *never* had I noticed this!

"And for very good reasons, O Jandar of Tellus," the fat priest chuckled. "I am one of the Mind Wizards of Kuur, dark shadowy Kuur that lies beyond Dragon River amind the Peaks of Harangzar, *on the other side of Thanator.* * *My people share a curious science, a mental discipline that permits us to read the thoughts and minds of other beings. As you can well imagine, this art gives us an unusual advantage over the other races of Thanator, an advantage we are not hesitant to employ.*"

"*That's* how you led the Chac Yuul into Shondakor!" I cried.

"Of course," he chuckled. "An archivist possessed knowledge of the secret tunnel beneath the river and the outer walls, and thus I gained ascendancy over Arkola and a place in his councils, by bartering the secret of a safe road into the Golden City for—*power.*"

A cold flash of reptilian greed shone momentarily in his slitted eyes.

"We are a small, a dying race; but we have a mighty power over the minds of other men, a power which, if used adroitly, can lay an empire within our reach. I found my way into the inner councils of the Chac Yuul by means of my mind power, and the Chac Yuul seized a kingdom. That iron man of war, bold Arkola, thinks he rules the Black Legion, but it is *I* am the master here!"

"Then using your mind power, you were able to still suspicion of your race in the brain of every man you met?" Lukor asked keenly. "That is why it never occurred to anyone to wonder who and what you were, with your yellow skin and slant gaze?"

His bald pate nodded sleepily.

---

*As pointed out in *Jandar of Callisto*, Jandar's knowledge of the world of Thanator is limited to the same hemisphere wherein he first materialized. Neither he nor any of the Thanatorians with whom he has become friendly has any knowledge of the other side of the planet, which is why he was able at various times to pretend his homeland lay on the other side without risking exposure.—L. C.

"True, Ganatolian. It is but the least of my abilities. When this gallant warrior here came into Shondakor, I knew him from the very first as a man from another world. His is a strange tale, and it will have a stranger ending, as I somehow seem to know—"

"Know you aught of the mysterious power that guided me to this world?" I cried, for the mystery of my coming hence had long plaqued me. Reluctantly, Ool shook his head and his cold eyes were dull and opaque.

"Nay. There are things hidden even from the probing skills of a Mind Wizard: but someday you will know the answer—if you live." He smiled.

"From the first, I knew of your true identity and of your cause and mission," he said sleekly, animation returning to his keen gaze. "I did not reveal you to my lords, for it amused me to see you play this little drama out to its end. But that end has come, aye, the last act is upon us even now, and I fear me you shall none of you live out the scene to its final curtain."

I lifted my cutlass into view.

"Have you forgotten, Mind Wizard, that I bear cold steel and you are unarmed?" I said tensely. His smile was mild and bland.

"And would you strike down an old man in cold blood?" he murmured. I shrugged.

"I will kill any man who stands between me and the woman I love," I growled. "I have naught against you, Ool; naught have you done to oppose me in my quest, therefore I am willing to let you live. Only do not get in my way—"

"Alas for your quest, O Jandar, it is not my will that you rescue the Princess of your heart," he smiled.

"You mean—"

"I mean that for all these months I have been working towards a certain end," he replied, and I knew then that I would have to kill him.

"What end, Mind Wizard?" I asked.

"I am not here by chance or accident, but by plan. We of dark Kuur must subjugate this hemisphere, and since we are few, we must set nation against nation, weakening them through endless wars, so that we may carry off the victory in the end. According to the decision of my Masters, the Prince of the Chac Yuul weds the Princess of Shondakor, thus provoking war between the Sky Pirates and the Black Legion. Out of that war, one victor shall arise—and we of shadowy Kuur shall dominate that victor. Alas, our plans have no room in them for Jandar of Tellus, or Koja of the Yathoon Horde, or Lukor of Ganatol—or even for the Ku Thad."

Suddenly I saw everything, clear and plain as if it were written on the wall.

It was the meddling little Mind Wizard had set Prince Vaspian and his father at odds, had cast the seeds of suspicion into their minds, each of the other. For surely, if the mind wizardry of Ool the Uncanny could blot a question of his race from the minds of those he met, that same grim art could *insert* a thought into the minds of others just as easily.

A sense of futility arose within me. All that we had striven for, all our plans and hazards, had been but as a game played out for the amusement of this fat, sinister little priest!

He had known when I despatched poor brave doomed Marud to the Lord Yarrak with my letter which revealed the secret tunnel under the walls and the river. That was true— now I remembered!—it had been *Ool's men* who caught Marud on his return!

But why on his return? Why let him get to the warriors

hiding in the Grand Kumala at all, when Ool could just as well have seized him ere he entered the secret passage? Why let him pass the letter to the Ku Thad, unless—

—*Unless the Golden Warriors were walking into a trap!*

"You are not stupid, O Jandar," the little Mind Wizard chuckled. "Indeed the mighty Yarrak and his gallant warriors will find themselves entrapped when they come through the tunnel this day and gamble all on one last, brave attempt to reconquer Shondakor! For I shall alert a full cohort of the Legion to wait hidden by the secret entrance of the tunnel, and as they emerge into the streets of Shondakor, they shall face the last battle and the doom of all their kind."

Grimly I stepped in front of him and set the point of my sword over his heart.

"You have just signed your own death warrant, wizard!" I said.

His cold, clever eyes probed deeply into mine, and his gaze was not worried but placid and serene and smiling.

"Think you I am a fool, O Jandar of Tellus?" he said softly. "Think you I came here to explain everything, to put myself into your power, without a means of escape? I am not a fool, Earthling; nay, 'tis you who art the fool. You should thrust home with that clumsy sword, and speak after. *Now it is too late.*"

And then a thunderbolt struck me directly between the eyes and I fell forward into a sea of black gloom.

Agony lanced through my skull as I swam groggily back to consciousness again. I could feel the gritty stone flags against my cheek, and the dank odor of musty straw was heavy in my nostrils.

Blearily I opened my eyes and strove to see what was happening.

Behind me, Koja and Lukor lay crumpled on the stone pave. Ool had struck them down even as I had been felled by his mental bolt. The power to read and to manipulate minds must include with it the strange and awful skill to employ the mind as a weapon. Ool's trained mind was able to project a stunning mental blow before which any lesser mind was helpless.

Why, then, had my own unconsciousness been but a momentary thing? Why did I rouse to wakefulness, while Lukor and Koja lay sprawled in the grip of an eerie mental paralysis?

Perhaps the answer lay in my own nature. I was not native to this jungle moon of Thanator; my body, my brain, had evolved upon a far-off planet. The bolt of mental force which the fat little Mind Wizard of Kuur had projected had stunned, but had not thrust me down into full unconsciousness. Perhaps the intensity of that stunning bolt had been attuned to the frequence of minds native to Thanator. Perhaps Ool the Uncanny had, for a moment, forgotten my extra-Thanatorian origin. It was a small thing to forget—doubtless, it had seemed of no great importance. But it seemed, after all, that the fate of a world hung on that little error he had committed in his complacence.

I resolved that he would feel the full weight of that error *now!*

Springing to my feet, snatching up the cutlass where it had fallen from my hand as I fell, I faced Ool, who had been bending over Lukor and who now started around with amazement written all over his placid, buttery features.

My brain throbbed abominably—I had the great-grandfather of all headaches—but I grimly thrust the consciousness of pain from me and sprang upon him, sword in hand.

From under his voluminous robes, Ool drew a rapier. So

he was armed after all! His pretense at being unarmed was just another deception—just one more lie. It would benefit him little: I had learned the art of the blade from Lukor himself, and he was one of the greatest masters of that art on all Thanator. The fat little man could not long stand against my flashing steel, and now he knew his mental bolts had but a momentary and passing influence on my alien intelligence.

We fought without words, the little Mind Wizard and I, with no one to watch. Our only audience consisted of a dead man and two unconscious warriors.

It was a strange duel. In many ways, it was the strangest battle that I have ever fought.

Ool knew hardly anything of swordplay; his soft, plump hands were not accustomed to the grip of a sword hilt. Nor was he used to violent physical exercise. In no time his fat jowls and bald brow glistened with the sheen of perspiration and his breath came in panting gasps and his arms trembled from weariness and exertion.

But Ool could read my mind, and he knew in advance where I would direct every thrust and stroke—and his blade was there ahead of me!

It was an odd sensation. In a way it was like fighting yourself, like battling against a mirror image, pitting your blade against an adversary who knew precisely every move you would make even before you made it!

A cold horror gripped me. I had faced powerful swordsmen ere now; it was absurd to feel qualms of dread, crossing steel with this fat, puffing little priest. But so much depended on the outcome of this duel that my mind was a dizzy turmoil of fear and tension. Koja and Lukor lay helpless, mentally paralyzed by the bolt of uncanny mind force: if Ool slew me, my helpless friends would follow me down to Death's amazing kingdom. The woman I loved would be forced into the arms of a sneering coward, the gallant warriors of Lord Yarrak would walk directly into a trap, the small, peaceful kingdoms and cities of Thanator, cities I had never seen, would fall to the cunning of the Mind Wizards—*a world lay helplessly in bondage if I were slain!*

I wonder if ever before, in all the history of Thanator or of any other world, so much rested on the outcome of a single duel. The fate of a world, the destiny of many nations, depended on my quick thinking, steady hand, and flashing sword!

I tried to fence automatically, without conscious thought, relying on the sheer force of training and instinct alone, hoping in that way to overcome the advantage Ool's unearthly mind power had over me. Alas, it was in vain: whatever the nature and extent of his telepathic skills, he continued to anticipate, by a fraction of a second, my every thrust, parry, and stroke.

Perhaps his mental probe went deeper than I even guessed. Perhaps he could read me clear to the depths of my unconscious and could scrutinize those fighting instincts, those trained responses, on which I now relied. Perhaps he was alert to those tiny triggering impulses of nervous energy as they set into action the twitching of my muscles, long ere those muscles moved in actuality. I know not. I only know that wherever my point flashed, the flat of his blade was there.

Only the Lords of Gordrimator know what would have been the eventual outcome of this weird battle of strength and steel against mind magic.

Perhaps my very superior endurance would have won out in the end, or perhaps Ool's strange powers would have gained the ascendancy in the duel, and he would have struck at me, using some tactic of advanced swordsmanship drawn from my own brain to strike me down.

At any rate, it was not my hand that slew him, but the hand of a dead man that struck his doom.

As I advanced, plying my blade in a glittering dance of death, the little wizard retreated, shuffling along backwards. Around the huge square stone chamber we went ... and then the hand of Fate struck.

The corpse of Bluto lay where I had struck it down. A puddle of cooling gore splashed the rushes. His dead limbs lay asprawl, and as Ool shuffled backwards, retreating from my point, he struck the dead hand of Bluto with one foot, staggered off balance, and fell over backwards, striking his bald pate on the cold stone pave.

His skull split like a ripe melon ... and thus the weird duel of sword skill against mind magic came to an end, and death came to Ool the Uncanny at the hand of a corpse!

BOOK FIVE

THE BOOK OF DARLOONA

CHAPTER XVII
THE FALL OF HOOM

As Valkar sprang down the steps of the high altar and drew back his arm to plunge his blade directly into the back of the robed and hooded little wizard-priest, Ool turned and looked him full in the face, and Valkar gasped, and paled, and his blade went wavering to one side.

"Jandar!" he cried in astonishment.

Was it relief—or joy—or amazement—that flared in the emerald eyes of Darloona?

"Jandar—?" she echoed wonderingly.

At her side, Prince Vaspian blanched, and turned an incredulous gaze on the hooded figure who stood a few steps above him.

"Jandar!" he gasped bewilderedly.

I laughed and threw back my hood, tossing the heavy robes aside, and stood above them, grinning with reckless humor, the heavy cutlass in my hand.

For, of course, it was I who had emerged from the far side of the Hall of Hoom, muffled in the thick robes I had taken from the corpse of Ool the Uncanny who lay dead in the Pits of Shondakor. Hunched over so that I seemed no taller than the fat little Mind Wizard, shuffling along in imitation of his waddling stride, I had gained a place close to Darloona without a single person in all that mighty hall guessing my identity. But the rasp of Valkar's buskin against the stone step had made me turn—just in time to let him see and recognize my face under the shadowing cowl, and turn his blade aside before it drank my heart's blood.

After Ool fell and split his skull, ending our uncanny battle in the Pits, the spell which had subjugated my comrades, Lukor and Koja, was broken. Donning Ool's robes as a handy disguise, I had swiftly found the nearest entrance to the maze of secret passages that lay within the walls of the royal palace, and we made our way to the Hall of Hoom where I knew Darloona was to be found.

Prince Vaspian saw the look in my eyes and the naked sword in my hand, and realized suddenly that this was the end of an imposture. His lips curled in a sullen snarl, and he tore his rapier from its jeweled scabbard, but I disarmed him with a practiced twist of the wrist and he fled from me, abandoning the Princess.

"Jandar—is it really you?" she whispered as I put my arm about her shoulders and turned to hold the astounded throng at bay.

"It is I, my princess," I replied calmly. "Think you that Jandar would not move heaven and earth to protect you from the arms of that weakling? Fear not for your helpless people— Vaspian will not very long be in a position to harm them!"

Valkar spoke from behind us in a clear, penetrating voice.

"Jandar entered the city pretending to be a mercenary and won a place in the ranks of the Black Legion in order to rescue you, my princess," he said. "His daring and courage, his cool head and quick mind, have saved you from a hideous parody of a marriage! Now you must come with us, swiftly, without argument—"

But just then we had no time for talk. Arkola, his face a savage mask of ferocity and rage, thundered a command at his bewildered guards who came charging up the stair towards where we stood. Valkar and I met them with flashing steel and drove them back a pace.

Darloona, however, would not obey our wishes and retreat to the top of the altar level where it was safer. The brave girl snatched up the rapier the cowardly Vaspian had let fall in his ignominious flight and stood beside us, adding the strength of her blade to our own.

Within seconds, four guards lay gasping out their life on the bloody steps and we had won a moment's respite from the assault.

But a hundred stout warriors of the Black Legion thronged the hall in a guard of honor and Arkola thundered commands that snapped them from their paralysis and sent them charging up the flight of marble steps in a massed body.

Our swords flickered and played like summer lightning, and men fell screaming, splashed with gore, but others came charging over the flopping bodies of the fallen, and we were hard pressed and retreated, step by step, holding our own only by advantage of superior height, as we stood higher on the stair than did they who sought to assault us.

Still, it was only a matter of time before sheer weight of numbers dragged us down. As I fought, I wondered desperately—where were Koja and Lukor? They had hidden in the antechamber as I went out to impersonate Ool and seize the Princess, but surely they had heard all the commotion by now and knew we were fighting for our very lives here on the steps below the altar of Hoom!

I dispatched an opponent and turned to see if Darloona was safe.

She was not only safe, but fighting like a tigress. How glorious she looked, her red-gold hair streaming about her lithe body like a tattered war banner, the fire of battle shining in her splendid green eyes, her full red lips parted with the excitement of the moment. In a second her flickering blade cut down the warrior she had engaged and she turned her enigmatic gaze on me.

"This is all madness, Jandar—yet, well met! I had not thought that we should ever meet again, save perhaps in the spirit, when our souls should travel on that long journey to stand before the tall thrones of the Lords of Gordrimator," she said.

"I could not desert you, my princess," I said.

"It was very brave of you to seek me out amidst the legions of the Chac Yuul," she said somberly. "Yet now all my plans are ruined, and my people are doomed—"

"I could not stand idly by and see you wed to a man you loathed!" I protested. She shook her head fiercely.

"But I must! Else my people will suffer!"

"Let us await the outcome of this day," I suggested. "For I managed to get word to your uncle, Lord Yarrak, of a secret tunnel beneath the Ajand and the city walls, and ere long the Ku Thad will enter Shondakor in force, and mayhap your people and not the Black Legion will be the masters here before this day ends."

Hope flared suddenly within her glorious emerald eyes, and her warm full lips parted breathlessly as if to speak—but then they were upon us in strength again, and we were both too busy for further conversation just then.

They pressed us hard, ringing us about with flashing steel,

and although we fought magnificently, I knew in my heart that it was but a matter of time before superior weight of numbers would crush us down.

Yet it was not in me to complain of my lot. For indeed, were I to fall here, I could not think of a better way to die than this—battling for my life beside the woman I loved, a sword in my hand, grim laughter on my lips, Darloona beside me!

We fought on, but without hope....

Suddenly the warrior whose sword I had engaged fell back a step, dropped his point, and cried out in fear. His features paled and his mouth sagged open, and his eyes went beyond me and froze as if fixed on some fearful apparition which stood behind my back.

"The god—*moves*," he cried with horror.

The other warriors about us staggered back from us now, their gaze transfixed with terror on something behind us.

"The god—*lives!*"

Risking a sword between the shoulders, I turned swiftly and cast a swift glance behind me. What I saw made me start with astonishment!

Above us on the flat dais stood the hideous stone idol of Hoom, devil-god of the Chac Yuul. Very horrible was Hoom, with glaring eyes, pot belly, leering fanged jaws gaped wide in a gloating grin, monstrous arms spread as if to crush us puny mortals in his multiple embrace.

And Hoom ... *moved!*

Even as I stared in amazement, the arm which was extended out over the stairs *lifted* into a position of command!

And a deep, hollow voice boomed out, filling the great hall with rolling echoes!

"LET THEM GO FREE," it thundered.

Swords wavered and fell; men stared up with expressions of utter astonishment frozen upon their pallid features.

I sprang into action. I knew not what had caused this weird and inexplicable phenomenon, but I seized the opportunity for escape which it held out to us. Valkar and Darloona stood, gripped in the same amazement that held the others petrified. I signaled them frantically.

"Come! The panel—*now*, while we have the chance!"

We sprang up the steps to the dais, and Vaspian saw us.

He was no less the superstitious savage than his fellows, but jealousy and suspicion colored his mind. His features distorted into a vicious snarl as he saw us eluding his vengeance, and he came leaping up the stair after us, sword lifted for the kill.

But it was Hoom who slew!

The great stone arm that was lifted in a commanding position came smashing down—and crushed his skull. Vaspian fell dead on the steps of the high altar in a welter of splattering gore, and the room erupted into fury!

"Kill them all!" Arkola thundered, waving his great blade. A host of swordsmen sprang howling on our heels.

I darted around behind the idol, and found a stone door open in its back. Within, his hands working a series of levers, sat Lukor, his merry eyes dancing with delighted mischief— and Koja, whose deep metallic voice, through a wooden trumpet arranged so that the words seemed to come from the very mouth of the idol, had supplied the booming command.

In a flash the entire mystery was revealed. The image was hollow and a simple system of weights and counterweights enabled whoever sat within to move the idol's arms up and down through slots and grooves. Doubtless this was the secret of Ool's authority over the Black Legion—he struck at them through their superstitious terrors of the unknown.

I learned later that Koja and Lukor had lurked in concealment, awaiting my return, until the sounds of the uproar caused by my unmasking alerted them to peril. They had hurried out to a new position of concealment behind the idol, and by accident had touched the secret spring that opened the hidden door in the idol's back. The discovery had offered them a more powerful method of assisting us than merely adding their swords to our own. But now the imposture was over, and half a hundred warriors were charging up the stairs to pull us down. I thought swiftly. If the massive stone idol were hollow instead of solid, then it was not as heavy and immobile as it looked—

"Here—with me!" I said curtly, and I set my shoulder against the back of the idol and—*heaved!*

Valkar, Koja, and Lukor grasped my plan instantly, and lent their strength to my own while Darloona stood, hands pressed to her heart in an agony of suspense.

Would our desperate scheme work? There was no time to think of an alternate. I clenched my jaw and threw the full weight of back, arms, and shoulders into one last terrific effort.

And Hoom—moved.

The idol shuddered, slid forward on its dais with a grating of stone against stone, struck the horns of the altar, and toppled over!

Men were crushed beneath its ponderous weight, for even though Hoom was hollow, still he was fashioned of massive stone. The monstrous idol came sliding and crashing down the steps, spilling men to either side, squeaking and crunching over the buckling stair. Then it crashed full length and went rolling down the steps like some colossal juggernaut of destruction. The multiple stone arms broke away; fragments of stone went flying to every side; I saw one mammoth stone hand spin away and smash a fleeing warrior to bloody ruin, for all the world as a man might crush a fly with the palm of his hand. Dozens were crushed to death; scores were maimed or injured.

Midway down the stair, Hoom struck an obstruction and shattered. His grinning head cracked and broke off and went skipping horribly down the steps, straight for the place where Arkola stood, his strong face frozen in a mask of incredulous horror.

The head smashed full into him and skidded on, leaving him a broken, dying thing.

Thus died Arkola the Usurper.

CHAPTER XVIII

THE CONQUEST
OF SHONDAKOR

We saw no more of Hoom's murderous fall, for we seized the opportunity afforded by his juggernaut-like passage down the stone stair to duck into the secret panel from which Valkar had sprung.

I seized Darloona's arm and thrust her ahead of me, with Valkar going before and Koja and Lukor at my heels. We ran through dark passageways and it seemed, from the uproar, that the entire palace was filled with the clamor of battle. Had the Ku Thad struck at last? We came out onto a broad and level terrace overlooking the city and gazed with delight upon what we saw.

Down every street came yelling mobs of Shondakorians, brandishing clubs, sticks, tools—whatever they could lay their hands on.

Before them, scattered units of the Black Legion retreated in confusion. And in a moment we saw the reason why—for there, in the forefront of the howling mobs, battled the warrior nobles of the Ku Thad with mighty Yarrak in the fore, his beard blowing on the wind, his great sword catching day-fire as it rose and fell tirelessly, smashing down warrior after warrior of the Chac Yuul.

In truth, the Ku Thad had come at the best possible moment, and half the city was theirs!

I laughed, weeping with delight, shaking Valkar's shoulder, yelling and pointing. Darloona's eyes shone with fierce, queenly pride and her lips trembled. Koja and Lukor recognized the bold warrior lords of the Golden People and shouted with joy and triumph.

But there was much fighting to do before the city was truly ours, for the Black Legion, although taken by surprise, still vastly outnumbered Darloona's warriors, and although the populace of the city had recognized Lord Yarrak and had risen in arms to join the battle for their beloved princess, they were poorly armed and could not stand up to Arkola's trained and disciplined troops. Even as we watched, the progress of the loyalists slowed to a crawl as Chac Yuul units sped to reinforce their sagging lines.

Then the inexplicable intervened.

A dense black shadow fell over the embattled streets below and before any could look up in surprise a deafening explosion and a blinding flash of flame erupted in the very midst of the thickly packed Chac Yuul warriors.

Another explosion—and another! We stared up to see the skies filled with fantastic flying vessels which had appeared over the embattled city as if by magic.

It was the Sky Pirates of Zanadar, and they had launched their long-impending attack against the Black Legion at last!

The ungainly flying contraptions of the City in the Clouds were like great wooden galleons, made fantastical with carven poop, fluttering banners ornamental balustrades. They hung aloft on immense, slowly beating wings, buoyed up against the pull of gravity by the powerful lifting force of the mysterious gas wherewith their hollow double hulls were suffused.

To the eye of the uninitiated, the sky ships of Zanadar were a thrilling and unbelievable sight, a fleet of enormous galleons that rode the golden vapors of Thanator's skies as the galleons of another world might ride the blue waves of the sea. But Lukor, Koja, and I had labored at the wheels of similar vessels but months before, and we knew the ingenious system of weights and pulleys that manipulated those vast ungainly wings, and the unique structure of the flying galleons which were made of compressed paper instead of wood, and thus weighed only a fraction of what their ocean-going counterparts on another world would have. Still and all, they were an incredible achievement, and had it not been for the rapacious greed and cruelty of the Sky Pirates, who used their aerial armada to prey off the merchant caravans of weaker peoples, I could have applauded their amazing skills with undimmed enthusiasm.

Nothing on my world had ever equaled the fantastic achievement of the Zanadarians, although that mighty genius of the Renaissance, the immortal Leonardo da Vinci, had sketched out plans for just such wing-powered ornithopters in his secret notebooks. And had he had access to the powerful lifting gas wherewith the Zanadarians nullified the weight of their flying ships, and had he also possessed the secret of the strong, molded, and laminated paper construction, the skies of old Earth might well have seen such a flying navy as this, half a thousand years before the triumph at Kitty Hawk.

Never before had I seen the ornithopters of Zanadar actually engaged in battle; now I saw the immense tactical advantage the fantastic flying galleons of the Sky Pirates possessed over land armies, and a qualm went over me. Unless some unexpected disaster intervened to demolish the imperial ambitions of Prince Thuton of Zanadar, his aerial navy could conquer all of Thanator and subjugate her peoples with ease.

Indeed, the Sky Pirates of Zanadar formed, if anything, a far greater menace to the peaceful nations of this jungle world than did the Mind Wizards of Kuur, who were few in number and who lacked military might.

Hovering on their slowly beating vans, the ponderous flying machines hung against the golden skies like something in one of the nightmarish paintings of Hieronymus Bosch or Hannes Bok. Far above the reach of spear, arrow, or catapult they hovered, and from the safe vantage of their height they rained down explosive missiles on the crowd-thronged streets below.

It was the hated Chac Yuul they were attacking, luckily for us, and the fire bombs wreaked a terrible toll of the beleaguered Black Legion warriors. Before my gaze the defensive lines about the palace were crumbling and the victorious ranks of the Ku Thad pressed forward, beating back the broken and demoralized forces of the foe.

Ere long, it seemed likely that the surviving Chac Yuul warriors would take refuge within the palace itself, which was constructed on the lines of a fortress, and which could be held indefinitely against siege. It was needful, then, for me to carry word to Lord Yarrak concerning the secret entrance into the palace—the hidden route whereby Valkar had often found his way into the network of secret passageways and thus to the suite of the Princess Darloona. For unless Yarrak made swift use of this secret door, he would exhaust his strength in a costly and time-consuming siege of the palace.

There was no time to lose.

I seized Valkar's arm and swiftly drew him aside, suggesting that he withdraw to a secluded corner of the terrace and guard the safety of the Princess, while Koja, Lukor, and I sought to fight our way through the battling mobs to the side of Lord Yarrak.

Valkar protested that there was no reason why he should remain behind in security while we risked all, but, I had no leisure in which to argue the point and tersely said so.

"Take care, Jandar," the Princess begged. I made no reply, but after one long look into her emerald eyes and a brief salute, I turned away and swung out over the balustrade of the terrace and began clambering down the outer wall of the palace, followed by Koja and Lukor.

Obviously, it would have wasted much time for us to have attempted to work our way out of the palace through the mazelike network of secret passages. This route was much shorter and swifter. It was also, of course, much more hazardous: but I had faced a thousand perils in the service of my princess ere now, and I was not likely to flinch from one more danger.

Fortunately the outer wall of the palace was encrusted with elaborate sculptures. I have noted before the considerable similarity between the architectural style of Shondakor and the fantastical stone structures of the enigmatic ruined cities of Cambodia, such as Angkor Vat and Arangkôr. The surface of the walls was covered with enormous stone masks which stared down like so many carven gods on the embattled streets below. Stone devils and dragons, gargoyles and gorgons, leered and laughed from between the calm features of graven divinity, and their profusion of horns and beaks and claws afforded us a broad choice of handholds and toeholds wherewith to clamber down the two stories to the street level below. Thus without any particular difficulty we reached the broad plaza before the main gate of the palace.

I found that matters had gone in the very direction I had assumed they might, and that the main forces of the Chac Yuul had already retreated into the palace, while small groups of surviving Black Legion warriors sought similar refuge in one or another of the stone buildings of the city. From these citadels they were fighting a twofold battle against the Ku Thad in the streets and the Zanadarians aloft in the skies.

Arkola had erected a rude defense against the impending attack of the Sky Pirates during the last days of his regime. Rooftop catapults had been set in readiness to do battle against the flying machines of Thuton, and as I gained the ground at last I saw to my surprise that the embattled Chac Yuul warriors had actually managed to bring down at least one of the great aerial galleons.

A well-placed stone missile, hurled with terrific force from one of these rooftop war engines, had smashed the control cupola of this galley, and grappling irons, securely hooked into the ornamental carvings, figurehead, and deck balustrade, had drawn it against the roof of a nearby building, from which bonds it was not likely to escape. Even as I gazed the Chac Yuul archers swept the decks of the captive ornithopter with a deadly rain of arrows, and thus the flying armada of Zanadar was lessened by at least one vessel.

But now Chac Yuul warriors, fleeing in broken rout before the victorious advance of the Ku Thad, were all about me, and I had no time to observe further events. For I was busy fighting for my life against the panicking warriors.

With Koja at my left hand and gallant old Lukor at my right, we formed a flying wedge and cut our way through the fleeing rabble to the forefront of the advancing Ku Thad. We three made a magnificent team, and the terror-stricken Chac Yuul melted out of our path, helpless to oppose us for long.

It was a scene of strange and terrible beauty, apocalyptic

in its grandeur and destruction. The streets were filled with battling men, and they rang with the steely music of clashing swords, the shouts and war cries of the victorious, the howls and shrieks of the injured and the dying. Corpses lay all about, amidst the rubble of shattered stone, and the air was darkened with a pall of drifting smoke from burning buildings. The heavens resounded with the deafening explosion of the bombardment of the Sky Pirates, and their mighty winged ships darkened the ground with their monstrous gliding shadows. All about me men were fighting, falling, fleeing. The day of vengeance had come at last for the Black Legion, and the day of victory had dawned for the brave warriors of Shondakor.

We fought on through a scene of nightmarish splendor and power, while all about us a dynasty died and a new age was born.

At length we recognized the grim features of Lord Yarrak as he fought at the forefront of his warrior nobles, his beard flying in the murk, his eyes ablaze with victory, his great sword rising and falling tirelessly as he cut down the squat, swarthy men who had long held his city in their merciless grip, and who now received no mercy from his avenging blade.

He knew me at a glance, and his eyes lit with amazement to see me here in the streets amid the struggling hosts. Swiftly I drew him aside and satisfied his apprehensions, assuring him that Darloona was in a place of safety, guarded by his own valiant son, for which he gave heartfelt thanks to the Lords of Gordrimator.

"But as you can observe," I said tersely, "most of the surviving Black Legion warriors have already retreated within the walls of the palace, from which vantage they can safely hold the gates against a thousand warriors, while picking off your men with well-placed archers."

"That is true, Jandar," he nodded in grim assent.

"There is, however, a secret entrance into the palace, which was discovered by your own son, Prince Valkar," I informed him. "If you will follow me, we can be within the palace before the Chac Yuul are aware of it, and can open the gates to the body of your warriors."

"Lead on, then!"

Summoning a small band of picked swordsmen to accompany him, Lord Yarrak, Lukor, Koja, and I swiftly made our way to the secret door whose hidden place Valkar had disclosed to me many days before. I do not think that a single eye marked our progress, for the bombardment of the Zanadarian flying machines had set afire several nearby buildings in their efforts to destroy the rooftop catapults which imperiled the safety of the aerial fleet, and the drifting smoke of the conflagration effectively hid us from view as we crept along the outer wall of the royal citadel to the small stand of ornamental sorad trees whose thick dark foliage concealed the secret door from discovery.

My fingers fumbled along the rough stone of the wall and within but moments they had found and depressed the secret spring. A mighty slab of stone sank soundlessly into the earth, revealing the black mouth of a secret passage which yawned before us. With a reassuring word to Lord Yarrak and his nobles, I stepped forward without hesitation into the throat of the hidden passageway and within moments we had vanished from sight. The stone slab rose behind us and once again became part of the walls of the citadel.

*   *   *

It would be to no particular purpose to bore my reader—if any eye but mine own shall ever peruse these pages—with a lengthy and complete account of the battle which ensued.

Suffice it to say that, once we had breached the walls of the palace by means of the hidden entrance, our flashing swords swiftly cut down the astonished guards the Chac Yuul leaders had set over the palace gates, and it was but the work of moments to remove the massive bolts which had been set in place to hold the gate secure against the entry of the Ku Thad.

And once the gates were opened, and the victorious forces of Lord Yarrak poured within, the palace fell to us without a prolonged and costly battle. For, although those of the Chac Yuul who survived sought to blockade the hallways and corridors, and to make us pay dearly in the lives of our warriors for every advance, they were helpless to oppose us for long. Yet once again, I thanked whatever gods might be that I had spent so many weary hours in the exploration of the secret passages within the massive walls of the palace. For by means of this network of hidden ways, I was able to circumvent every attempt by the Black Legion to block our progress. Each time they sought to seal off a corridor or close a suite of apartments against us, I simply sought and found a hidden panel in the walls and led a force of Ku Thad warriors through the labyrinthine maze, coming out *behind* the barricade to strike down the surprised Chac Yuul who guarded it.

In this manner we very swiftly invested the entire palace from top to bottom, slaying a vast number of the Black Legion, and taking captive those whose prudence or cowardice was sufficient to overcome their stubborn sense of superiority and who laid down their weapons and surrendered to our advance.

The battle had taken hours and it was now late afternoon.

But—save for a few scattered pockets of resistance, where a handful of Black Legion warriors still held out and refused to surrender—before nightfall the Golden City of Shondakor was conquered and the victorious Ku Thad reigned again in the mighty metropolis of their ancestors there on the shores of the river Ajand.

CHAPTER XIX
VICTORY—AND DEFEAT!

The weeks that have passed since the conquest of Shondakor and the victory of the Ku Thad and the destruction of the Black Legion have been quiet, but not exactly restful, for we have labored long and mightily to repair the damage wrought by the great battle and to bring into some semblance of order the chaos and confusion into which Shondakor fell during the struggle among the three forces.

The bombardment of the Sky Pirates of Zanadar was actually less destructive than it seemed at the time, for the main goal of Prince Thuton was obviously to crush the Black Legion rather than to level the city of the Ku Thad. Thus most of the fire bombs had been directed at mobs of Chac Yuul warriors in the streets, and only those buildings which housed the rooftop catapults had been assaulted by the Sky Pirates. Only a few buildings had suffered any extensive damage from the aerial bombardment; and since by far the greater number of structures towards the heart of the city, in the area around the royal palace, were built of stone, the fires caused by the Zanadarian bombs had not spread.

It had, of course, crossed my mind at the time that we might succeed in destroying the Black Legion only to find ourselves locked in battle against the Sky Pirates. Fortunately this did not prove to be the case. In fact, even while we were still engaged in crushing the vast vestiges of Chac Yuul resistance within the royal palace, the bombardment ceased— the armada lifted—the Sky Pirates suspended their attack upon Shondakor and rose into the upper air, wheeling slowly above the city, with the obvious intention of sailing off to their distant stronghold, the City in the Clouds.

This cessation of the attack, this withdrawal of the vast flying contraptions from the skies over Shondakor, was most puzzling. At the time I could not account for it. It was only later that the dread truth burst upon my consciousness and I realized the ghastly reason that had occasioned this inexplicable retreat of the Sky Pirates. . . .

The golden skies of Thanator darkened swiftly with the advent of night, which falls swift and suddenly upon this jungle world. Huge Imavad ascended the skies, glowing against the dark like a vast rose-red lamp. Tiny Juruvad, as the peoples of this world call Amalthea, the innermost moon of the planet Jupiter, was also aloft, a minute flake of golden fire. Ere long the shimmering lime-green sphere of Orovad, or Io, would soar up into the heights of heaven.

But before Orovad rose over the horizon, the city was ours.

Great was the joy with which the citizens of Shondakor hailed the triumphant warriors of the Ku Thad. Ten thousand voices rose up to chant the stately measures of the anthem of the immemorial stone city by the river Ajand. Surely the measured thunders of that noble and ancient song were audible to the last of the Sky Pirates of Zanadar as they sailed off down the darkling sky, bound for their far-off mountaintop

fortress amidst the mountains of Varan-Hkor which rise hundreds of *korads* away, beyond the trackless jungles of the
Grand Kumala, on the borders of that unknown and boreal
wilderness called The Frozen Land.

I could almost think that the music of that mighty anthem
rang against the cold and watchful stars that peer down in
redundant remote scrutiny on the little dramas played out by
mortal men across the small stage of this little world.

More than one half of the Black Legion perished in the battle
of Shondakor.

Arkola, the Warlord, and his son, Prince Vaspian, and
many of the clan leaders and high commanders of the Black
Legion died there in the Hall of Hoom, either crushed beneath
the rolling juggernaut of their fallen devil-god, or slain by
the swords of Valkar, Darloona, and myself, when we held
the stair against their advance.

Leaderless, a milling chaos of confused and frightened
men, under attack from every side, the common warriors of
the Chac Yuul fell in their hundreds and their thousands before the mobs of angry citizens, the disciplined swords of the
Ku Thad, or the rain of death and fire from the flying navy
of Zanadar. Over a thousand were slain by Lord Yarrak's force
within the palace itself.

The small number which remained of the once-mighty
conquering bandit horde were broken and demoralized. They
were disarmed and captured with little effort; many of them
laid down their weapons and surrendered rather than continue the unequal struggle any longer.

Lord Yarrak could have had the captured remnants of the
Chac Yuul slaughtered. It was no less than they deserved, and
in this barbaric world, mercy was a rare phenomenon. However, the great Baron spared all those who had been taken;

he expressed himself as being weary of killing, sick of slaughter, and as the few who had survived the destruction of the Legion could never again form a menace against the peaceful nations of Thanator, he set them free and drove them forth from the gates of Shondakor into perpetual exile, never again to return to the lands of the Ku Thad on peril of death.

Thus the Black Legion passed forever from the great stage of history; scattered bands of them infested the mountains for some little time, preying on merchant caravans, but these small bands dwindled and soon were heard of no more. Rarely has a more decisive and total victory been recorded in the annals of warfare.

In the weeks that followed I have set down this narrative account of my deeds and adventures on the moon Callisto, and now I am almost at the end of my story.

Lord Yarrak has promised me that when I have concluded this history, a band of his warriors will carry it from the gates of Shondakor through the jungles of the Grand Kumala to that enigmatic ring of monoliths which stand as eternal guardians over the Gate Between The Worlds. They will set the bundle of manuscript within the circle of the standing stones, and will watch as the cycle of the moons comes again to that hour when the mysterious sparkling beam of unknown force blazes forth once more to link this world of Thanator and my own Earth, the planet whereupon I was born, with its weird and inexplicable shining pathway.

And for the second time a bundle of manuscript that is a true narrative of my remarkable adventures upon the surface of this strange and terrible and beautiful world will dematerialize into a sparkling cloud of energy and go flashing up that weird ray to vanish from the knowledge of men in the dark places between the stars.

Will this record of my adventures find its way across the limitless void? Will it cross unharmed the vast distance of some three hundred and ninety million miles of space to re-materialize once more in the Lost City of Arangkôr amidst the trackless jungles of Cambodia, on the planet Earth?

I cannot know for certain.

I can only hope that this record of my discoveries and deeds will survive that mysterious trip through space, and come to the attention of some person of my own world. For I should not like to think that this account, wherein I have so laboriously preserved the lore of another world, will be lost forever in the darkness between the stars.

There is a curious blending of nostalgia and sorrow in my heart as I set down these last few words.

There is a restlessness in me, and a hunger to visit again the fair and splendid cities of my youth, to see dawn break crimson over the green jungles of the Amazon and the stars glimmer faintly in the clear gliding waters of the Oronoco, to drink raw gin in the fetid back alleys of Rio, and taste the indescribable savor of fresh black coffee and frying bacon on the cold winy air of a little camp high in the Rockies.

I would like to see the fabulous lights of Broadway beating up to dim the few faint stars above, and to see the mighty shaft of the Empire State lift its flashing crown of searchlights against the gloom, and to wash down a sizzling veal scallopini with a bottle of tangy Chianti in that Italian restaurant on Bleecker Street in crazy, cluttered Greenwich Village.

All of these things I would like to do, and all of them I could do, if I truly wished.

Yes, for I could accompany that band of handpicked Ku Thad warriors across the jungles of the Grand Kumala to that ring of stones that marks the place where I first set foot on the surface of this world of Thanator.

Then I was naked as a babe, alone and friendless, lost in a weird and hostile world of savage men and hideous monsters.

Now I have a multitude of friends: somber Koja with his great eyes blazing like black jewels in the featureless casque of his gleaming, inhuman features; gallant old Lukor, that chivalrous and gentlemanly master swordsman; brave, noble Valkar and wise Zastro and stern, kingly Lord Yarrak—good friends and gallant comrades all, tried and true, and tested in a thousand battles. They love me well, that I know, and will stand beside me in peace or in war.

And, although they have heaped me with honors, ennobled me with the high rank of a *komor* of the Ku Thad, thus giving me a place in the lordly nobility of Shondakor, and although I know that the Golden people of the Golden City will be proud and pleased to offer me a home amongst them for however long I wish to stay ... I also know that they would not stand in my way if I should desire to make that long trek through the jungle country of the Kumala and stand naked amidst the standing stones of the Gate, to bathe again in that shimmering force that will whisk me across millions of miles of space to the world that is my home.

My departure would grieve my Thanatorian friends and my old comrades would miss me at their high councils and on the ringing plains of war, we who have so often stood shoulder to shoulder, a smile on our lips, a sword in our hands, facing together the onslaught of our enemies.

They would mourn my departure, but they would set no obstacle before it.

But of course I shall not enter the Gate Between The Worlds.

It well may be that I shall never again stride the shores of the Oronoco, the back alleys of Rio, or the busy sidewalks of Broadway.

Perhaps, someday, I shall return, but not yet and not now. For now Thanator is my home. Here on this jungle world of war and battle and intrigue, I have found good friends, a cause for which to fight, and a woman to love.

Never shall I leave Callisto until she stands once again at my side.

If that longed-for day ever comes, if she truly yet lives, if I have succeeded in rescuing Darloona from the clutches of her enemies—then and then only will I think of going home once more.

My days are busy, assisting my friends in the rebuilding of war-shaken Shondakor. My afternoons and evenings have been devoted to setting down, however crudely, with what poor skill I possess, this record of my experiences.

My nights are given over to—*dreams.*

And my dreams have a soft, generous scarlet mouth, a splendid and womanly figure, clear, tilted eyes of emerald flame, soft warm flesh of amber gold, and a savage mane of rippling, red-gold splendor, like a mighty war banner.

Never can I forget her heart-shaking beauty, her peerless courage, her strength and fierce pride.

Never shall I forget my last glimpse of Darloona. The joy and horror and heartbreak of that cataclysmic moment echoes yet within the depths of my being.

The palace was finally ours and the last dejected survivors of the overwhelmed and broken Chac Yuul were disarmed and bound, our helpless captives.

We raced through the corridors, Yarrak and Lukor and Koja and I, to the broad terrace where I had left Darloona under the protection of Valkar's sword. All about us lay scenes of carnage and devastation; corpses lay strewn about the hallways amidst the wreckage of broken barricades.

Bands of the Ku Thad paced vigilantly the hallways of their retaken citadel, herding groups of Black Legion captives before them or seeking out the last pockets of resistance. Swords were naked in their hands and the joyous light of victory shone in their weary faces.

At length we reached the level terrace and looked out over a city rejoicing in the first hour of its freedom. Here and there a building in flames cast a drifting pall of black vapor across the skies, but the streets were cleared now and the gold and crimson banners of imperial Shondakor shook out upon the night winds their heraldic colors in token of victory.

Through the smoke-veiled skies the last few ornithopters yet circled the vast metropolis, ere rising to the heights of the sky for their long return voyage to Zanadar, the City in the Clouds. One mighty vessel yet hovered close above the palace. I recognized it as the *Kajazell*, the flagship of the aerial navy, Prince Thuton's own ship.

We searched the broad terrace with eager eyes, but strangely enough we did not see either Valkar or Darloona.

The ghostly chill of apprehension touched my heart.

Then I heard a stifled cry from behind me. It was Lord Yarrak, an expression of consternation on his face. With a trembling hand he pointed to a crumpled shape that lay huddled in the shadow of a mighty pillar.

It was Valkar!

His eyes were closed, his limbs slack, and a thread of scarlet fluid leaked from a great wound on his brow to stain the deathlike pallor of his features.

My heart racing, I knelt beside his sprawled figure and laid my palm against his breast. He yet lived, for the throbbing of that vital organ beat however faintly against my touch.

"Valkar! What has happened!" I cried as my comrades gathered about us and Lukor knelt to set a cup of water from his canteen at the white lips of our injured friend.

His eyelids flickered and a trace of color came into his marble cheeks.

"Jandar," he whispered hoarsely, and in so faint a voice that I had to bend low to catch his next words.

"They sprang on me ... from behind ... three of them I ... slew ... but there were ... too many," he whispered feebly.

"And the Princess?" I cried in an agony of suspense. "What of the Princess? What of Darloona?"

"Seized ... taken," he whispered, and then he spoke no more. The effort had drained what small reserves of energy his body retained, and he fell back in my arms unconscious, although not seriously injured.

"Taken!" Lord Yarrak repeated, horror written upon his stern and kingly features.

"But by whom?" Lukor asked, rendering vocal the question that throbbed in the hearts of each of us.

And then the answer came—in a woman's cry!

"*Jandar! O Jandar!*" came a faint, far voice. A voice that I knew. A voice that brought me swiftly to my feet, the sword ready in my hands.

"*Darloona?* Where are you?" I shouted, and the answer came, faintly as if from afar, "Here!"

And then I turned, and looked up, and saw her.

Her eyes looked longingly into mine; her warm lips were opened in a tremulous smile and her arms reached out as if to clasp me. My heart leapt within me, and her next words— the last words I was to hear from her lips—echo within me to this very hour, and shall remain in my memory so long as life endures: never had I dared to hope that I should hear her speak those words to me, and that I have heard them from her very lips is a precious memory which I shall shore up against whatever empty, lonely years of bitterness and despair lay ahead for me.

"O Jandar, my beloved, my gallant warrior—I love you! I love you! I shall love you until I die—"

A thunderous burst of emotion shook me to the core and rose to overpower me. I stood speechless, heart-shaken, basking in the glory of it—that my own hopeless and unspoken love was returned by my peerless and incomparable princess! *She loved me!*

My heart was too full for speech. But my eyes gazed deep into her own, and I doubt not that the eloquence of my gaze of longing and adoration communicated my feelings to her heart.

It was a magic moment, but already she was receding from me, her face dwindling, a pallid oval against the deepening dusk.

I stared after her, heartbreak and longing written on my anguished features. For as long as we remained within sight of each other, we continued to gaze deep into each other's eyes.

But it was not very long.

For, locked a helpless captive in the clutches of Prince Thuton, who grinned down at me with cold gloating triumph written in his cruel face, Darloona was swiftly borne away from me as she stood on the deck of the *Kajazell*, the flagship of the Zanadarian fleet, which rose from hovering above the terrace of the palace, circled us briefly once, and then rose again to fly at a vast height, dwindling down the sky, bound for Zanadar, the mountaintop fortress of the bold and powerful Sky Pirates of Callisto.

EDITOR'S NOTE

And it is at this point that Captain Dark's second narrative of his adventures on Thanator comes to an abrupt end.

In editing his manuscript for publication by Dell Books, I have striven to retain wherever possible his own precise phrasing. What changes I have made have been for the purpose of simplification. And, of course, wherever Captain Dark has inadvertently made an error in word usage or spelling, grammar or punctuation, I have corrected it.

It will be understood that, marooned as he is on the fifth moon of Jupiter, our author does not have easy access to a dictionary.

In concluding my version of this second volume at this point of tension and unresolved conflict, I wish I could assure my readers that the remainder of the story will yet be told. But this I cannot know for certain. It may be that this is the last word we shall ever receive from the first Earthman in history to explore the marvels and mysteries of that remote world. Or it may be that a third manuscript will materialize in that weird jade-lined well in the Lost City of Arangkôr in the unexplored jungles of Cambodia.

Only time will tell. . . .

Lin Carter

A NOTE ON THE
THANATORIAN LANGUAGE

B oth in *Jandar of Callisto* and in this book which serves
as its sequel, Captain Dark reveals a considerable
amount of information about the language spoken on
Thanator.

While he is not trained linguist and does not convey language data in anything even roughly approximating a working
vocabulary of the Thanatorian tongue, sufficient information
is given in the course of his narrative to tell us quite a bit
about the language. He himself comments on the unusual fact
that the identical language is spoken by all the human and
nonhuman races of the jungle moon, and that not only is no
other language known upon Thanator but the very concept
of "another" language is difficult for the Thanatorians to
grasp. In this respect, I call to your attention the incident in
Jandar of Callisto, Chapter 4, where Captain Dark describes
the immense difficulties he had, not so much in learning the
universal language of Thanator under the tutelage of Koja of
the Yathoon Horde, but in getting across to the friendly ar-

thropod the very fact that he did not know the language and required tutelage in it.

From what the two Callistan books reveal, it would seem that the common tongue of that world bears no relationship to any terrene language; at least, I have shown the following data on Thanatorian words to two language experts, Dr. Ralph Morton Jamieson of my old alma mater, Columbia University, and Professor Alton Aimes of the Department of Languages of Brooklyn College. Both experts are willing to be quoted in saying that the Thanatorian vocabulary which follows does not seem allied to any of the terrene languages, as a comparison of cognate terms reveals. (Professor Ames thought it looked more like a derivative of Esperanto than anything else, but I am not familiar enough with that famous synthetic language to agree.) Both acknowledged that the language is obviously agglutinating not unlike Turkish or Hungarian, but bears no other similarity to those languages.

I have prepared the following brief glossary from my study of the two manuscripts, and it follows.

Lin Carter

A GLOSSARY OF THE THANATORIAN LANGUAGE

AKKA-KORMOR: seems to mean, literally, "high-chieftain"; and as far as Captain Dark informs us, the term is used only among the barbaric warriors of the Yathoon Horde.

AMATAR: possession, a prized but soulless "thing."

ARKON: among the Yathoon, at least, this seems to be the title of the supreme chieftain, perhaps cognate with "king."

A NOTE ON THE THANATORIAN LANGUAGE

Captain Dark unfortunately does not give us the originals of the Thanatorian words he translates as "prince," "queen," or "king," so we cannot be certain this word is used by others besides the Yathoon, who in many respects have a separate vocabulary all their own.

BICE: a gold coin of considerable worth; beyond mention of the bice, Captain Dark reveals nothing of the coinage or currency of Thanator.

BORATH: a tall tree found in the jungle country of the Grand Kumala. Captain Dark mentions only two other forms of arboreal life on Thanator.

CAPOK: an impolite colloquialism by which the baser elements of the various human races of Thanator refer, derogatorily, to the Yathoon insectoids; cognate to "bug."

CHACA: the color "black."

CHACA YUUL, THE: Captain Dark translates this term as "Black Legion." A bandit horde under elective leadership, which Captain Dark likens to the Don Cossacks or the *condottieri* of the Italian Renaissance.

DELTAGAR: a monster of the Thanatorian jungles which Captain Dark describes as a twenty-foot super-tiger with scarlet fur and a lashing, whiplike tail edged with jagged serrations. It has enormous canines like those of a terrene sabertooth, two curling horns sprouting from the brow, and a ruff of coarse mane which stands up around the base of the skull. Captain Dark killed one in the arena of Zanadar (see *Jandar of Callisto*, Chapter 12).

GORDRA: the Thanatorian word for "eye." Note that it is possible this word is the plural; Captain Dark seems uncertain on this.

GORDRIMATOR: The name by which the Thanatorians call the planet we know as Jupiter. Conjecturally, I suggest that the name means *gordra ima tor* or "world of the red eye," so-called from the prominent feature called The Great Red Spot which has been noted by terrene astronomers. The gods of the Thanatorians are called "the Lords of Gordrimator," which suggests that the priesthood of Thanator (if such indeed exists, for Captain Dark's narratives thus far contain no reference to any such, save for the cunning little devil-worshipper Ool the Uncanny), in whatever religious doctrines they have evolved, teach that Jupiter is the home of their pantheon of gods. On this point, however, we can only conjecture; for Captain Dark himself frequently points out that he has learned precious little about the religious practices of the jungle moon.

HORAJ: the word wherewith Koja alerted Jandar to the importance of the news he carried, as described in Chapter 12 of the present book. The word means "urgent."

HOREB: a naked Thanatorian rodent of repulsive habits; the word is used in a derogatory sense much as we use the word "rat."

IMA: the color "red."

IMAVAD: the Thanatorian name for Ganymede, the fourth moon of Jupiter. Captain Dark explains that Ganymede appears rose-red from the surface of Thanator (Callisto), and he further notes that the name means, literally, ima vad, "Red Moon."

JARUKA: this seems to be one of the more common trees of the Thanatorian jungle country; Captain Dark describes it as having a gnarled black trunk and branches and weird scarlet foliage. No tree of this description is native to Earth, and a botanist whom I have queried points out that red foliage would preclude the existence of chlorophyll in the leaf structure, which makes it difficult to see how such a tree could live.

JURU: little or small.

JURUVAD: the name by which the Thanatorians refer to the moon Amalthea, the smallest and most inward of the Jovian satellites, visible from the surface of Thanator as a minute flake of golden fire. The name means "Little Moon."

KAJA: the sky.

KOMAD: a military rank which Captain Dark explains is inferior to that of a full chieftain; in other words, a subchieftain, or captain.

KOMOR: the military rank of "Chieftain." Superior to the rank which is equivalent to captain, it would seem to equate with major or colonel.

KORAD: a Thanatorian unit of distance which Captain Dark says is about the same as seven miles.

KUA: the color "golden," and perhaps the metal as well (?).

KU THAD, THE: the name by which the amber-skinned, flame-haired, green-eyed race dominant in Shondakor denote themselves. The term translates as "The Golden People."

LAJ: the Thanatorian word for "sea." Captain Dark's narratives describe two inland seas, or land-locked lakes, on Thanator; the larger of the two is known as Corund Laj and the smaller as Sanmur Laj.

LAJAZELL: a small winged reptile of which two distinct species exist on Thanator, the first inhabiting the desert regions (see ZELL), and the second, the shores of the inland seas. *Lajazell*, the lakeside species, Captain Dark aptly terms "seagulls."

OLO: a small knobbed wooden club worn at saddleside wherewith the Thanatorian mounted warriors keep their unruly mounts (see THAPTOR) under control.

ORO: the color "green."

OROVAD: the Thanatorian name for Io, the second moon of Jupiter. Captain Dark explains that Io appears as a globe of frosty lime green from the surface of Castillo, hence the name, which translates as "Green Moon."

PALUNGORDRA: a peculiar form of communications device known only to Thanator, and the lone example of a higher technology than that usually found in the Thanatorian cities. Captain Dark describes it as a "television crystal," and explains that the name means "the far-seeing eyes." For an account of one of the *palungordra* (the name seems to be plural) in action, see *Jandar of Callisto*, Chapter 11.

QUARRA: in *Jandar of Callisto*, this is described as a potent liquor, perhaps something like brandy.

RAMA: a color Captain Dark described as "silver," but whether the same name is used to refer to the metal I cannot say with any surety.

RAMAVAD: Europa, the third moon of Jupiter. Captain Dark has described its appearance from the surface of Callisto as "a luminous globe of frosted azure" or "silvery blue;" but I assume that the name translates as "Silver Moon."

SORAD: a rather rare tree with crimson wood and black foliage, the reverse of which is far more common (see JARUKA).

THAD: from its use in the name *Ku Thad*, I deduce that this word means "people" in the singular. The plural form would seem to be *thana*, but this is only my conjecture.

THANATOR: the moon Callisto, a satellite of Jupiter. Terrene astronomers record that Callisto, fifth of the Jovian moons, is about 2,770 miles in diameter, 8,702 miles in circumference, and some 4,351 miles from pole to pole. Those astronomers whom I have consulted personally, at New York's Hayden Planetarium, assure me that while Callisto is one of the very largest moons in our solar system, it is far too small and has much too weak a surface gravitation to retain anything like a breathable atmosphere. As well, being more than five times farther away from the Sun than is our world, it receives a correspondingly slight amount of sunlight and heat, and should, by all accounts, be an airless and dead world, frozen in the eternal cold of space. So much for the opinions of the scientists. Captain Dark does not, to my recollection, explain the meaning of the name, but I deduce that it may be translated as *thana tor*, "world of the peoples."

THAPTOR: a beast used by the Thanatorians much as we use the horse. Captain Dark describes it as a wingless, four-legged bird about the size of a terrene horse, with a stiff rufflike mane of feathers, clawed feet spurred like those of a terrene rooster, a sharp yellow beak resembling that of a parrot, glaring eyes with orange pupils and a black iris. He further remarks that the nations of Thanator have not succeeded in fully domesticating the *thaptor*, and they retain unruly, half-wild habits (see OLO).

TOR: the Thanatorian word for "world" or "planet," combined in such agglutinating words as *Thanator* and *Gordrimator*.

UHORZ: a term which may be rendered as "indebtedness." Among the primitive Yathoon warriors, who seem generally to be devoid of the nobler sentiments and do not have any conception of friendship or love, the word *whorz* has a very special meaning in that it is about as close to "friendship" as their barbaric mentality has been able to come.

VAD: the Thanatorian word which may best be translated as "moon," as in *Orovad*, "Green Moon." Note that the Thanatorians have only a rudimentary knowledge of astronomy, and seem to be aware only of the four satellites between their own world and its primary. But Jupiter has, in all, twelve moons, the outermost seven of which are either too

small or too distant to be clearly observed from the surface of Callisto by the unaided eye.

VA LU ROKKA: a phrase which Captain Dark renders as "it was destined," and which, among the warriors of the Yathoon, expresses a fatalistic philosophy rather similar to that of the Arabic people who use the word "Kismet" to express much the same notion.

VASTODON: the elephant-boar of the Grand Kumala jungles. Insofar as Captain Dark has yet discovered, this is the largest mammal on Thanator. He describes it as having a slate-gray leathery hide, with squat, thick, columnar legs ending in flat pads, and a head like a wild boar, with vicious pig-like eyes and coarse black bristles on a long, prehensile snout. It is a dangerous beast to encounter and is armed with fierce tusks of gleaming yellow ivory. Captain Dark records a hand-to-hand battle with a vastodon in *Jandar of Callisto*, Chapter 6.

YATHRIB: the dreaded dragon-cat of the jungle country. It seems a peculiar combination of tiger and reptile, its rippling catlike body clad in tough emerald scales which pale to tawny yellow at the belly plates. Its feet are armed with terrible bird-claws and a row of jagged spines line its backbone to the tip of its lashing snaky tail. Captain Dark was rescued by the Yathoon chieftain, Koja, from a monstrous yathrib as he reports in *Jandar of Callisto*, Chapter 3.

ZELL: a winged, flying reptile inhabiting the desert countries. A similar species inhabits the beaches of the two inland seas (see LAJAZELL).

The above forty-four words or terms represent all that we know of the Thanatorian language at the present time, and probably this slender sampling of the Thanatorian vocabulary

is too small to serve as the basis of a scientific study of the tongue.

Any more extensive knowledge of the language, then, depends on what further information Captain Dark may give us in the future. But as communication with Callisto is erratic at best, this tantalizing brief glossary will probably be our only source for knowledge of this, the first language of another world ever on record.

But, then, who knows what the future may yet unveil?

Lin Carter